THE FORSAKEN CRYPTS
THE FROST FILES 2

TERRY C. SIMPSON

Golden Arm Press

www. terrycsimpson.com.
Printed in the United States of America
First Edition
ISBN: 978-1-939172-27-3

To Kai: Always and forever in my heart.

Be sure to visit terrycsimpson.com for free book offers and to join Terry's Facebook reader group. Just search for Storyteller Terry C. Simpson's Void Gate. Free swag, updates, chapters, ARCs, regular chats with Terry, beta reads, input into Terry's worlds and books. You might even get towns, creatures, and people named after you.

So come on over and join up.

MAP OF MIKANDER

CHAPTER 1

"Do you ever think about the outside world?" Standing at a window of their Upper Ward hotel room, Blaze stared out at Downtown Brooklyn, dawn's pallid glow framing her slender form through the sheet draped over her shoulders.

"Outside world?" Frowning, Dre sat on the edge of the bed in his boxers.

"Yeah. You know… the world outside the NAR. The rest of the world that we used to be able to travel freely. You ever think about what it's like?" Her dark hair fell in braids atop the white sheet.

Dre shook his head. "Maybe when I was a kid. I usually don't dream that big anymore. I got enough trouble dealing with the world we're in."

"No doubt. But you were out there before, weren't you?"

"Yeah. When I was six. Just before they banned all international flights and closed down the public airports." He'd been back in Barbados at the time. It was a memory he preferred not to dwell on.

Dre stood and strode across the room, bare feet slapping on the heated marble floors. When he got to Blaze, he wrapped his arms around her waist from behind. "The most I thought about it since were stories Pops told me about Barbados. Or how the USA used to be before it became the NAR. I used to be fascinated about life back in the days, before the War of The Americas, the Climatic Shift, or the superstorms."

She snuggled closer into him, tilting her head back and to the side of his chin. He leaned his head down, her braids soft against his cheek. Dre

1

inhaled long and deep, relishing her shampoo's vanilla aroma. He sighed. He could stay in this position, in this room, with her forever.

Up here on the two hundredth floor, the only vehicles zipping along on the massive invisible skyway outside were Personal Transports. Drones emblazoned with NYPD or SDF hovered at regular intervals, silent and foreboding. All other traffic, from Airbus to Maglev, was relegated to below the Upper Wards.

Sunlight weakened by the city's perpetual smog glinted off the other skyrises. Far below, pedestrians on skywalks were little more than dots. In the distance was the mist-shrouded ocean and the dark stain of the massive seawall eating the coast.

"I dream about the world all the time." Her voice was soft. Longing. "I want to go out there one day. See what it's like."

Dre could understand her feelings. Even if he couldn't exactly relate. Blaze was a DeGen. He paused when he thought of the word, hearing her correct him gently as was her habit of late, telling him she was a Lifer. That's what they called themselves in the Bottoms. Lifers. She was born in the First Ward, and had lived in the Bottom Wards for the majority of her life. Suffering was a part of her.

She had the scars to prove it. Ribbons of raised tissue ran down her spine, her left side, and along her left leg. He'd asked her about them, but she'd said they were nothing, a product of recklessness. He suspected there was more to them than she let on.

Closing his eyes for a moment, he considered the stories told of the Lifers, the things he'd grown up believing to be true. The government had labeled them DeGens, the worst of the North American Republic. Many of them were illegal immigrants who'd come to the city during the Great Migration, fleeing both the Second Civil War and the War of Americas. They had hidden themselves away beneath cities, in places unfit for humans to live. Later on, escaped criminals had joined their ranks. Gangs had formed.

When he saw Lifers on a broadcast, they were dirty, disheveled, emaciated, and riddled with disease. Such displays always labeled them as criminals. Murderers. Thieves. Rats. Dre knew some of it was propaganda, lies told by the likes of Sidrie Malikah and those in power.

Blaze and Pops' tale in Void Legion was proof of those lies. If someone

2

had told him he could feel so much for a Lifer he would have laughed in their face. Not now.

He opened his eyes, gaze drifting to the blanket of smog and clouds blushed by the distorted coin of a sun. "Maybe when this is all over, we can all go one day. You, me, Mom, and Kai." *And Pops,* he thought.

"Maybe." She sighed.

Despite it being a ridiculous thought, an impossible dream, he wanted it to come true. He felt good saying it.

"I never told anyone, but getting away is one of the reasons I game so much." Her chest heaved. "I can go anywhere. Fly anywhere. Do anything. I can be as strong as I want to be as long as I'm willing to work hard. My troubles fade away. I can be someone else. I can *be* someone."

"I'm sorry." Dre gave her a comforting squeeze.

"Sorry for what? You're not the one making us suffer. Making our lives worse." Her voice hardened. "They are. Why? Just because they can? Because they think we're weak? Don't we endure enough? We just want to be left alone to live our lives, be able to build our society, and not be beholden to the Corps, or bowing and scraping to skyrisers for food or shelter."

Dre had no words to soothe her. To reassure her that things would get better. He let silence stretch, leaving her to her thoughts, hoping that holding her, listening to her, was enough.

After a while, Blaze let out a slow breath. "I can't wait to get back in the game."

"I understand *exactly* what you mean." Dre smiled. He was more at home in-game than IRL. He enjoyed being one of the top dogs, exploring, fighting, clearing dungeons, and visiting exotic locales.

"Speaking of the game, I heard some disturbing rumors." She lifted the back of her head off his chest.

"What did you hear?"

"Remember they mentioned the risk of brain damage from in-game death? How brain function stops for an instant IRL?"

"Yeah."

"I heard it's worse than they let on. A few Total Immersion testers who died in-game ended up as invalids. They can't walk, can't talk, can't see, or hear. They just sit there."

"That's fucked up." Dre couldn't even begin to imagine such a fate.

"Same thing I said."

"Where'd you hear this?"

"Players I know."

"How'd they find out?"

"It happened to their friends. They picked up on it because of the mystic's rez spell. When a mystic rezzes a player, they don't return to life at that moment. The person can either stay in that spot for a few hours, appearing barely conscious, or they can choose a respawn location."

Dre thought it was a weird way for resurrection to work, but he knew the reason. "That's because the devs wanna make sure TNT has done its job effectively. A precaution."

"No doubt. But these players who died never came back in-game. They didn't respawn. Equitane delivered them to their homes. When their friends went to visit, they found the ex-players bed-ridden or in wheelchairs."

Dre was speechless. At the same time, he wondered how Equitane was keeping a lid on such news. Until he thought about the NDA and his own situation.

Blaze sighed. "Funny thing is that a part of me finds the risk exciting while another part is scared shitless. Especially since we *have* to play."

Without giving the idea much thought, Dre knew his feelings ran deeper. "I'd still play regardless. Particularly after experiencing Total Immersion. And seeing Pops. He's worth it all by himself."

"True." She brought her hands up and placed them over his at her midsection. "I don't even know why it bothers me at all. I mean, I know why, as in no one should be getting hurt doing what we do. But for me, I'm not worried. I'm fully capable of playing without dying."

Dre grunted derisively. "Somebody's feeling themselves."

"Hey." Blaze shrugged. "I can't help it if I'm *that* good."

"You're too damned cocky." Dre chuckled.

"Trust and believe I got every right to be."

Dre grew serious. He kissed her head. "There's another reason you shouldn't worry. There's no way I'd let you die."

Blaze leaned away, twisting until she could glance back at him over her shoulder. She smirked. "Let? Pfft, boy, you better go somewhere with that."

She straightened, facing the window again.

"Yeah… let." Dre smiled down at her. "I promise not to *let* you die."

"Oh, now we're promising?" She shook her head, voice tinged with mirth.

"We sure are."

"I feel you." She nodded appreciatively. "I'll *let* you have that one." They burst into laughter. When their mirth subsided, she added, "I won't let you die either."

The idea warmed Dre's insides. He grinned like a big kid. They remained in that position until the sun set the smog and clouds on fire.

Blaze turned to face him, dark angled eyes staring up into his. "It's about that time." Her voice carried a hint of reluctance. "You're going to see your Mom, right?"

Dre nodded. "And my sister. I wanna spend a few days with them before we play Void Legion again. What're you gonna do?"

She got up on her tiptoes, planted a kiss on his lips, then slid her face past his cheek until her mouth was at his ear. "Do some research on old school puzzles in games, and deliver the first protocol," she whispered.

He matched her timbre. "Be careful."

"No doubt."

They hugged for a bit longer. Finally, they separated and got dressed. Before they left the room, they shared a long kiss.

******

Blaze's mind was preoccupied with thoughts of Dre as the elevator made its way down toward the Mid Wards. She didn't understand why she felt the way she did for him. Keeping business and pleasure separate had been what kept her alive over the years. She prided herself on the ability. But though she tried with Dre, she couldn't help her feelings.

At first, she'd thought it was just an in-game thing. When she watched him play, she was immediately drawn to his skill, command, and quick thinking. The fact he hadn't judged her as a girl but simply as a player had made the attraction even easier to accept.

But IRL, it had become more than that. She liked him from the very first day she watched him, studied him on his way to and from Downtown

Brooklyn. His tall, slim but fit frame, low fade haircut, impeccable waves, broad nose, thick eyebrows, caramel complexion. They all seemed so… right.

Sure, he was young, turning seventeen in a few weeks. But then she was young also. And in this life, the way the world was, time waited for no one. She or he could easily be dead in a few months if caught in the wrong place during a superstorm despite the advantage of the seawall.

Making matters easier, or more complicated, depending on how she looked at them, he hadn't been grossed out when he discovered she was really a Lifer. He'd opened himself to her all the same.

She shook her head. Maybe her mind was just playing tricks on her. *So why is he always in your thoughts? Why do you think about his lips, his hands, his voice, his smell?*

The elevator stopped. Floor 100. Center of the Mid Wards. The door opened on the skywalk side, letting in a blast of frigid early November air.

Dismissing Dre from her mind, she hunkered into her jacket and strode out onto the skywalk, mist drifting into the air with her every breath. She needed a clear head for the work at hand.

Androids mingled among people who bustled by on their way to work or school or shopping, for those who still felt the need to physically do such activities rather than use the Grid's plethora of VR facilities. She understood the sentiment of the ones making that choice. Sympathized with it. Certain things made you feel more alive. Even if it meant coming outside on a cold ass day.

Walking and smiling like she was a tourist or a Bottom Warder enthralled by the soaring glass facades, the many PTs, hover vehicles, and EVTOL craft, she headed to her destination, certain Equitane security was tracking her as they did every other tester. The monitoring was routine. She did not want it to become more than that. Draw attention to herself.

So, she practiced the same habits whenever she'd come up from the Bottoms, gave the same impression of herself: a girl of low status caught in the wonder of great society. The thought almost made her scowl.

Equitane's teams relied on the city's numerous cameras for monitoring. Cameras on everything from buildings to signs to droids to the drones hovering overhead. She found comfort in knowing they had to resort to such means for her rather than through direct contact by way of implants. But for the lone chip on her finger for ID and biometric tatts, both of which she had scanned to make sure there were no transmitters, she had no other wearables.

Her current smile was for the frustration security displayed over the years as she'd removed anything they planted on her. It had made for a great game of cat and mouse. A game she always won. Eventually, they'd given up.

What damage could a poor little Bottom Ward girl do anyway? What damage, indeed. She smirked.

"The city's amazing, isn't it?" A man with a too perfect goatee, dressed in a bright green sweater and khaki pants, looked from her to one of the other skyrises. The blue light of implants flashed in his eyes and was gone. "I try to come once a year."

His accent and choice of clothing would've given him away as someone not accustomed to the cold even before he said that bit. The regular New New Yorker wouldn't have donned body heat wearables until the temps were in the single digits.

"No doubt." She nodded curtly.

"I fly in from Boston." He was at the partitioned edge of the skywalk, gazing below at the many levels all the way to the crumbling brick build-ings and asphalt that made up the First Ward. "You can't begin to imagine what the countryside looks like outside the cities. I never imagined we could've avoided as much damage as we did or grow as quickly as we have after all the madness. Says a lot about being American. As we used to say back in the day, God Bless America."

Blaze slipped among the pedestrians before he turned back to her. She made her way to her favorite spot since she'd become a tester. Skybucks, a quaint little coffee shop that was a throwback to yestercyar.

She entered the Skybucks to the strum of soft jazz music. Two CX3 droids manned the counter while another busied itself making certain ev-erything was clean. All three had the new synthetic skin most companies had adopted in an effort to make bots more acceptable. More human. One was dark-skinned, one white, and the other was Asian like Blaze.

Blaze passed the cushioned bench seats near the front; the pairings of stools and single round tables; sofa, armchairs, and small table set up in the middle of the room; and headed all the way to the rear that held another set of benches against a wall. She chose her usual corner and sat.

A holo popped up on one side of the table. It displayed a selection of drinks. On the other side was another holo with access to the Grid. Between them was a set of Smart Glasses.

With a flick of her finger, she scrolled down the list and tapped to select a drink. Caramel peppermint latte. Yummy. They didn't have drinks like these in the Bottoms so she got one whenever she came up

The credits deducted automatically from her Equitane account. With her other hand, she hovered over Grid content selections for entertainment, news, or info.

Her first hand now rested on the tabletop near the connection she needed for her ID chip's second and true function. Built by the best Lifer techs to specifications given by Alphonso Taylor to imitate Equitane's real one, it circumvented the Grid's security, allowing her to pass messages and data on the old system hard-wired into this very table. The internet. Banned by the NAR to limit outside world influence. And blamed by many for the USA's downfall.

With a tap of her finger, she could pass on the code stored in her head to Gridrunners like herself, waiting beneath the city. With the first protocol, they were truly on their way to righting so many wrongs. To ridding themselves of a threat to their lives. She raised her finger.

And stopped.

A little voice in the back of her mind said to wait. A second voice chided her.

You worry too much. Nothing's worth doing if there isn't risk.

Considering the importance of her work, the second voice was tempting. She almost gave in. Almost. Until she recalled a time she hadn't listened to the first voice. A time she had almost lost her life. She'd been left with a memory of agony, knife wounds, and blood. Scars. Mental and physical.

Struck by an idea borne of the Sanctum's maze, she tapped the holo for the Grid and picked up the dark-tinted Smart Glasses. She didn't like the idea of wearing them, but doing so was the fastest way for memorization.

She put them on. Her mind and the Grid joined in a once weird synchronization that had now become common.

Although her inner thoughts were her own, she could issue commands by mere gestures or by thought projected at the Grid. Recalling all the time she spent with Alphonso Taylor, and his admissions in the Sanctum, she asked for a list of old game companies beginning with NCSoft, EA, Ubisoft, Rockstar, and Blizzard. She checked the wikis of the companies' games for any puzzles and secrets.

Using her contacts from when she fenced goods, she managed to snag a collection of old games including the likes of World of Warcraft 2, Lineage 3, Overwatch: Endgame, Diablo Immortal, and a few others. Her hopes were partially dashed when she saw a few of them were online only with no current servers or versions accessible on the Grid. She settled in to play the others, starting with Diablo.

It was odd playing a game that wasn't in VR. More than odd, it was unsettling. The one saving grace was the ability to still use the Smart Glasses and virtual controls.

After quite a bit of tinkering, she got the hang of the game. Soon, she was engrossed in ancient hack and slash glory.

Blaze didn't know what time it was when someone tapped her on the shoulder. She assumed it must have been hours. It certainly felt that way.

She took a last look at the cow king in the game, smiled, and removed the Smart Glasses, severing her connection to the Grid. She rubbed her eyes for a sec then looked up.

Two Equitane security officers loomed over her. Their hands rested on their sidearms.

The taller one spoke, a familiar man with a too perfect goatee. He looked like he was pissed off. Blaze smiled at him. "They need you in the pod room. Right now."

******

Sidrie scares me. Be careful of her. Mom flipped the pencil over and erased the message.

Leaning over the paper on the clipboard, one shaking hand partially hiding the words, she scribbled another sentence. As she worked, her biometric tattoo's dark stain seemed to shift along the caramel skin of her arm.

Your father had issues with her. He was scared too.

She erased the words. After a furtive glance at the open bedroom door, the shift of her head causing her single brown ponytail to fall down her back, she scratched out another message, her hands moving faster this time. Desperate.

We must avoid talking about it in here. You must always believe she's either tracking you or has us or this apartment bugged. She might be watching now. And definitely recording us.

All of our conversations going forward must appear normal. The one thing working in our favor is that she seems to need you. Or us.

If she asks about this paper, tell the truth, that I was warning you to be careful of her. She knows I never really liked her.

We'll do whatever it takes, until we can find a way out of this. Okay?

Mom erased everything. Hand shaking, she pulled the paper from the clipboard, tore it into tiny pieces, reached over to the tray sitting atop an AGC, and dropped it into the glass with the remnants of her orange juice. She looked to Dre with round, brown eyes. Eyes that brimmed with tears. Fear. She took a deep shuddering breath.

Staring into those eyes, Dre took her hands in his. They were cold to the touch, but at least they stopped shaking. He ached inside with the need to tell her about Pops' holo in Void Legion.

"Whatever it takes," he repeated.

She squeezed his hand, if a bit weakly. "Good." Though somewhat hoarse, her voice had improved from the day when he'd first returned from playing Void Legion to find her awake. She leaned back onto the bed whose upper portion was raised at an angle for her comfort.

Dre glanced over to Kai. His little sister was sitting at the bottom of the bed with her Holotab, watching Munsters and Minions. She wore pajamas imprinted with the show's yellow and purple creatures. Giggling, she covered her mouth.

Their new accommodations, an apartment on the hundred and eightieth floor of Equitane Towers, was complete with three bedrooms, a large living room, kitchen, expensive furniture, and anything else they might need. The apartment's systems were controlled by an AI named Rachel.

They even had a maid in the form of an MX4 droid named Mariel. The whiff of stew chicken emanated from the kitchen.

Their current circumstances seemed a dream. However, despite its Upper Ward location, the apartment was little more than an expensive prison.

Dre braced himself, fighting down fear at the question he was about to ask. "What happens if we're deported? Will they take Kai? And what happens with the FPC, then?"

Mom looked up into Dre's face, brown eyes steady. "We just have to hope Sidrie keeps her word. We're in no position to prepare for the alternative. Everything's gonna work out. Okay?" Mom squeezed his hand.

Dre let out a shuddering breath. "Okay."

"Mrs. Taylor," Mariel's voice called from the bedroom door.

Dre looked up. The droid was wearing a short-sleeved deep blue dress and had a white apron tied around her waist. As with all droids from MX4 models and up, she appeared almost human, particularly her synthetic skin and red hair, which was done in a bun.

"What is it, Mariel?" Mom glanced over.

"Lunch will be ready in twenty minutes, ma'am." Mariel offered a smile that showed off perfect white teeth.

"Thank you." Mom dipped her head. "We'll be along shortly."

"Yes, ma'am." Still smiling, Mariel nodded demurely, turned, and left.

Dre regarded Mom with a frown. "You sure you should be walking around?"

"I certainly don't plan on staying in bed. Besides, a little exercise would be good for me."

"Is that what the doctors said?"

Mom chuckled. "You sound like me with the questions." Stroking the top of his hand, she offered an encouraging nod. "I really meant what I said yesterday. The crash wasn't your fault. It was me who told you to drive. Praise the Lord that Alphonso's old company had someone working in the area.

"And although it was them who were involved in the accident, we might not be alive otherwise. Sometimes, what seems a curse is a blessing in disguise."

Dre stiffened at the mention of the crash. Stroking his Two Ring, he fought back the painful memory. His shoulders sagged. He replaced his melancholy with the thought of the crash being more than a simple accident. It had been one of Sidrie's ploys.

A fire rekindled in his belly. "I know. But I can't help feeling bad. We coulda all died."

"But we didn't. Silver linings. Take them when you can."

"I'll try, Mom." Dre reached over and rubbed her round belly. "How's Regi and Rayne?"

Mom shifted her hand to below the prominent swell. She practically beamed now. "The doctors said they're healthy. Which I believe, from the way they were kicking my ass like usual this morning."

Dre cracked a smile seeing her like this. And at the idea of the twins' health. "How long before they're here?"

"Just over another month." Mom's expression grew distant. Then fresh joy creased her features. "Thinking of them makes me remember when you and Kai were babies. It also makes me want you here, not in that damned game. What did you call it again?"

"Void Legion."

Mom shook her head. "Nice name, but I still don't like it."

"But–" Dre began.

"But your gift for gaming is the reason they gave us the care we needed." Mom sighed. "The reason the twins and I are still alive. Why Kai's alive." Her gaze was on Kai, who was giggling again.

So far, Sidrie had kept her part of the deal. Dre wondered if she would do the rest. He agonized over it, had constant images of himself and Mom's deportation. Or of Mom being turned over to the Family Planning Corps for breaking the Better Tomorrow Law. Vigorously rubbing his Two Ring, he fought against those nightmare scenarios by telling himself Sidrie would keep her word. She would do the right thing.

"Why do I get the feeling that you just want to play?" Mom arched a brow.

A ghost of a smile touched his lips. "Cuz you know me. Gaming's always been part o' my life."

"Don't remind me. I once tried to talk to your father about it becoming a bad habit, but he wasn't trying to hear me."

"Bad habit might be an understatement." Dre snorted. "When I couldn't game, it was like I couldn't breathe."

Mom shook her head slightly. "And you got all moody. Pouting all the time like a big baby. When are you going back in?" Even as he made to speak, she continued, "And that's another thing I don't like... those pods you mentioned and the time you'll be gone."

"They aren't so bad." Dre shrugged. "As for when I'm going back in... I kept my part o' the deal, so Sidrie's gotta keep her word and gimme a decent amount o' time with you and Kai. But if you really don't want me to play at all, then I won't. I'd rather be here with y'all."

"So, who's the girl?" Mom abruptly switched gears, knowing brown eyes focused on him.

"Girl?" Dre frowned before he understood. "I don't know what you're talking about." Clearing his throat, he looked away from Mom.

"Is that why you can't look at me?" Mom's tone dripped with mirth. She lowered her voice. "I can smell her on you."

Dre snapped his head around, eyes wide. "Smell?"

"Her perfume." Mom wrinkled her nose. "And something else. Something I wouldn't say with your sister so near." Mom jutted her chin toward Kai.

Heat flushed across Dre's neck, face, and ears. One thing came to mind. "Nah, you can't smell... stop it." Without thinking, he sniffed but came up empty.

Mom covered her mouth, cheeks puffed up, her eyes sparkling as she tried to hold back her laughter. "I sure can. And I hope you were safe about it. Your father said he had the talk with you when you turned fifteen and again at sixteen."

"I was as safe as I coulda been." Dre remembered the talk all too well. He hoped Mom interpreted anything she saw on his face or his reactions as him telling the truth.

"It's alright." Mom sighed "I'm not mad. Even if I think you're too young. My mother had me when she was your age and I turned out fine." Dre opened his mouth. "And don't mention how you'll be seventeen in a few weeks. This day had to come sooner or later. I'd just rather it had been later. I'm not ready for grandkids. Keep that in mind."

"Yes, Mom." Dre hung his head. He couldn't believe they were having this conversation.

"What's her name?"

Dre lifted his head. "Blaze."

"Blaze? That's her real name?"

"It's what she goes by."

"A gamer like you, I suppose." Mom raised a questioning brow. He nodded. "At some point you're gonna have to let me meet her." Mom gestured toward the room. "This isn't the ideal place or situation, but it's what we've got to work with. I'd rather meet her than not."

"Yes, Mom."

"With that out of the way." A mischievous smile creased Mom's features. "I think you should go take a shower before we eat lunch."

"Alright." Blushing, he hurried off toward the bathroom, only too happy to get away from the conversation and Mom's knowing smile and eyes.

Thinking of Just Blaze got him to wondering what she was doing. His heart fluttered every time he thought about her. If he closed his eyes, he could feel her, smell her, taste her, see her toned body, honey-colored skin, small beautiful face with a dainty chin and angled eyes. Long box braids. An Asian picture of beauty. Exotic.

Unlike himself.

He shook his head, wondering what she'd seen in him. The only thing they had in common as far as looks would be that his skin color wasn't far off from hers. He was maybe a shade darker. More caramel. But he knew his face all too well and didn't need to look in a mirror to picture his blob of a nose and average features.

When Dre entered the bathroom, Rachel spoke. The AI's voice was soft. Melodic. "Welcome, sir. Should I run a bath or shower."

"Shower." He closed the door behind him. "And play some hip-hop. Jay-Z's album. Four Four Four." It was Pops' favorite classic from 2017 that Dre had grown to love.

The first song, Kill Jay-Z, pipped into the bathroom. The music was low and clear and sounded as if it were everywhere.

"Water temperature?" Rachel chimed, her question followed by the shushing sound of the shower.

"Lukewarm." He closed the door behind him and got undressed. Immediately, the musky fetor of old sex hit him. He sighed. *I knew I shoulda bathed at the hotel.* But both he and Blaze had been in a hurry. Him, to return to Mom. Her, to deliver the protocol.

Remembering his hair, Dre opened a nearby linen and amenities closet, hoping to find a durag to cover his waves. There was none. With a sigh, he crossed the warm ivory-tiled floor to the large shower positioned beside the bathtub, both sectioned off and enclosed in translucent glass. He slid aside the glass door, stepped under the shower, and closed the door.

Jets of water shot from the shower heads along the three walls. Relishing its warmth and soothing feel, he thought of Blaze and Void Legion as he recited the lyrics to Kill Jay-Z. He couldn't wait to get back in game and see Pops, experience SR in all its glory, and explore the wonderful world Pops had helped to build. And he was even more excited at the prospect of playing with Blaze again. He could picture her character, Gilda Mordian, even now.

"Add soap for a few moments." His voice echoed.

"Scent?" Rachel asked.

"Start with vanilla. Finish with mint."

In the next instant, the water became foamy and filled with the bouquet of vanilla. While lathering, his train of thoughts drifted to Pops' revelation that Dre was the first gameborn. He fully intended to experiment, discerning how his learning and activities in-game translated to the real world.

He had so many questions about TNT and Uncle Kim's Whole Brain Emulation work. Though himself and Pops were examples of the tech at work, Dre still found the ideas near unbelievable. They were those things you saw in a movie that you thought might always be fiction.

He couldn't begin to fathom all the applications, but the mere thought of becoming smarter, stronger, faster, and more skilled in a shorter period of time was extremely enticing. The possibilities seemed endless.

No wonder Sidrie killed for it.

He shuddered. His thoughts made him wonder about the protocol downloaded through his Two Ring, the black aether ring replica Pops had bought him. The code was there, in the back of his mind, a set of instructions he could recite despite his ignorance of the meaning or function.

15

He stopped lathering. *Shit. The protocol. Blaze. Had she gone to deliver it already?* An anxious flutter rippled through him. He prayed she hadn't. Particularly if Mom's suspicions of Sidrie's surveillance proved to be true.

He tilted his head to the side, thinking of Blaze's last few words, whispered in his ears. *Did she know?* He let out a slow breath, trying to drive away the dread rising within. But it lingered.

On edge, Dre hurriedly rinsed, grabbed a towel from the linen closet, and dried off. He rushed to his room with the towel wrapped around his waist. Standing in front a closet filled with clothes to fit his medium build, he chose faded denim jeans, a plain black Tee, got dressed, and headed for the dining area. He'd enjoy a quick lunch with Mom and Kai then go looking for Blaze to warn her. Her apartment on the floor below his would be a start.

Mom and Kai were already seated at the frosty-colored dining table. Mariel was placing dishes atop its glass surface. A righteous aroma rose from the combination of brown stewed chicken, rice and peas, and asparagus. A glass pitcher in the middle of the table was filled with sparkling water.

Dre's stomach grumbled. He licked his lips. He was on the verge of taking a seat when the doorbell chimed. "I got it, Mariel." He crossed the room, turned down the long hall, and headed for the front door, hoping it was Blaze.

Dre took a look at the holo projection hovering from a panel beside the door, displaying the hall outside. Staring directly into the camera with those dark, predatory eyes, Sidrie Malikah was standing beside a short stern-faced man in a blue suit who carried a small folder in one hand. Stomach knotting, Dre stroked his Two Ring. The sight of the man and Sidrie left a sour taste in his mouth.

CHAPTER 2

Two days with his family is more than enough, Sidrie Malikah thought. In truth, she would have cut Andre's time even shorter if not for the Void Legion update. Having the first protocol made her want them all as soon as possible. They were the keys to how Simulated Reality, Tissue Nanotransfection, and Whole Brain Emulation could work together. They were the keys to Equitane's future, to her future.

She hated the idea that anyone controlled something she owned. That someone was preventing her from doing as she desired. Thwarting her. Holding power over not just her but her life itself. Even if he was effectively dead.

If what she'd gleaned from the hotel room was any indication, forcing the issue with Andre had the potential to solve her problems in one fell swoop. She tried not to get her hopes too high. Only to have them dashed. She'd been there countless times over the last decade.

She was still staring at the entrance cam when the door swung inward. Andre Taylor stood just inside, an imitation of his father, Alphonso, with his slight frame, caramel skin, brown eyes, and a nose that was too large for his narrow face. The resemblance made Sidrie's lips curl.

A short hall opened into a larger room behind Andre. His expression was flat, but his eyes were dark daggers.

"Hello, Miss Malikah." Dre's gaze shifted from her to Mr. Risenor. "Sir." He dipped his head then returned his attention to her.

Sidrie arched a brow. He had purposely called her Miss Malikah rather than Sidrie as she'd asked. Like his father, the boy was ready to dig in. Well, if he wanted to play, so would she.

Putting on her best distressed expression, Sidrie gestured to the man in the cheap suit beside her. "We're here with news for your family. This is Mr. Risenor, a senior official with North American Immigration Logistics."

Dre paled once she mentioned NAIL. He opened and closed his mouth. His eyes darted from her to Mr. Risenor and back again. His fear was almost palpable.

Sidrie loved every minute of it. She knew his mind was working, calculating if the news was good or bad. If she had kept her part of the bargain. Or if the NAIL official was there to deliver orders for deportation.

"That's a wonderful smell." She inhaled, long and deep, savoring the spicy bouquet wafting from the apartment. "Is that Jamaican stew chicken?" Knowing Dre was caught off-balance by his concerns and the seemingly innocuous question, she used that moment to sweep inside and by him before he could answer.

Wearing a wolfish smile, she strutted down the hall. Two sets of footsteps followed on the tiled floor in her wake. She passed the pristine stainless steel and white kitchen, crossed the living room, and entered the dining area. Theresa and Kai were sitting at the long glass table before an array of enticing dishes. Mariel, the MX4 droid assigned to housekeeping, was serving them.

"Theresaaa." Sidrie spread her arms as if greeting an old friend rather than a woman she knew despised her. She put on her warmest face as she approached. "So glad to see you up and about. My doctors said you had almost fully recovered. I had to see for myself. Amazing."

The almost bronze of Theresa's skin said she was quite healthy now despite all she had suffered. Not that Sidrie did not know this. The cost in resources and credits for the woman's recovery scrolled down one side of Sidrie's optics. A few million for such an unremarkable piece of flesh. It grated Sidrie's insides.

Smiling broadly, Sidrie stopped a couple feet from the table and shifted her attention to Theresa's daughter. "And hello, Kai. You're so beautifulll."

"Thank you." The little girl smiled shyly.

"Hello, Sidrie." Theresa's stolid expression matched her voice. Her brown eyes took in Mr. Risenor for all of a moment. "I'm glad you're here, so I can thank you in person for helping my family. For saving the lives of myself and the twins."

"You're most welcome." Sidrie inclined her head.

Dre took up a position beside his mother, eyes shifting from Sidrie to Mr. Risenor. He was stroking a little black ring on his pinky finger. Sweat beaded his brow.

Good, Sidrie thought as Dre agonized over the visit. Aloud, she said, "It was sheer luck things worked out the way they did. Providing assistance was the least I could do to honor your late husband, who was our top AI engineer." Sidrie caught Theresa's split-second grimace at the mention of Alphonso before the woman straightened her face. "I regret my absence from the funeral. I was stuck across the country due to a storm."

"Not your fault." Theresa shrugged. "Care to join us for lunch?" She gestured to the food with an open palm.

"On any other day, I might, but I have some pressing matters." Sidrie indicated the short pale-skinned man beside her. "The first of which was to come here with Mr. Risenor. As I told Dre, he's a senior NAIL official."

Theresa's eyes narrowed at the mention of NAIL. Dre rested his hand atop his mother's shoulder. Theresa brought her hand up to cover his in an act of comfort, nervousness, or a bit of both.

"Good morning, Miss Taylor," Mr. Risenor said in a nasal voice. "How are you today?"

Theresa stared directly at the man. "I'm fine, thank you, Mr. Risenor. And yourself?" Her voice gave away nothing.

"I'm good. Thanks." Mr. Risenor dipped his head.

Sidrie admired the woman's fortitude even if she would never admit it to Theresa. Another person in a similar position as Theresa would be in a panic right now.

"As you know," Sidrie began, "your son and I had an agreement, the details of which I'm certain he has already informed you. I had to go about it in a rather forceful manner, but sometimes such things are necessary." Sidrie swept her hand out, palm up. "This apartment, your health… all were a part of the agreement. As was the petition I filed with NAIL on your family's behalf. A petition which they approved."

19

Theresa's eyes widened at those words. She squeezed her son's hand on her shoulder. Dre let out a relieved whoosh. Sidrie allowed herself a ghost of a smile.

"Thank you." Theresa's voice was breathy. She wiped at the corner of her eyes.

Dre cleared his throat. "Thank you, Sidrie."

The change in Dre's tone and attitude was refreshing. Sidrie offered them no more than the slightest dip of her head.

Mr. Risenor strode over to Theresa. He opened the small folder and removed three blank cards made of a slim yet sturdy transparent plastic. "These are your new Green Cards. I just need to scan your biometrics. If you'll call your daughter over?"

Theresa motioned for Kai to join her and Dre. A few minutes passed as Mr. Risenor positioned himself at each person's right shoulder and asked them to lift their sleeves to expose their biometric tattoos. The blue light of implants flashed in his eyes as he scanned their tattoos followed by their faces and retinas. Each of the cards lit up in green upon activation.

"As usual," Mr. Risenor said in a bored voice, "you don't need to travel with the physical cards. They're just for emergency. Your new status is logged on the Grid."

"I don't know what to say." Theresa was shaking her head, brown eyes sparkling as she regarded Sidrie. "Thank you so much."

"Thank your son." Sidrie gestured to the boy. "He performed admirably. He's well on his way to becoming one of Equitane's prized employees."

"Employee?" Dre repeated, brows drawing together.

"Yes. How else do you think I was able to petition for your family?"

"I—" Dre began.

"It's not what you expected." Sidrie formed a steeple of her fingers in front her midsection. "I get it. Particularly since we got off to such an early misunderstanding."

"It was more than a misunderstanding." Dre scowled. "You threatened me."

"In your eyes, perhaps. For me." Sidrie pressed her palm to her chest. "It was a matter of stating the steps I would take after being denied by someone I saw as ungrateful. I do not take such things lightly." She regarded him impassively. "And I'm even less tolerant of anyone who forgets themselves and touches me in a hostile manner."

Theresa tilted her head up and to the left to regard her son disapprovingly. "Dre! Is that true? Did you try to put hands on her?"

Dre's mouth downturned. He nodded glumly.

"Apologize." Theresa glowered at her son.

"But she—" Dre began sullenly but cut off at his mother's raised brow. One hand balled into a fist, he took a deep breath, looked toward Sidrie, and grumbled, "Sorry."

Sidrie dipped her head. "Apology accepted." She gestured to their surroundings. "I hope this apartment, your new resident status, keeping your family away from the dangers you would face in the Bottom Wards, your mother's health, as well as a two-hundred-thousand-a-year salary, convinces you of my good intentions."

"I'm sure it does," Theresa said.

Dre averted his eyes. For all of a second there had been a glint within them, as if he intended to say something, or if some feeling had overcome him.

"Well, congratulations to your family." Mr. Risenor dipped his head to the Taylors. He turned to Sidrie. "I have some other pressing business to attend, so I'll be on my way."

"Certainly." Sidric nodded once.

"I will see him out." The MX4 droid left from beside the table and followed Mr. Risenor.

The NAIL official was halfway across the living room when he stopped. He faced the group. His gaze shifted to Dre. "I almost forgot. Make certain you remain in Equitane's employ. Your status is dependent upon it." He turned and departed with Mariel on his heels.

"Aren't you worried he'll report me to the Family Planning Corps?" Theresa asked the moment Sidrie heard the front door close.

Sidrie shook her head. "I would not have brought him here if the FPC were a concern."

Theresa appeared to relax. "Fair enough. This work of yours that my boy's doing… it involves playing that game?"

"Yes."

"For the record, I don't like it. I never liked it."

"Be that as it may, it's my requirement for services rendered." Sidrie shrugged. "If it makes you feel any better, then I promise to make certain no harm comes to him."

"I'll take you at your word." Theresa stared at her icily. "And you should take me at mine. If *anything* happens to my son, I *will* find a way to make you and your corporation pay."

Sidrie laughed. She could not help it. Theresa had said the words with such conviction. The woman truly believed them. As preposterous as they were. It took a few moments for Sidrie to gather herself. "Your warning has been duly noted."

"I hope it has."

Despite the desire to put the woman in her place, Sidrie offered a derisive smile instead. "I have always admired people who have such love. It's a strength."

"As I've always pitied those who never got to experience it," Theresa retorted.

Sidrie fought back a scowl. Yet again, she found herself wondering why she had listened to Dr. Redmond and saved Theresa. Until she glanced down at the woman's round belly. Sidrie smiled instead.

"I will leave you to your lunch." Sidrie eyed the boy, ready to deliver the true reason for this visit. "Dre, you're to report to begin prep within the hour."

"What?" He threw his hands up. "I've barely been back for two days. You said I could spend time with my family."

"Isn't that what you're doing now?" Sidrie motioned to the Taylors. "At no time have I broken our agreement. Besides, completing prep should give you a day or two more."

"What if Mom goes into labor while I'm gone?"

"I promise to pull you from the game if she does. She still has two months, according to my doctors."

Dre made to open his mouth, but it was Theresa who spoke. "It's alright, Dre. I'll be fine. We'll be fine. Beggars can't be choosers. Besides, Miss Malikah gave her word. Let's just enjoy the time we do have together. Silver linings, remember?"

22

Sidrie met Dre's glare. "See you downstairs in the prep room. Theresa, it was good to see you well again." She gestured to the MX4 bot. "I will let myself out."

"Sidrie." Theresa's face was blank now. "I kinda understand the route you took with my son in order to get him to test this game of yours. He's stubborn. And he made a promise to me and his father that he wasn't going to break. Plus, knowing him, he'd not only want to be with his little sister, but he'd also want to be here the moment I woke up.

"But I'm awake. Did it ever occur to you to ask him now?" Theresa grimaced. "To ask *me* now? I owe my family's life to you. It's not something I'd forget. Throw in the offer of a job paying the credits you mentioned, and I might have agreed." Theresa let out a breath, obviously calming herself, and shook her head slowly, her expression radiating pity. "Yet, you didn't ask. You *still* chose what amounts to extortion, no matter how much you dress it up."

Sidrie made to give a scathing reply but stopped. Dre wore a small smile. She wanted to wipe it and Theresa's expression from their faces. Sidrie schooled herself to calm. Or as calm as she could manage. She pictured Theresa's twins as gameborn. The image helped.

Face a mask, she regarded Theresa. "Extortion is a strong word. As well as a crime. You should be careful of such accusations. What I have done is simply cut to the chase, disabusing you of the notion there is a bargain to be made. A middle ground. I am the one in control here. I could have simply made him do as I wished without any compensation. That option is still available."

Sidrie allowed the threat to hang for a moment. "Do not take my kindness for weakness. Besides," she added, allowing a small smile that did not touch her eyes, "beggars can't be choosers." She spared a glance for Dre. "A tech will be waiting for you outside." She turned on her heels, strutted back the way she'd come, and left the apartment.

Her mood improved as she imagined having all the protocols, and the things she would do once she no longer needed the Taylors. If she had to provide extra incentive, even in-game, then so be it. She'd treat Dre like a pet hound, pointing him in whatever direction she wished.

A notification lit up her optics. A communication from Keenan

Costace. She accepted. A video of the coffee-skinned former NAR soldier turned head of Equitane security popped up in the corner of her vision. The man had arms that threatened to burst through his sleeves, a chiseled face, and gunmetal eyes that missed nothing.

"Miss Malikah." He dipped his clean-shaven head.

"Yes, Keenan?"

"The assault's a go. Four days from now. We're gonna start in the Bottom Wards of the Seven's main buildings and work outward. It'll most likely take a few days just to cover Downtown Brooklyn. Plan to sit in on the op?"

"Of course. I would not miss this for the world."

"Alright. See you upstairs, ma'am."

Sidrie severed the connection and smiled. The DeGens had to be hit hard. They had to feel the repercussions for daring to attack her.

With a little luck, the assault might yield Hank Kim and his work. A thrill built at the thought. She crushed the feeling before her hopes got too high.

Up on the two hundred and fortieth floor, Sidrie Malikah sighed and disconnected her tether from the MX7 prototype. The clone would follow regular parameters, enacting her daily activities.

Exhausted, she closed her eyes as Doctor Shorin worked, adjusting TNT levels. "How long?"

"Six months." The doctor tapped an IV tube. "Perhaps a year."

Sidrie smiled mirthlessly. "Ironic, isn't it?"

"What is?"

"I'm head of the greatest tech company humanity has known. Because of me, we've made all kinds of breakthroughs. Marrying TNT with artificial brains. Brain emulation. Developing cures for almost every disease known to man.

"I'm the reason for the NAR, the reason North America survived. My work, driven by my dire need, has saved countless lives. But I lack the means to save my own."

She grimaced. She hated feeling sorry for herself. She hated *feeling*. Period. *I deserve to live. After all the things I have done for humanity, I deserve to live.*

In turn, the DeGens deserved to die. They were the reason she was in this current state. Her disease had come from them. Decades searching for a cure among them had proven futile. Now, her survival relied on a thread of hope. On a man who was supposed to be dead. And another who had disappeared.

******

Smiling, Dre watched Sidrie leave. When he heard the door close, he came around in front of his mother, shaking his head, amazed at how she'd dealt with the CEO. "Mom! What was thattt?"

"What?" Mom shrugged, a sheepish expression on her face, yet her eyes twinkled.

"Whatever happened to what we spoke about a little while ago?"

Mom snorted. "Because you're worried or fearful of someone, or because they're richer than you, doesn't mean you let them walk all over you. Or that you can't tell them about themselves. Even the powerful need to be put in their place from time to time."

"She might hold it against us," Dre argued.

"She might. But she gave her word."

"And a person is only as good as their word," Dre finished.

"Exactly." Mom nodded. "We taught you well. Now, let's eat."

"Yes, ma'am." Dre grinned.

CHAPTER 3

Nomarch Setnana Botros hurt. It was a pain of three pieces. The first was the pain of memory as she relived the moment Perihy had transformed into a draconid grunt. The second was the pain of a broken heart, for she'd lost the flawless Perihy she loved dearly. The last was the pain in her head. Mental anguish. A combination of the first two and the knowledge of his possible fate. A fate she swore to fight until her dying breath.

The thought brought on visions from the days after the last voidstorm when the Gray Death ran rampant. She relived the slaughter, the giant pyres, the burning of thousands of corrupted. She could smell their cooking flesh, hear their piteous cries even now, the echoes of their misery.

But there was hope, however slight. All she needed was for one of her contacts to provide information on the whereabouts of Adesh Hamada, Dante Blackblade, Saba Nerubi, Gilda Mordian, or Drelan Frost. Or anyone inquiring after the empowered spells. Either one would lead her to the zhua, Benediction. Perihy could yet be saved. He would have his horns, unblemished features, and chocolate skin again.

Why else would there be this accursed Cure quest for the zhua? Or the other, named Saving Perihy? Both objectives lingered in her mind, making her as much a prisoner of her pain, as she had made Perihy a prisoner in the Temple of Nif.

"You did just enough to atone for your many failures." Bakui Assam's nasal voice broke Setnana from her thoughts. That voice grated at her ears despite the fact it was only coming through the Comm Orb.

Scowling, she could imagine Bakui Assam's smug expression as if he were present. His projection of authority. His condescending manner as if he stood above the world entire.

She clenched her fist, barely staving off the inadvertent summoning of aether lightning. *Botros show no weakness. Strength always.* Papa's mantra calmed her.

Breathing deep and slow, she reminded herself of the truths she'd come to realize. Bakui Assam was not as smart as he thought himself. Neither was he as handsome or as strong as he believed. The hitch in his gait, the blemishes on his horns, his thin hair, said he was well past his prime. All he had over her was his position as Exarch.

And Aishani.

Setnana grimaced. Soothing herself with the notion Aishani loathed the man, she refocused on his voice.

"You acquired a Genesis Engine for us." Glee dripped from his tone. "I hope you did as I commanded and told no one. Kill everyone who saw what it was before you brought it out of the Sanctum. And I do mean everyone. Have the Engine transported to Modra's Keep. Aishani and I will meet you there when I'm finished with this… this… *issue…* you created in Kituan."

Those last words were a reminder of her failure. Of broken rules. Bruised egos. Of amends to be made to Kalarch Stadius Voculo and the humans.

Two objectives bloomed in her head. **Kill the Witnesses** and **Delivery to Modra's Keep.**

Wine glass in hand, she studied the other two women in the room with a flat expression. "Bakui Assam has ordered your deaths."

Major Neferna stood with her head high, dark horns resplendent. Clad in the Blackguard's namesake colors, she seemed at peace. Neither her hands at her side nor her hard eyes betrayed any emotion. As a reaver of considerable skill, she might last twenty seconds if she decided to fight.

Vindicator Dita Paresh, on the other hand, licked his lips. His already pale turquoise skin had grown even paler. His ossicones trembled. His blue eyes shifted to match the near indiscernible movement of his head as if he yearned to look over his shoulder where Ihuet and Khafra waited in the shadows. For a person who had walked all sorts of battlefields, had seen all sorts of carnage, it was ironic that death frightened him.

Or perhaps that knowledge was the very reason for his fear. Horrific memories of such endings.

Grand korae, quick to condemn others without a thought for their own fate. Or their shortcomings. Setnana took a sip of the sweet red Kelsial Valley vintage to hide her disgust at Dita Paresh's lack of horns.

"I live to serve you and the Hand, my nomarch." Neferna was still expressionless. "If my death serves, then so be it."

"I, too, live to serve." Vindicator Dita swallowed visibly. "But are these orders the Hand's will? And what purpose would it serve to sever a mystic who possesses almost all the requirements to cure the Gray Death?"

"I asked myself the very same questions. But I had made my decision even before then." Setnana nodded to Major Neferna as a sign of respect. "Major, I would not kill someone who has shown nothing but loyalty no matter what I asked."

"Thank you, my nomarch." Neferna bowed.

Setnana turned her attention to the Vindicator, met the man's gaze with ice, and allowed herself a mirthless smile. "As for you, Dita Paresh, you can still help my Perihy with his affliction once we get our hands on a Benediction."

Dita sucked in a slow, shuddering breath. He averted his eyes. "I look forward to redeeming myself, Nomarch Botros."

"Good." Setnana tucked her hair behind one of her horns. "Bakui Assam's order tells me he wants the Engine kept secret from everyone. He did not tell the Five Fingers. If he had, one of their Shadows would have been here in Aprunis to meet us." Setnana shivered with the thought of the cutthroats no one ever saw coming. "And he did not demand the Engine be taken to one of the Hand's strongholds. Instead, he named Modra's Keep, his little private enclave hidden away in the Kaigake Desert. He covets the Engine for himself.

"We *will* do as he ordered with the Engine. When he arrives at the keep, we can discuss the dilemma with him. And state our terms. Make the necessary preparations. We leave at first light."

"Yes, nomarch." The grand kora man and erada woman bowed and took their leave.

When the door closed behind them, Setnana sagged into her favorite cushioned chair. She emptied the glass and looked to her personal Battleguards. "What do you think?"

They glanced at each other. And then back to her.

"You did the right thing." Khafra stood with his hands crossed at his waist, korbitanium vambraces on display. "And you should have us kill Bakui."

Burn scars marred Khafra's indigo face. He'd refused to have them healed, saying they were a reminder of what happens when a man underestimates his opponent. A strange kind of beauty existed in those scars.

"I agree with Khafra." Ihuet's quiet voice, lithe build, unassuming manner, and penchant to dress in mundane garb might make a person think less of him. Many had taken such thoughts to the grave. "The Fingers respect shrewdness, power, and ruthlessness above all else. This is an opportunity to improve your status. Opportunity waits for no one. You must seize it."

She sat back and gazed up to the vaulted ceiling. If there was ever a time to chase her dream of becoming Kalarch, to fulfill that quest, it was now. And Ihuet was right. **Ranks of the Hand** was an objective for as long as she could remember. The very traits he mentioned had seen her attain Disciple status, the fourth rank, in a short period of time.

How exactly to proceed? That was the question. If she did the deed, it had to be in a manner that would not cause undue suspicion from the Coalition.

She had the spark of an idea. "Ihuet, there should be two gargants outside, waiting for an audience. Send them in."

Ihuet left to obey. Moments later, he returned, leading Esben and Frida.

Upon entry, the two gargants were forced to duck their furry heads despite the fortress' tall doors. Esben was the color of old blood and his loose-fitting robes did little to hide a round belly. Frida was the opposite in size, her fur like new grass. Looking at the thick fur made Setnana itch.

Setnana had disliked the idea of relying on more outside help in her desperate attempt to cure Perihy, but in this case, it was the best option.

The only one. Her hierkaneers and alchemists had all failed. As had the grand korae. As had Dita. And she was certain Esben and Frida were no different, but they had discovered something else, something she could use.

"Nomarch Setnana." As they spoke, the gargants offered the slightest of bows.

"Esben, Frida, so glad to see you." Smiling, she beckoned to them. "You said you had news. Good news, I hope. After all the credits I paid for your services."

Esben looked to Frida, who nodded. His fearful eyes shifted to Ihuet and Khafra for a moment.

"They are just my personal guard." Setnana lounged in her chair and waved off Ihuet and Khafra as if they were inconsequential. "I assure you that anything said here is said in confidence."

"Very well." The alchemist's voice was a deep rumble. "We tried every possible spell and potion we could think of. We even went so far as to have one of your hierkaneers strengthen our concoctions by way of the Genesis Engine. Nothing worked. The poison flowing through your son only became stronger. So strong that the corruption could be passed through ingestion of his blood."

He produced a belt from the folds of his robes. Leather slots ran the length of the belt. Stoppered vials occupied them. "These contain the tainted blood. We intended to destroy them, but you had already warned us that anything of your son was to be brought directly to you on punishment of death."

"You did the right thing. Thank you for your honesty." She gestured to the table. "Leave the belt there."

Esben stepped forward and placed the belt on the oak table. "We have done all we can. We are truly sorry we could not do more."

"Me too. Thank you for the effort." She clasped her hands and dipped her head. "My steward, Resena, will see to your payment. Ihuet, see them out and tell a servant to take them to Resena."

After a last slight bow to her, Esben and Frida departed in Ihuet's company. Setnana sighed. Killing those two was a waste of talent, but it was another of those necessary things to preserve her secret. At least the lupines would be pleased.

Her Comm Orb dinged in time with Ihuet's return.

Citri Madiga's shrill voice and Purian accent piped through. "Nomarch Setnana. Come to the temple, now. Hurry. It's Perihy. He—" A scream cut off her voice.

Heart racing, Setnana leaped to her feet, Perihy her immediate concern. "Something has happened at the temple. Go!" Dread was a claw squeezing her heart.

They dashed through the fortress, servants scrambling from their path. As soon as they exited the building, they blew their drake whistles. Screeches echoed in the night.

They hurried down the stairs to the flagstoned courtyard. The wait seemed to take forever. Urgency and fear pressed down upon Setnana. She battled frantic thoughts as her leg shook with impatience.

In the next few minutes came the sound of beating wings. Three drakes shot over the fortress, banked, and lowered to the ground.

Setnana clambered atop her mount, a sky-blue drake that matched her skin. Ihuet and Khafra rode a green and a red, respectively. She pulled on her reins, and with a great beat of its wings, her drake took to the night sky.

Heading toward the city's radiant ocean of bloomglobes and glimmerwands, they left the acropolis' towers and spires behind. They sped over the Noble Domain's villas and orchards into the Obsidian Quarter. Veins of black rock glinted beneath them.

As an arrow from a bow, her drake's snout pointed at the statue of Nif where it reached into the sky. She kicked her bolsters, coaxing more speed from the beast. They shot past the Radiant Quarter, the crystal orb of the Great Timesphere, and over the temple grounds.

The moment her drake touched down at the entrance to the rearmost buildings, she leaped from its back. Ihuet and Khafra were a step quicker. She Flickered past them, worry an undigested meal settling in her gut.

Their trip down the corridors was a blur. Up ahead was the room where they had kept Perihy. The metal door lay in the hall. Scorch marks marred the walls. The reek of something burnt drifted on the air. As did another, stronger fetor.

Blood.

Ihuet and Khafra reached the door first. She was a step behind.

Slaughter greeted her.

Something had torn the two guards and the grand kora mystics to pieces. Limbs and guts covered the floor. The table upon which Perihy had been shackled was empty. The chains had been snapped.

Steeling herself, she made to step into the room. Ihuet's hand on her arm stopped her.

"Look." He pointed at a corpse.

It took but a moment for her to understand who and what she was seeing. The person was Citri Madiga. Part of her face and a chunk of flesh was missing from her neck.

But it was her skin. Gray splotches stood out on her pale, yellow skin.

A rustle from the adjoining room startled her. Ihuet had his storm lance in hand. Khafra faced the room's open door in a defensive stance, korbitanium vambraces ready.

They crept to the doorway. Setnana gasped.

Perihy was there. Or rather, the draconid grunt with metallic gray skin threaded with a network of green and blue veins beating in time with his heart. Eyes closed, he was curled at the foot of the Genesis Engine, his body giving off a faint glow.

"We must get him out of there," Setnana whispered.

"That will be a challenge." Ihuet matched her tone. "Not only will he fight us, but if a spell hits the Engine, the explosion would take this entire place with it."

"I have a solution. Wait here." Khafra stalked down the hallway to another room.

He returned minutes later carrying two sets of chains and shackles, these ones crafted from korbitanium. He passed them to Ihuet. "I will fetch the little one and hold him. You put them on."

"Are you certain?" Ihuet raised a skeptical brow.

Khafra smiled. "Yes. My days of underestimating the opponent are behind me." He turned to Setnana. The smile faded. "I will need to be rough, so I ask for your approval, my nomarch."

Though Setnana dreaded the idea, she understood the necessity. "Do as you must."

Khafra nodded once and turned to the room. "Keep to either side of the door." With those words, a thick, transparent, multifaceted surface crept down his face, his neck, the uncovered portion of his arms, and hands. Bloomglobe light reflected from the layer. He'd invoked his Diamond Hide.

The Battleguard sucked in a deep breath. Beneath his Diamond Hide, his skin bloomed to a brighter indigo. He strode across the room to Perihy, snatched the boy by his ankle, and even as Perihy's eyes shot open and the boy flailed, Khafra dashed back to the door at several times his normal speed.

Khafra now held both of Perihy's shins to one side of him outside the room, while blocking the doorway. Screaming, Perihy lashed out at Khafra's back. But even if Perihy's claws managed to pierce Khafra's armor, they could not penetrate the Diamond Hide.

Ihuet shackled Perihy's ankles. In one swift move, Khafra stepped through the doorway and into the corridor, dragging Perihy with him. Setnana let out a whimper and covered her mouth when Ihuet jabbed Perihy's jaw with the butt of his staff, knocking the flailing boy unconscious. Ihuet chained Perihy's wrists.

"Sorry, my nomarch." Ihuet dipped his head to her.

She waved him off but did not speak, taking a moment to compose herself. Tears moistened her cheeks as she regarded her boy.

Perihy's face was peaceful. If she looked hard enough, she could make out the Perihy she remembered despite the metallic skin and network of vibrant green and blue veins. Where his body had been emaciated while corrupted, and slim before the Gray Death, it was now rife with defined muscle.

Although his current state hurt, there was one change which affected her more than any other. His missing horns. They had been splendid, dark and curved, always polished to a shine. Now, two lumps protruded on either side of his head. His hair was growing back in, so perhaps it would hide the deficiency.

"My nomarch?" Ihuet's tentative voice broke her from her thoughts.

She regarded him for a moment with wrinkled brows. Another few moments passed before she realized they awaited her instructions.

Gathering her thoughts, she nodded toward the carnage in the first

33

room. "At least my son saved us the trouble of having to kill them. We cannot afford any more surprises or waste time. Order guards to be placed outside the temple. Only people approved by myself or you are to enter.

"Have the hierkaneers cover the Engine, pack it up, and fly it to Modra's Keep by simurgh. Khafra, you and the Sky Swords will escort it. Ihuet, you and I will travel by wagon with Perihy since no flying beast will accept him.

"I will also send word to Resena to clean up this place before the hierkaneers arrive. She should be done with the gargants by now.

"Come, bring Perihy into the room down the hall. I will wait there with him until you return with the wagon."

The two Battleguards lifted Perihy gently and carried him to the room in question. As they left to do as she bid, Setnana activated her Comm Orb to pass more orders. When she was done, she settled in to wait, ready to cast Immobilize should Perihy wake and go into a frenzy.

Hours later, she and Ihuet rode in the lead wagon, well on their way south toward the Kaigake Desert and Modra's Keep. Perihy's wagon was behind hers. Every so often, she eased back the curtain and peeked out the window to make certain all was well.

Satisfied, she sat back and took a deep breath. All was going to plan at last. Two days would see them reach the keep.

A resounding boom rocked her wagon. She yanked the curtain aside. And gasped.

The wagon carrying Perihy was nothing more than smoldering bits of wood. The driver and the guards were strewn about the ground.

Perihy was sprinting across the grassy plains, an apparition of vibrant blue and green veins glowing in the night. Several Azureguard drake riders gave chase. Perihy vanished.

CHAPTER 4

The techs required two days to complete Dre's prep. Each day, a tech would escort him to the logistics room and back home again. He wasn't given a chance to leave the apartment to go anywhere else. If he tried, a guard waited outside to deny him.

Frustrated and worried about Blaze, he spent as much time as he could with his family. He'd play or watch Munsters and Minions with Kai. At others times, he'd watch movies with Mom, although they had to resort to the holo versions because Mom wanted no part of VR. He did manage to convince Mom to take a peek into VR when they watched Star Wars, Episode Twelve: Legacy of Jade. Smiling, he recalled how she'd almost jumped out of her skin. When not with Mom or Kai, he indulged in Hop-hop or soca music and surfing the Grid. On the third day, the techs took him toward the Total Immersion test room.

Dressed only in tights, an aural bud in one ear, Dre stood on the observation deck in a line of similarly garbed testers. Techs fussed over pods in the room below. Some studied holos, while others helped men, women, and children climb into the pods.

A part of him regretted having to leave his family again. The other half looked forward to seeing Pops. Dre sighed, the thought of the holo that was his father a painful reminder.

He'd need to find some way to tell Mom about Pops in Void Legion, about what Equitane had done. Preferably after she gave birth to Regi and

Rayne. He'd hate for the shock of such news to be the cause of further complications.

Dre got up on his toes, hoping to see Blaze either in front, behind, or down in the pod room itself. But he saw no one with her tell-tale box braids.

The buzz of numerous voices rose all around him. Techs passed by, often stopping to scan testers' biometric tatts. After the scans, another set of techs ushered testers into one of two glass elevators with clear views into the pod room. Dre tried and failed to pick out Blaze's pod.

"Good day, testers," chimed a female voice through Dre's aurals. The woman had a thick New York accent. The room quieted. "I'm Zhi Yin, one of the head developers. Some news. First, we've updated the game based on the feedback you gave. We've fixed some bugs and exploits.

"The major change has been to Information Memory," Zhi Yin declared. "Many of you complained about an issue between Simulated Reality and real life. A disconnect. The feeling of something missing. Something intangible."

Dre nodded. He knew the feeling too well.

"As we're trying to perfect Total Immersion, we reduced the scope of Information Memory. The general concern was an overabundance of knowledge, history, and lore at one's fingertips, which took away from the exploration, the learning, the discovery of the world. The wow factor, as some of you put it.

"To some of you, it felt too much like a game in that regard. You wanted things to be more organic. While some aspects concerning stats remain, we've curtailed many other parts of IM. We hope we've done enough to soothe those concerns and look forward to your take on the changes."

Numerous murmurs of agreement emanated from the testers. Quite a few smiled. Including Dre. The change made him look forward to the game even more.

"The second bit of news is the focus of this phase. As often happens after a first clear, more groups have gone on to kill Emperor KiGyaba and pass Imanok Sanctum. We congratulate you all and offer you the next challenge: The Forsaken Crypts of Puria.

"The scenario around the Crypts is part of one of many unique world events connected to Mikander's lore. And by unique, not only will the event not happen again, but the Crypts themselves will only be in their current form until cleared. Some bosses will move on to pursue their interests, evolving, growing with the world. Some rewards like titles and items cannot be attained again."

A chorus of ohs and ahs swept through the corridor. Dre had to admit even he was impressed and excited by the prospects. Hopefully, the devs had balanced the unique items.

"You must be level twenty to enter. Your group cannot be more than five until the place is cleared. Then you can bring in others. Unlike with Imanok, which was an open dungeon, this is an instance, which means each group will have its own private version. At least until the summit.

"Also, it does not scale per encounter. It scales by entry and based upon the highest-level person in the group. But if you're above level twenty-five, you won't get any loot or exp. Not even from chests. As for the bosses? You'll see when you get there.

"One last thing. Bonus information based on a ton of questions we received.

"Many of you mentioned seeing the foundation of a Genesis Engine in the Sanctum. You also wondered if you had the ability to craft the low-level shards and weapons, stating it was unfair or bad design to have to wait until you were high enough level to get past the Front to use the Engines there.

"Rest assured that there was an Engine in the Sanctum. Once a dungeon is fully cleared, the actual areas or rooms with Engines become open. Not just open to anyone, but also Open PVP, meaning any player can attack another not in their group. There's no limit to the number or level of people who can be in the area and engage in the fight.

"We made this choice based on the impact Genesis Engines have on the game. They are among the most powerful artifacts.

"Engines can be destroyed. They can be taken and moved to another place if the players or NPCs have the skill to do so. If destroyed, they don't respawn. Any other info as to their origins or the ability to build them will remain a mystery you must uncover.

"Good luck. And have fun."

Dre cocked his head to one side. The info on the Genesis Engines was worth remembering. As was that of the Crypts. Although the dungeon was another new addition, it had been listed on Pops' protocol map from the Void Gate room. The map Dre had committed to memory.

Fifteen minutes later, Dre was standing next to his pod, the A200 lettering standing out on its side. His stomach fluttered as if it were his first time. But this time, the flutter was more anticipation. Excitement rather than fear.

He climbed into the cylindrical pod and lay facing up. The door swung down seconds later and sealed with a hiss. Machinery droned. A helmet maneuvered atop his head. A black-tinted visor slid over his face. The whirr of needles that would introduce the nanites and Tissue Nanotransfection into his system echoed all around him. He gritted his teeth, bracing for pain. The needles stabbed into him all at once. He stifled a cry. The pain faded.

A light appeared, joined by a voice moments later. "Welcome to Ataxia Online 2, Void Legion." The world shot forward.

******

He was standing in an empty room. There were no mirrors, but iterations of himself surrounded him like vivid reflections.

He was Drelan Frost, a roughly seven-foot tall erada with dark magenta skin. His black mane was done in cornrows, the plaits weaving a roadmap between his curled ram-like horns and falling down his back. A shadow of a beard hugged his chin and crept up the side of his face.

His attire consisted of knee-high leather boots, black pants, a matching thigh-length gambeson, a mahogany brigandine, and a deep brown hooded cloak. He also had matching greaves on his shins, cuisses over his thighs, and bracers on his wrists.

He checked to make certain he had his Two Ring, the black aether ring that came with his character. It was a memento of the real world, one that every player had some version of, a clone of something they held precious IRL that would keep them grounded in-game so they would not lose themselves within the experience of Simulated Reality. The aether ring was Pops' creation.

And it had a secret purpose.

If he turned it counter-clockwise twice on his finger, it activated a field that scrambled his location and anything within the field's vicinity, preventing the game's security systems or admins from tracking him. It also caused a diversion in the form of the simultaneous appearance of an anomaly elsewhere in the world.

Frost glanced down. At his feet was Deadeye. He picked up the rare aether cannon, its quality revealed by a blue tint provided by IM. If he stood the weapon beside him, it would stretch from his shoulder to the floor. He cradled the cannon, again immediately reminded of DOOM's BFGs or some massive, large-barreled weapon straight out of a sci-fi movie.

Frost thought about his stats. IM was there to greet him.

Strength: 20
Agility: 25
Vitality: 29
Aether: 30

He recalled that for each level from one to ten, he'd been granted two points per attribute. Algorithms based on genealogy and then his own practice with Replenishment and skill use had provided an additional bonus to his aether. He chalked up the disparity in agility and strength to the fights, to running and dodging, where he had to rely on his speed and Cannon Kata.

Thinking about the numbers had IM provide him with the stats derived from his attributes and gear.

Physical Attack Power: 42
Movement Speed: 50
Haste/Attack Speed: 2
Aether Power: 110 – 135
Stagger Resist: 3%
Damage Reduction: 5%

Frowning, he considered the lack of numbers for things such as dodge, health, or aether capacity. He expected IM to be there with details, but it was not. He gave the idea some thought and drew to a few conclusions based off his experience so far.

For health and aether capacity, he recognized it was a matter of feeling.

To put it simply, he felt like shit when he was wounded. Aether capacity was a sense of fullness which depleted upon skill use or increased by way of Aether Absorption or Replenishment.

He had one explanation for the lack of a hard percent for dodge. Dodge was skill-based. A player didn't automatically dodge attacks. He had to practice like a boxer or other combatant.

Curiosity piqued by the disparity in attributes, he focused on vitality first. He ran the numbers, considering the passive two-point stat allotments. After a moment, he smiled.

One calculation made sense. Vitality, strength, and agility were linked. According to his math, five points of agility or strength equated to one point of vitality.

He knew movement speed and haste or physical attack speed were the product of agility. But they converted in opposite directions. While every point of agility equated to two points of movement speed, twenty points of agility accounted for one point of haste. He assumed he could increase haste through practice, but there was no need unless he decided to train in melee weapons as the attack rate of cannons had been constant so far.

For a moment, he wondered how a player would increase spell haste, thereby decreasing the time needed to cast a spell. Practice, he assumed, which seemed unfair when compared to melee, but casters did have the advantage of range.

Considering Deadeye's damage ranged from fifty to seventy-five, then his total aether power was a matter of doubling his aether stat and then adding it to the weapon's lower and upper damage levels. Physical attack power used the same multiplier, and his Braided Loop rings provided the additional two points.

His armor accounted for four percent damage reduction; the steadfast bracelets two percent stagger resist total. Brows furrowed, he ran the numbers again, seeking the explanation for the extra percentage point of stagger resist and damage reduction. Typically, strength also affected defense.

After a couple minutes, he nodded, recalling stat changes while leveling to ten. Every twenty points of strength added one percent damage reduction. Twenty points of agility did the same for stagger resist.

IM dinged to make him aware of a new available skill.

Leap:

All Mikanderans gain an affinity to the world by way of aether usage. This affinity causes special aspects to activate as the Mikanderan grows. The first such aspect is Leap, which allows Mikanderans to cover distances several times their own height when they jump. The act of jumping itself activates the skill. With practice comes greater control.

Epic, Frost thought. He wondered what the skill would be like in combat. He could see it being difficult to adjust to, but once mastered, it offered an entirely new dimension.

Excited to be on his way, he checked his exp and credits. He needed forty thousand more experience points to level eleven. He had fifty-five hundred KDC and nine thousand two hundred and fifty IDC.

Satisfied, he said, "Begin."

******

He spawned in a cavern, identified by the light filtering in from its mouth. The first thing he noticed was the air. It was thick, humid, pressing down on him, and smelled of wet earth and musty animals. Winds howled from outside. A quick look around said he was alone, although he couldn't see into the cavern's deeper darkness.

He clicked. Echolocation confirmed his solitude. The skill also unveiled the cavern continued behind him for at least some three hundred feet, the maximum distance of the ability's range. Not far from where he stood was the remains of a dead campfire. A quick inspection revealed a collection of flint, tinder, and clumps of dry grass.

Frost turned to face the cavern's maw. Outside, the sky was fifty shades of ash. Lightning etched the ash with livid scars. Cradling Deadeye, he strode forward until he stood in the opening, the wind billowing his hooded cloak. He confirmed a suspicion that crossed his mind the moment he spawned.

He was where he had left the game. Daggerspine Mountain on Maelpith Island. Before him was a ledge wide enough to hold four men shoulder to shoulder. It led up and down. Beyond its edge was open air.

The land sprawled far below him. To his right was the lake that held Imanok Sanctum, its green murky water hiding the dungeon. Straight ahead were plains and forests, stretching all the way to the coast where waves crashed and the sapphire of the Empyrean Sea clashed with the leaden sky.

Squinting, he made out numerous ships and sails. A bit inland were clusters of buildings Dagrun had shown him. They made up the Coalition's base of operations.

Frowning, he wondered where everyone had gone. He barely had the thought when the Communication Orb dinged in his mind, informing him of a message from Meritus Killgain.

"Yo, my dude, it's ya boy." Meritus' nasal voice piped through the Orb. "Hope you're alright. I'm still over here in Korbash, leveling and keeping an eye on Tia. Although, I doubt she needs me. The eradae in the stronghold have practically adopted her."

Frost smiled. Knowing Tia was in good hands was refreshing.

"Yo, did you know the gargants had libraries as good as those in the Aetherium? They call them the Halls of Illumination. I've been over here doing as much research as I can to help me make more credits. You know how I do. I gotta be the richest player in game.

"Anyway, ya girl, Gilda, had a courier deliver a message to me for you. She's somewhere in Lothal."

The mention of Gilda gave Frost instant relief. Knowing she was in-game, and well, meant the world to him. Meritus' voice became a distant thing as Frost pictured Gilda, cerulean-skinned and lithe. Her green eyes and beautiful face put the 'ex' in exotic. In his mind, she twirled her dagger as he stared at her. Frost sighed.

Meritus' voice drifted back into focus. "They left Maelpith because they weren't sure if or when you'd be back with all that you got going on with your Mom. She said if you spawn in the same cavern as they did, the one y'all took Sigrid to, that you'll find a chest with supplies in a corner to the far right of the entrance."

A quick glance at the location revealed the chest. Its coloring and position were such that he might have overlooked it.

"She also said the safest way off the island was to get a young drake. To find one, you'll need to go up the mountain from the cavern until you reach a saddle with a waterfall and lagoon before the summit. That's where the drakes live.

"Oh, and she said not to try sneaking onto one of the Coalition ships and passing for a returning expeditioner. They have special passes." Meritus chuckled. "Guess she knows what kinda reckless dude you can be sometimes.

"Nomarch Setnana still has lupines and trackers searching for y'all. Even got a bounty on your head, naming you in the attack on Kituan and claiming that you're a Blue Sky agent. As soon as Gilda can afford a Comm Orb, she'll message you.

"Stay safe, homie. Looking forward to when we hook up again. Holla at me when you get a chance. Oh, and… shaddup." Meritus chuckled once more.

"Shaddup," Frost repeated with a smile.

Relieved the others were fine, he strode over to the stone-colored chest. He flipped open the lid. The first thing to catch his attention was a sword belt with a sword in a plain leather scabbard. He wasn't much of a swordsman at the moment, but the weapon might still prove useful. He buckled the belt around his waist, the sword hanging near his right hip.

Acquired weapon: Expedition Sword
Level: 5
Damage: 60 – 70
Force: none
Special: none
Available shard slots: none

In his mind, IM gave the weapon a white tinge, marking it as common. Frost removed the sword and took a few one-handed practice swings with Deadeye in his other hand. The weapon felt a bit odd. As if his body wasn't yet accustomed to it. Unlike when he held the aether cannon.

He concluded the effect had to be some innate weapon mastery that would only improve with time and use. The idea fit with everything else he'd experienced to this point.

On a whim, Frost checked his stats. Sure enough, his physical attack power had increased to match the sword's upper and lower ranges.

Further study of the chest's contents revealed a canteen of water and potions. There were five of each pot. He'd used all his consumables to defeat

Emperor KiGyaba. He took them, sparking IM.

Health Potion

Regain 500 health instantly.

Reuse: 2 minutes

Rejuvenation Potion

Regain 1000 health over 30 seconds.

Reuse: 2 minutes

Purification Potion

Cleanse one adverse effect.

Reuse: 2 minutes

Coulda used some vials too, he thought. *But as Mom would say: 'beggars can't be choosers. Silver linings.'* He stuck the pots into a few of the quick access pouches on his belt.

Returning his attention to the chest, he noted strips of dried meat. He took up a strip and sniffed it. The meat had a smoked odor. He bit off a chunk. Indeed, the flavor was smoked, the taste similar to beef. Chewing, he stuffed the remainder of the meat into his belt pouches. He took a swig of warm water from the canteen to wash down the meat then placed the metal container into its satchel beside the pouches.

At the bottom of the chest was a set of drake reins, large enough to fit a neck as wide as Frost's arms could stretch to form a circle. Frost smiled at Gilda's foresight. He hadn't considered that he'd abandoned the last reins back in Soleb. He picked up the set.

Acquired item: Young Drake Reins

Allows for basic flight

Young drake required

Recalling that possessing the reins and finding drakes were only one part of his problem, he put the reins in his inventory and took a stock of his belongings. Benediction stood out. Not only because it was a zhua—a long staff topped by a silver korbitanium claw—but the genesiswork hierka also had a barely discernible violet glow. A color that marked its quality as epic.

A schema made from thick paper contained violet-tinged instructions on how to craft more zhua like Benediction. Not all of the listed materials had their origins or locations attached.

Acquiring korbitanium and blood from void beasts appeared simple enough. Of greater concern was dragonwood, forsaken bones, and void beholder's eyes. Dragonwood typically grew in the Dagoda Front and beyond. A place too high for his current level. He had no idea where to find the mobs that dropped the bones or the eyes.

Additionally, the hierka could only be crafted in a Genesis Engine, which meant needing a hierkaneer. And most likely battling draconids.

He smiled at the thought of such fights. Particularly at end-game when it meant venturing into the Dagoda Front and beyond to face some of the strongest creatures in Mikander. He sighed longingly at the loot to be found. *Epic players do epic things*, he thought, before shaking off the idea. It was a challenge for another time.

But there was one thing he *could* do. "Activate Comm Orb." He didn't need to say the words. Thinking was enough, but saying it out loud felt natural.

A list of In-Game Names popped into his head, each IGN with an @ before it. People he had partied with the last time he was in-game. All the IGNs were grayed out but for one. "Meritus Killgain. Voice message." A ping announced its readiness.

"What up, homie. It's Frost. I can't thank you enough for all your help. And you know I don't like asking, but I need another favor. Play a mystic like you used to.

"I got this epic weapon that scales with the owner, both by level and by usage. A zhua named Benediction. Its special allows it to channel void energy to cure the Gray Death. I also got the schema to craft more of them. We'll need forsaken bones, void beholder's eyes, void beast blood, dragonwood, and korbitanium. And of course, a Genesis Engine since it's a hierka. It also needs three specific empowered spells to activate the cure.

"The spells are Empowered Ameliorate, Empowered Suppression, and Empowered Rejuvenate. I know we can find the skill-effect shards in Imanok Sanctum, but keep an eye on the Auction Market in case they show up. Or for word from any merchants or scavengers about where else we might find them."

Frowning, Frost paused. "Come to think of it, there's gotta be more weapons like this for every class. Look into that also. Until then, level up. I'll send for you when I'm ready. Or if you hear anything, let me know."

"Holla at ya boy. And… shaddup." Smiling, Frost commanded the message to be sent by a mere thought.

Absently stroking his aether ring, Frost imagined what it would be like to possess an aether cannon similar to Benediction. His mind ran through dozens of possible specialties it might have. Almost as important would be the leveling. With the weapon's ability to grow in power, he might not need another.

Goaded by the possibility, Frost set his focus on getting off the island. Reaching level eleven to gain an additional three points in stats seemed the smartest move. *Might be a good idea to also do some calisthenics and shadow boxing to increase strength and agility. Maybe, a couple hours a day in the morning.*

Nodding to himself, he checked his ammo. He was all out of korbitanium shells. Sighing, he cradled Deadeye and went outside.

He looked once more toward the murky lake that hid Imanok Sanctum. Melancholy sat heavy on his chest. He wished he could visit the Sanctum again. For no other reason than to see Pops, hear his voice, talk to him in the Void Gate room.

Frost took a long slow breath, remembering Pops' words about other Void Gate rooms. He longed to find the one in the Forsaken Crypts.

"Won't do that sitting around here," Frost said aloud.

Following Meritus' directions, he trudged up the ledge, which soon became an old path of shale and dirt. A part of him was tempted to give the new Leap skill a try, but the howling wind buffeting him toward the edge said it would be the absolute worst idea. Battling the wind, he pulled on his hood and held it in place.

He reached the crest over an hour later. The air had grown a bit cooler, foggy, and wet. A constant roar emanated in the distance. Lightning radiated in fitful spurts among pregnant clouds, but there was no accompanying crack or angry rumble of thunder.

Cloak fluttering, he wiped his brow and took in his surroundings. He stood on a saddle, the land dipping into a gradual slope, flattening to a plain of hardy grass, shrubs, and stunted trees for several thousand feet, before rising again into wind-scarred cliff faces whose stony foreheads were crowned in gloom.

To his left, frothy water gushed from a cliff covered in moss and algae and crashed down into a lagoon with roaring effervescence. The lagoon sprawled from the foamy collision like a turquoise sky. Several rivulets ran from the end of the lagoon near him, forming a stream that spilled downhill, meandering its way across the plain before disappearing where the land fell away to his right.

His stomach clenched as his fear of deep water swelled when he looked toward the area into which the waterfall churned. Yet, there was a beauty to the violence, the foam and froth. The white. A counterpoint of peacefulness. The crescendo of the falls, enough to leave him mesmerized.

A screech snapped his attention to the gemstone of a pool. A red and black drake, several times Frost's size, was drinking from the water. When it had its fill, the drake lurched into the air.

The drake glided like an exotic dancer in red and black, body undulating with each flap of leathery wings. It headed far left to one of many caves pockmarking the cliff face, well away from dozens of similar openings. Movement along the cliffs and at the caves resolved into scores of drakes. Above the waterfalls' roar came the raucous dissonance of their screeches.

With the discovery of the drakes complete, he set about his next task. Leveling. A quick perusal of the saddle revealed several forms of wildlife. He dismissed the korbitoises and their spiked shells, the sight of them immediately making him think of Dante who had called them Bowser's babies. Smiling, he wondered what the big crimson-skinned, lion-faced gurash was doing.

Probably off somewhere looking for some action. Frost could hear Dante's high-pitched voice even now.

The smile became a frown. Frost wondered what had become of Adesh Hamada and the goblin, Ryne. Adesh had completed his task as an NPC, but Ryne was still Frost's bodyguard. *Had Ryne gone off to do his own thing?*

Sidrie had claimed the game world was persistent. If left to their own devices, NPCs and mobs could make decisions for themselves. Decisions independent of programming. Zhi Yin's talk about Crypt bosses hinted at the same thing.

Frost shook his head, still finding the idea hard to believe. But if it was true, then the little black-robed shadowmancer was probably summoning defilers, boasting of his prowess, while rhyming as if he were a traveling bard. Or looking to do bad things to gnomes.

Chuckling, Frost decided to practice Leap now that he'd found a place to level. Only a fool went into battle without a sense of a new skill's capabilities. Fools often ended up dead. At the risk of brain damage, dead was the last thing he wanted to be.

Focusing on the idea of a regular hop, he jumped. He lifted about a foot off the ground, just as he'd envisioned. On the next try, he pictured something a bit higher and jumped some three feet straight up. There was an airy sense for all of a split second.

Thinking back to workouts in real life and sims, or days when he practiced MMA, he imagined box jumps. He considered putting down Deadeye, but almost every moment in-game would be with the cannon. Whatever he did needed to be practical to Void Legion.

In his mind, he saw the heavy foam plyometric box before him. Above chest high seemed a good place to start. He bent his knees and pushed off in one quick motion. He sprang up, nearly doubling the previous distance. The airy sensation was there in earnest this time.

Frost landed with a thud and grinned. He was certain the last sensation was the activation of Leap.

Over the next hour, he increased the Leap's increments. He also practiced in different directions. Leaping back, to the side, or forward were all a rush, the movement swift. Eventually, he was Leaping twice his height, his feet moving as if he walked upon his descent. To the back and sides were much shorter in comparison to up or forward.

With an idea in mind, he picked nearby solitary trees or rocks and fired off Aether Shots during Leap. His aim was abysmal. As in real life, shooting and hoping to hit a target while jumping was not practical. At least not with single target abilities. AOEs might work better, but the last thing he wanted was to draw any attention to his presence. He promised to work on it another time.

Comfortable with his progress, he returned to the matter at hand. Leveling. Although they might be easier to deal with, killing korbitoises would be a waste. Not only did he lack an adequate means to skin them or remove their shells, but he despised the idea of skinning altogether. That left the other two types of mobs.

The largest and most fearsome of the two were the lamias. They measured perhaps fifteen feet from head to serpentine bottom half. The four-armed upper body was humanoid, shapely, complete with a beautiful woman's face and flowing hair in various colors. That portion stood six feet on average, but midway down, where the hips curved, the human form melded into a scaled body the tail of which ended in a spike.

The other set of mobs were arkets. Taller than Frost by a foot on average, tanned and black-spotted, they reminded him of hyenas. If hyenas walked like men. Occasionally, an arket threw back its head and let out a boisterous chortle. Two fought each other near the stream, rolling on the ground while barking, clawing, and snapping.

On the far side of the area, a lamia was fighting off a drake. The drake tried unsuccessfully to attack from the air. Its target proved too agile. When the drake landed and charged with its wings spread, the lamia was equal to the task, slithering faster than the drake could run. Eventually, the drake abandoned the chase.

Another lamia, its head low to the ground, slithered through shrubs not far from a korbitoise. The korbitoise stood on its hind legs, neck stretched up. In a blur of movement, the lamia dashed to the korbitoise, wrapped its serpentine half around the creature, slammed its claws beneath the korbitoise's chin, even as the end of the tail whipped around and stabbed the korbitoise in the jugular notch.

Mouth agape, Frost could only stare as the tail expanded and contracted. The korbitoise grew sallow. Its skin sloughed. The lamia fed.

Frost turned away from the sight. He picked the smallest arket, one a good distance away from the others, and headed toward it. He was almost in Staggering Shot range when he stepped on a twig. He froze. But it didn't matter.

The arket had eyes only for him. Frost aimed Deadeye.

The arket chuckled. It disappeared.

Grass, dirt, and debris swirled where the arket had been visible. A whirlwind taller than the average erada shot toward Frost.

CHAPTER 5

Frost made to jump away but was too slow. Howling, the Whirlwind struck his left side, flinging him back several steps, his cloak flailing around him. Pain shot through his body.

Not waiting to discern the damage done by way of his weakness, Frost snagged a rejuvenation pot from his belt, popped the cork, and drank the bitter liquid. He grimaced even as the potion's first tick refreshed him.

"Just my luck that I picked a caster. One that can Conceal too." He shook his head.

Circling to his right, he kept Deadeye aimed. He let out a soft click. Echolocation responded, revealing a silhouette perhaps two hundred feet away, creeping in the opposite direction.

"Got ya."

Frost fired off a Staggering Shot, the deep blue beam hurtling through the air with a whine. While the disorienting skill was zipping toward the silhouette, Frost squeezed the trigger again to release an Aether Shot. Deadeye coughed out a bullfrog whomp. A cyan bolt followed its darker cousin.

A one-second charge saw him unleash Divergence, the five beams blasting from Deadeye just as the Staggering Shot hit the Concealed arket. Another second and Frost had fired Piercer, a red streak.

Staggering Shot knocked the arket from Concealment. The beast wobbled where it stood. The single blue Aether Shot and one of the five from Divergence blasted into the creature in quick succession, the other four beams continuing through the air before dissipating.

A moment later, Piercer's streaking red ripped through the arket's canine head. The beast crumpled. Deadeye's Improved Cannon Kata kicked in upon the arket's death, increasing Frost's movement speed by fifty percent for the next six seconds.

Elite arket slain.

Gained 400 experience points.

"Elite." Frost nodded. "No wonder that bastard was so tough." Killing these mobs weren't an ideal situation, but the exp was worth it, even if the arkets might prove to be a pain in the ass with their casting and invisibility.

Aether drifted into the air from the corpse. It swirled for a moment before thickening into a band and darting across the distance and into Frost. The energy from the Aether Absorption joined that within him, bringing him to three quarters capacity. Some of the aether diverted into his Overload reservoir.

While Frost strode toward the remains, he focused on the air around him. He could feel the aether. A living energy that tugged at him, swirled and dived and danced like playful sylphs. Concentrating on the aether within and without, he formed a connection. Aether trickled into him by way of Replenishment.

He bent and checked the dead arket for loot, hoping for something good. There was nothing.

Remembering the red and black drake, an idea came to him. He grabbed the arket by its ankle and dragged it toward the blue-green gemstone of a lagoon. When he got up on the flat slate-colored rocks, Frost dropped the carcass. He lay Deadeye behind him and drew the Expedition Sword.

Frost kicked the arket's arm until the limb extended straight out from the creature's body. Crouching over the carcass near the shoulder, he braced himself. "Just remember it's a game. It's just a game." It was ironic how he could fight and kill in the heat of the moment, but to deliberately maim as he intended left a queasy feeling in his stomach.

He committed the joint of the arm and shoulder to memory, inhaled the fresh air, closed his eyes, and swung. Chunk. He opened one eye. He'd managed a relatively deep cut but nothing more. Frost deflated.

Blood welled out from the wound. Thick. Ruby. Viscous. Swallowing at the sight and pungent odor, Frost took aim, pretended he couldn't see, and swung. Chop. He swung again. And again, ignoring the wet, sickening sounds. The arm parted from the body.

He let out a breath he hadn't realized he held. After he wiped the sword on the arket's fur, Frost slipped it into the scabbard, picked up Deadeye, and made his way back to the hill.

Rather than hunt more arkets, he decided the lamias might be the easier target after all. Due to them being melee, he might not need to rely on Crowd Control abilities like Staggering Shot. If the lamias weren't too fast, he could kite them.

Before he began, he imagined the strategy. For kiting, he would start at max range from his target, pump out as many initial shots as possible, and then run away while firing off occasional attacks until the creature died. If the lamia got too close, he could always fall back on the Staggering Shot.

For the most desperate situations, he had two more Crowd Control skills in reserve. The disorientation from Aether Bomb and stun of Concussion Blast.

But they were both Area of Effect skills that involved explosions. Using either AOE wasn't the best idea if he wanted to avoid drawing attention. But like Gilda often said, ya gotta do what ya gotta do.

A part of him wished he was playing a sorcerer. Or had a few sorcerer skills like Glacial Eruption, which had two CC effects: stun and slow. And the skill was a noiseless one. The fights would've been so much easier.

"Gotta work with what you got, dawg."

His Comm Orb dinged. Frost expected a message from Meritus. Instead, it was a notification. A powerful man's voice bloomed in his head.

WORLD FIRST KILL

A group led by Kazuto Morow of the WaR guild defeated Bragash the Bender, a void revenant that had been terrorizing the people of Aesernia, a small town in the western Ignis nome of Sutrium. As a reward, the Coalition has bestowed the title of Sutrium Protector unto Kazuto and his group members, Meileen Elune, Saigo Thrall, Vash Quickdraw, and Aizen Shadowblade.

The notification vanished. Frost smiled. He had to admit to being a little jealous of the achievement despite having the World First on Emperor KiGyaba. He wanted to be first for every kill.

"Ah well." He shrugged and returned to the task at hand.

From his vantage, he picked out the nearest area with lamias. As he approached, he chose one of the smaller reptilian-humanoid hybrids. Staying low, he used stunted trees and brush as much as he could until he was in range.

He took aim and unleashed a Staggering Shot, Piercer, Divergence, Aether Shot combo. The lamia wobbled in place on the first hit. The other abilities blasted into its chest and head in quick succession. He was ready with another Aether Shot after its two-second recharge time, and still had Aether Bomb and Concussion Blast. A part of him wished Aether Overload was full for him to use Stand and Deliver, despite knowing the skill would be overkill.

However, he needed none of them. The lamia no longer had a head. Aether formed a small mote, streaked through the air and into Frost.

Elite lamia slain.

Gained 400 experience points.

"Easy peasy. Only ninety-eight more kills."

He chose another lamia and repeated the sequence with the same results. After eight kills he'd exhausted his aether despite the amount regained from Aether Absorption, the percentage return from his abilities, as well as calling upon Replenishment on his way to the next target.

He sat among the grass and meditated. Replenishment accelerated. Within a minute, he had the sense of fullness again, like a stuffed belly. As he made to get back to leveling, he noted his reservoir for Aether Overload had already begun to decay, but not his aether pool.

Once more, Frost started up on the lamias. After the first couple kills, Aether Absorption had almost filled Overload once again. And it had done so faster than Replenishment. The decay rate had also lessened while he was actively engaged. He made a mental note of the difference.

A drake screeched when he was on his thirtieth kill. Lamia carcasses were strewn about the ground. He still hadn't been lucky enough to find any loot.

Another screech joined the first. And another. Glancing up, Frost tracked three large drakes as they circled the turquoise lagoon.

From their size, he assumed they were GUMs. But no title popped into his IM to designate any of them with the boss or mini-boss status of a Giant Ugly Mofo. A part of him was sorry they weren't GUMs. He'd already envisioned himself riding atop one and the admiration such a feat would've brought.

Unlike their smaller brother or sister below them, the three drakes were solid-colored. Green. Blue. Gray. Wings beating, they descended toward the rocks near the carcass.

The red and black drake was already there, sniffing at the arket, stalking one way then the next as if uncertain what it should do. It was oblivious to its kin's approach.

Wings beating the air, the newcomers descended to the ground. Hissing and snapping, they charged the red and black drake. Red-and-black raised its wings, let out a growling squawk, and waddled away.

The others turned to the carcass and tore at it. Red-and-black made to return. They attacked the drake again. With a flap of its wings Red-and-black flew to the other side of the lagoon.

Hissing and screaming amongst themselves, the bullies resumed their gorging. When they finished, only bits of bone and meat were left. They took turns nudging the remains into the lagoon with their snouts. The turquoise water reddened for a moment.

Together, the three drakes looked toward Red-and-black, raised their snouts, and emitted croaks that reminded Frost of chuckling. Wings flapping, they took to the air.

"That was mean. I guess even animals in a game can be assholes." Shaking his head, Frost marveled at their AI. He could not have imagined such lifelike interactions. The creatures seemed too real.

Red-and-black crossed back over the lagoon. It sniffed at the red-stained area. After a moment, the drake headed to the water's edge. Head cocked, it stared into the murk. It made a sad cooing sound and hung its head before lurching into the air and flapping over to its aerie.

Disheartened by the encounter, Frost turned toward the most recent lamia carcass. Most of the others had now despawned. He grabbed the creature by the tail and dragged it to the stained area. With a few swings of his sword he chopped off part of the tail. On the way down he refilled his canteen from the stream.

Frost returned to leveling. New mobs had spawned. He fully expected them to have adjusted to his strategy. At first, he could not tell if they did. He was too strong. They succumbed to the same method, dead before they could react. But it wasn't long before he realized their numbers had diminished.

That was when he noticed the burrows. If a lamia saw him first, it would slither away and into the holes in the ground. Most of them remained close to those habitats.

Frost adjusted his strategy, using any cover he could find to get in range. Sometimes, he crawled on his stomach. When he'd killed a few in a row he cut off the snake portion of the body and made a small pile.

At kill number fifty, he discovered a skill shard, this one in the shape of a teardrop gemstone, the aether coiling lazily inside. Frost pumped his fist.

Skill acquired:

Homer

Requires level 12

He nodded his approval. Frost tucked the shard into his inventory and resumed the hunt. From time to time, he stopped to wipe sweat from his brow, eat a bit of dried meat, and take a swig from his canteen. He continued to work on Leap, increasing its distance, his body quickly growing accustomed to the skill.

Lost in the monotony of the process, he refined his Replenishment and Echolocation. He used Cannon Kata to speed up his target engagement. When he checked his stats again during a meditation session, his aether had increased by one to thirty-one.

The distorted coin of a sun was past the midway point when a cry announced Red-and-black's return to the lagoon. Red-and-black was soon followed by the bullies. The scenario played out in a similar fashion.

After the three bullies left, Frost picked up one of the tails he'd set aside. Holding the tapered bottom end in both hands, he whipped his arms around, and tossed the tail up toward the bloodied spot at the lagoon. Staying motionless, he waited.

Red-and-black's attention snapped toward Frost. The drake tilted its head. It let out a sound trapped between a growl and a squawk. It peered from the meat to Frost and back again.

Soon enough, the drake flapped across the pool and landed near the morsel. It looked to Frost again. With a sudden move, it dashed to the tail, snatched it up, and flew towards its aerie.

The three drakes met it in the air. They attacked from multiple directions until Red-and-black dropped its meal. One dived down to feast. The other two chased off Red-and-black.

Frost sighed. He retrieved another tail, placed it in the same spot, then got back to the grind. Soon enough, he leveled.

Level 11 gained
Attributes increased by 3 points
Strength: 23
Agility: 28
Vitality: 32
Aether: 34

Frowning, Frost pondered why there hadn't been an extra increase in vitality. He'd gained six total points between agility and strength. One conclusion made sense. Agility and strength counted individually. Not combined.

Noting he now needed eighty-five thousand exp to level, he continued to grind. He relished the fact the increase in aether meant more power, faster kills, and the use of more abilities before he needed Replenishment.

The day died, giving way to evening. Wanting to push to the next level, Frost took on extra fights. He paid for the mistake several times, forcing him to kite a lamia or chug down a pot.

On one occasion, two beams from Divergence had struck additional lamias. With no way to successfully kite three mobs, Frost was left with no choice but to use Concussion Blast. The explosion cast a fiery white haze on impact, stunning one lamia and killing the other two. Frost cursed himself. When he finished off the last creature, he waited a while before resuming the grind.

Evening birthed velvet night and a sky immersed in a panoply of radiance, fitful spurts of voidstorm lightning. Or rather, the remnants of the last voidstorm. With night came the cold. Exhaustion set in. Frost shivered. He'd tried to wait for Red-and-black to show again, but the drake had not returned.

Frost killed one more lamia then cut off its tail. He placed Deadeye in his inventory, the cannon disappearing as if by magic. Dragging the tail behind him, Frost made to head toward the gurgling stream. He stopped, mouth agape.

The air above the lagoon's surface burned with turquoise fire. Such was the glow that it lit the area. Insects flitted through the radiance like snowflakes in a squall.

Enthralled, Frost did not know how long he stood there staring. A wind carrying a chill like death and the pungent odor of rotten eggs knocked him from his trance. As did a long lingering roar of something on the hunt farther up the mountain.

Remembering his prior task, he filled his canteen from the stream, and drank a few mouthfuls of cold water, relishing its fresh taste. After refilling the canteen, he took one last look at the lagoon, grabbed the lamia tail, and trudged downhill in the direction of the cavern.

As he walked, he took in the distant coast and the tiny lights marking the Coalition expedition's base of operations. He wondered what had become of Nomarch Setnana Botros. He still had quests that concerned her. Namely, **The Black Hand** and **Vengeance For Anefet.**

When Frost arrived at the cavern, he built a small campfire by way of the flint and tinder. He chopped the lamia tail into chunks, skewered some of them, and placed them in the fire. Smoke rose into the air, giving off a righteous scent of roasting. His stomach grumbled.

While chewing on the tough lamia flesh, he decided on which quests to pursue, the main lines being **The Cure** and **The Black Hand.** Those chained into others, many of which were unidentifiable.

He took a quick look at some of the others, pausing at a sub-quest titled: **Kill Umesh Madara.** He scowled as he considered the massive GUM who had held Tia prisoner. Even if he hadn't promised Umesh's death to Nepia, he still would have seen to it.

Despite the draw of each objective, none raised his interest like the Forsaken Crypts. It might be a while before he found the quests to direct him to the dungeon, but he already had a reason to venture into its depths. Pops. The Crypts had been on the list of locations to acquire the second protocol.

Frowning, Frost took a look at the chest. *I coulda sworn I left that closed.* He got up, strode over to the chest, and flipped the lid shut. He glanced around, wondering if someone had been in the cave.

His Comm Orb dinged.

Meritus' voice was breathless with excitement. "An epic zhua? A hierka that levels with the owner? Come on, dawg, you didn't even have to ask. I got you. And curing the Gray Death? Wicked. Just wicked. Might be able to convince the Coalition to lift the bounties if we pull it off.

"I already bought a bunch of mystic skills and a scepter, and I'm putting in the work. I'll hit up my contacts about the empowered skills to see what mobs we can farm for them besides those in the Sanctum.

"Also, the gargant Highseekers gave me access to one of the upper levels of their Halls of Illumination to help. A few books claimed hierkaneers can craft the skill-effect shards by way of a Genesis Engine. I'll research the details and find out if anyone can confirm it. Keep you posted. Good luck and see you soon, my dude. Meritus out."

Frost smiled at his best friend's enthusiasm. He finished his meal and washed it down with water. His tiredness abated. With the fire crackling, the wind howling outside, he stripped down to his pants and leather boots. He removed his greaves, cuisses, and bracers.

After he limbered up by hopping from foot to foot and shaking his arms, Frost worked through a series of stretches. When he was loose enough, he lost himself in pushups, pistol squats, shadowboxing, and various core exercises. All things he'd done when Pops had hired trainers to teach him MMA, both IRL and by way of sims.

Remembering the few sessions he'd had on the basics of swordsmanship, he retrieved the blade. He ran through several drills. Time passed, the weapon growing a bit more comfortable.

As Frost practiced and exercised, adding Leaps in various directions to his repertoire, he devised a strategy to capture and ride a drake. The hunting roar echoed again.

CHAPTER 6

Standing upon the battlements of Modra's Keep beneath an unforgiving sun, Setnana felt broken inside. Pain gripped her heart. She had not slept. Unbidden tears streamed down her cheeks. She cursed Bakui Assam regularly, blaming him for her presence at this godforsaken place on the border of Puria, Lothal, and Khertahka.

Every time her Comm Orb dinged, she hoped it was news she yearned to hear. News of Perihy's retrieval.

But the reports were the same every time. Failure. No more than a glimpse of her son.

At first, she thought Perihy was faster than should have been possible. A thought she dismissed when she considered he was no longer a true erada, no matter how she denied it. He was a draconid. Drake riders were the only ones able to keep up, but he vanished whenever they drew close.

She had spent the entire night and day following on a drake. West. Always west. The same direction chosen by many corrupted when the Gray Death first spread. She wished she knew the reason for the choice.

Eventually, her Azureguard trackers were forced to stop. Perihy had crossed the border into grand kora territory. The last sighting was of him heading into Puria by way of the Isfet Mountains.

Gazing longingly at the distant peaks, she spoke into her Comm Orb, the message directed to Khafra, who was leading the search. "I cannot ask Aishani to arrange safe passage through the Isfet. Too many questions would be asked. I was already forced to concoct a story to Bakui Assam concerning our presence there.

"Return to me but have the Azureguards skirt the mountains and wait for Perihy to emerge on the far side. Stress to them the importance of remaining Concealed. If the grand korae capture them, they might as well kill themselves." She ended the message.

"Major Neferna." Setnana faced the Sky Sword leader who waited atop an owl-faced zephyr. The major was dressed in scale armor and a cloak, its hood secured to keep her face and horns hidden. "Take the company to the border between Lothal and Puria. Help the trackers once Perihy is well away from the grand kora strongholds. Be careful. Fight if you must, but if anyone falls, make certain there is nothing left to identify them. They must think you are humans not eradae."

"As you wish, Nomarch Setnana." With a pull of her reins, Neferna sent the zephyr into the sky, its diaphanous wings spread wide.

I will never give up, my sweet Perihy. Your mother will find you and save you. Even if she has to raze everything in her path, it will be done.

Her Comm Orb dinged. Without even thinking to see who it might be, she was prepared for disappointment. She frowned. The messenger wasn't a tracker. It was Sid, one of her Trade Conglomerate contacts, Sid. As Setnana listened to Sid relay the information, she could not help her smile.

******

Half a day and several simurgh Velocity Surges later, she, Ihuet, and Khafra arrived in Ezaki. Despite being a rather small Lothal town, it brimmed with activity, primarily gurash miners who were seeking fortune in the distant Jurojin Mountains. Following Sid's directions, they soon located the store in question.

She was on the verge of approaching the establishment when Ihuet grabbed her arm. He jutted his chin toward a nearby stall.

Her eyes widened. She could not believe her good fortune. After all she had suffered, all the obstacles, all the trials, all the unanswered prayers to Nif, Gilda Mordian had strolled into her path.

The girl was a slim erada, her color that of a clear afternoon sky. Soft. Not quite unlike Setnana, and yet not as beautiful.

Gilda's color was the only thing seemingly gentle about her. The girl carried two chakrams on her belt and often twirled a dagger as if born with it. She moved with a fighter's grace. Her long twisting horns and face spoke of youth. Her average features spoke of a commoner. Barely better than a sceeve.

Setnana grimaced. To think these sceeves were the reason she had failed to secure Benediction. The reason Perihy had turned. And thus, the reason Perihy was lost.

The horrific moment rose anew. The failed healing. The impossible contortion of Perihy's body. Perihy's skin bursting apart like a rotten fruit. The revelation of scaled metallic skin, the infection of gray, deep green, and electric blue veins that belonged to a draconid grunt. She squeezed her eyes shut against the images.

Hands folded into fists, Setnana let out a shuddering breath. She opened her eyes. The girl was still haggling with the vendor.

Setnana smiled grimly, again pleased with her luck. And for contacts like Sid. She almost praised Nif. Almost. She grimaced. *This isn't Nif's work. The gods care nothing for my worldly problems. This is my doing and my doing alone. My will. My love.*

Scowling, she recalled Aishani's attempt to steer her from this course, trying to convince her Perihy was past the point of curing. But Aishani was wrong. Setnana would find him and fix what was broken.

"Give it up," Aishani had said. "You'll ruin everything if you don't. You're letting love blind you. I told you time and again, show me a man in love, and I'll show you his weakness."

Setnana shook her head. *If I do not give it my all, what kind of a mother am I?* Her all began with the girl.

Gilda Mordian must have sensed something was wrong, because she spun and snatched the chakrams from her belt loop. The great circular discs lit up with aether-infused power. Aether Shields shot up around her arms.

But it was too late.

Ihuet appeared beside Gilda, stepping out of Concealment. His body was a mass of crackling energy as if he were the walking embodiment of lightning. He touched the exposed flesh of Gilda's arm.

The girl did a jittery dance where she stood. The chakrams fell from her limp fingers, clanging on the cobbles. Gilda collapsed to the ground and writhed.

Setnana strode over to the helpless girl. Eyes cold and pitiless, she stared down into Gilda's face. "You will tell me where Benediction is, the location of its schema, and you will give up the location of your friends."

Teeth gritted, Gilda stared Setnana down with defiant eyes. "Not a chance."

Setnana allowed a ghost of a smile to play across her lips. "I will enjoy breaking you. You will know my Perihy's suffering."

CHAPTER 7

Early the next morning, Frost woke beside the campfire's dying embers, his cloak balled beneath his head. He rolled his neck to work out a little stiffness and climbed to his feet, screwing up his face at the stench rolling off his body.

Promising himself to bathe in the lagoon, he repeated the stretch and exercise regimen from the previous night. He again worked in Leaps.

Hunger gnawed at him by the time he finished well over an hour later. He ate some of the roasted lamia and washed it down with water.

After breakfast, he got dressed in his undershirt, black thigh-length gambeson, and mahogany brigandine. He pulled on the close-fitting, knee-high, soft leather boots, strapped on his greaves over them, and then secured his cuisses to his thighs. Lastly, he cinched the bracers on his wrists. Smiling, he rubbed his Two Ring, thoughts drifting to Pops for a moment.

Shaking off the reverie, he made a makeshift sack of his cloak and bundled chopped bits of lamia tail into it. He'd thought about putting the chunks in his inventory, but the sack felt more practical. With one last look around the cavern, he tossed the sack over his shoulder, and departed.

Today would be his last day on the island.

Mist and cool air greeted him outside. Beyond the mountain, the mist was dirty milk blotting out the land. The war of lightning among the clouds was muted. From above came a lament of drakes' screeches.

When he crested the hill, he immediately became aware of numerous drakes circling the open area, most of them larger than the ones he'd seen the day before. At a quick glance he could tell they were hunting. Frost dropped the makeshift sack and retrieved Deadeye from his inventory. He sidled up against the steep slope to his left, got flat on his belly, and studied the encounters.

Most drakes attacked the speedy lamias. In twos or threes, they would swoop down time and again until they managed to snatch a lamia with their claws. Some flew off to the aeries when successful. Others gorged on the spot.

The majority of the arkets had fled to the far right corner of the saddle among several rock formations. Squinting, Frost could just make out caverns like the one in which he'd spawned.

Arkets caught out in the open proved to be no easy meat for the drakes. Relying on Concealment, they often escaped. But the drakes followed doggedly.

The bolder arkets flung Whirlwinds at their assailants. Others hurled Gust, an aether-infused half-moon of wind as tall as a man. The drakes flapped away every time.

Frost wondered why the drakes bothered. Hunting arkets seemed such an annoyance. Particularly since the lamias were much easier.

To escape the onslaught, the lamias had taken to their burrows. But some weren't fast enough or chose to help a nearby counterpart fight off a drake. More often than not, such attempts failed.

By Frost's estimate, the hunt lasted half an hour. No carcasses were left when it was over. The drakes either picked them clean or flew off with the remains.

Frost had kept an eye out for Red-and-black. It wasn't among the others during the hunt.

While he waited for the mobs to return to their normal haunts, he watched Red-and-black's aerie. Sure enough, it appeared at the opening. It didn't leave until the other drakes had settled in their aeries.

Frost picked up the sack and dashed to the lagoon. He emptied the chunks of meat onto the rocks. Focused on Red-and-black, he crossed to the lagoon's opposite side.

A shadow passed over the land as Red-and-black banked and circled the plain. Unlike its predecessors, the drake made no noise but for the flap of its leathery wings. And unlike its predecessors, it did not seem to strike fear in the hearts of its would-be prey. Neither the lamias nor arkets attempted to flee.

Red-and-black must have spotted the meat at the lagoon, for it abruptly veered off its path and descended toward the waterfall. A blast of Gust shot up and exploded into the drake. With a plaintive cry, the drake pitched from the air.

"No!" Frost was off and running before he gave any thought to the action.

The drake plummeted. Moments before it slammed into the ground, the drake managed to spread its wings and regain a semblance of control. But Red-and-black had fallen too fast. The angle was too steep. The drake hit a thicket and tumbled to the ground. It rolled a few times before coming to a stop.

Legs pumping, Frost had almost made it to the drake when two seven-foot arkets appeared out of Concealment some distance away. They let out chuckles and broke into long loping runs toward the hapless drake.

Growling, Deadeye cradled in his arms, Frost willed himself to run faster. His chest heaved. Each breath was louder and harder until he was huffing. He sprinted by Red-and-black.

In one motion, Frost drew to a halt, aimed Deadeye, chose Aether Bomb, and squeezed the trigger. The one point five second charge seemed to take forever, the cyan luminance growing at the cannon's muzzle until it was the size of a basketball. With a whoosh, the Bomb launched.

The Bomb hurtled across the distance. It exploded when it struck one of the arkets, leaving a conflagration in a ten-foot radius. Afire, both creatures ran around aimlessly, yelping.

Frost squeezed the trigger again, this time having chosen Concussion Blast. A white beam flashed from the cannon, exploded near the arkets, staggered them, and launched them into the air. The moment they slammed back into the ground, Frost hit one with Staggering Shot, leaving it incapacitated, swaying from side to side. He lit up the other with a combo of Aether Shot and Divergence. It did not get up.

One of Divergence's five-shot spread had struck the first, knocking it out of the stagger. Retreating step by step, Frost pumped Aether Shot after

Aether Shot into the yowling creature as it stumbled toward him. The arket crumpled to the ground.

Chest heaving, Frost kept Deadeye level and aimed in case more of the beasts were Concealed. He clicked to make certain. Satisfied when Echolocation revealed no threat, he turned to the drake.

Red-and-black was gone.

Frost scanned the area. He didn't see the drake. A motion in the corner of his eye caught his attention.

The drake was hobbling alongside the lagoon. One wing dragged on the ground. Red-and-black disappeared through the waterfall's foamy spray.

Following the drake, Frost Leaped atop the rocks. Creeping along so as not to startle the beast, he approached the roaring waterfall, wary of the dangers of the pool itself and the slippery rocks. The wind gusted, sending out swaths of misty spray.

Frost stopped adjacent to the effervescent water curtain. He could just make out movement behind it. And a pair of eyes. A snorting growl resonated, barely audible amid the water's rage. Frost backed away slowly.

Concerned for the extent of Red-and-black's injuries and blaming himself, Frost retraced his steps, and circled to the lagoon's other side. He ambled over to the area with the chunks of lamia meat. One by one, he picked them up, tossed them farther up the wet rocks near where the waterfall spilled over the cliff, and then hurried to them.

He picked out a spot where the falling water abated, where it was little more than several trickling lines. Beyond the trickles of water, he saw a ledge, a hollow carved into the cliff.

Red-and-black was pressed up against the far corner. Its fangs glinted in the dim light. As did the gold of its circular iris and convex pupils, which were surrounded by the black sclera of its eyeballs.

Frost picked up the meat and hurled it through. The drake's head shifted to track the meat, but its golden pupils, contrary to the head, were still on Frost. Red-and-black made no move toward the morsel.

"Eat." Frost pointed at the meat. The drake stayed in position. "Go on… eat." The drake didn't budge.

Frost sighed. "Don't worry, buddy. I'll protect you until you can fly again. Least I can do." Although disappointed, he found a little solace in the idea the drake would not want for food or water.

He headed back to the plain, intent on grinding out his level while keeping an eye on the drake. Before he started, Frost took a swig from his canteen. He wiped sweat from his brow then spent a few minutes meditating for Replenishment. When he was at full capacity, he chose the lamias, and got to work.

Within the first thirty minutes he had left a trail of carcasses. A part of him wished he had bought a skinning knife. He could have at least come away with some hides to sell or for future use. Until he considered that like everything else, skinning would be an imitation of real life. He grimaced at the gore involved with the work.

Brushing away the thought, he considered that there had to be rare herbs like those Saba had mentioned the last time. Although Gilda had said gathering was simply a matter of engaging in it, he didn't know where to start. He sighed. *Gonna have to fix my life skills and professions after all.*

The hours dragged on, the mist burning off, the day producing a swelter. Frost gained yet another point in aether, raising it to thirty-five. Hot and sweaty, he dragged a lamia tail up to the waterfall. He chopped it up and flung a few chunks behind the water.

Again, he tried to coax the drake into eating. But Red-and-black merely delivered snorting growls of warning. Frost took note of the old food's absence.

Frost left the rest of the lamia just outside the trickling water. He paused for a moment, face held up to the foamy spray's welcome respite. With a sigh, he refilled his canteen and got back to grinding toward level twelve.

Whenever Frost heard a drake screech, he'd worry, thinking the three bullies had found Red-and-black. Or that any of the others had done so on occasions when they landed at the lagoon. Frost stopped the grind during those times, an expectant breath held. But the drakes would drink and fly back to their aeries.

Bored of the lamias, he sought out the arkets. This time he took more care in approaching his target. A combo of Staggering Shot, Piercer, Aether Shot, Divergence, and Aether Shot put the creature down without fuss.

Frost checked the carcass. His mouth fell open. A skill shard.

Skill acquired:

67

Concealment

Cast time: Instant

Recharge Time: 1 minute

Consumes: Aether

Available shard slots: 3

Effect: Allows user to become invisible until user cancels the ability or takes damage. Environmental aspects and situations can affect invisibility in adverse ways. Concealed attacks do fifty percent less damage due to the inability to properly focus aether while invisible.

Frost absorbed the shard. He had always loved the idea of stealth, of cutthroats in general. He was less enamored with the penalty for the skill and was positive it didn't exist in the game's old version.

But then, classes were restricted in Ataxia One. In Void Legion, all a player needed was to hit the requirements, be it stats, levels, or weapons to use a particular skill. Concealment, like many of the dash skills that covered great distances in a blink, had no weapon requirement.

While he continued with his leveling, Frost practiced Concealment. The advantages of the skill seemed amazing. But he also became aware of the flaws. Concealment did not mute his footsteps. Or breathing. And while Concealed, he noticed the stink of his unwashed body.

On one occasion, an arket heard him coming and had also Concealed. Frost considered clicking for all of a second. Instead, he studied the arket's location. Minutes passed. Frost frowned. He swore he could see something there. A distortion. Eventually, the arket reappeared. Frost killed it.

On a whim, Frost cut off the arket's arms. He returned to the waterfall. He threw one bloody arm onto the wet ledge halfway between him and the drake.

One wing still hanging awkwardly, the drake dashed forward and snatched up the arm. Making growling sounds, it ate. Bones crunched. Those golden pupils were still focused on Frost.

"The little hyena bastards are a delicacy for you, huh?" Frost smiled.

He reached out, his hand passing through the cold dripping water, and held out the other bloody arm. Red-and-black finished off the first arm in a series of swallowing snaps. Its gaze tracked Frost and the other arm.

"Eat." Frost waved the arm.

After a moment, the drake took one tentative step. One became two. Two, three. The drake leaned forward, its neck stretching, mouth open. It snatched the food and backed up.

"Good boyyy. Eat."

He waited until the drake finished. Smiling triumphantly, he refilled his canteen then headed down to the arkets. He continued with the grind, using Cannon Kata's speed boost after every kill to sprint to a new target. His sprints using Kata as well as his constant Leap practice saw his agility increase by one. By evening he had a good collection of arms wrapped in his cloak.

He'd also gotten two more skill shards. One for Concealment and the other for a sorcerer's Infernal Spear. He was certain they'd be worth some credits on the Auction Market.

On his last kill, he leveled up.

Level 12 gained
Attributes increased by 3 points
Strength: 26
Agility: 32
Vitality: 37
Aether: 38

He nodded at the additional vitality outside of the three-point allotment. It proved his theorycrafting for conversion rates between agility and strength was correct. He absorbed the Homer skill shard.

Skill Acquired

Homer:
Cast time: Instant or chargeable
Recharge Time: 15 seconds
Consumes: Aether
Available shard slots: 2

Effect: Instantly fire an Aether Missile at a target locked onto when aiming. Range up to 400 feet. Charging the skill creates additional missiles. Two missiles per one second charge up to a maximum of eight missiles. Recharge time is constant regardless of firing method. Gain 2 percent aether for each successful hit.

Evening had bled into night's inky cloak. The hunting scream from the previous night echoed farther up the mountain. It sent a shiver through Frost.

Gripping Deadeye tight, he peered toward the sound but only deepening dark greeted him. Lightning radiated at the summit in fitful spurts.

Shaking off the unease, Frost headed up to the waterfall with his spoils. The lagoon glowed with unearthly turquoise splendor, insects flitting like playful specters in its radiance. He paused to admire the spectacle before striding up to the edge of the hollow. The luminance allowed him to see Red-and-black in the far corner.

Frost dropped the makeshift bag of arms. He picked up two and tossed them toward the drake. "Eat." Frost did his best impression of tearing flesh with his teeth.

When Red-and-black moved to the morsels, Frost picked up the bag, and stepped through the spray. Red-and-black froze. A snorting growl rumbled low in its chest. The black of its eyeballs glinted with the lagoon's blue radiance even as the golden pupils tracked him. But the drake made no move. Neither of aggression nor to flee.

Frost sidestepped over to the corner with the bag of arms. Willing himself to relax, he took a seat and placed Deadeye across his lap. Within the hollow, the crash of the waterfall was thunder, the sound of an entire stadium cheering a team. Soon enough, the clamor became a part of his surroundings.

With a snort, the drake returned to its meal. It made short work of the food. The drake looked to Frost, but its eyes shifted to the bag. Frost leaned forward, grabbed an arm, and tossed it. The drake caught the arm in mid-air and swallowed it whole.

Frost threw a few more on the ground between him and the drake, each time instructing it to eat. Watching the beast feed reminded him that he, too, was hungry. Frost removed the chunks of roasted lamia from his inventory and had himself a meal, his attention on the drake, who had worked its way to each arm until it was within spitting distance of Frost.

When Red-and-black finished, it made a gurgling sound. Its eyes shifted to the bag.

Frost smiled. "You sure can eat." He finished his lamia, reached into the bag, took an arm, and held it out.

Red-and-black stretched its neck out. Frost pulled back a bit. The drake took a step forward. Frost held his breath. Red-and-black took the food and ate.

The drake was so close now that Frost could touch it. Its musky odor was strong. Animal. Heat emanated from its body, a heat that reminded Frost of the chill in the air. Frost shivered. He'd hoped there might be an area in the hollow dry enough to support a campfire, but the light mist in the air dashed such thoughts.

Red-and-black gurgled once more. Frost handed it another morsel. When the drake took it, Frost eased to his feet. Reaching out, he stroked the drake's head as it ate. Red-and-black made a soft noise in its throat. A noise Frost could only interpret as contentment.

This close, Frost noted that the injured wing was higher up, closer to a more natural position to match the other side. He placed the last two arms on the ground before the drake.

Frost walked around the beast, trailing his fingers along its shoulder, back, and down to its tail. He admired the little he could make out of its mottled color in the poor lightning. He could only imagine the splendor of the red and black scales up close in the day.

The day's grind and the cold finally crashed down on Frost. He made to leave, to head back down to the cavern and build a fire. To rest.

A roar stopped him in his tracks. A roar only as far as the hunting plain. Something was doing just that. Hunting. A pungent odor drifted on the air. The odor of rotting eggs.

Red-and-black let out a low rumble, deep in its throat. Clicking, Frost stretched his Echolocation as far as it could reach beyond the waterfall. The falling water itself either killed visibility with its violent froth or blurred the outside world with its translucence.

With Deadeye aimed, Frost side-stepped until he stood in the middle of the hollow. Red-and-black positioned itself beside Frost, its attention focused outward.

On occasion, the drake would bare its teeth. But it made no sound. Frost waited, his breathing loud to his ears, heart thumping, the waterfall's roar somehow seeming muted. He was ready to unleash every skill in his arsenal.

Frost stretched his Echolocation to its farthest range, some three hundred feet. Something massive approached the lagoon. Its footfalls reverberated. A shadow engulfed much of the turquoise luminance. The rotten egg stench grew near unbearable.

Frost froze. Holding his breath, he prayed the monster could not see or sense him or Red-and-black. The shadow shifted.

In his mind's eye, Frost swore a head had swiveled toward him. Eyes like flames burned into his. The beast snorted. There came the lap, lap, lap of water-drinking. The massive shadow receded.

He let out a relieved breath. But he still kept Deadeye aimed. He stayed in that position, pressed against the wall and the drake.

Time passed. Frost couldn't tell how long, but it must have been at least an hour. The monster's roars had become sporadic. With his arms tiring, he resorted to resting Deadeye across his legs, ready to bring it to bear at any moment.

He fought against the urge to relax. The urge to sleep. He could not afford to do either. With Deadeye's handle in a death grip, he swore to remain awake, to remain vigilant. Their lives depended upon it.

Vision blurry, he squinted at the waterfall and the turquoise glow beyond. *Was that a shadow?* He leaned forward. He snapped his head up when he realized he'd been dozing.

Battling weary bones, he busied himself with thoughts of Gilda. *What's she doing now? Is she leveling somewhere? What new spells has she gotten? Does she miss me as much as I miss her?*

A roar reverberated. How close, Frost couldn't tell. Chasing away the wayward thoughts, Frost tried to focus. He hoped morning would soon come.

CHAPTER 8

Frost snapped his eyes open. Something screeched. No, not one thing. Many. He brought Deadeye up and aimed at the waterfall.

Frowning, he considered his position. He didn't remember sitting or lying down. But he was sitting, back against the hollow's wall. A mound of warmth beside him resolved into Red-and-black, curled up, slumbering, head facing toward the waterfall and the brightness beyond.

Brightness. Frost narrowed his eyes. Early morning, he realized. The screeches were the drakes in their daily hunting ritual. As much as he'd tried, he'd failed to stay awake. They were lucky to be alive.

Yawning, he lowered Deadeye. He tilted his neck to one side and then the next to loosen it. Frost paused, head still tilted. He'd stretched out of habit, expecting pain, soreness from all the activity, the leveling, and especially the two days of calisthenics. An onset of DOMS like in real life. But he felt no such discomfort.

He checked his stats. Strength and agility had increased by one point. He was uncertain of the algorithms used to convert exercise to attributes, but the increases convinced him he was on the right track. As aether had readily shown: improvement on certain aspects was a matter of usage. As in real life, so it was in-game.

Frost glanced at the drake whose musky odor filled the hollow. Red-and-black was at least four times his size. Its body rose and fell with each deep breath. Frost made to take his drake reins from his inventory and snap it around the creature's neck but paused in the middle of the action.

How'd you feel when Sidrie basically shackled you? Forced you to do what she wanted. Frost sighed.

Red-and-black snorted. The drake climbed to its feet and shook itself. Its neck curled a bit to the left, black eyes and convex gold pupils shifting backward to regard Frost. The drake let out a low gurgle.

Frost was uncertain if the sound meant something good or if it was a show of aggression. "Heyyyy, boyyyy." He smiled uneasily even as his heartbeat quickened.

Red-and-black gurgled again. The drake flicked its head toward the outside.

"You hungry? Me too." Relief eased through Frost once it became apparent the drake meant him no harm. "But we gotta wait until your friends are done."

On cue, the hunting drakes screeched. Red-and-black turned its head to peer outside. It whined. A sound Frost interpreted as disappointment. The drake settled back down on its stomach.

Frost's Comm Orb dinged.

"What up, my dude, you know who it is," Meritus' nasal voice piped into Frost's ear. "Got some great news. Not only did I get a lead from my Trade Conglomerate buddies on those empowered skills, but you were right about the weapons like Benediction according to tomes in the Halls of Illumination. There're more of them for different classes.

"Even better, a gurash relic hunter named Nakada Masami in the Lothal dominion claims he got the info we need about both. It'll cost us, of course. I can swing the credits, but there's some items he wants in return.

"When we have the payment, we'll meet him in Kojin, the Lothal capital, to make the trade. I'll hit you with the list of items he wants in a little while. Then we can link up at an inn called the Wandering Man in Kikonai, a southern Lothal town in the Daiko nome.

"I also confirmed that hierkaneers *can* craft the empowered skills by way of Genesis Engines. Takes twenty of the normal versions and certain gems imbued with aether. If we decide to go that route.

"And in case you're asking where the hell do we get access to another Engine outside of the Front. I heard the Engine in the Sanctum isn't the only one hidden away in a dungeon.

"The bad news is there's only one Engine per location. So, whoever takes an Engine gets to keep it until someone takes it from them. Or it's destroyed. They don't respawn.

"That's all for now. Lata, homie."

The news made Frost think about the Genesis Engines. Due to their design, he could see them being the cause of major PVP. Hell, perhaps even faction or dominion wars if the Coalition decided to stay out of such squabbles.

Time dragged as he and Red-and-black waited. Stroking his aether ring, he found himself worrying about Mom and Kai. His third day in game meant almost nine days away from the real world. He hoped they were both fine. Despite any misgivings, he had to believe Sidrie would keep her word. She would pull him from the game if Mom went into labor.

But what if she didn't?

Frost shook off the thought before it festered. Instead, he imagined what Gilda and the others might be doing. He smiled as he saw blue-skinned Gilda, cocky as ever, twirling her dagger. Then there was Saba, the dresdor centaur with her habit of swishing her tail, and finding excuses to avoid fights when possible. Dante, the crimson-skinned gurash was Saba's opposite. He'd rush into any battle. Thinking of them did make him miss his days as leader of Soldiers of Chaos.

Maybe I should start the guild again after all.

He was lost in thought when Red-and-black nudged him with its nose. Frost looked up. The morning had brightened. No drakes screeched.

"Let's get some food then." Frost stood.

The drake's nostrils spread wide. It turned its head away from Frost, its golden pupils narrowing, and made a sneezing noise.

"What?"

Red-and-black leaned forward and pushed Frost away again. It repeated the same sneeze. The membrane around its nostrils opened and closed.

Frost's eyebrows shot up as understanding dawned. "You trying to say I stink?" He shook his head. "You don't exactly smell like flowers either."

The drake's tail curled around and bumped Frost to the side. Red-and-black gurgled.

75

"Fine. Let's go." Frost assumed the drake meant for them to get a move on. His belly was rumbling something awful.

He led the way from behind the waterfall. As usual, a gray sheet riddled by radiant lightning hung over them. Today, the heat was a bit more oppressive, such that he appreciated the swirling wind.

Red-and-black came to stand beside him at the lagoon's edge. Frost stared at the drake. Up close, in daylight, its color took his breath away. It was a mottled yet rich red and black with a sheen as if the scales were oiled. A dark scar stood out beneath one eye. Its previously injured wing was healed completely.

Cradling Deadeye, Frost headed toward the arkets with Red-and-black stalking beside him. Frost Concealed. He made to tell Red-and-black he was still there, but the drake was staring directly at him.

Could it see through Concealment?

Frost shifted left then right. The drake's black and gold eyes tracked him. He circled around the creature. Red-and-black's eyes shifted with him.

"Interesting." Frost nodded, impressed by the seemingly natural ability.

Still Concealed, Frost made his way to the closest arket. As usual, he opened up with Staggering Shot. The arket died to Piercer and a single Aether Shot.

Red-and-black let out a gurgle. Its focus was on the dead beast.

"Go on." Frost jutted his chin toward the carcass.

The drake cocked its head and regarded Frost with those deep black and gold eyes. It gurgled again.

"Hmmm." Frost imitated biting into the meat. "Go on. Eat." He pointed at the carcass.

Red-and-black bounded forward. In moments, it was tearing at the arket.

Smiling, Frost watched for a bit before he found and killed another arket. This time, he cut off a leg. He left the rest for the drake.

Frost ventured over to some rocks not far from the lagoon. He took the tinder and flint from his inventory, found some dried grass, and started a fire. He added some twigs. He sawed a chunk of meat from the upper thigh, skewered it on the sword, and roasted it, turning it to make sure it cooked well. Juices sizzled and dripped, making his mouth water.

Red-and-black's shriek made Frost snap his head around. The drake was chasing a lamia. Body shifting in a wavy undulation, the lamia bolted for a burrow. Red-and-black clawed at the hole.

With a wry smile and a shake of his head, Frost turned back to his meal. He removed the meat from the fire and settled down to eat.

Soon enough, the drake joined him. In its jaws was a dead lamia. Red-and-black dropped the carcass next to the fire. The drake looked from Frost to the lamia and back again. It kicked at the lamia with a claw.

"For me?" Frost chuckled. "Thank you."

The drake returned to its hunting.

After he ate, Frost made his way to the lagoon, deciding it was time for a bath. He stripped naked, forced the old fear of drowning down into his gut, took a breath, and waded into the turquoise pool. The water was cold at first, but his body soon adjusted. Frost basked in the moment. If not for the circumstances, he could have seen himself living in-game. He let his imagination run wild with the idea.

Angry screeches broke him from his reverie. The three bullies soared above Frost, headed toward the plain. Frost scrambled from the water. Heart thumping, he dressed as fast as he could manage, attention diverted between Red-and-black and the three drakes.

Red-and-black had stopped hunting and frolicking. Teeth bared, it stared up at the three newcomers. It shrieked a warning.

Fully dressed, Frost sprinted toward the confrontation. The bullies landed and approached Red-and-black from three directions, spitting and hissing. One of them faked a pounce. Another attacked from the opposite side.

The moment Frost was in range, he fired a Staggering Shot at the closest drake, the blue one. A second later, he followed the attack with Piercer at the gray drake.

Red-and-black chose that moment to charge the green drake. Snapping and snarling, they fought. Though smaller, Red-and-black was quicker and stronger. The green drake let out a piteous cry and darted away. It took to the air.

Frost turned back to the other two. But they had recovered and flown off. They headed in the direction of the aeries. Frost had a horrible feeling in his gut. He ran to Red-and-black.

"They're gonna bring them all, aren't they?" Frost didn't expect an answer, but Red-and-black was already staring after its cousins as if it had the same thought.

Red-and-black whined. And did the most unexpected thing. It got down flat on its stomach, eyes focused on Frost.

"You want me to climb on?" Frost's brows rose in wonderment. "I think we need these to make that work properly." He produced the reins from his inventory and stored Deadeye.

Frost opened the reins, placed them around Red-and-black's neck, and snapped them closed. The reins transformed. They became a circle of near indiscernible aether, powdery blue like a clear sky. Straps of aether grew from the circle, creeping down either side of the drake's neck to where the torso began. The straps flowed down beneath the belly.

Impressed, Frost nodded. "Wow. That's different."

Screeches echoed from the direction of the aeries. Drakes took to the skies like flies lifting from a corpse.

"Shit." Frost scrambled onto Red-and-black's back.

He reached out and gripped the reins with both hands. The moment his fingers closed around the circle, the aether coiled up his hands and around his wrists. The effect was similar to a simurgh's harnessing ability. Something gripped his thighs and ankles. Glancing down, he saw aether had locked him in. The coils of it around his ankles reminded him of bolsters on land mounts.

"Epic." Grinning, Frost leaned forward into the drake's neck. It seemed the natural thing to do.

With a flap of its leathery wings, Red-and-black leaped into the sky. Swirling winds streamed by Frost, ruffled his hair. The ground dwindled below.

A Drake In Need
Objective Complete
Help abused drake:
1000 experience points
500 Ignis dominion credits
Capture a Young Drake:

Objective Complete
1000 experience points
500 Ignis dominion credits
500 Khertahka dominion credits
Earn Your Wings:
Objective Complete
Learn how to fly a drake:
1500 experience points
500 Ignis dominion credits
500 Khertahka dominion credits

Frost nodded his approval for the quest completions.

Drake screeches echoed. Hundreds of them. Darkening the sky, the lament of drakes sped toward Frost and Red-and-black.

Frost had the urge to use the reins in his grip to direct Red-and-black. He could head out to sea as fast as possible. But they'd be just as dead if they didn't find land. He needed to get his bearings first. Realizing this wasn't the first time Red-and-black had to flee from its own kind, he let the drake have the lead.

With the ground a blur beneath them, Red-and-black banked sharply and aimed at the mountainside away from the chasing drakes. It followed the meandering stream and shot out into open space. The stream became another waterfall below them. Red-and-black dived, an arrow streaking down, skimming the falling water.

The move and speed sent Frost's stomach lurching up into his mouth. Frost squeezed the reins tight. He leaned forward and down onto RnB's rough scales, the drake's musky odor filling his nostrils. His eyes teared up in the whipping, howling wind that drowned out all other sound.

Red-and-black veered left. It swept around rocky outcrops and past several more waterfalls. The drake beat its wings and climbed. Up. And up. And up, they soared. The air chilled. Above them, lightning radiated within the gray murk like frenetic strobes. Finally, the drake leveled out. It landed on a mist-shrouded plateau.

Heart still racing, Frost took a long, slow breath. And screwed up his face at a stench as if someone had eaten eggs and farted.

"I hope that wasn't you, homie." Frost smiled as he rubbed Red-and-black's neck. "Looks like we lost them." The drake screeches were distant things below.

Peering out into the open space, Frost swore he could just make out the Coalition base far in the distance. Beyond it, the sapphire of the Empyrean Sea yawned to meet the azure sky. A dark line sat on that intersection point. A line that meant the mainland. The continent of Marang.

The foul rotten egg odor rose again, this time a bit stronger. Struck by a sudden sense of danger, Frost yanked on the reins and kicked his legs, activating the bolsters. The drake leaped forward off the plateau's edge. Frost snatched a look over his shoulder.

Less than a hundred feet from where they'd stood, a massive reptilian face peered out of the mist. Ruby scales glinted for a moment. Black and silver void energy crackled around the head. Eyes like flames stared at Frost.

IM named it Imanok. A GUM. A void dragon.

The monster tilted its head to the gray mantle above. Lightning spewed from its maw.

Frost had no time to relish their narrow escape. A drake screeched below. A glance down revealed the three bullies and a dozen others making straight for Frost and Red-and-black.

But Frost had the advantage of several thousand feet of height. Angling Red-and-black down added its momentum to its flight speed. Their pursuers dwindled behind. Grinning, Frost allowed himself to relax.

Maelpith Island Trials
Escape Maelpith Island
Objectives Complete
Discover a way off Maelpith Island:
2000 experience points
500 Ignis dominion credits
500 Khertahka dominion credits
Maelpith Island Trials passed:
5000 experience points
1000 Khertahka dominion credits
1000 Ignis dominion credits

"Thanks, homie." Frost stroked the drake's neck. "Couldn't have done it without you." The drake gurgled. "I was thinking that if we're gonna be together, I'm gonna have to give you a name." Frost pondered it for a moment. One thing made sense. "I'll call you RnB. Yeah, I like that."

With the quest completions, Frost contemplated the items on which he might spend his credits. He remembered he still owed Meritus for Deadeye, Stand and Deliver, and the Comm Orb. He'd have to find a roundabout way to repay Meritus, or else his best friend would just return the credits. Perhaps some skills or items. Or clothes. Meritus had a thing for clothes.

Gotta get something for Gilda too. Flowers, maybe? Girls like that kinda stuff. Nah, she's not like other girls. She's too hard for flowers. Probably better off if I take her on a hunt. He nodded at that last.

Thoughts of Gilda sent his mind wandering. He missed her cerulean skin and lithe body. Her smarts. Her attitude. He couldn't wait to see her again, both in-game and IRL. He basked in the memories of their lovemaking.

Frost activated the Comm Orb. A simple thought drew out the intended address @GildaMordian. But the address didn't illuminate. Frost sighed. He'd keep trying. Sooner or later, she would acquire an Orb. He hoped it would be sooner.

Stroking his aether ring, relishing the feel of the cool wind, Frost considered how well his leveling had gone on the island. He'd seemingly hit the sweet spot where a person could readily solo the island's low-level elite mobs. Having RnB meant he could come and go as he pleased as long as he stayed away from the drake area and the Coalition.

"Maybe I can shoot for level fifteen. Go find Dagrun, Gunarr, and Sigrid... see if they have any of that chimera scale armor. Or maybe get some korbitanium to take back to Marang and have a smith make me a shitload of projectiles. What do you think?"

The drake made a cooing sound.

"Yeah, I agree. Sounds like a plan." Gripping the reins, Frost tilted his hands to the right, causing RnB to bank and circle back toward the island.

His Comm Orb dinged.

"Yo... what up, homie." Frost froze at the melancholy in Meritus' voice.

"It was supposed to be a surprise. I'd linked up with Gilda. We were in Ezaki, completing quests and farming the materials Nakada Masami wanted."

There was a long pause.

"But now she's gone. She went to deal with a merchant but didn't come back. He said someone took her. Claimed it was most likely slavers."

Frost barely heard the rest of the message. Turning his hands, he made RnB circle back out to face the sea. Images of Gilda filled his mind. Worry was a weight on his chest.

He aimed RnB like an arrow at the dark line that split the azure sky and the sapphire sea. Above him, the fitful gray murk of the voidstorm's remnants bled into the bowl of heaven before disappearing entirely. Below, the ocean was a frightening expanse of undulating hills, valleys, and white-capped teeth.

Memories of almost drowning tried to form, but Frost pushed them away. He had one focus.

"Activate Comm Orb. Voice. @MeritusKillgain. I'm on my way."

CHAPTER 9

Frost flew all day and all night. He spent the night battling sleep, battling nightmares where Gilda's captors mutilated or killed her. He sent messages to Meritus, asking for news, hoping the original report had been wrong, hoping Gilda had shown up, or praying she'd escaped her captors. The response was always negative.

He inquired after her kidnappers' identities. And the details as to how they'd managed to take her. Meritus didn't know. Frost was certain of one thing: the kidnappers were much stronger than Gilda, despite having her outnumbered. He had that much confidence in her fighting ability.

He lost himself in thought amid the rhythm of RnB's wings, a sweep and then a glide, a reliance on aerodynamics Frost didn't quite understand, but which kept them aloft without the need for constant flapping. The mainland had grown from a line to prominent features: forests, mountains, shores, landmarks, and distant colored lights that spoke of civilization.

Frost snapped his head up from a doze. Night had given way to the pale pearl of dawn. Land was to his immediate right, but RnB still soared over the sea whose frothing mouths of white teeth gnashed at a beach. He made to steer RnB toward land even as he allowed his gaze to follow the coastline, head turning until he saw over his shoulder.

A landmark stood out. A peninsula. Not just any peninsula. It was the spear that gave The Glaive its name. That meant the land to his right was Ignis. Ignis meant being too close to the humans, to the Coalition, and the debacle he'd fled in Kituan.

Frost stared ahead. The ocean appeared as an endless sapphire in that direction, and the gnawing in his stomach, his stiff legs, and his thirst said he needed to land. RnB had to feel the same. But Frost knew if he continued on this current line for several hundred miles, he would see the great curve along Lothal's eastern coast. Rescuing Gilda required him to push on.

Disheartened by the distance left to travel, Frost occupied his mind by practicing Replenishment although his aether pool was full. Meditating on the connection between himself and the world allowed him to sense aether, the living power of Mikander, the near invisible swirls and bands. He siphoned it. In minuscule increments, excess aether collected into Aether Overload's reservoir. With Overload, he could activate his most powerful ability, Stand and Deliver.

Smiling, he recalled using Stand and Deliver to defeat Emperor KiGyaba. In his mind's eye he looked like a Vindicator, dressed in high level silver and gold armor, suffused in a blue glow, abilities flying from the cannon too fast to follow, lighting up the air like fireworks.

The power he'd experienced in that moment had been incredible. Overwhelming. He promised himself to experiment with the skill, to see which combos sped up the cyclic rate to maximum in the shortest period of time.

The day dragged on, its heat growing. The sun beat at his back. Frost asked Meritus for updates, but the answers remained a disappointment.

Frost checked his empty canteen for the tenth time. Sighing, he welcomed any cool breeze carrying the ocean's briny scent. Squawking gulls swooped by, none daring to come close to RnB.

His thoughts wandered to Mom, Kai, and Pops. He reminded himself to find a way to tell Mom about Pops' holo. He smiled as he considered the holo now. Pops was the ghost in the machine.

A part of him wished he was back in the real world with them. Another anticipated seeing Pops again. Yet another yearned to simply enjoy Void Legion.

84

He scowled whenever he thought of Sidrie. Combatting the loathing he had for her, for what he knew she had done to Pops, was beyond difficult. Particularly since he had to trust her to keep her word.

As time dragged on, Frost resorted to stretching as best he could, checking his inventory, his stats, theorycrafting about various skills, and weapons. Looking toward the expanse of land to his far right, he tried to name cities and locales from his old memory of Ataxia One, although there was the likelihood some had changed.

Eventually, there was only so much he could do to distract himself from the lengthy trip. Hunger crashed down on him. As did the stiffness in his legs.

"RnB." He petted the drake's neck. The drake gurgled. "It's time we land. You gotta be as hungry as me and probably need to stretch your legs too."

Choosing a lake not far inland, he steered RnB to his right, swooping over waves that frothed onto the shore. A lake of the sort ahead meant fresh water. And wildlife. Wildlife meant food. Frost pushed down on the near indiscernible aether reins. Wings spread, RnB descended in a glide.

As the ground drew closer, Frost made out a few creatures wandering in a nearby marsh. Giant green or blue scorpions came to mind, complete with two claws, one massive and the other much smaller, a barbed tail, and segmented bodies. IM identified them as swamp scorpids.

Frost considered hunting them for all of a second. As usual, he had no way of telling their level or strength. They could be elite, for all he knew. When RnB flew over the scorpids, they scuttled along on eight legs, tails swaying back and forth.

Refocusing on the lake, Frost soon discovered that which he sought. A herd of deer-like cervin were busy grazing among grass, shrubs, and occasional trees. Frost aimed RnB at a shore downwind from the cervins, making certain not to fly over the animals and spook them.

RnB landed gracefully. As much as Frost wanted to leap from the drake's back, his stiff legs wouldn't comply. He was forced to lift one leg over and slide off RnB's back.

It was like heaven when his feet touched ground. Yet, they almost failed him. They felt numb and didn't immediately respond to his body's need for support. He steadied himself by leaning on RnB.

Moments passed and the unsteadiness vanished. As did the numbness. Frost took one tentative step, then another, and soon was strolling among the spongy grass. He performed a few practice sprints and Leaps to make certain all was normal.

Once satisfied, he made his way to the water's edge, squatted, and scooped up a handful of the clear water into his mouth. He sighed at the heavenly taste, made more so by his parched throat. Beside Frost, RnB lapped up his fill, gurgling in contentment.

After filling his canteen, Frost headed toward the grassy area with the cervins, RnB following some ways behind. Staying low, he crept along until he was almost within range of his prey. He took Deadeye from his inventory.

Frost glanced back to tell RnB to wait, but the drake was gone. Brows furrowed, Frost looked all around. But there was no sign of RnB other than the drake's musky smell. Assuming the drake had flown off, he returned his attention to the cervins.

Frost Concealed. He took a few tentative steps forward to get within range of the animals. He aimed at an older buck with weathered horns. A doe was just on the other side of the buck.

Selecting Piercer, Frost took a slow breath and squeezed. A red bolt streaked across the distance. The whine of its discharge echoed a moment later, startling the herd.

But the bolt had already struck. It blasted through the buck, the doe, and continued on for some distance before dissipating. The two animals crumpled. The herd scattered.

Frost deactivated Concealment. He took one step forward when RnB appeared up ahead next to the cervins. Mouth agape, Frost stopped and stared. *Had RnB also Concealed?* He grimaced in doubt but couldn't deny his eyes.

Shaking his head, Frost strode over to the kill. He pointed to the buck. "That one's yours, boy. Eat." RnB gurgled and tore into the cervin.

Smiling, Frost slid the sword from its scabbard and chopped up the doe. He dragged the haunches over to one of the large trees in the area.

Frost cleared a space in the tree's shadow, collected some dry grass and twigs, got his flint and tinder out, and started a fire. Soon enough, he was roasting skewered meat. When he'd finished cooking, Frost kicked dirt over the fire to put it out.

As he ate, Frost basked in a late afternoon breeze that carried a medley of fragrances from the lake and nearby blooms. Birds piped high and low in a harmonious ballad, the tree leaves murmuring in applause. When Frost finished the meal, he stored some extra food in his inventory, reclined on the spongy grass, and stared up at the sky.

RnB strutted over and settled down on his stomach near Frost, his head and tail curled inward until they almost touched. In moments, RnB was snorting and snuffling.

Brows raised at the sound, Frost propped himself up on his elbow and studied the drake. RnB's red and black body rose in a steady rhythm. Frost almost laughed. The damned drake was snoring. But even as Frost watched, something odd happened.

RnB disappeared. But the snoring said the drake was still there.

Without thinking, Frost let out a series of clicks. Echolocation activated. The world within three hundred feet was revealed to Frost's second sight. RnB became a shadowy mass in the shape of a drake.

Separating his sight from Echolocation, Frost studied the spot. He knew certain creatures like defilers could see through Concealment, and RnB had displayed a similar ability, so it might be possible for him to do the same. Squinting, he tried to pick out a difference between the space occupied by the Concealed drake and the air around it.

RnB shifted. The instant the movement occurred, there was an almost imperceptible distortion in the air. A blur, framing RnB. The trees and grass seen beyond was like looking at a steamy mirror.

The effect reminded Frost of the time he'd picked out the Concealed Redthorns by way of the rain falling on them. Or more recently when he thought he'd discerned the same from the Concealed arket.

He smiled as the thought sparked a memory from a movie. One of the Jedi in Episode Twelve, Legacy of Jade, had a similar skill. Hughey had argued that the old Predator movies made the ability look way cooler, and in fact, LOJ had copied from Predator. They'd argued for hours, pulling whatever references they could from the Grid.

The blur shifted upward. Frost deduced that RnB must have stood. A snorting growl rumbled from the drake.

Eyes narrowed, Frost scanned the field. A man approached from a copse some distance away. He was tall for a human. Well-built. He was dressed in dark trousers, a tan shirt, and a long cloak. The stranger carried a staff in one hand, using it almost like a tall walking stick.

Although Frost could not see the staff's base, the light crackling down its length marked the weapon as a storm lance. He had to assume the man was a stormcaller.

Cold fingers slithered down Frost's spine. *What're the chances of running into someone with a hierka out here? Was he a player grinding levels? An NPC? Or is he trying to gank me?*

Again, Frost wished a way existed to discern levels or player type, some kind of identification like there was for mob names and GUMs. But then what difference did it make? None at all if this was some Player Killer.

And if he's a PKer much higher level than me, I'm most likely dead anyway.

Frost always hated the idea of ganking. Whether it was by using unfair numbers or taking advantage of higher levels to kill lowbies, ganking sucked.

True PVP was more his thing. Challenging players who were of a similar level or range of equipment. A sign of player skill.

Frost considered trying to leap onto RnB's back. For all of an instant. Not only was the drake Concealed, but in all likelihood the stormcaller could hit him with a thunderbolt before Frost was able to get airborne.

Aiming Deadeye in the stranger's direction, Frost inched backward. His advantage was range.

As if reading Frost's mind, the man Flickered. One moment he was on the field's far side, and the next, he was halfway across it. Blue electrical arcs crackled around the man's body.

Frost stepped behind the tree, Concealing the moment he was out of sight. He darted around the tree trunk, returning to the spot he'd vacated.

As Frost had anticipated, the man had Flickered again. The man was in the spot Frost had abandoned.

Frost aimed Deadeye at the middle of the man's back. "If you move, I'm gonna take it as a threat and kill you."

Storm energy flared. The man made to spin.

Frost fired a Staggering Shot into the stranger's back. He followed with an Aether Shot. The first attack blasted a hole through the man's chest. The second took half his head. Gore splattered the ground and tree trunk, followed by the heavy thud of the man's corpse.

Frost had the sudden urge to vomit. Gritting his teeth, he fought down the sensation. He chalked it up to his distaste with the kill as well as the heightened emotions the game injected into players.

Guess he wasn't that much higher in levels after all. He strode toward the dead man.

RnB reappeared a few steps from the corpse. He gurgled but made no attempt to move closer.

By an effort of will, Frost ignored the gore and rolled the dead man onto his back. An emblem stood out on the man's left breast. It depicted a storm lance and a great sword, the weapons pointing up, crossing each other to form an X. Nestled in the topmost V of the X was a shield. In the bottom, between the handles of the weapons, was a brazier with a flame.

Abruptly, the body dissolved. One moment it was flesh and blood, and then it was a bunch of bones. A player, Frost concluded, recalling how the Battleguards killed by him, Gilda, and Saba had remained as flesh for some time.

The player's belt, clothing, armor, and weapon remained. Frost emptied the belt pouches.

Health Extract:

Level 10

Regain 1000 Health instantly

Reuse: 2 minutes

Rejuvenation Extract:

Level 10

Regain 2000 health over 30 seconds

Reuse: 2 minutes

He found three of each. In another pouch was a red and green card. Expedition Pass was stenciled in bold letters.

Did he follow me from Maelpith? Frost pocketed the Pass for future use.

A thought made him stop looting the corpse. He recalled the trailer and demo mentioning new Player Killing penalties.

IM was there to provide an answer. Self-defense and fulfilling a bounty did not incur penalties. Neither did accepted challenges to a duel, nor any killings in Open PVP zones, which were a few designated areas within the Coalition's immediate jurisdiction, and anything beyond it, starting from the Dagoda Front and continuing north across the entire Akufa dominion. Anything else was considered murder and allowed for the placement of bounties. A second murder, or committing too many crimes, resulted in the person becoming fully chaotic, punishable by diminished exp, town and city bans, and guards automatically trying to kill or capture the criminal.

Brows furrowed, Frost wondered why this player had been willing to take such a risk. Some players liked the idea of the outlaw life, but they were typically max level and had some OP armor and weapons. It was then Frost remembered the bounty Meritus had mentioned.

He was hunting me. Tensing, Frost studied the stand of trees from which the man had appeared. *What if he hadn't been alone?*

Frost aimed Deadeye, ready to defend himself. RnB perked up at the motion but offered no other concern. Frost waited for perhaps a minute before deciding the man had been alone. If not, his associates would have attacked by now, especially when Frost had been distracted with looting the corpse.

Relieved, Frost bent and took the man's storm lance. Crafted from thick wood, it reached Frost's shoulder. The hierka had a blue tinge to it, marking it as rare.

Frost frowned. If the Expedition Sword had felt odd, the storm lance seemed as if it did not belong in his hands at all. The energy creeping up and down the weapon tingled his skin, raised the hair on his arms.

Acquired weapon: Luminance
Level: 10
Damage: 75 – 100
Force: 15
Special: Increases Flicker range
Available shard slots: 2

Seeing the damage and force, Frost was glad he had avoided a strike. He would have been the one needing to respawn somewhere. Or worse, he might have ended up like one of those invalids.

Shaking off the morbid thought, Frost put the storm lance in his inventory. The rarity and power of hierkas meant a good price on the Auction Market.

A quick inspection of the green brigandine left behind revealed it to be no better than Frost's own. He put it in his inventory. The clothing and robes, he left where they lay. Deciding to look for the player's drake, Frost made to head toward the trees when his Comm Orb dinged.

"Yo, it's ya boy." Meritus' voice had that somber tone again. "I found out who took her. It was Nomarch Setnana Botros and her goons.

"I don't know what else happened besides the thing in Kituan, but she's got it in for the crew. She's been torturing anyone suspected of knowing where y'all might be. Heard she wiped out an entire dvergar village on the island.

"Change up your look somehow. I checked the bounty boards when I got the news. Your pictures are up there. So, it's not only NPCs after you but players also. The reward is five thousand credits of any type.

"If there's any good news from all this, it's that Dante and Saba contacted me. They both have Comm Orbs now. They're all in on helping to save Gilda. How exactly we're gonna do it? I don't know. But knowing you like I do, you'll come up with something.

"I'll look into where they're holding Gilda. Until then, meet up with Dante. He's in Nalanda, a mid-eastern Lothal town not far from the coast in the Fujin nome, which is where you should be heading in from anyway. Saba's on her way to meet me."

Message ended.

Scowling, Frost removed his brigandine and replaced it with the dead player's green one. Pondering how best to prep for the fight to come, he decided his first need was a map. One could be found in the nearest town. A visit to a bounty board was also a must.

He undid his braids and let his ebony hair fall around his face, down to his shoulders. It was a poor disguise, but for now, it would have to suffice.

CHAPTER 10

An hour later, pushing hard southwest across a sky marbled with gold and wispy white, Frost passed the great cliffs and curve in the land marking the borders of Khertahka and Lothal. A town sprawled not far from the coast, its roofs wood or red tile, the main thoroughfares made of cobblestones, while its lanes and alleys were dirt. Figuring it would be as good a place as any to stop, Frost made to follow several other drakes.

The hyoo, hyoo call of kirins echoed from behind. Frost frowned and peered down and back. He shouldn't have been able to hear kirins from this high in the sky.

Something large swept by from above. Winds buffeted him. Even as he turned his head, another form darted by. And another. Several more followed.

Frost gaped. Blinking, he tried to reconcile his sight with his thoughts.

A company of gurashi were flying kirins. Frost had always thought the one-horned creatures were restricted to the ground. Their equine faces and bodies helped reinforce the idea. But that was where all similarities to a horse ended.

Rippling in the wind, the kirins' spiky manes flowed upward and ran down the creatures' backs to meet with bushy tails that tapered at the end. Equally spiky beards sprawled from their chins down to the curve of their necks. Tufts of hair fluttered around the backs of each leg. But what held Frost's attention was the wisps of electric blue and white energy emanating from all growths of hair.

As the last kirin flew by, Frost picked out a depiction of crossed long-hafted axes on the cloak of its rider. Deluth's Crossed Quakers, symbol of the Lothal military. The company of kirins continued on a path to a private Landing and Aviary.

Frost shook off his awe and continued down to the common Landing. An Aviary attendant with glowing glimmerwands directed his descent.

Upon touching down, Frost dipped his head to the green-skinned Flightmistress. "Good day, my lady. What town is this?"

Dressed in a dusty kimono, she was a bulky lion-faced gurash who'd seen better days. If her eye patch and one broken canine was any indication. "I'm not your lady and this here is Madurai," the Flightmistress grumbled. "And unless you have a whistle to send that thing off and call it back, you'll have to take it with you." She grimaced in RnB's direction. "We have no more stables left."

The drake growled, the sound like a hungry belly.

"Thing?" Frost arched a brow. "You talking about my drake?"

"If that's a drake, then I'm a gargant."

"What does that mean?"

"Well, gargants and gurashi are colossuses, but we sure as shit aren't the same." The woman jutted her chin to RnB, the side of her mouth with the good canine curling up. "All our drakes come from the Isfet or Ouroboros Mountains or Mount Setep. He might be some sort o' drake, but his coloring isn't right. Neither is his size. Too big for one so young. Never seen one colored like that before. Mixed and what not. Guess he's like the guralim." She hawked and spat on the dusty ground.

Frost narrowed his eyes. "Guralim?"

"Bastards like them over there." Grimacing in obvious disgust, the Flightmistress jutted her head to the left.

Three gurashi, a man, a woman, and a child, were picking through a mound of garbage in an alley. When they found what they sought, in this case bits of cast aside food, they stopped to eat, stuffing their mouths as if they hadn't seen a meal in days. All three were marble-skinned, the two adults green and red, the child, brown and green. Their kimonos were in tatters.

"Good for nothing. Not even to be named as us." The Flightmistress snorted. "Either too dumb to work a proper job or always wanting to fight."

"Whatever." Frost shot the woman a dirty look. He couldn't help but to

93

think of DeGens when he looked at the guralim. "Come on, RnB."

Heading for the alley, he stalked across the Landing, the drake strutting beside him. He stopped at the mouth of the alley from which the stench of garbage wafted. Frost grimaced at the fetor. RnB shook his head and blew out his nose.

The family cowered away from Frost, but there was a glint in the hulking father's eyes. A warning not to come any closer. Frost took two chunks of roasted cervin from his inventory.

He held out the meat. "I'm not gonna hurt you. Just wanna give you some food."

The man approached tentatively. One half of his face was mottled in red, while the other half was mostly green. His mane was matted. Golden eyes shifting from Frost's face to the food, he got within arm's reach, the stink of shit and piss rolling off him.

Despite the stink, Frost allowed a smile to grace his lips. He waved the meat encouragingly.

Emboldened, the gurash slowly reached a bony hand out and took a chunk of cervin. He sniffed it first, golden eyes still on Frost. He took a bite. His eyes widened. The gurash outcast snatched the other bit of meat from Frost. He turned and signaled to his family, who shuffled over.

They tore the meat between them and quickly ate. By the time they were finished, Frost had taken the other chunks from his inventory and placed them on the ground in as clean a spot as he could find among the alley's muck. He smiled, bowed to the man, and turned away.

Objective complete

Help the Helpless:

1000 experience points

400 Lothal dominion credits

A deep voice echoed from the alley. "Thank you."

Frost turned back. "You're welcome."

"Can I know your name?" The gurash man was standing straight and proud despite his filthy clothes.

Frost thought about giving the man an alias, but on a whim, he decided against the lie. He glanced around to make certain no one else was within earshot. "I'm Frost. Drelan Frost."

The man bowed from the waist. "I am Matsuta Tsujii. I will never forget, Drelan Frost."

Smiling, Frost bowed in turn. Chest puffed up, he left the family to their meal. Frost thought about riding RnB, following the example set by many others leaving the Landing, but he was sure the drake could use a rest. Besides, he liked the feel of RnB next to him. Enjoyed the company. RnB was like a friend who didn't talk too much and never got in the way.

He noticed every other drake was of a solid color. White. Green. Blue. Brown. Black. Red. Those were the most common, but a few yellows or oranges were sprinkled among them. The shades varied. But always solid.

People gave RnB odd looks, most often in awe or curiosity. Some pointed. A few folk shied away from him.

As for the other mounts? Most kept their distance or deliberately moved out of his way. One or two hissed or growled. None seemed friendly. The kirin they passed paid RnB no more attention than they did to any other drake.

Frost grimaced at the reflection of his encounter with the outcast family. At some point he'd have to get to the bottom of it, but his immediate concern was the map and the bounty board. He strode down the main avenue, asked a fellow erada for directions, and headed toward the trade district.

Madurai was quite busy for not being a city. People of all sorts crowded the streets. Horned eradae, lumbering bushy-maned gurashi dressed in kimonos and sandals, fair-skinned humans, and centaur-like dresdori their equine portions covered by barding. He even saw a few blue-skinned undines, water stalking along their skins like snakes. The air practically buzzed with their voices. And scents. Frost chalked up their presence to the town's location, so close to the border of two dominions as well as the coast.

"Bless?" A silver-haired human in robes shuffled up to Frost. He held out a vial with golden liquid. "Do you wish to buy a Bless? Protect your goods from cutthroats with a Bless. From theft or identification. Only one thousand LDC."

"Not interested." Frost shooed the man away.

Frost had taken but a few steps when something tapped him on the leg. He looked down.

A gnome stared up at him, eyes twinkling. "Hey, buddy." Voice high-pitched, the gnome graced Frost with a gap-toothed smile. "Wanna join my guild?"

Frost shook his head. "Sorry, I like to play solo."

The gnome crossed his arms. "That's because you've never been in an awesome guild before. Or at least not one as awesome as Pwnage Inc."

Frost made to speak, but the gnome overrode him. "We have a ton to offer. Power-leveling noob guildees, guild dungeon runs, raids, PvP, castle sieges, and when the battlegrounds and the arena are finished, we'll be there too. At the top, pwning everyone. You look strong. You and your mount. We could use someone like you. So, wanna join Pwnage? I'll even make you an officer."

The gnome had spoken so quickly, Frost hadn't been able to get in a word. Not wanting to be rude, Frost smiled and dipped his head. "Maybe another time. Thanks, though."

"Okay." The gnome's shoulders slumped. Before Frost took a step, the gnome had darted over to someone nearby. "Hey, buddy, wanna join my guild?"

With a shake of his head and a wry smile, Frost continued on his way. He stopped when he encountered a tailor's stall, the wares spread out in front on tables or hanging from stands. The vendor was a burly gurash with a round gut not even his sheet-like kimono could hide. His gut fell over his sash. He kept peering at RnB, thick brows bunched as if he were trying to decide exactly what he was seeing.

"How much is that cloak?" Frost indicated the black knee-length piece with a large hood.

"Two hundred LDC. Double for any other types of credits."

Frost winced. He considered going to a credit changer, but time was against him. "Two hundred LDC, it is then." Lothal dominion credits appeared in his hands in the form of pale red paper with a likeness of Kalarch Amari Kisa, her ruby skin standing out.

With a tilt of his head, the vendor took the credits and passed the cloak. "Thank you, sir."

Frost nodded, slung the cloak over his shoulders, tied it off around his neck, and strode away. He pulled the hood up over his head.

His next stop was at a cartographer. He managed to haggle with the man for a map of Mikander. Wanting to keep his few LDC, he paid two hundred IDC. When he received the map, it immediately became a part of IM.

Frost focused on the idea of the map. And stopped in his tracks, eyes wide.

An overhead rendition of Madurai had appeared, populated with districts, streets, lanes, and buildings. Most of them were unidentified, except for those he'd already passed. The latter had names attached. Striding forward revealed more. In awe, Frost shook his head and continued on, mapping the town.

He paused at a nearby building. *Message,* he thought, activating his Comm Orb. Dante's and Saba's IGNs were both highlighted now. Choosing Dante, he spoke in a low voice, "Yo, this is Frost. I'm on my way to meet you in Nalanda. Keep your head down until I get there." *End Message.*

Frost set off again, sticking to the long shadows cast by buildings around him. He soon located the trade district and the Auction Market, a three-storied building. Outside the Market there was a long hitching rail separated in sections. Mounts of all sorts were tethered. Drakes, zephyrs, kirins, non-flyers like crevids and lupines, and even a four-tailed fox.

Unlike many other mounts, tethering a flying beast didn't require a leash of some sort. The reins did the work. If he simply set the drake where he wanted, it would remain there until he returned. Frost made to place RnB beside a green drake, but it hissed.

RnB gurgled. A sad sound if Frost was any judge. RnB hung his head.

"It's alright, boy." Frost shot a scowl at the offending drake, petted RnB on the head, and took him two spaces away. "Stay here, I'm gonna be right back."

Knowing the typical location for the bounty board would be outside the Auction Market, Frost headed to the building. The board was located to one side of the front door. No one was near it.

Imitating the confident stride of a man with nothing to hide, Frost ascended the stairs. He stopped before the board and studied the papers upon it. Each paper had names, bounties, and pictures of the wanted, approved by the Coalition Tribunal.

Not all the bounties were for murder. Some of the wanted people had committed other crimes like treason, arson, bribery, and theft.

He frowned. Murder and theft were rather common. The latter more so than the former. While the murderers ranged in class, the vast majority of the thieves were cutthroats. Frost wondered how many on the board were NPCs and how many were players.

Running an index finger down the list, it wasn't long before he found himself, Gilda, Saba, Dante, Adesh, and Ryne. Their last location was given as Imanok Sanctum. As Meritus had said, the bounty was five thousand each, except for Adesh Hamada. His was fifteen thousand.

Bringing them in dead or alive also mattered. The bounty was cut in half if they were dead. Their crimes were murder, theft, and treason against the Coalition as members of the Blue Sky Network.

A pack o' fucking lies. Frost seethed.

IM flashed, letting him know the bounty board was now part of its archive. He could access updates on-demand in real time without having to visit another board.

The functionality made sense. A means to prevent a killing should the Coalition's Tribunal absolve a person of their crime. Or if the wanted person had paid all necessary fines and penalties and were no longer considered chaotic. Or if someone had simply canceled a bounty.

Seeing himself and his friends on the board made Frost glad for the way the game worked now. For the inability to identify players through a Heads-Up Display. The lack of such information on a HUD made survival probable.

In the old version of the game, a chaotic player's name would be in bright red when you looked at them. He wondered how the new functionality affected the game's AI, if the guards suffered the same deficiency. Did they need to be shown the criminal first? The idea made sense, considering the Lothal soldiers who'd flown by had not chased him.

He headed into the Auction Market, intent on acquiring a new weapon, ammo, armor, and jewelry. Rows of small partitioned booths lined the interior, each row separated by a walkway large enough for two people to walk abreast of each other. Attendants in green jackets had the symbol of a hammer on their lapels. Frost studied the patrons, noting that many bore an emblem either on one side of their chest, on their shoulder, their cloak, or a combination of the three.

Choosing a booth in a corner away from any other patrons, he strode over and sat on the chair provided. A thought connected him with the Auction Market interface.

"Welcome to the Auction Market, shopper. I'm your host, Marie." A fair-skinned, two-foot female asrai popped into Frost's mind. Wings buzzing, she flitted this way and that. She stopped in front of Frost and graced him with a smile.

"Hi, Marie. I'm Frost."

"Helllooooo, Mr. Frost. Brrrrrr." She rubbed her arms and giggled. "Since this is your first time here, it is advisable to run the tutorial. It will give you a grasp of bidding, selling, longs, shorts, base pricing, duration, pick up, delivery, and other nuances needed for a good experience. Do you wish to run the tutorial now or skip it?"

"Skip it."

Marie's lips curved down in obvious disappointment. "Awwwww. Have you purchased a warehouse to have your items delivered? Smaller items can go directly into your inventory, but weapons, construction materials, and certain other things must be delivered to your warehouse where you can retrieve them."

"I haven't yet."

"Would you like to purchase one now?" She perked up, wings flitting faster as she darted around Frost. "Your warehouse will be accessible in any town or city. Certain villages also have the capability. But this applies only in Coalition-owned territory."

"What're the prices?"

"Five thousand credits of any currency for a basic warehouse. Ten thousand for mid-range. Twenty thousand for deluxe."

Frost winced, knowing he had no choice in order to get a new weapon. "Fine. I'll go with basic and pay in IDC."

"Yay!" Marie clapped. "Ignis dominion credits it is, for a basic warehouse. Say yes to confirm the agreement."

"Yes."

"Congratulations, you are now the owner of a basic warehouse!" She flew in circles before returning to hover in front of Frost.

IM dinged. Notifications informed him of the warehouse's size and location. A demo showed it to be more like a storage shed in a building on the town's outskirts.

"Happy bidding and selling. Goodbye!" The asrai flew away before disappearing in a poof.

The Auction Market interface popped up with types of items listed at the top from left to right. Each had an icon. Weapons, Armor, Jewelry, Ammunition, Hierkas, Skill Shards, Skill-Effect Shards, Gems, Schemas, Materials. Letting his vision drift over one or another provided an additional range of options for sorting or searching.

Identifying rarity was done by color. Common was in white, superior in green, rare in blue, epic in violet, legendary in orange, and relic in red. Hierkas fell in a classification called genesiswork, started at rare, and ended at genesis, which was dark purple, and one level above relic.

Frost chose hierkas. Options opened up for bidding or selling. He chose bidding. Next, he picked level range from ten to twelve. Ignoring all the other hierka types, he settled on aether cannons. A list opened up with available aether cannons that met his criteria.

Frowning, he looked for a way to input skill boosts connected to a weapon. He saw none. On a whim, he thought about searching for a hierka with added Cannon Kata. The search returned no results. Frost sighed.

"Any type of cannon from level ten to twelve."

The first list returned. Frost roved down the choices. The damage according to level was identical on all of them. So was the force. All but one. A level twelve epic cannon called The Stunner. Its force was thirty. Its special was five percent chance to stagger on a hit. A note from the buyer said it was a drop from Emperor KiGyaba.

He chose to see the cannon. In his mind's eye, a live version of the weapon appeared. The Stunner was longer than Deadeye by about six inches. Its barrel was broader, black, and sleek. The battery pack was on the top right, midway down the weapon. The trigger assembly and handle were at the rear, apparently a common aether cannon feature.

Frost whistled at the price. Ten thousand credits of any kind for an outright purchase. The bids started at a thousand. He'd be almost broke if he chose the weapon. And yet, he couldn't let the chance slip by. Nor could he wait for the end of bidding in three days. With a sigh, he clicked buy.

The asrai popped up. "Are you certain about this outright purchase?"

"Yes."

Marie clapped her hands joyfully. "Awesome! How do you wish to pay?"

Frost took a look at his credits.

7050 IDC

8000 KDC

"Split evenly between IDC and KDC."

"Sold! You may pick up your purchase at your warehouse." Poof, she was gone again. As was the image of the cannon.

His credits diminished accordingly. After a deep breath, Frost took a look at his other needs. Buying any piece of armor or jewelry was out of the question. So were skill and skill-effect shards. Those were insanely expensive.

His next skill, Strafe, was at level fifteen. He sighed. Having it now would have saved some time, but the seller wanted six thousand LDC.

Hoping for some luck, he searched for any of the empowered spells for Benediction. The results came up empty each time.

With a shake of his head, he spent a thousand of each credit type on korbitanium projectiles. Two thousand projectiles popped into his inventory.

Thinking of a way to increase his power by utilizing shard slots, Frost took a look at the gems. They came in two main forms: precious and semi-precious. The first consisted of diamonds, emeralds, rubies, and sapphires, all high level, and none for sale. There were quite a few of the second type, including tourmalines, peridots, topazes, amethysts, and citrines. When placed in a shard slot, they boosted various weapon or skill properties. It was the lesser version of empowerment. The cheapest to be found started at three thousand credits. Frost sighed.

He closed out the gem menu and proceeded to miscellaneous. There, he bought a drake whistle for five hundred IDC.

Acquired item:

Drake Whistle

Bonds with owner's drake. With this item, the owner can call his drake to

101

him from up to a distance of twenty miles. Once taught to fly away, the drake will remain within range. Blow the whistle while touching the specific drake to create a bond. Once bonded, the whistle only works for that drake.

He decided to keep the rest of his credits for emergency. Frost took the storm lance, Luminance, from his inventory. He listed it with a starting bid of two thousand credits. Outright price was ten thousand. Perhaps he could make back what he'd spent for The Stunner.

Marie reappeared. "Hello, again, Mr. Frost. If you would be so kind as to give the item to one of our attendants, who will take it to our warehouse until it is sold." She gestured toward the booth's doorway.

A gurash man waited, dressed in the Auction Market's green jacket over a yellow kimono. Frost passed Luminance to him.

"If you have other items for sale, you may list them," Marie said.

Frost considered listing the skill shards before deciding to keep them. "That's all I'm selling today."

"Thank you." Marie vanished once more.

The gurash bowed, turned on his heels, and strode away. A ding returned Frost's attention to the auction interface. Luminance had appeared as an icon listed under Frost's name.

Frost disconnected from the Market. As he was about to leave, his Comm Orb dinged. It was Dante, his high-pitched voice more than a little excited.

"Hey, bro. Glad you hit me up. I'll be right here with Ryne. Can't wait until you reach so we can get down to some real action. We're staying at an inn called the Creeping Man on Dervish Street. West end of town. Second floor. Room two-oh-two. If we're not in our rooms, we'll be in the bar area, playing shevla. See you soon."

A smile crept onto Frost's face with the thought of Ryne. Dante and the goblin were the last two people he would have expected to be together. Shaking his head at the thought, he left the building and made his way to pick up RnB. Only to find several people inspecting the drake.

RnB had his head down and seemed utterly depressed by the attention. He perked up when he saw Frost. Seeing the drake's misery, Frost called RnB over with a simple wave.

One of the people, a human woman, approached Frost as he was mounting RnB. Dressed in a long, flowing, green silk dress with shimmering sleeves and a cloak to match, she reeked of riches. "Hello, good sir." Her voice was a wind chime.

Frost turned RnB to face her. The woman didn't shy away from the drake's maw. Not even when RnB snorted.

Her face was angular, brown-skinned, her skin smooth. Beautiful. Her hazel eyes were particularly intoxicating. It was as if she drank him in.

"Hello." Frost tossed his hood back and inclined his head.

She smiled and returned the gesture. "My intention wasn't to bother you, but my guildmaster collects rare drakes. He'd be especially interested in this one. You would be greatly compensated."

"It's no bother, but I'm not interested." Frost shrugged. "Sorry."

"Twenty thousand credits of your choice wouldn't interest you?" Her eyes said she was serious.

Frost's brows shot up. He thought of the gear he could buy with the money. But almost immediately, he heard Pop's voice, warning him of things that seemed too good to be true.

"Forty thousand?" She smiled. Even her eyes twinkled.

Frost narrowed his eyes. If the woman was willing to pay that much, RnB had to be special in some way. Extra special, probably. "Nah. This guy's more a friend than just a mount. Money can't buy friendship. Thanks for asking, though."

"Fifty thousand." Her voice was flat now.

"No thanks. And not meaning to be rude, but I gotta go."

"Very well. Can I at least know your name for when we meet again?"

Frost almost replied with the truth before he caught himself. "I'm Lan."

She looked to Frost, brow furrowed, a few moments passing before she added, "And your last name in case my guildmaster wishes to contact you with an even better price?"

Frost ground his jaw. "Just Lan, ma'am. And good evening."

"Well, Lan, if you should change your mind, my name is Meileen Elune. You can reach me by Orb. I'm sure we shall speak again. Good evening." She turned and glided away, her cloak hiding her form. Emblazoning the cloak's back was a crossed storm lance and a greatsword, a shield, and a brazier with a flame.

Frost frowned at the design. Two men Frost had not noticed before stepped forward to meet the woman. They wore the elaborate signature silver armor of Vindicators. Their cloaks bore a tan mountain split by a blue river. The Coalition's Mountain and the Aetherstream.

Frost licked his lips at the sight of the Vindicators. A prickle of fear eased through him. *What if she'd been to the bounty boards? What if she had recognized me?*

Sweat beading his forehead, he turned down an alley and hurried toward his warehouse. He had to flee this town as soon as possible.

CHAPTER 11

As Frost approached the warehouse, he linked RnB with the drake whistle. While touching RnB's neck, he blew the whistle three times. There was no sound Frost could hear, but RnB immediately gurgled. IM alerted Frost of the active bond.

Rather than use the hitching rail out front, Frost circled behind the warehouse to a copse of trees. When he found a spot where he thought RnB would be hidden, he dismounted. With a thought, he released the part of the reins that served as RnB's tether. This way RnB could escape should someone try to take him.

Frost preferred for the drake to fly off and wait for him to whistle, but he needed to teach RnB some sort of command to leave in the first place. Still, at least there was the bond. Something was better than nothing.

"I'll be back in a few minutes, boy." Frost reached up and stroked RnB's head, the drake having snaked it down toward him. RnB gurgled.

As Frost strode away, footsteps on the soft ground alerted him to RnB's presence. Frost turned. RnB stopped. The drake was several feet away from the trees, watching Frost, eyes glinting gold, head tilted to one side.

"You gotta stay here." Frost help up his hand, palm outward.

RnB tilted his head even more. He released a series of gurgles like a complaining belly.

"Alright." Frost nodded. "Whatever you just said. But I still need you to stay." He held up his palm again.

When RnB voiced no other complaint, Frost turned to leave. He made but two steps before snapping his head around. RnB froze, but the drake had definitely taken a step of its own.

Frost strode over to the drake. RnB lowered his head level with Frost's face. The drake snorted, breath positively rancid. Frost wrinkled his nose.

"You can't come into the warehouse, and I don't want people bothering you." Frost stroked RnB's snout. "Come on." He gestured for the drake to follow him and strode away. RnB turned and walked alongside Frost.

When they reached among the trees, Frost stopped. "Please stay, alright?" He held up his palm. RnB snorted. "I'll take that as a reluctant yes."

Frost smiled, turned away, made to take a step, and spun back around. He caught RnB with a leg raised. Smirking, Frost looked from the leg to RnB's face and shook his head. The leg lowered to the ground. RnB gurgled.

"I'd rather you be with me also. I promise I'll be back soon." Frost took in those intelligent golden pupils and irises surrounded by black sclera. "Stay. Pleasssseeee." He held up his palm once more.

RnB hung his head. He gurgled once, a quick sound that cut off abruptly.

Frost acted as if he were leaving again. When he made a sudden turn back to the drake, RnB had not moved.

"Thank you." Frost gave the drake a sad smile, sighed, and departed with a heavy heart.

Halfway across the field, he checked behind him once more. RnB had not moved. The drake was well hidden among the trees.

Frost hurried to the three-storied building and entered. He spoke to one of the attendants, this one a female goblin with smiling eyes. The goblin led Frost to the warehouse, a ten-foot square room with shelves along two walls. The aether cannon was sitting on a shelf. Frost picked up the sleek black weapon.

Acquired weapon: The Stunner
Level: 12
Damage: 120 – 140

Force: 30
Special: 5% chance to stagger on a hit
Available shard slots: 3

He equipped The Stunner, replacing Deadeye as his main weapon. The jump in his total damage brought an appreciative nod. One hundred and ninety-four to two hundred and fourteen. He looked forward to how fast he could drop enemies now and the chance to stagger them without using a skill.

Frost turned to the attendant. "What if I wanted to leave my old weapon here?"

"You could." The goblin gestured to the shelf.

"And if I wanted to put it on sale in the Market?"

"We have a link to the Market. We would be alerted of the listing and place the weapon in the system."

"Thanks." Deciding to keep Deadeye with him as a backup, Frost placed the cannon in his inventory. With The Stunner resting atop his shoulder, he left the establishment.

Outside, he brought the whistle to his lips and blew. As before, he heard no sound, but moments later flapping wings and a familiar cry announced RnB's arrival. The drake landed next to Frost, kicking up dust. With The Stunner in hand, Frost climbed onto RnB's back. He took a hold of the reins, pulled up, and RnB took off with a great beat of his wings.

A mere thought brought up the map of Mikander and its two main continents, Marang and Korbash. It was akin to looking at a fully color-ized render with his location on Marang marked as a red dot. Across the Empyrean Sea was Korbash, about a third the size of Marang.

The world's eight dominions were listed in white with the battle-scarred mountain range of the Dagoda Front separating the draconid-controlled Akufa dominion from Nimri, Ignis, Khertahka, Puria, and Lothal. In Korbash, there was the gargant dominion of Ostenia, and the yurid mountain and sky home, Lantano. Each dominion was further separated into nomes, with some cities, towns, forests, mountains, oceans, and various dungeons or places of interest clearly marked.

If he focused on a location, he could zoom into it, but there were no details for most of them. Only shadow. From experience, he knew the details of the cities and towns only became visible after he'd visited them.

He assumed the many shadowy spaces on the map worked in the same fashion. Most of them were beyond the Dagoda Front or in Korbash.

Right now, he needed to find Nalanda. In response to his query, the town's name glowed yellow. Nalanda was directly south from his location. Judging by the distance he'd already covered, he could make it there in a few hours, a tad after nightfall.

Frost coaxed as much speed as he could from RnB. The drake's wings beat a constant rhythm, the ground below a blur as they sped across a sky whose clouds burned with the burnished hues of early evening. The cool wind whipped Frost's black cloak behind him.

Concern for Gilda crept into Frost's mind. He tried to chase away the worry by thinking about times they'd spent together. He smiled as he recalled their fight against the Azureguards in Snakewood Forest. Then, there was the dreamleaf they'd fed to the Sky Swords. The mad dash to Marna. He had particularly fond thoughts of her prowess and knowledge when they'd fought Azonoth and cleared Imanok Sanctum, killing Emperor KiGyaba.

He saw her now, flitting around him during the battle with the emperor. She employed her Aether Overload skill, Song of Ice and Fire, an oval cyan Aether Barrier surrounding her, red and blue Aether Shields on her arms repelling almost every attack against him.

Most of all, he remembered their time outside the game. First, in Equitane Towers, surrounded by a hut made of MX1 boxes, their lovemaking steaming the air. Then, in the Hotel Manzania after Mom had come out of her coma.

Thinking of those moments made him want to be with her now, right here in game. He wondered how different the sensations would be. Need tried to rise, but he pushed it away.

Daylight died a slow death, the western horizon swallowing the sun. Night crept in like a cold worm slithering across his skin. A hunter's horn of a moon had taken its place in a sky that had donned an ebon dress sprinkled with glittering jewels.

Below him, myriad lights marked towns and cities. The colors varied from the orange flames of torchlight to the blues, whites, and yellows of short glimmerwands, longer glimmerstalks, or the circular luminance that were bloomglobes. A quick look at the map showed he was still on a direct line with Nalanda. Not long afterward, the town appeared at the edge of a forest's stygian stain.

Message @DanteBlackblade.

"What up, Dante. I'm about to land in a few minutes. See ya soon."

Frost directed RnB toward a square field on the outskirts, certain it was a Landing. If the lone person wielding one red and one green glimmerwand was any indication. Sure enough, as RnB began its descent, the person waved the green glimmerwand and directed them until they touched down.

The attendant approached. To Frost's surprise, he was a gurash boy, the short mane suggesting he had to be in his early teens. Slight for a member of the race, he had deep brown skin, which had an odd look to it beneath the mixture of the colored glimmerwands. The boy's leonine features spoke of tiredness.

"Hey, mister." The boy yawned. "Kinda late to be flying in. Do you need a stable for—" He stared at RnB, rubbed his eyes, then looked again.

"For my drake?" Frost waved the boy off. "No. He stays with me."

"Fine. I hope he's tamed. If he bites somebody, the guards will most likely kill him."

"Not gonna happen." Frost meant that more toward possible action on the part of the guards.

"If you say so." The boy moved out of the way, but his gaze followed RnB.

Frost rode into town where the streets were mostly empty. Music drifted on the air. As did the echo of raucous songs from some nearby tavern. A group of drunken gurashi staggered from an establishment, boisterous voices echoing.

On a whim, Frost focused on the map again. It had changed from a world view to Nalanda alone, filled with streets, lanes, and buildings. Location names unveiled as he rode, adding to those already uncovered by his flight.

He was on Osian Avenue, a main thoroughfare. Heading due west, he kicked the bolsters, encouraging more speed. Soon, they were running at a decent rate, RnB's claws clicking on cobbles, Frost's cloak fluttering in the cool breeze. When he got to the intersection of Osian Avenue and Dervish Street, he stopped.

"Which way, RnB?"

The drake gurgled. Frost stroked his aether ring while trying to decide. He considered asking one of the few people strolling along the avenue.

To his right, two guards approached, both gurashi dressed in leather armor, the hilts of large two-handed swords jutting above their shoulders. Well aware of the bounty on his head, Frost tensed, ready to flee should the need arise. But the guards paid no more attention to him than to anyone else.

Breathing a relieved sigh, and again glad for the design of identification, Frost rode over to the men. "Heyyy there, fellas. Which way to the Creeping Man?"

The bigger of the two jutted a thumb back in the direction from which they'd come. "Two intersections over."

"Thanks. Goodnight." Frost dipped his head and set off.

The Creeping Man was a five-storied building. A sign outside declared the name in red letters. Yellow and white bloomglobes lit the exterior. Music and laughter drifted from inside. Four drakes and several kirins occupied sections of the hitching rail. Frost got a spot for RnB, petted the drake on the head, and then strode into the tavern.

A short blue-skinned gurash woman, which meant she was about Frost's seven feet, greeted him at the door. "Welcome to the Creeping Man."

Her eyes were the purest silver. Her shape was quite svelte despite her beige kimono. She wore an oversized sash, cinching from her waist to a hair below her breasts. "Do you wish to rent a room or are you here for entertainment?"

"Looking for a friend. Friends, really. A crimson gurash about this big. Red mane." Frost gestured to indicate a height a foot taller than himself. "Totes a large black axe most times. Has a really high voice. Like a girl. Probably will be with a cocky goblin who has way too many muscles and has a habit of speaking in rhymes."

"Oh." The woman smiled warmly. Even her eyes twinkled with delight. "Chaotix and Aximand. They're in the bar. Back right corner." She pointed to a door from which music, voices, and laughter filtered out.

Frost smiled at the names, glad he hadn't used their real ones. At the same time, he shook his head because Dante had not mentioned their aliases in the Comm Orb message.

He made to cross the room when the door to the bar exploded in a spray of wooden shards. The body of a green rough-looking gurash crashed into furniture. A blue one followed. Neither moved from where they'd fallen.

From inside the bar came the clash of steel on steel. Someone cried out. Women's voices screamed. Men yelled.

In a flash, Frost had The Stunner out of his inventory. He aimed the black cannon at the door, ready to let loose if need be.

The fighting stopped abruptly. The yelling died down. Whimpers followed.

A broad chain-mailed back and a shaggy red mane appeared at the shattered door. "Sorry for the trouble, Tiya. I'll leave some credits for the damage."

Frost smiled at Dante's high-pitched voice.

Ryne strode through Dante's legs, the short sleeves of his robes revealing bulging arms. His hair was still in the same top knot and his wispy beard was a bit longer.

The blue gurash was creeping across the floor, struggling to rise. Ryne's foot landed a precise kick to the chin. The gurash crumpled.

"Chaotix! Aximand!" Frost laughed.

Dante turned, grinning madly. His red mane fell around his face. "Oh, hey, Fro—hey, buddy. Long time no see." He rested the black-bladed, long-hafted crescent axe on his shoulder.

Ryne did a little hop step over the unconscious gurash's head, voice like a rumble of thunder when he spoke. "Hello, friend. Glad to see you didn't meet your end."

"Same here." Frost shook his head as he took them in. "I actually didn't believe you two would be together, considering how y'all went at it before."

"The little guy and I have an understanding." Dante smiled fondly at the goblin.

Ryne jabbed a tiny thumb up at Dante. "Indeed. He understands I

111

provide a need. He's reckless. I'm here to clean up his mess."

"What can I say, bro?" Dante shrugged. "You know I'm all about the action, right?" He crossed the room, clapped Frost on the shoulder, and gave a friendly squeeze with fingers like iron.

"Right." Frost winced and tapped Dante on the hand.

Dante snatched his hand away. "Sorry, bro. I tend to forget my strength."

"It's all good. What happened?" Frost nodded toward the unconscious gurashi.

"I'll explain in a sec." Dante strode over to the woman. He passed her a wad of Lothal dominion credits. "Sorry about the mess, Tiya. Tell Angrim if he needs anything else to send word." He glanced toward a hall with stairs. "Let's go. Their friends will be down soon." He spared a glance for Frost. "Let me add you to the group real quick. And I hope you've got a flyer outside."

"I do."

They hurried from the Creeping Man.

CHAPTER 12

IM informed Frost he was part of a group. The moment they ran through the front door, Ryne and Dante put whistles to their lips. Hoots and screeches echoed in the night. Beating wings followed.

"Where's your flyer?" Dante headed toward the open space near the hitching rail, carrying his massive axe as if it were a twig.

"There." Frost pointed toward RnB, an electric excitement creeping into him.

"Good. Ryne, CC their mounts." Dante blew his whistle again and ran toward the rail in those lumbering gurash strides.

Ryne Flickered ahead. A green drake swooped above the goblin then lowered itself to the ground. At the same time, Ryne stretched a hand out toward the other flying mounts hitched at the rail. The black shackles of Immobilize encircled their bodies. The captive drakes and kirins cried out in protest. Ryne climbed atop his mount.

Sprinting beside Dante, Frost grinned at the sight of tiny Ryne atop the large drake. "So, what was that about?"

"A little difference of opinion." Dante chuckled.

"About what exactly?"

"Shevla and politics. They didn't like losing to a draconid hand."

Frost's brows shot up. "A draconid hand? I woulda been pissed too. You shoulda known better than to take the situation lightly, card game or not."

"No rules were set, bro," Dante protested. "And their leader threatened to take me to his boss if I didn't return double the amount of credits they lost." A kirin landed gracefully a few steps ahead of Dante, blue and white energy swirling up from its yellow hair, particularly its bushy mane.

"They're almost at the door." Ryne was focused on the Creeping Man.

"His boss is one o' the worst pieces o' shit in recent gurash memory." Dante heaved himself atop his kirin. "Umesh Madara. Who is only topped by the bastard above him, the traitor, General Dakshi Asamar."

Frost swung up onto RnB, The Stunner in one hand. "I've seen Umesh's work. He slaughtered most of a village I passed through." A quick look at the Creeping Man's first floor windows revealed shadowy figures crossing the front room. "I had to save Tia from him. Promised to bring his head to a friend. Even got a quest for it."

"Count me in for that one." Dante tugged on his reins.

The three of them had barely lifted from the ground when several gurashi burst through the Creeping Man's front door. Frost smiled. Pulling on his reins with his left hand, he fired a Concussion Blast into their midst. The white streak exploded, tossing them into the air.

Looking down at the gurashi, Frost steadied The Stunner across his left arm, which still gripped the reins. A cyan globe formed at the cannon's tip, growing to the size of a basketball in the 1.5 second cast time. The Aether Bomb spit from the muzzle with a whoosh, rippling diagonally toward the gurashi who were just now slamming into the ground from the Blast. The Bomb exploded on impact, setting them afire.

"Nice shot." Dante's falsetto voice piped through group chat. "Let's get to hell outta here before more of 'em come."

"On my way." With a kick of his bolsters, Frost sent RnB flapping after Dante and Ryne's mounts into the night sky.

Assuming his friends had a plan, Frost followed them, the howling wind ruffling his cloak. Every so often, he glanced over his shoulder, expecting pursuit. Any dark blotch in the sky, any screech of a drake, hyoo of a kirin, or call of some animal below them set him on edge. He kept The Stunner ready.

A couple hours' worth of flight saw them pass several farms, ranches, homesteads, villages, towns, and cities. The night air grew cooler, the wind picking up. Finally, they descended toward a home with a barn near it, located within a hundred feet of an obsidian forest.

114

They landed outside the barn. Dante led them inside. Despite the darkness, Frost still made out a few things. Along the walls were several wooden pens, complete with food and water. Dante rummaged along a wall to their right. A bloomglobe flickered to life. Dante ventured farther inside and turned on another.

"This your spot?" Frost took in the training area at the back of the barn. He squinted, and then his brows shot up. "Yo, is that a weight bench and an Olympic bar. Hold up… hold up… hoooolldd up… you had someone make some plates too? And dumbbells?"

Dante laughed in that high voice of his. "Yeah, bro. A man needs to stay fit. Especially if Sidrie's claims about TNT are true. Plus, any type of exercise we do enhances our attributes over time. Besides." He nodded toward the goblin. "You seen Ryne's guns? I can't have his pythons outshining mine." Axe in one hand, Dante got into a quick single bicep pose.

"No doubt." Frost glanced from Dante to Ryne, forehead wrinkled. This was the second time Dante called Ryne by name rather than making reference to the goblin as gnome to get under Ryne's skin. "How'd you come by this place?"

"Built it. All you do is claim a plot and file it with the Coalition. Once approved, you can farm your mats and build."

"Sweet." Frost was already considering where he might do the same. He loved the idea. His eyes narrowed. "You sure this place is safe, considering there's a bounty on us?"

"A friend filed the claim for me, so this place isn't in my name. Stable your drake." Dante gestured to the pens before he returned to his kirin and led it to the first enclosure.

Frost followed suit in the second pen, whispering soothing words to RnB. The food was meat of some sort. RnB busied himself with the meal.

"That's a strange one you got there." Dante strode over to Frost. "Hold on, is that the one from the aeries on Maelpith? The one the others kicked around?"

"Yeah." Frost shrugged. "I didn't like seeing him get bullied."

Dante chuckled. "You always had a soft spot for that stuff. Come on, let's go inside, get a bite to eat, and you can lay this plan of yours on me." Dante strode toward the door.

115

When they left the barn, Frost took a quick look up at the night sky but saw no flyers. Out of habit, he clicked. Echolocation revealed the immediate area was clear.

Breathing in the fresh cool breeze that set the trees and grass murmuring, Frost sighed, the last bit of adrenaline bleeding from him. He followed the massive gurash and his tiny counterpart to the large house made of wooden logs, the two of them carrying on with playful banter.

Once inside, Dante activated two bloomglobes set in sconces along one wall. Soft yellow light illuminated a spacious room complete with an area rug, a center table, four cushioned armchairs, a sofa to match, and paintings. The perfume of incense threaded the air. A dark hall led into the rest of the house.

"Welcome to my humble home." Dante gestured around him. "Have a seat. Relax. I'll be right back." He headed deeper into the house, another light blooming moments later.

Frost eased into a chair. He eyed Ryne, who had climbed onto the sofa. "How come you two ended up together?" As Ryne's services were still contracted to Frost, the NPC's actions were intriguing.

Ryne leaned back into his seat, skinny legs showing past the bottom of his robes. "The night we were celebrating your victory in the Sanctum, you four disappeared. One moment you were there, the next, elsewhere. Exactly where, I had no clue, but I had this urge to wait for you."

Stroking his wispy beard, Ryne paused, green forehead furrowed. "And so, I waited, breath bated. I spent time hunting and helping Dagrun, Gunarr, and Sigrid as more of their people came. Some in good health, some wounded, some lame. Then, a day later, Dante, Saba, and Gilda returned, looking like new. But not you." The look he gave Frost was almost accusatory.

"That was outta my hands." Frost shrugged.

"So Dante said. He said a lot of things then and since." Ryne's expression became studious. "Some things that were hard to believe."

Frost regarded the goblin with a raised brow. "What did he say?"

"I told him where we were from." Dante was standing at the hall to the rest of the house, balancing two platters of food and bread on his large hands. Tin plates were tucked under one arm.

"You did what?" Frost gave the red-maned, lion-faced gurash an incredulous stare.

"Told him we were players. Explained the game to him." Dante crossed the room in two strides and placed the food and plates on the center table. "Sidrie liked to boast about the AI, so I figured I'd put it to the test. I don't see the harm in it."

In truth, Frost didn't either. "I guess."

"I'll get us something to drink." Dante left again.

"I was not surprised to learn you were dreamers." Ryne hopped off the sofa and waddled over to the table on spindly legs. He took a slab of meat in his tiny hands. "The way you talked about your skills, some of the things you said… they were… different to anything I lived or read.

"I'd heard some of it before from people who claimed to be dreamers, but some of them were mere schemers. In the end, I followed my nose, because where there is smoke, there is likely to be a fire. And solutions to mysteries of which I do not tire." Ryne popped the meat into his mouth and chewed, bright eyes regarding Frost.

"Interesting." Frost took a step to the table, picked up a plate, and loaded it with meat and bread. "How'd you decide what to do." He bit off a piece of meat. It was cervin, basted in a sweet sauce. He nodded his approval.

Ryne shrugged. "I ignored the biggest urge driving me. The need to wait for you specifically. The thing in my head that said I must, that you were my boss, that I shouldn't even venture out into the fields to hunt if I was hungry. You see, it wasn't telling me about duty. There was no true reasoning other than you were my boss."

"What happened then?"

"Dante convinced me that leaving with him was best. Part of a test." Ryne filled a plate. He returned to his chair, put the plate up first, then climbed after it. "And the stories of this outside world intrigued me. Buildings made all of glass. Mechanical beasts that fly as fast as a simurgh. What do you call them? Airplanes? Mechanical mounts with wheels that are faster than any lupine, crevid, or kirin. Weapons not unlike your aether cannon."

"He told you all o' that?" Frost sopped up sauce with a bit of bread.

"Yes. But I would not want to live in your world, I don't think." Ryne bit off a piece of meat, chewed, and swallowed. "It seems boring. You have no aether. No magic. Life must be dull without magic. Why else would you come here?"

"Facts. But our world does have its moments."

"Facts?" Ryne repeated.

"Oh, sorry." Frost smiled. "Facts is like saying you're telling the truth."

"Oh, okay." Ryne shrugged. "Anyway, once I left with him, I suddenly felt freer than I ever did before. Mikander seemed bigger with so much more in store." Ryne grabbed a bun.

"Good for you." Frost smiled, curious to see where the change led. Sidrie's claim of a persistent world might even be better than she thought.

Dante returned with a pitcher of purple liquid and three ceramic cups. "Plum juice." He placed them on the table, then he eyed Frost. "What do you think of what he said?" His gaze shifted to Ryne and back.

Frost stroked his aether ring. "The fact he thought outside his programming is amazing. Gonna be something to see."

"Same thing I said." Dante took some food, poured a drink, handed it to Ryne, did the same for himself, then took a seat. "Now, let's hear how you plan to get Gilda back."

Frost got himself a drink and sat back. He took a sip, savoring the plum juice's sweet taste. "Can't have a plan until we find out exactly where she is. But it'll probably involve kicking ass."

"And taking names," Dante finished and held up his cup. "I'll drink to that."

"You plan to steal someone's name?" Ryne glanced from Frost to Dante, innocent green eyes searching their faces.

Frost chuckled. "No, it's just a saying. The literal meaning is we're gonna beat some people up and make a list of who's next to get whupped."

"But usually there's no actual list." Dante thumped the empty cup on the table. "Definitely lots of ass kicking, though."

"Yeah." Frost nodded. "But sometimes there's no actual fighting either. It can mean to just be awesome."

"Ah. Okay," Ryne said, obviously confused. He took a bite of his food.

Frost smiled. Watching Ryne, he tried to figure out where the little three-foot goblin was putting all that food. His Comm Orb dinged. He listened to the message. When it was over, he looked to the two men.

"That was Meritus. The relic hunter he was doing business with when Gilda was taken claims he knows where she is but won't say until he receives the goods Meritus promised in a deal."

"What kinda deal?" Dante asked.

"The hunter was to supply us with info on where we can farm the empowered spells needed for Benediction, the materials required in the schema, and the location of other epic weapons like it."

"Damn." Dante winced. "Does this hunter know about Benediction? That we have it?"

"Of course not. Meritus didn't give reasons. He only mentioned the things we were looking for."

"Good. What's his name, again?" Dante cracked his knuckles. "We should just go beat it out o' him."

"I agree with Dan." Ryne wiped his mouth with the back of his hand.

"Dan?" Frost snorted. "You're calling him Dan, and he's calling you Ryne?" He shook his head in disbelief. "Y'all have really come a long way."

"For the best." Ryne held up his cup to Dante.

"For the best." Smiling, Dante repeated the gesture.

"Y'all gonna make me throw up." Frost chuckled. "Anyway, his name is Nakada Masami. And Meritus already said beating it outta the guy isn't gonna work. Not only has he gone into hiding, but he's got contacts in the Coalition. We got enough trouble with them as is.

"And trying to retrace Gilda's steps from where they took her means exposing all of us. So, we're gonna help collect the things Nakada asked for."

"Sounds easy enough." Dante pushed up from his seat. "Let me get in a quick workout then get some sleep before we head out."

"I'll join you for an hour." Frost stood. "Then I need to practice some more with my drake and the whistle so I don't need a hitching rail."

"Me, three." Ryne leaped down from the sofa, exposing spindly legs once more.

"Hey, Dan." Frost glanced over to the gurash and jutted his chin toward Ryne. "What kinda friend are you, letting him skip leg days?" Frost and Dante burst into laughter.

Ryne looked from one to the other, waddling along, a frown creasing his features. "Leg days?"

"Never skip 'em," Frost quipped, wiping tears from his eyes. Laughing, he headed out to the barn.

CHAPTER 13

Even before the first pearl of dawn, Frost, Dante, and Ryne headed out. They flew northwest to meet Saba and Meritus at Ina, a mining town below the Jurojin Mountains at the border of Lothal and Khertahka. Upon arrival well after noon, Frost had an immediate sense of longing. If he flew directly north over the Jurojin, crossed No Man's Valley, and continued on for a few hundred miles, he would reach Niba, his old home.

The realization sparked memories of the fateful day Anefet died in the fire. A fire began by those who served the Black Hand. Frost ground his jaw, frustrated because he was not yet powerful enough to complete the **Vengeance for Anefet** quest.

When they landed, Frost gave RnB instructions by blowing the whistle once. The drake gurgled and took off. Ryne did the same for his drake, and Dante for his kirin. Meritus Killgain and Saba Nerubi arrived moments after the flyers departed.

"What up, people," Meritus greeted them cheerily.

Of average height, skin like burnished copper, Meritus was dressed in a plain tan shirt and pants that made his face even more forgettable. A mystic's scepter hung from a loop on his belt.

"Hey, y'all. Long time no see." Saba bent her forelegs a little, a centaur version of a curtsy.

She had shed her typical crupper, flanchard, and peytral for a simple dark-colored barding that fell around the chestnut equine portion of her body like a robe. She wore a shirt on her bronze-skinned human half. Her hair was no longer honey-colored or cropped short. It was the purest white and fell down to her shoulders. A golden longbow was slung over her back. Arrows jutted from a quiver like a pincushion.

"Hey, guys!" Dante clapped Meritus on the back. He winked at Saba.

Grinning, Frost approached his best friend. "What up, dawg."

"What it do, babyyy!" Meritus stepped forward, and they gave each other a dap, ending by touching their right hand over their hearts.

Grinning, they peered at each other and as one, they said, "Shaddup." They burst into laughter.

After Frost composed himself, he nodded to Saba. "Hi, Saba. Looking good."

"Thanks. You, too." Saba smiled shyly and nodded in his direction.

"Always the disrespect in all aspects for the Little People." Ryne harrumphed from below, voice a deep rumble.

"Oh, hi, Ryne!" Saba and Meritus looked down at the same instant and burst into laughter.

Ryne grumbled something unintelligible, before glancing at Saba, frowning. "I'm trying to guess why the dress."

Saba scowled. "It's not a dress."

"Fine, my equine. Why the whatever it is?" A mischievous smile spread across Ryne's face. "You would look better natural."

"As you would if you didn't look like Baby Hulk," Saba retorted.

Ryne's brows drew together in confusion. "Whatever this Hulk thing is still does not answer my question."

Saba sighed. "Centaurs aren't horses. The civilized among us have certain feelings about being naked."

"Naked?" Ryne grimaced. "Don't you always wear a coat?"

Saba groaned. "You win, Ryne. Youuu win." She blew out a breath, tail swishing in annoyance.

Ryne took a bow, black robes spreading about him. "Call me Undefeated."

"Knock it off, Ryne." Meritus wagged a finger at the goblin. "Before I send you on a new contract far away from here."

"Those days are no longer for meee. I'm freeee." The goblin did a little twirl.

"Wanna bet?" The threat in Meritus' voice was obvious.

Ryne stood there, arms crossed, expression serene. He stared at Meritus as if daring him to follow through. The moment stretched.

"What the hell's going on?" Grimacing, Meritus looked to Frost. "I tried but I couldn't assign him to a contract. What's up with that? And he isn't listed as one of mine. Even when I loaned him out, he'd still be there. Is he still under contract to you?"

Frost chuckled. "Nah, he isn't. I'll explain later. It's all good."

"If you say so." Meritus shook his head. "Let's get a move on. I got a caravan waiting. And Nakada Masami's man, Kensai, is in town, waiting for delivery."

"Did you get the dvergar?" Frost followed after his friend.

"Of course, dawg. I had planned to get them even before you asked, seeing as they're the best miners and prospectors in Mikander."

"Sweet." Frost nodded.

The group wove their way through a boisterous crowd of eradae, humans, and towering gurashi, most of them dressed in clothing soiled from sweat and labor, their fetor as loud as their voices. Many were hard-looking men, but there were women among them whose countenances matched or surpassed their male counterparts. Some led heavily laden unguls, whose faces had much in common with donkeys but for the three short tentacles that made up their noses and constantly waved to sample the air.

When the group reached a square rife with shops, stalls, and vendors, they stopped. All types of wares were too be had. Pickaxes. Shovels. Hammers. Chisels. Pans. Potions, vials, and extracts. Name it, and it was available to be bought. There were even explosives of some sort, but they could only be purchased by engineers.

Meritus gestured around them. "This is the best spot to grab health pots and quests. You can clear all of 'em where we're headed. Also, get a Bless or two if you got anything valuable in your inventories. A day doesn't go by without someone crying about some thieving cutthroat."

"Alright." Frost nodded, but his thoughts were on Gilda.

"Thieves." Dante scowled in disgust. "I wish one of 'em would try me." He made a chopping motion with his axe.

"It'd be better if they didn't, seeing as most of the cutthroats known for it are at least level twenty. And unless you're that level, you're as good as got, and there won't be much you can do about it." Meritus' gaze swept across them. "What level are y'all anyway? I'm fifteen and Saba's seventeen. I'm pushing for twenty to get into the Crypts."

"I don't get the obsession with the place, truth be told." Saba swished her tail. "The stories about some weird energy makes me want to stay far away. That's on top of the talk about void beasts and people infected by the Gray Death heading there. I even heard rumors of some draconids." She shuddered.

"Shiiiiitttt," Dante said. "That just sounds like crazy fun to me. Add in epic loot and I'm good to go. As for level, I'm the same as Saba. Be right back." He headed toward the closest NPC.

"Saba," Frost said, "I wonder about you sometimes, about why you're even playing."

She shrugged. "Same reason as most people. To escape. I love anything about the world that doesn't involve having to fight monsters. I fight because I need to, but exploring, crafting… those are my things, truth be told."

"I hear that." Frost nodded appreciatively.

Meritus motioned to Frost, but Ryne spoke first, smiling in Meritus' direction.

"I'm thirty-two, which makes me higher than you. Stronger too." The goblin flexed his disproportionate biceps.

Meritus gave the goblin a dubious look. "You realize you don't level, right."

"Is that so? That's not what I know."

Meritus rolled his eyes. "Look, you're just an NPC."

"I wouldn't say just anymore," Frost interjected, smiling at the exchange. "He's a little different now."

"I'm starting to get that vibe," Meritus admitted. "And I don't know if it's better or worse."

"I'd say better. I think he's still finding himself."

"Really?" Meritus glanced down at Ryne, brow arched. In turn, Ryne regarded his old boss with feigned innocence.

Frost nodded. "Yeah. I'll tell you about it when we're outta town. And as for my level, I'm the lowbie of the group, sitting at twelve."

"Dammmnnnn." Wincing, Meritus shook his head.

Frost shrugged. "What can I say? I missed an entire day at least. Plus some of y'all had another day or two head start before I began playing altogether."

"You got a point," Meritus conceded. "Which is why you need to get some quests from these vendors, my dude. You'll probably hit fifteen by the time we're done today. Saba and I'll wait here."

"Sounds like a plan." Frost gave his friend a dap and set off.

He weaved his way through the raucous crowds and bickering vendors to the Auction Market. Ina's AM assistant was a yurid with shimmering blue-green feathers, her eyes tilted up in contrast to her aquiline beak. She introduced herself as Danica.

He checked on Luminance. There was a bidding war, the highest current offer listed at seven thousand IDC. Smiling, Frost added Deadeye, starting bids at fifteen hundred with an outright price of seven thousand credits.

Next, he searched for the Strafe skill shard again, but the price was still six thousand LDC. He looked for the next cannoneer skill, available at level eighteen. Aether Barrage. It was priced at ten thousand of any credit. With a sigh, he disconnected from the Market and headed out to the vendors in the square.

By the time Frost returned to the group, he'd picked up several quests, a few of which had collection objectives for korbitanium or some other precious stones or metals. Others involved getting hides. He cringed at the idea of skinning but still bought a skinning knife for two hundred KDC.

One quest in particular had gotten his attention. Ten people reported their loved ones had died at the mines and blamed some monster named Krator the Klaw. They'd each asked Frost to bring back its head. The quest, **Avenge the Dead**, was worth five thousand exp and five hundred LDC from each person upon its completion. He itched to get to that one.

"Everyone good to go?" Meritus looked to each of them when they returned. They gave various affirmations. "Alright, I'll start the group." He paused. "Unless you wanna lead, Frost."

Frost waved him off. "Nah, dawg, I'm good with following along. Plus, you're the one who knows where we gotta go."

A moment later they were in a group. They made their way through the town and exited at the north end. Meritus took them to a caravan of four wagons pulled by crevids. Next to them were six unguls laden with supplies.

Armed guards on crevids or lupines rode alongside the wagons. Most of them were humans, but there were a couple gurashi and eradae. A shield and a fist emblazoned their cloaks.

"Call your mounts." Meritus put his whistle to his lips and blew.

The others followed suit, except for Saba, who preferred to ride in the lead wagon. Meritus' flyer arrived first, a majestic white zephyr with an owlish face and diaphanous wings. Ryne and Frost's drakes arrived next, followed moments later by Dante's kirin.

"Yo, your zephyr's beautiful, homie." Frost nodded his approval as he climbed atop RnB.

"Thanks, dawg. Cost me a bunch but was well worth it." Meritus peered at RnB. "You picked him up on Maelpith? I don't think I ever seen a drake that color."

"Yeah. People and other mounts been acting funny toward him, too." Frost shook his head glumly. "Like he got the plague or some shit. Hurts his feelings and pisses me off."

"F 'em." Meritus waved a hand. "People hate what they don't understand."

"Facts," Frost said.

"Captain Vallen." Meritus waved to a guard with a weather-beaten face. "We're good to go."

Vallen raised a hand. He gave an order. Beneath a boiling sun, they set off along a wide, crowded dirt road surrounded by fields and occasional trees. Ahead loomed the Jurojin Mountains' green mantles, rocky shoulders, and cloud-wreathed crowns.

"Already got the dvergar working on a mine I took off a prospector," Meritus shouted above the beat of crevid hooves and rumbling wagon wheels. "Had no choice but to buy the damned thing since the Sioziri clan owns the biggest operation here and pays good credits." He gestured to the crowds. "Most of these people work for them." He nodded to one of the guards. "I also had to hire the Charged Shields. A protection guild. Got a bunch of level twenty NPC guards from them."

Frost narrowed his eyes, concerned by the need for an escort. "Why?"

"The area we're heading into is an Open PVP zone. Been a lot of competition up in the Jurojin for korbitanium and gems. If you're not strong enough, you can have your mine taken. Also been a group of bandits going around robbing folks. And there's talk of missing miners."

"The Krator the Klaw quest?" Frost brought up the objective in IM. Beyond the requirement to kill it, there were no details as to what Krator might actually be.

Meritus nodded. "Yeah. And before you ask, I don't know what Krator is either. Or how strong it might be. Never seen it. Seen the remains of a few of its kills, though. It literally rips people apart. The few who survived an attack were delirious and just kept talking about a big claw."

"Sounds like crazy fun." Dante rode up beside them with Ryne on his other side. "An epic battle for the win."

Chuckling, Meritus shook his head. "I should've expected you'd want in on something like that."

Dante shrugged. "You know I'm all about the action, boss."

"So, we will be ass-kicking and name-taking?" Ryne looked hopeful.

The players burst into laughter. To which Ryne appeared utterly confused. Which brought another round of mirth.

After they calmed, Frost answered. "Yeah, we're gonna kick some ass and take some names."

"Awesome." The goblin beamed.

The day dragged on, the sun beating down to the point Frost wished he wasn't wearing the green brigandine and the gambeson. A shirt alone would have been just fine. He wiped his brow with the back of his hand. Studying the people around him, he took out his canteen and took a swig to quench his thirst and soothe his parched throat and dry lips.

The folk traveling toward the Jurojin almost encompassed the entire width of the road. Those returning were sparse and mainly kept to the edges. Many carried weapons or wore armor like those in his group. Others had the tools of the mining trade on their pack animals, drays, or wagons.

Frowning, he turned to the other group members. "Those crests some people wear on their right or left breast. Or on their cloaks. Is that like a faction they joined?"

"Guild emblems," Meritus answered.

"Ohhh, alright." Frost nodded. "Makes sense." In other games he'd played, there was typically a guild tabard. "Who's the guild with the shield, storm lance, greatsword, and the flame? Been a lot of 'em."

"WaR. Short for Wrath and Retribution. Current top PVP guild." Meritus waved to someone he knew. "Top guild, period. They nicknamed their emblem the Herald of WaR."

"Truth be told, most of them are a bunch of assholes." Saba was lying in the back of the wagon, peering out at them.

"Yeah, I agree with Saba, bro." Dante propped his crescent axe on his shoulder. "Avoid them like the plague."

Frost snatched a look at one or two of the WaR members to see if he spotted a familiar face. "I had a run in with one of them. Two, really."

"What?" Meritus snapped his head around to Frost.

The others were eyeing Frost too. All except Ryne, who appeared completely disinterested.

"One tried to gank me, so I smoked him." Frost shrugged. "The other was a woman with two Vindicators as escorts. Tried to buy RnB."

"RnB?" Meritus repeated.

"My drake."

"You named your drake after music?" Dante glanced Frost's way with an arched brow.

"No, fool. That's his colors. Red and black." Frost paused. "Although now that you mention it, I like the idea of it being after music. Yo, in fact, when we need a nickname for me, I'm Hip-hop."

Saba snorted. "That's wack."

"Facts," Dante chimed in with his falsetto.

"Shaddup," Frost said glumly.

"It's not that bad." Meritus shrugged but his sheepish expression belied his words.

"Fine." Frost blew out a breath. "When I need an alias, call me Lan."

"Dai Shan?" Meritus exclaimed with a terrible English accent. "That's a classic. Both the book and the TV series."

"One of my faves," Frost agreed.

"Mine too, dawg. Now, back to these WaR members. Where'd you come across the one who tried to PK you?"

"Not long after I got to the mainland. He had an Expedition Pass, so I'm pretty sure he followed me from Maelpith. I'm assuming he mighta been searching for me on the island, either found the cave, or caught a glimpse of me somehow, and tracked me from there. Although, it makes me wonder why he didn't try to PK me on the island if that was the case."

"And the woman?" Meritus was stroking his chin now.

"In Madurai."

"What did she look like?"

"Human. Really pretty." Frost pursed his lips as he recalled her. "Her clothes were expensive, but it was her eyes that caught me. They were the most beautiful shade of hazel. You think you know her? Wait, she gave me her name. Lemme check my Comm Orb."

Meritus lowered his voice. "She's Meileen Elune, co-leader of WaR, and wife to their leader, Kazuto, a badass dementer."

"I guess that explains why she was willing to pay fifty thousand credits for RnB," Frost said.

"Fifty thousand credits?" Dante whistled. "Damn, bro, your drake must be pretty rare." He eyed RnB.

"Seems so." Frost rubbed RnB's neck, thinking back to Madurai. The drake gurgled in contentment.

"Definitely got to look into that," Meritus said. "Our best bet would probably be the Aetherium whenever you manage to get off the Coalition's bounty list. If that fails then we can hit up the Halls of Illumination."

"I can't believe you guys," Saba said. "You're more concerned with the drake than with WaR and the bounty. You're acting as if we aren't heading into an Open PVP zone. To make it worse, you three haven't really changed much about your appearances." Her accusatory gaze shifted from Ryne to Dante before settling on Frost. "And you're probably on WaR's KOS list now."

"She got a point," Meritus agreed. "We have to assume they have pics of you. Maybe even shared on the guild's notice board."

"In my defense," Dante said, "my coloring is of noble descent, so I'm shown respect rather than suspicion."

Pondering the dilemma, Frost stroked his aether ring. If he was max level, he wouldn't have been concerned about being on any guild's Kill On Sight list. The Coalition bounty was another problem entirely.

He drew his hood up over his head. "Dante, you and I'll dye our hair like Saba. Ryne, you're gonna need to give up those robes you like so much. Switch to pants or something. And get hooded cloaks. Light ones, considering the heat."

"I got one." Dante retrieved a light brown cloak even as he spoke. He flung it over his back, tied it at his neck, and pulled up the hood. "You know we'll have to deal with this problem at some point, right. Can't hide forever."

"Cross that bridge when we get to it. Right now, we have a goal." Frost found himself thinking about Gilda again as they rode toward the Jurojin Mountains. He occupied his mind by explaining the change in Ryne's behavior to Saba and Meritus.

CHAPTER 14

Haladie in hand, Setnana stood over Gilda, the naked erada girl shackled to one of two stone slabs within a few feet of each other. Blood stained Gilda's slab. Trickled from it to drip on the dusty ground.

The dark beam of Life Link stretched from Setnana to Gilda to a dvergr miner lying unconscious on the other slab. Vindicator Dita continually healed the miner, who moaned from time to time.

Sweat trickled down Setnana's face. A pittance compared to that covering the girl. With a flick of the haladie, Setnana peeled off a strip of Gilda's skin along one leg. Gilda cried out. She writhed, but the shackles held her firmly in place.

Days had gone by since Setnana captured the girl and brought her to the keep. Days of torture. Days of the girl not relenting. Not surrendering her friends' whereabouts, the whereabouts of Benediction. Days of Gilda spitting defiance in Setnana's face.

It was so tempting to kill the girl. It would be easy. Less than easy. But every time Setnana had the thought, she reminded herself of Perihy.

As much as the memory of Perihy's transformation evoked pure odium, the desperate need to heal him tempered the hate. No matter how slim the chances of success were, she had to do everything in her power to try.

"Pardon me, my nomarch." The deep voice belonged to Ihuet.

"I said I was not to be disturbed."

131

"I know. And I would not have done so if it was not of the utmost importance."

"Speak." She removed another strip of skin from Gilda's leg. The girl shuddered.

"Two things. First, we found Perihy."

Setnana's breath caught in her throat. She had to fight to bring her emotions under control. "Where's my son?"

The sky-colored Blackguard leaned on his storm lance. "Our trackers picked up his trail from the mountains. He is still headed west. They believe he is going to the Forsaken Crypts like so many of the draconids and corrupted since this all began."

Setnana frowned. "Why there?"

"The trackers spoke to one who was in the early stages of infection, when the corrupted are still coherent. The corrupted claimed something draws them. Something only they can feel."

Setnana stared ahead, thoughts straying to Perihy and her fervent desire to heal him. "Tell the Sky Swords to head directly to Apur while the trackers follow Perihy. As soon as we have Benediction, that is where we will go. What was your other bit of news?"

"The very thing you just mentioned. A gurash relic hunter claims he can deliver Benediction, Drelan Frost, and the others."

Setnana froze. Her heart thumped. This was the reason she had appointed Ihuet. The man knew her so well. It took all of her willpower to remain calm.

Staring into Gilda's eyes, which shifted frantically, Setnana allowed herself the ghost of a smile. "I might not need you after all." She turned to Dita. "Let her suffer for a while." Without acknowledging Dita's response, Setnana gestured for Ihuet to lead the way, the thrill of anticipation running through her.

When she returned to Gilda's side, Setnana was full of hope. Vengeance was hers. And so much more.

She plucked a vial from a pouch on the belt that once belonged to the gargant alchemist, Esben. The blood in it was a deep purple threaded with black and silver, the latter shifting of its own volition. Smiling cruelly, she unstoppered the vial and emptied the contents into a gash on Gilda's stomach.

"Now, you will suffer as my son did." Setnana waited for the first screams, for the first gray splotches, the first signs of corruption.

CHAPTER 15

Connected to Keenan Costace's cam feed, Sidrie watched the end of the assault on the First Ward in Downtown Brooklyn. Random chatter from various sources piped in through the feed. There had been numerous fire fights.

Smoke billowed from a few structures. Old style weapons fire and the discharge of pulse weapons echoed sporadically. Soldiers in full tactical gear emblazoned with NAIL or SDF stalked down streets, pointing weapons this way and that. Human-like MX5 androids scouted buildings.

Watermarks from superstorm floods stained every structure. As did moss and algae. The marks reached up to the tenth floors, the divide where the First Ward ended and the Bottom Wards began.

She sighed, disappointed that her men had failed to find where her former employees were hiding. Or the bulk of the DeGens. She was even more upset at no sign of Dr. Hank Kim or his work.

The few DeGens they encountered had led NAIL, SDF, and her personal troops on a frustrating chase through the city's bowels, often popping up in the many crumbling buildings along the abandoned streets of Downtown Brooklyn and Manhattan. None of the buildings had revealed anything about their homes, much less their headquarters.

Until now.

Keenan's company had taken the rusted, derelict remains of the Barclays Center stadium and apartments. The fight here had been the most intense. They'd killed at least a score of DeGens and were now in the old subway system beneath the stadium.

The subway's roof was missing. The entire structure was hollowed out. As Keenan looked up, Sidrie saw the space led into the belly of the old stadium with its rings of rusted seats where mold and moss flourished like spongy green skin. Along one crumbling wall were the words Brooklyn Nets and the dark stains of watermarks.

The ceiling above the seats held her attention. Hanging from beams, an intricate network of wooden partitions, scaffolds, pulleys, and catwalks connected together to create structures with wooden floors hundreds of feet in the air. It was an engineering feat she'd not have thought capable by such uneducated beasts as the DeGens.

"You seeing this?" Keenan's baritone piped into the comms. "We might finally be on to something after all the decoys."

"I hope so." Sidrie inadvertently tilted her head as if she was standing beside Keenan. "Can you get up there?"

"One sec. This is Commander Costace. Send a dropship to my coordinates." Keenan paused. "Yes, the Barclays. I'll meet you outside on Atlantic Ave in front the old mall."

Keenan pulled out a round black device the size of a hockey puck. He pressed its center and flung it across the ground. It bounced several times before coming to a stop some hundred feet or more inside.

The commander turned to his fellow soldiers. "Haven't picked up anything on infrared, but if something moves up there that ain't us, kill it."

"Yes, sir," the men answered, voices muffled by their oxygen masks.

Keenan made his way through a series of halls, the walls of which were covered in mold. Water and sewage had settled in many places. Sidrie could only imagine the smell.

A rat the size of a dog bounded from a dark passageway. Sidrie jumped. Keenan did not react. The rat bared its teeth then fled. Keenan continued up and out of the remnants of the Atlantic Center Mall by way of broken staircases and the skeletons of escalators.

One of Equitane's EVTOL Personal Transports lowered to the ground, its engines humming. Two men stood at the wide, open side doors. Several more soldiers were seated inside the PT.

Head down, Keenan jogged to the PT and climbed aboard with the assistance of the waiting men. The vehicle lifted off.

Drones hovered above the oval building that was the Barclays, missiles like porcupine quills. Keenan turned his armored forearm to expose a rectangular display. He swiped over the screen.

"Activate scanner and track."

A holo flickered to life from the display, hovering above his forearm. It was a replica of the stadium's interior. A red dot blinked in the area of the subway tunnel.

"Transfer to ship's logistics." He paused, attention still on the holo. "G Thirty-two Hundred," he yelled over the whine of the PT's engine. "I sent the info from the tracker to you. Go to that spot."

"Got it." The pilot gave a thumbs up.

The PT drifted slowly toward the stadium's east end. The holo showed the PT in green, gaining on the red dot. The two merged.

"In position," G Thirty-two Hundred called out.

Keenan signaled to the four waiting soldiers. Like him, their gear had SDF on the chest and back in white letters, although they belonged to Equitane. "Place some shape charges, then come on back."

The four soldiers moved to the doors, threw out ropes, and rappelled down. In a few minutes, they'd done as Keenan ordered. When they returned, Keenan nodded.

Explosions rumbled from below. The crash of glass and debris followed. When Keenan looked down, there was a gaping hole on one side of the roof. Smoke drifted into the air.

He gestured to the men and pointed down. "Shouldn't be any contact, but keep your eyes peeled." He took his pulse rifle from his back, inspected the weapon, replaced it, then took two steps to the door.

The four men joined him, two on the PT's opposite side. They rappelled down to the roof. A strong wind buffeted the men, howling in Sidrie's ears.

Watching this type of work sent a thrill through her. One of excitement and fear. The soldiers lowered themselves into the building's guts.

Keenan touched down on one of the catwalks, surrounded by dappled sunlight and shadows. He held onto the rope. The dark interior made Sidrie marvel at Keenan's ability to identify things around him and wonder how it was he made out anything. Until she reminded herself that what she saw with normal vision through the cam, Keenan was seeing with infrared and motion detectors.

Keenan adjusted his rope then jumped up and down on the four-foot wide walkway. It hardly budged. He gave the men a thumbs up, disconnected his rope, and then swung his pulse rifle from his back, brought it up shoulder high, aiming as he panned it from left to right.

One soldier brought up his rear. The other three were on catwalks to his left and right. They crept toward a doorway in one of the many partitions, Keenan's breathing loud to Sidrie's ears.

Keenan moved like a snake through the open door, pulse weapon quickly swinging one way and then the other before again pointing directly ahead. "Clear in here. Looks like some kinda living quarters." His head shifted and Sidrie caught a glimpse of cots.

"I always wondered how the DeGens who failed to report to the Bottom Wards survived the storms," Sidrie mused. "Now, I know."

"Clear. Clear. Clear." Each call was from a different soldier. They all reported living quarters.

"Move in, nice and slow. How's it looking from down there, G Forty Thirty?" Keenan slunk forward.

"Still nothing on infrared. And only you guys on motion detectors."

They continued along the catwalks, traveling a quarter of the way across the stadium. They encountered more living spaces and a couple of dining areas. In the next space was some sort of gym with makeshift weights, ropes, and calisthenic bars.

"Hey, commander," a man's voice chirped. "I found what looks like a main breaker box. Orders?"

"If everything looks good then flip those switches, G Forty-two Fifty. Infrared off, folks."

"Yes, sir."

Minutes passed. Then several soft lights flickered on. The bulbs hung from wires that stretched up into the rafters.

"Hmmm," Keenan said. "G Thirty-two Hundred, do you see lights in the stadium from up there?"

There was a pause before G Thirty-two Hundred replied, "Only where y'all breached. The rest is dark."

"Thanks." Keenan aimed his pulse gun up into the rafters. A flick of his thumb turned on a light along the barrel. The beam illuminated a thick black material like a sheet. "Gotta give it to these DeGens. They're smart. They covered the interior of the roof so the light wouldn't show."

Sidrie scowled at the admiration in Keenan's voice.

After he turned off the beam, Keenan continued ahead. The next room contained several tables and wooden lockers. A few empty magazines were on a table. The same in the lockers. There were also spare parts for weapons. Barrels. Carry handles. Stocks.

Keenan inspected the equipment. "On your toes, boys. Found some HK Four Thirty-three parts."

"The news is worse over here on the left flank, sir."

"What'd you find, Jer?"

"Parts for a Ma Deuce."

"You sure?" Keenan sounded both shocked and concerned. "A Browning fifty cal? An M2?"

"Yep."

Keenan whistled. "Shit. Kinda lucky we didn't run into one o' them fuckers."

"Agreed," Jer said.

"Alright, fellas, you heard what Jer found. Forward. Head on a swivel. Forty Thirty, how we looking?"

"So far so good."

The five of them continued on, discovering various aspects of life for the renegade DeGens who called themselves the Gridrunners. And then they all entered a large room located above the stadium's center. There were a dozen chairs at tables upon which sat old style LCD monitors. Keyboards with built-in mouse pads sat in front of the displays. Lines of wires ran to banks of hardware. Neither the hardware nor the screens were powered on.

Keenan stopped. "Are those computers?"

"Looks like one of those old data centers," Jer said. He and the other three men had entered doors to Keenan's left or right.

"Send in a tech. We'll make sure everything is secure. Forty-two Fifty, head back to pick him up." Keenan moved in toward the racks of computer hardware, gun aimed. He checked the spaces around and between, stopping at wires and devices. "No sign of booby traps."

"All good on this side, also," Jer said.

When Keenan returned to the front, the other three men were there also. Twenty minutes passed before Forty-two Fifty returned, leading another man in full tactical gear from head to toe. The tech introduced himself as G7000.

"Alright, Seven Thousand." Keenan strode in front of the hardware. "What do you think? Is there a way to fire this stuff up?"

"Gimme a sec." G7000 strode up to the racks. He peered around and then headed between them. He could be heard rummaging.

The screens and hardware flickered to life. Fans whirred. Power sources hummed.

"Fuck, yeah," Keenan said.

G7000 returned. He took a bow.

"Good job." Keenan nodded in the tech's direction. "Now, let's see if you can crack into this system and see what they've been up to."

G7000 headed over to the closest display and keyboard, removed his gloves, and took a seat. Keenan followed him. A boot sequence was still in effect. Seconds later, a penguin in a seated position popped on the screen. The display went dark, but there were a few lines and a blinking cursor.

"They're running Linux." G7000's fingers flickered across the keyboard. "A very old version, but luckily all our techs are trained in it. It's what was used to build the Grid after the war."

G7000 continued to type. The screen changed to lines of code or commands on the left. On the right was what appeared to be folders, drives, and the like.

Sidrie muted Keenan's part of the feed. "Estela, record everything and analyze. Tell G7000 to plug in to that system so you can scan it. Look for anything on Dr. Kim."

"Yes, Miss Malikah."

As was the norm, Sidrie kept her hopes in check. A part of her knew it was only a matter of time before she gained the information she required on Whole Brain Emulation as well as the remainder of Alphonso's protocols. But time was the one thing she did not fully control, the one thing she did not possess in abundance.

Minutes passed with G7000 typing away. Folders opened and closed.

G7000 stopped. "Holy shit." He leaned forward.

"What?" Keenan bent over him and peered at the screen.

G7000 pointed. "This here is a list of comms between the SAC and whomever ran this place. The latest is from six months ago." He clicked on one.

A video played. A Hispanic man in a dark suit with his hands behind his back was staring at the screen. He was clean-shaven with hard eyes.

"Commander Carlson, be patient." The man had a thick South American accent. "My people have assured me the supply shipment will reach you by the end of September. It takes time to avoid the drones and cameras along the border wall. And going under or over the sea walls is near impossible."

"We're trying our best, President Esteban." Carlson's voice was deep. Cultured. "But we're dying here. We need help. The sooner we can hit at least one silo, the better the chance we have of survival."

"I understand, Commander." Esteban raised one hand, palm up, and dipped his head in recognition. "And believe me when I say you have my sympathy. No one should have to endure such suffering. I wish we could speed up the process. But your leaders are stubborn. More so now than ever. Until we can get them to listen to reason, this is how it must be. Some wars must be fought from the inside first. This is one such."

Through her optics, Sidrie selected her connection to Governor Morrison. He and his entire cabinet would be watching. She'd made certain to provide the governor with access to these feeds.

"Well, Richard, here is your proof," Sidrie declared. "It's past time we treat this as what it is. War. Unless you people want the country to revert to what it once was, overrun by drugs and crime. I much rather preserve the utopia we have built."

CHAPTER 16

Early afternoon saw the fields around Frost become expanses of rock and shale, only the hardiest vegetation able to take root. The crowd split into groups, heading toward their respective mines or prospecting areas, the largest contingent continuing straight ahead to the Sioziri operation.

Meritus veered off to the right. They rode for perhaps half a mile, up through a pass, then into a small valley. They rounded several rocky outcrops and hills before they reached Meritus' mine.

The mystic drew his zephyr to a halt on the trail and pointed down a slope at an area with sparse grass patches and dirt like rust. "Dante and Frost, if you got the quest for basilisk hides, then those are yours."

The lumbering basilisks looked like massive green-gray lizards with rows of armored ridges running down their backs. Horns jutted from the sides of their heads, below their eyes but back toward their necks. Each had a long tail with a wedge-shaped slab at the end.

"Don't worry about the korbitanium and the gems," Meritus said. "The dvergar will get those for us. I'll send one of 'em over to help skin the basilisks too."

"Thanks, homie, because I doubt I woulda been able to do any skinning. That shit's nasty." Frost dismounted and blew his whistle, sending RnB away.

"I figured." Meritus chuckled. "I don't blame you either. Skinning's one of those things that's too close to reality to be enjoyable."

"Ha! Speak for yourself, wussy city boys." Dante pointed at them with his axe while his kirin flew off.

Ryne was smirking in their direction. He shook his head slowly, clearly disappointed.

"You two can shaddup," Meritus shot back. "And Ryne, I'll be dropping you from group so your level don't stunt their exp."

"Fine by me." Ryne gave a sullen kick of his legs and directed his drake toward a lone tree.

Meritus turned to Frost. "Saba and I'll take the caravan to the mine so the helpers can start packing the ore. Then we'll give you guys a hand." He urged his zephyr into motion, ambling down the path to a clearing where the mine's dark mouth cut into a cliff above which rose the Jurojin's wind-and-rain-scarred body.

Leaning his black-bladed crescent axe on one shoulder, Dante massaged his butt while striding over to stand beside Frost, facing the basilisks. "Finally, some action after all that riding."

"Yeah. I was getting kinda bored." Frost studied the basilisks. He frowned. "Is it me or do these look... less defined." He shook his head. "Like less muscular, less detailed than the mobs on Maelpith?"

"They're not elite."

"Ahhhh," Frost said with a nod.

"Tell me something," Dante said, staring off at the basilisks. "You and Meritus with this shaddup business... What's that about?"

Frost smiled. "An inside joke from IRL. We were in a store one day, and this big muscle-bound dude was trying to get the attention of the scrawny worker, an Arab guy, who was helping another customer. I guess he thought his size and money meant he would get served right away.

"The worker is steady ignoring dude. Finally, muscleman steps to him with his voice raised, demanding service. The scrawny guy glances at him with this expressionless look, and in the thickest accent you ever heard, he calmly says, 'Shaddup.'

"Muscleman turned red. He looked like he would choke. Now, he's all up in the little guy's space, towering over him, pointing and yelling, cussing him out.

"And little man just repeats it, 'Shaddup. Shaddup.' The big guy is beyond pissed now. And he decides he had enough. He swings. Little guy sidesteps, sticks his foot out, and just uses the big man's momentum to push him on by.

"The big guy slaps his head into the wall. Bam. Out cold. Slides down like a sack o' shit.

"Little dude peers at him. 'Now you shaddup.' Everyone in the store bust out laughing. Ever since then, we used the word."

Dante chuckled. "Now, I get it. I wish I was there to see that." He shook his head.

"Yeah, man, still one of the funniest things ever at the time."

"You ready to get these basilisks?" Dante limbered his arms and legs.

Frost aimed The Stunner and nodded. "Let's do this."

Dante's color oozed from crimson to bright scarlet with his activation of Frenzy, tripling his power and speed. He bounded forward, becoming a red blur by way of Raging Rush, covering the distance between him and the nearest basilisk some fifty feet away in a blink. He slammed into the beast, striking its head with his axe, and turning it to expose its flank.

Frost had begun charging Homer the moment Dante engaged Frenzy. A cyan glow swelled at the cannon's muzzle. He counted seconds in his head as the aether brightened. At four, when Dante was chopping at the basilisk, Frost released the trigger. Beams of aether in the shape of missiles shot out in eight directions. As they sped across the distance, Frost fired off an Aether Shot followed by a Korbitanium Projectile burst.

The missiles converged and exploded into the basilisk's head and flank with repeated booms almost too close to separate. The Aether Shot and the Projectiles struck moments later. With a plaintive mewl, the basilisk dropped onto its belly.

"Piece o' cake." Dante's high-pitched voice piped through group chat. "DPS for the win."

Mountain Basilisk killed.

Gained 600 experience points.

Group bonus 450 experience points.

Frost whistled. "That's some sweet exp. That's like what… a seventy-five percent bonus for being in a group?"

"Yeah," Dante said. "Because we're within five levels of each other.

Would be double exp in a full five-man set up the same way."

"Ninety-six more kills 'til I level." Frost looked forward to that moment. And the next. He wanted to consume himself with it all so he wouldn't think about Gilda.

"Let's get going, then." Dante was already heading for the closest basilisk. "Pew, pew." He Frenzied and Raging Rushed.

Over the next few kills, Frost got to experience The Stunner's special. On occasion, any ability could incapacitate a mob. The effect was all chance.

Frost and Dante had killed ten basilisks by the time Meritus and Saba returned with two dvergar. The little rockform men started skinning the carcasses.

"How's it going up there?" Frost asked Meritus.

"Pretty good." Meritus jutted his chin toward Dante, who was on his way to them. "How about here?"

"Not bad. I got an idea on how to level much faster. Would take you, Saba, and your Servitors if you already have the skills."

"If?" Meritus gave him a sidelong glance. "You should know better than to sleep on me, dawg. You know how I roll. I got every single skill for my level and some for a few levels ahead too."

"Let me guess." Saba smirked at Frost, one hoof pawing the ground as Dante joined them. "This idea will be something reckless."

Frost snorted. "Nothing reckless about it. Not with Dante and the Servitors tanking, Meritus healing, and the two of us using skills that also CC. Just gonna be a whole lotta fun."

"I'm always wary of your idea of fun." Saba sighed.

"Don't worry, little lady." Dante puffed out his chest. "I got Maim and Gravity Crush, now, which means I'll be able to slow a bunch of 'em, and they won't be able to move me."

"Fine." Saba huffed. "What's the plan?"

Frost called Ryne over. He explained his idea. The big gurash grinned madly as he listened. Saba swished her tail. Meritus just nodded.

Ryne muttered something unintelligible under his breath before he spoke aloud. "Although I'm worth two men, I get to be backup again?"

"Exp." Frost shrugged and continued with the details. When he was done talking, he led them down into the center of the basilisk grazing area.

He scanned the mobs surrounding them. "This is a good spot."

Meritus summoned his Servitors. The Bulwark was a hulking black-furred gargant some twelve feet tall. The Duelist and Shaman were both female yurids a little taller than Meritus, one with leathery wings and the other with blue plumage. A moment later, Meritus cast Aura of the Nomarch, a group buff which lasted an hour and increased the groups' defense and vitalization gained from heals.

"Set up about a hundred feet to our right." Frost pointed out the spot. "Saba and I'll pull a bunch from that side first."

"Got it." Dante strode away, the Bulwark following him.

"Saba, place the traps between him and us."

Saba trotted out into the space, perhaps some fifty feet. She bent in one spot. The crackling glow of a Lightning Trap materialized. She took a few steps to her right and placed another trap. Chains appeared, the metal glinting in the sunlight. With the Crowd Control skills in place, Saba made her way back to the group.

Frost hefted The Stunner and took aim at the basilisk beyond Dante. "I say we lure about ten and see how it works out. Ready?"

"Always." Meritus stood with his Duelist and Shaman beside him.

"I'm ready, but let me say again that this is a bad idea." Saba's tail swished harder than before.

"I hear you." Frost smiled. "That's why we got Ryne."

Ryne shook his head and let out an annoyed breath. Grumbling to himself, he got his haladie and began cleaning his nails with one end of the double-bladed dagger.

"Pulling in three... two..." Frost aimed at a group of three basilisks. "One. Pull." He fired a Concussion Blast. The white beam was still streaking through the air when he loosed an Aether Shot.

Saba's bowstring strummed. In rapid succession, volleys of wooden, ice, and fire arrows flew across the distance to different targets. The volume, range, and speed of the attacks were advantages of the marksman to make up for their lack in power and AOE ability. It was due to a plethora of instacast skills with little to no recharge time.

Frost fired off a Korbitanium Projectile burst at one more target. Saba had pulled six on her own.

Frost held up a fist. "Stop firing and wait."

The basilisks charged toward him and Saba, those recovering from the Concussion Blast bringing up the rear. They were a lumbering gray-green wave of armor and thrashing tails, mewling as they came, the thunder of their feet quaking the ground.

Dante was a lone figure between the charging monsters and the rest of the group. He Sentinel Shouted, fortifying his health and defense. The space between him and the basilisks closed. His skin flared to bright scarlet.

The moment the first basilisks reached Dante, he spun, his crescent axe held out before him. Aether spilled from the blade's edge. Dante spun in three revolutions, cutting into the basilisks. Not only did Dante slow the basilisks by way of Maim, but the attack also caused them to change aggro, dropping Frost and Saba as their targets, and choosing Dante instead. The last of the basilisks waddled among the others.

Dante Soul Screamed, the sound echoing. Meritus' Bulwark repeated the ability. Frost and Saba forgotten, the ten basilisks attacked the two tanks in earnest. A deeper yell was Dante unleashing Enfeebling Bellow, weakening the basilisks.

"Now." Frost squeezed his trigger, letting off another Concussion Blast. He followed with Aether Bomb and the five Aether Shot spread of Divergence.

Saba unleashed a Quadruple Barrage, four arrows streaking to different targets. Then she settled into a rhythm with single and double shots, her bowstring thrumming faster than before. The Duelist Servitor was firing single target fire globes one after the other. Blue motes of Mikander's Tears flew from both the Shaman and Meritus.

All around Dante, the basilisks died. Swirls and motes of aether shot off in multiple directions before flying into Frost and friends.

"That was epic!" Dante pumped his fist. "Let's do it again!"

"Guess it wasn't that reckless after all, huh, Saba?" Frost smiled in her direction.

She rolled her eyes. "We're just lucky this game doesn't have friendly fire."

Frost chuckled. One day he was going to get Saba to give him some credit.

"I think Dan could handle five or ten more," Ryne said.

Meritus' head snapped around. "Dan?"

Saba stared at the goblin also, looking as shocked as Meritus.

Frost laughed. "Yeah… Dan. That's a story those two gotta tell. They're buddies now."

"I can't wait to hear it." Meritus shook his head, mirth in his voice.

"That pull was worth ten thousand five hundred exp for me." Frost broke into a wide grin. "Beautiful. How much did y'all gain?"

"Eleven five." Meritus nodded in approval.

"Twelve five." Saba pranced. "Would be better for those of us who're higher level if the mobs were higher also, but I can't complain too much."

"Hey, Dan," Frost yelled, smiling at his use of the nickname. "Ryne says you can handle five or ten more mobs."

"Piece o' cake!" Dante shouted. "More action, boss! More DPS. Moooaaarrrr!"

Frost chuckled. "No prob. We're gonna do a few more pulls, then give the dvergar a chance to skin."

"Bring it on." Dante swung his axe in a chopping motion.

Contemplating the possible needs for a larger pull, Frost eyed Meritus. "Aether Absorption after the kills won't be enough, so hit us with Aether Infusion on the next two pulls. That should see us through."

Meritus nodded. "I got you."

"If you manage this, I'll go take a nap," Ryne grumbled.

"Find you a good spot," Frost chided, "and watch us work."

"And you call me cocky, Meritus." Ryne shook his head.

A ghost of a smile curved Frost's lips. "Alright, Saba, we're gonna keep pulling until we have fifteen. Meritus, hold off on the Bulwark's Soul Scream to get any stragglers."

Frost counted down again. They started the pull the same way as the first time. Frost added extra Korbitanium Projectiles to snag a few more basilisks. As he fired, he reveled in the feel of the aether cannon, the ease with which he could wield it. It was as if the weapon were an extension of his body.

They waited a bit for Dante and the Bulwark to gather all the mobs together. In that time, Meritus cast Aether Infusion, which pulled from his

147

aether pool and the air itself to add to Frost and Gilda's aether. The two DPS unleashed their skills. A minute later, the fifteen had died, Aether Absorption delivering much needed aether into the players. They repeated the process several times.

Soon enough, their regular aether pool was almost empty. But Frost had an idea. Aether Overload was still full. "One more pull." Frost raised his voice. "Dante, this time we're gonna pull twenty."

The red-skinned gurash pumped his fist. "Awesome, bro. This'll be crazy fun."

Frost nodded to Saba. "Use your Overload skill on this one."

The centaur's eyes lit up. "Sure thing."

They pulled the basilisks. When Dante and the Bulwark had the twenty beasts in place, Frost activated Stand and Deliver. He glowed blue. The Stunner let out a hammer drill and buzzsaw whine. Aether Shots and Korbitanium Projectiles spat out. Alternating. Slow at first. Whine. Whomp. Whine. Whomp. Frost's arms jerked with the recoils.

The cyclic rate picked up. Built. It became a rhythm, faster and faster until it was a solid whine. The rate eliminated the recharge on Aether Bomb and Divergence.

The air lit up as Frost unleashed hell. Beside him, Saba was a blur, her Arrow Battery firing at an uncanny rate.

Smoke and explosions hid Dante and the Bulwark. Frost and Gilda stopped firing. When the air cleared, basilisk corpses littered the ground.

"Damn, my dude," Meritus whispered in awe. "I just did like twenty percent of a level since we started. That level fifteen prediction I gave you might be too low."

"Epic players do epic things." Frost shrugged. Checking his exp, he noted he was two-thirds of the way to level thirteen. He raised his voice. "Dante, take a break and let the dvergar work."

"I think we need more dvergar." Meritus' gaze tracked the two diminutive rockform beings who ambled out to the carcasses.

"Facts." Frost nodded.

"Be right back." Meritus dismissed his Servitors. They slowly melted from the air. The mystic jogged off toward his zephyr.

"That was wicked," Dante exclaimed when he reached Frost and Saba.

Frowning, he glanced around. "Where's my lil bro?"

With a shake of his head at Dante's reference to Ryne, Frost pointed toward the goblin who was in a fetal position, hidden by the long grass beneath a nearby tree. "Over there sleeping. Said to wake him if we need him."

Dante chuckled. "Typical. He needs his beauty sleep."

"With his face, he could use tons of it," Saba said.

"I heard that." Ryne held up his middle finger.

Frost's brows shot up, and he snapped his gaze around to Dante. "Did you teach him that?"

The red-skinned, lion-faced gurash put on a sheepish look. "Guess I'm rubbing off on him."

Meritus returned moments later with six dvergar. They joined the other two, skinning carcasses, and piling the remains to one side. The smell of blood and offal filled the air.

"That's some nasty shit." Frost grimaced.

"I couldn't agree with you more." Saba looked as if she would be sick.

"Wussies." Dante waved them off. "Guess none of you ever went hunting."

"Whatever, homie." Frost gestured to the rolling green and tan plains leading to a tree line at the feet of the Jurojin Mountains. It was rife with basilisks. "That looks like the perfect spot over there. Lots of mobs to grind."

They left the rust-colored dirt and hardy vegetation behind and proceeded to the plains. Frost's legs swished through grass dancing to the cool wind's sigh. He picked out a spot from which they could readily pull the basilisks.

Once the group had set up, Dante got into position. Meritus summoned his Servitors, sending the Bulwark out to stand with Dante. The Duelist and Shaman remained. As before, Frost and Saba started the attacks.

Midway through the third group of fifteen, Meritus cast a new spell onto Dante. Korbash's Retribution. A ring tinged with gold and blue emanated from the ground around the gurash, stretching out dozens of feet in every direction. The ability drained health from the mobs, converting the health into aether, which shot off into the air much like Aether Absorption, before settling around the players in an aura.

"Level thirteen," Frost declared when the last basilisk died. He took note of his new stats, pleased with the extra two points in aether from his skill use.

Strength: 30
Agility: 36
Vitality: 42
Aether: 43

"Another two pulls for me to level," Meritus said.

"Same here." Saba stuck several arrows into the soft ground.

"What are y'all waiting for?" Dante shouted. "Let's kill shit."

Frost chuckled. "You heard the man."

They did another two pulls before they were completely drained of aether and needed to rest and replenish. Despite the three-minute recharge on their Overload skills, they'd been unable to use them due to the time needed to build Overload itself.

Meditating for Replenishment, Frost found his mind straying to Gilda. He banished the thoughts before they festered.

They returned to leveling and collecting hides minutes later. Whenever they could, they took advantage of their Overload skills, pulling an extra five to ten basilisks. The one disappointment about the grind was the lack of drops.

On several occasions they had to wait for respawns. And though the basilisks had adapted, sometimes attempting to flee, their need to defend themselves when attacked won out more often than not. The group continued to grind for several hours more.

Frost reached level fourteen and fifteen way faster than he expected. However, the fact he still had forty-five levels to go before max diminished his sense of accomplishment and leveling speed. In all fairness, he was still a noob. His level fifteen stats did bring on a smile.

Strength: 36
Agility: 42
Vitality: 50
Aether: 53

The agility brought his stagger resist to four percent, which was still paltry. He looked forward to the day when it would be extremely hard to stagger or stun him.

His friends also chatted about their levels. While Meritus had almost reached eighteen, both Dante and Saba had gotten to nineteen.

In anticipation of leveling, Dante and Saba had brought new skills with them. Saba's was Aura of the Pack, a buff that increased the group's movement speed by twenty-five percent. Dante had acquired Scythe, a one-hundred-and-eighty-degree attack that also added a bleed effect, draining the target's HP over time.

"You got Strafe, right?" Meritus regarded Frost with an arched brow.

Frost shook his head. "Nah. Couldn't afford it after I got the map, warehouse, and new cannon. Wish I knew where to farm for it."

"No biggie." Meritus shrugged. "You'll make enough off the quest rewards back in town. Buy it off the Market, then."

"Alright." Frost took a stock of all the hides and dead basilisks. The dvergar had brought over a wagon and were loading up the hides. Frost screwed up his face at the fetid stench of blood permeating the air. "We got enough hides for sure, but what're we gonna do with all this meat? Seems a waste."

"Could call in our mounts to feed them," Meritus suggested. "Or cook some and save it. But cooked food like meat spoils after two days in your inventory."

"Oh, shit." Frost checked his inventory and saw the old cervin meat was going bad. Nose wrinkled, he pulled it out, and tossed it. "Disgusting. Thanks, homie. I hadn't even looked into the inventory stuff or much of any tutorials I saw in IM. Even skipped the one for the Market."

Meritus' gave Frost a shocked stare. "You skipped the Auction Market tutorial? Bruh, come onnn, there's some good tips in there."

Frost chuckled. "Why do it when I can come to a pro like you with questions?"

"Facts." Meritus nodded slightly and stroked his chin, clearly pleased.

The drum of onrushing hooves drew Frost's attention. Frowning, he turned to the sound. A human on a lupine was galloping toward them from the direction of the mines. Frost brought The Stunner up.

Meritus placed a hand on Frost's arm. "That's Vallen."

Chest heaving, Vallen pulled up in front of them. A ragged tear ran down his gambeson, all the way through to his flesh beneath, exposing a bloody wound.

Wincing, he drew in great gulps of air. "Sir! It's Krator the Klaw. He's at the mine and has some men with him. They're killing the dvergar. The men are fighting them off around the caravan, but I don't know how long they can hold. No one's been a match for Krator."

Now the man had mentioned it, Frost heard the screams. The distinctive ring of steel on steel.

CHAPTER 17

"Saba, wake Ryne up. Add him to the group, Meritus." Frost blew his whistle, and RnB screeched in response, appearing above a nearby hill.

The centaur dashed toward the tree Ryne had chosen for his bed. She was a blur, a sure sign that she'd engaged Streak. A moment later, a notification said Ryne was now a part of their group.

In minutes, Frost was atop RnB and had taken to the skies. Meritus' white zephyr and Ryne's drake rose to meet him. Dante joined them moments later on his yellow-maned kirin. Saba galloped below them, hooves kicking up dust. They pushed hard for the Jurojin, goaded by the cacophony of the nearby battle.

With the dying sun at their backs, long shadows falling across the ground, they arrived at the mine. A path led down into a clearing and the tunnel cut into the cliff face. There, a battle played out.

Gurashi, humans, and eradae fought each other, either in front of the mine itself or not far from the caravan of wagons. Spells and cannon fire echoed. Steel clashed. Combatants cried out or bellowed, voices carrying on the wind.

A roar cut through the tumult. Frost's head snapped toward the sound. The battle paused, the combatants' attention riveted on the mine. Something massive dashed from the mine's dark mouth and into a sliver of sunlight.

Krator the Klaw was fourteen feet of humanoid sinew and muscle, wide as a shed, with a face like a lizard. If Ryne stood before Krator, the goblin

153

might reach its knee. A bushy mane ran from the crown of Krator's head down its back. Its skin was a dull gray. Vibrant red and blue lines criss-crossed the GUM's chest and upper body like a nebulous road map. Its pants were nothing more than torn leather. Silver greaves enclosed Krator's shins. Covering one hand was a silver dementer's hierka. A fist. The other arm was a massive crab's claw.

Frost directed RnB down to the wagons. The other group members joined him.

"I expected a GUM. But for it to also be a draconid overseer." Frost shook his head, trying to wrap his head around Krator's appearance.

Krator picked up a dvergr woman and tossed her at one of the human guards. That broke the trance. The fighting resumed.

Three guards charged the Klaw. The GUM slammed his fist into the ground, sending out a rolling semi-circular wave of earth and stone. The guards dashed away.

Saba pointed. "Those so-called bandits aren't exactly normal either."

The men and women fighting Meritus' guards were eradae, human, and gurashi. That much could be seen from their general appearances. But none of them had normal skin. The exposed portions of their bodies were rife with gray blotches and sores.

"They're infected with the Gray Death," Meritus said softly.

"We call them the corrupted," Ryne added. "They have been appearing since the last voidstorm. It's a surprise to find so many of them here with no warning from the Coalition."

"We can figure out the reason later," Frost said. "Right now, we gotta save the caravan. Dante, Meritus, and Saba, y'all take the Klaw while Ryne and I pick off the adds."

"Adds?" Ryne screwed up his face in Frost's direction.

"Additional monsters or minions of a boss." Frost nodded to the bandits.

"Oh." Ryne whipped out his haladie. "But no. Krator is mine. Just give me Meritus and his Servitors. The rest of you can deal with the... adds... and save the caravan."

Frost opened his mouth to argue the point but changed his mind, recalling Vallen's words. "You heard the man. Let's go."

Even as Frost kicked the bolsters to send RnB forward, two Summoned Defilers materialized beside Ryne, towering over the goblin. The wraith-like creatures wore hooded black robes. Clawed hands jutted from the sleeves.

Leaving Ryne to his task, Frost took aim at the nearest corrupted, a staff-wielding human woman, pus oozing from the blotches on her face. He fired an Aether Shot, a Korbitanium Projectile burst, and a single Homer in quick succession. He followed those a second later with Piercer. The first three attacks exploded into the corrupted's torso, knocking her back. Frost allowed himself a triumphant smile.

The corrupted cried out in pain. Pain that lasted but a moment. Body smoking and blackened from Frost's abilities, she snarled in his direction and brought the staff up. The staff head glowed white. She stretched out one hand toward Frost, fingers forming a claw.

Threads of arcing energy leaped from her hand like lightning cast sideways. It crackled toward Frost, illuminating the air. She slammed her staff into the ground.

Frost felt more than he saw the lightning strike descending. He yanked RnB's reins.

Arc Lightning and the Thunderbolt struck a split-second apart. The detonation knocked Frost from RnB's back. He slammed into the ground, ears ringing.

Wincing, Frost clambered to his feet, shaking his head to clear the noise. The corrupted was mid-cast, her staff head glowing, an electrical globe forming in the palm of her hand.

Frost took quick aim and snapped off a Staggering Shot. The ability struck and stunned her. He charged Homer for four seconds, two short of the stun duration, and released the trigger.

The moment the eight missiles flew into the air, Frost squeezed the trigger again. A second was all it took to charge the five-shot spread of Divergence and loose its cyan beams after the missiles. He finished with an Aether Shot, Korbitanium Projectile combo.

The corrupted woman died in a hail of explosions.

Chest heaving, Frost glanced around, expecting RnB to be wounded. But the drake was tearing into a corrupted a few dozen feet away.

155

Farther on, Dante tanked two corrupted while a pair of guards hacked at them. Saba kited another, galloping and firing her bow without pausing, always staying ahead of the monster. Arrows made a pincushion of the corrupted.

Ryne was in Ethereal Form, appearing like a darker translucent goblin. The skill reduced incoming damage. Ryne also had two Mimics of himself and his Summoned Defilers. The three identical goblins cast Shadow Globes, Nether Lances, and streaks of black Shadowflame that raced across the ground. The Shadowflame left a Damage Over Time effect, rising like black gas from Krator's body. Meritus and his Shaman focused on healing.

The Klaw dashed toward one of the goblins, body leaking silver and gray void energy and the deeper black of Ryne's DoTs. Frost hoped the goblin was a Mimic. Krator punched. A half-moon of cyan aether appeared, carving into the goblin.

In the next instant, Krator's giant crab claw shot out, snatched the goblin, and tossed him into the air. Krator Leaped, met the goblin at the apex of the throw, and punched. The impact was an explosion. Gravity Bomb. The goblin hurtled down.

With a resounding boom, the goblin crashed into the ground in an eruption of dirt, debris, and dust. As Krator landed, the goblin stepped from the dust cloud.

Smiling, Frost returned his attention to the fight near him. Several guards had retreated to the wagons.

Frost helped finish off the corrupted Dante was tanking. "Dante, taunt the one that's on Saba. We're gonna kill it then pick the others off one by one." He turned to the dresdor and waved. "Kite it this way, Saba."

The centaur galloped toward them. The moment she was within range, Dante Raging Rushed into the corrupted chasing her. This one was a gurash, matching Dante in size. Dante Soul Screamed. He gained aggro immediately, the corrupted now fixated upon him. Frost and Saba killed it with two attack combos.

Within the next ten minutes, all the corrupted were dead. Frost looked over in time to see Krator tumble to the ground. The vivid blue and red within the draconid's body dimmed. Then it went out. The residue of DoTs drifted into the air for a few moments longer before it, too, faded.

A cheer went up. Grinning, Ryne took an exaggerated bow, twirling his hand like a showman. Meritus smiled sheepishly.

Objective Complete

Avenge the Dead

Kill Krator the Klaw:

50, 000 experience points

5, 000 Lothal dominion credits

"Good thing we didn't try to fight the Klaw ourselves." Frost peered over at the massive corpse. "He musta been at least level twenty-five and elite."

"No wonder you let Ryne have his way," Saba said.

"I had a feeling," Frost admitted as RnB ambled over and sniffed at him while gurgling. "Especially after I remembered the guards are all level twenties and were having a hard time with the Klaw." Seemingly satisfied, the drake stalked over to a dead corrupted and nudged at the corpse with his nose.

Meritus and Ryne sauntered over to the rest of the group. The Mimics and Servitors trailed behind. A moment later, the summonses dissipated.

"Nice work." Frost acknowledged Meritus and Ryne with a nod.

"We got this." Meritus held up a weapon. "Fist of Fury."

The silver fist was aptly named. It would slip on like a glove, the joints made of a flexible material that adjusted to accommodate the wearer's fingers. Unlike other fists that had claws or blades, this one had raised studs adorning the knuckles.

"Epic loot," Dante exclaimed.

"Not quite." Meritus tucked the fist into his inventory. "This one's a rare."

"Bummer." Dante sighed.

"Still a hierka," Meritus said. "A genesiswork. As or more powerful than a normal epic weapon."

"Man's got a point." Frost glanced over to the wagons. "I'm thinking we should head back and turn in what we got before something else goes wrong."

"Might be too late for that." Saba's tail swished in agitation. "There's a few guys wearing WaR's colors up on the path. They pointed toward us."

Sure enough, three men and one woman atop lupines were on the slope leading down to the mines. Two were gurashi. One was human. The woman was a gargant. Frost squinted but couldn't make out the emblems on their chests.

The gurash woman turned and headed upslope. Billowing in the wind, her cloak displayed the Herald of WaR.

CHAPTER 18

"Meritus." Frost studied the three remaining WaR members as the woman disappeared around a corner of the trail. "When those guys focus on the rest of us, go tell your man, Vallen, and the dvergar, to take whatever they got here, meet the others with the hides, and head back to Ina. Tell 'em to ride into the night if they gotta."

"Alright."

"The rest of you, follow me and stare them down." Chest up, The Stunner held at an angle, pointing toward the ground, Frost strode toward RnB.

He climbed atop the mount, waited for Ryne and Dante to do the same, and nodded to Saba. At a slow walk, he led them toward the path, his gaze focused on the WaR members. The action forced the guildmates to watch his group. Convinced they were wondering about the group's intentions, he reached the path, stopped, and made a deliberate show of pointing RnB upslope toward them.

Echolocation told Frost when Meritus was done and headed their way. He waited for his best friend.

"I told him." Atop his zephyr, Meritus stopped beside Frost. "What's the plan now, dawg?"

"Want to take them on?" Dante hefted his axe.

"We can't." Saba's tail swished. "I mean, we could, but then we'd have their entire guild to contend with. We're not even sure they know who we are. Truth be told, if they did, they would've brought more people."

Frost gave her a dubious snort. "They aren't here by coincidence. They're

159

here either to take the mine or for us. And considering that one of them left, I feel we're gonna be facing more of them, or they just don't think much of us." He hoped it was the latter.

"You can let me kill them. This is an Open PVP zone." Ryne had taken out his haladie and was using it to clean his fingernails.

"Nah." Frost shook his head. "We need the caravan to make it to town so we can get paid. And to get the info from Nakada Masami."

"Frost is right," Meritus said.

"So." Frost rubbed his aether ring, mind conjuring potential ideas. "We're gonna head in the opposite direction from the caravan. If those guys want us, at least two of them will follow. The other will probably run to go tell their buddies."

"What then?" Saba asked.

"We're gonna keep leading them away." Frost looked at his map. "We stick together, but we won't fly. Even the dumbest person would eventually think Saba's the reason for the choice. We head south then circle back east, which should bring us within twenty miles of town, allowing Saba to be able to call to her drake. At that point we lose these fools then fly to Ina. We pick up our rewards, the info for the empowered spells, the hierkas, and Gilda's location."

"And dip before they even understand what we did." Meritus grinned.

"Dip?" Frowning, Ryne looked from Meritus to the rest of them. "Why would we dip into something?"

Frost laughed. "Dip… as in leave. Run away."

"Ahhhh." Ryne nodded.

"Ryne, this time I was as confused as you." Saba shook her head. "For the record, I don't like this plan."

"Any particular reason why?" Frost asked.

"Drakes. I don't like flying. Riding on the back of any animal feels stupid." She gestured to herself. "Just look at me and imagine it."

But Frost was already picturing the last time she rode the simurghs. Fighting the need to laugh, he wheeled his mount around. "You're gonna be fine. Let's go. When we ride past the caravan area act like we don't know anyone. Ryne, when we're out of sight, summon a Defiler, and let us know what those fools do."

"So asked. So done," the little goblin said.

Leading the way, Frost rode along the winding path down past the mine area where the wagons surrounded by Charged Shields were beginning to roll out. "Meritus, is there a way you can contact Nakada to tell him to expect delivery?"

"Yeah. By Comm Orb. I'll let both him and Kensai know."

"Good. This way there's no delay in getting our info."

The group followed the foothills until they rounded a corner. Ryne summoned his Defiler and Concealed it. The trundle of wagon wheels and beat of padded feet and hooves faded behind them. The sun was but a glowing ember far to the west, shrouded behind blood-orange clouds.

"All three are still coming," Ryne said. "They completely ignored the caravan."

"Good." Frost glanced at his map.

To the south, in their immediate vicinity, was an area called the Green Sea. Looking in its direction, he could see how it got its name. A veritable ocean of undulating grassland and brush stretched for miles, the occasional hill and tree jutting up to break the monotony.

He turned RnB to the greenery and urged him forward. "Let's speed up. Give them something to think about. If none of them turn back, then we gotta assume they have Comm Orbs also, which means we gotta act quickly."

The group broke into a gallop. Wind streaming by, mounts grunting, they sped across the grassland. The land dipped, flattened for a bit, then rose again. When they crested the hill, Frost snatched a look behind.

The WaR members weren't trying to hide the fact they were giving chase. Their lupines howled for blood.

Frost spoke in group chat. "Looks like we're gonna have to kill them and hope they didn't report to anyone with flyers or that they're dumb enough to believe they can take us."

"Want us to turn back now and do it?" Dante expertly handled his kirin with one hand, his long-handled axe in the other.

"Nah. Ryne, cast a Mirage of us when we're out of sight going down the next hill. Have it keep going as if it's really us. We're gonna dismount, hide, and ambush them as soon as they come over the hill."

As planned, after they had crested the rise and were headed downslope, they slowed, dismounted, and tried their best to hide behind the available brush. Ryne called forth a Mirage of them riding. The replica of the group continued down into the basin and then up the ensuing slope.

Lupine howls grew closer, echoing on the evening air. As did the shouts of the players urging them on.

Soon, Frost could hear the rhythmic beat of feet. He stretched his Echolocation as far as he could manage. In but a few moments, three forms crossed its threshold. Frost raised his hand.

The three WaR members galloped over the hill and down. Shouting, they kicked their bolsters, focused on the Mirage riding up the opposite slope.

Frost dropped his hand. The three WaR guildmates died to a hail of spells and cannon fire before they could react. Smoking and aflame, they fell to the ground and did not move again.

"Check the bodies, Dante and Ryne," Frost ordered. "Keep anything you find. Saba, best to call your drake now before their guildees come searching for them and us.

"Soon as it gets here, we're gonna head to town and lay low until the caravan arrives. When night comes, we handle our business and be gone before they know it."

"We slip and dip," Ryne declared proudly.

"Exactly." Frost chuckled.

Saba put her drake whistle to her lips and blew. It did not take long for the drake to arrive. Huffing and puffing, tail swishing, she climbed atop the green-scaled beast.

The sight of a centaur atop a drake was even funnier than Frost imagined. Everyone laughed. Frost was still wiping tears from his eyes when they took off.

They arrived in town as night fell. Rather than go to the tavern rooms he'd rented, Meritus took them to the house that once belonged to the old prospector. It had come with his purchase of the mine. He provided everyone with changes of clothes and armor from his stash.

Frost's was a black brigandine and blue gambeson. Unfortunately, the stats were the same as his previous armor.

Late that night, Vallen sent word of the caravan's safe arrival. As requested, he turned in the hides, precious stones, and metals to the appropriate merchants for their quests. Frost earned thirty thousand exp and another two thousand LDC.

Frost reached level sixteen, gaining an additional three points per each attribute, except for aether, which had increased by five.

Meritus had Vallen bring the goods meant for the relic hunter, Nakada Masami. He contacted Nakada, letting him know they had his korbitanium and precious gems. He also threw in news of the Fist of Fury as extra incentive. Not long after, he went out to meet Kensai to complete the transaction. Once Nakada confirmed delivery, the relic hunter was true to his word, and divulged the info on where they could find the materials they sought, which mobs dropped the empowered spells, and rumors he'd picked up on which dungeons held the special epic weapons.

Frost was interested in one thing. Gilda's location. Stroking his aether ring, he waited impatiently for Meritus to finish.

Meritus took a deep breath and glanced over at Frost. He shook his head solemnly.

"What is it?" Frost stopped stroking the ring, his chest tight.

"According to Nakada Masami, Setnana's been torturing Gilda. Word is she won't survive much longer."

Speechless, all Frost could think about was his promise to Gilda IRL. He couldn't allow her to die. He felt as if his heart stopped.

But slowly, his fear developed into something else. Something that rose inside him. Clawed its way up. A heat. A withering rage ready to be unleashed on Nomarch Setnana Botros.

CHAPTER 19

Frost spoke through clenched teeth. "Where's Setnana holding Gilda?"

"The dungeons at Modra's Keep," Meritus said. "A few hours' flight from here."

"Does anyone else think this could be a trap? Or that Gilda might already be dead?" Saba stopped stringing her bow and looked to each of them, one brow raised, her gaze settling on Frost. "I like Gilda. Obviously not as much as you do, but tell me you aren't going to walk into an obvious trap."

"We don't know that it is. And even if it is a trap, I don't see a choice." Frost shrugged. His conversation with Gunarr and Dagrun after the Sanctum ran through his head, conjuring images of the torture their people had suffered at Setnana's hands.

Saba smirked. "That's because you're thinking with your heart and not your head." She finished replacing the string with a few deft moves.

"More like thinking with the wrong head. That man's pussy-whipped." Dante made a whipping sound and motion before bursting into a laugh. When no one else joined in, and Frost shot him a scathing look, Dante smiled weakly and averted his eyes. "Sorry, bro."

"Asshole," Meritus grumbled.

Saba drew her bowstring to test it. "I just don't want to end up dead, truth be told. I don't know about you, but the idea of brain functions possibly stopping in real life scares me."

Frost scowled at Saba. "Why do you think we're doing this? That's *ex-*

actly what Gilda feared… what I don't want to happen to her. But I'll understand if you don't come."

"Don't you dare insult me." Saba glared, tail swishing with vigor. "I came to help. Hell, I flew when I hate flying. Not once, but twice. I'm just making sure you know what we're getting into. That you're aware Setnana's using your feelings against you."

"It is what it is." Frost shrugged. "But I'd take the same risk for any of you." He meant every word. He might not care as deeply for them as he did Gilda, but love was still love. He paused for a moment, frowning at that last thought.

"You know me, homie." Meritus gave him a dap, fist to fist. "Just point and I'm there. Always got your back."

"Appreciate it, dawg." Frost smiled at his best friend.

"We came to get Gilda." Dante's face was serious now. "So, let's go get her."

"Agreed. Now, how do we proceed?" Ryne took a seat on the floor, folding his spindly legs beneath him.

Frost nodded and pulled out a chair, overwhelmed by the sudden urge to sit. "We gotta make a move before WaR returns in force. We go out now separately, get any supplies we need, and meet back here." He jutted his chin toward Meritus. "You know anything about this keep or the area?"

"Just that it's part of an abandoned crada mining outpost northwest of Ezaki in the Kaigake Desert."

"Hmmm." Frost stroked his aether ring. "Maybe the dvergar might have an idea."

Meritus pursed his lips and nodded. "You might be right. I'll ask around when y'all go for supplies. I already got everything I need."

"Meet back in an hour. I'm gonna think up a plan by then." Frost got up, the chair scraping on the wooden floor. He looked to each of them. "I'm heading for the Auction Market. Don't forget to buy some dye, Dante. And Ryne… new clothes. Most of all, be careful."

"If you spot a quaker axe for auction, let me know," Dante said.

"No prob." Frost left the house.

Hood up, thoughts occupied by Gilda's fate, Frost kept to the shadows, doing his best to avoid the light from bloomglobes and glimmerstalks. He refused the temptation to take The Stunner from his inventory. Despite the protection the cannon promised, it would draw attention if any WaR member were on the lookout for him.

Following his map, he made his way to the Auction Market, running ideas through his head on how to rescue Gilda. When he entered the Auction Market, he kept his head down, hood shielding his face, and proceeded to a sparsely populated corner.

Danica appeared, the yurid's feathers a shimmering blue-green, her wings folded against her body. She informed him of two sales. Luminance had sold for ten thousand IDC. The timer on Deadeye's bids had expired with the highest at five thousand LDC. He accepted both sales. Danica took the AM's five percent fee on each transaction.

After taking the credits, he searched for quaker axes but found none. Disappointed, he scrolled through until he found his next target. A thought, and he'd purchased Strafe for three thousand LDC, smiling at the decrease in price due to several other sellers. He absorbed the shard.

Skill Acquired

Strafe:
Cast time: Instant
Recharge: 20 seconds
Consumes: Aether
Available shard slots: 2
Effect: Dash up to 60 feet in any direction. Immune to movement impairment and stuns while active.

Another search and he'd found the level eighteen skill, Aether Barrage. He purchased it for the outright sale of ten thousand credits, half IDC and half LDC.

The level twenty skill was also there. Aether Fusillade. A demo of the ability was available to view.

Selecting the demo, Frost watched as four red Piercers streaked from a cannon. The skill seemed lackluster until he saw the Piercers could be detonated just before impact for AOE damage. If they were detonated within a hundred feet of a Walker bot, which was a skill available later, the bot unleashed Ground Zero, firing an Aether Bomb at each detonation.

166

Frost whistled. Both at the skill and its list price. Fifteen thousand credits.

Dismissing the ability from his mind, Frost spent another five hundred LDC on korbitanium projectiles. He checked for armor or jewelry upgrades, but none were in an affordable price range. Settling for what he had, he sighed and turned to leave.

He bumped into a blue-skinned gurash man in chain mail wide enough for two men. The Herald of WaR stood out on the gurash's chest.

"Watch where yer going," the gurash drawled.

An erada woman clung to the gurash's arm. The gurash was stroking her horns, eliciting moans.

"S-sorry, friend." Frost bowed, glad the gurash was taller than him by at least a foot.

Heartbeat quickening, he skirted the large man and his woman, hoping the gurash took it as a sign that Frost was properly intimidated. The gurash muttered something under his breath and swaggered past. The erada giggled. Head down, Frost shuffled outside.

On his way home, he passed an apothecary who was closing shop. Remembering the dye, Frost hurried inside. The proprietor was a human with a humped back and an eye-patch who introduced himself as Igor.

"What can I do you for, young man." Igor hovered over the counter as Frost perused the wares through the glass.

"How much for the crimson dye." Frost pointed at the one in question. Almost every other dye had a price of fifty LDC.

"Ah, that one's special." The man's lips parted in a gap-toothed grin. "A relic from beyond the Front. A Vindicator killed a void dragon and harvested its blood. I made this from that blood."

"Sounds good. How much."

"Tree fiddy." Igor was still smiling.

"What?"

"Tree fiddy."

"You gotta be kidding."

Expressionless, Igor stared at Frost.

"No prob. I'll take it." Frost shrugged. It was his turn to smile. "But I don't have the credits right now. I'll gladly pay you on Tuesday—"

"Get out!" Igor's face looked as if he would burst a vein. He jabbed a stubby finger at the door.

"Alright. Alright." Frost chuckled. "Just give me the one that says plain red for fifty LDC." He placed the credits on the counter.

Chest heaving, Igor grumbled under his breath but retrieved the dye. He shoved the glass container to Frost and snatched up the credits. "Good. Night."

"Nice doing business with you." Smiling, Frost picked up the dye, turned and strolled to the door, flipping his prize up and catching it again.

On his way home along the dark streets, he practiced Strafe. He worked on controlling the distance and direction of the dash ability, often using it to speed to the corner of a building or to get from one shadow to the next.

When he arrived at the house, the others had already returned. Dante had colored his hair black. Ryne had gotten himself a plain blue pants, shirt, and had shaved. His bald head and clean face made him look like a new goblin. Saba had settled on chestnut hair, both on her head and her body's equine portion.

Standing near the table was a dvergr dressed in hides. He was half a foot taller than Ryne and had the wizened face and snowy hair of a man who'd seen a lot in life. He watched Frost with wary eyes.

"This is Raynor." Meritus gestured to the white-haired rockform man who offered a slight bow. "He used to work the mines at Modra's Keep. Says if Gilda's in the dungeons he can get us in through the mines. I think we can sneak her out without anyone knowing."

"I like that idea." Frost nodded, spirits higher than they had been when he left. He could see them rescuing Gilda. And maybe killing Setnana if he was lucky. He held up the red dye. "Lemme color my hair, then we can get to it." He headed for the bathroom.

******

Under a velvet sky sprinkled with glittering shards, they flew northwest for several hours. Frost wished Saba's Aura of the Pack worked on mounts like some buffs. The twenty-five percent increased speed would have been a boon.

Perusing his map, he noted the small towns, villages, forests, and farm-

168

lands, all of which gradually petered out, the terrain becoming savanna, and eventually rocky land with sparse vegetation. With the change, the air grew drier to match. And chilly, which surprised Frost.

They landed at the eastern edge of the Kaigake Desert. With Raynor leading, they rode the rest of the way, crossing from shale to sandy dunes. Frost pulled his hood up against the night's chill and to shield his face from sand when the wind swirled.

Raynor slowed near several towering rock formations. Signaling caution, he led them up a path between the rocks, deep shadows enclosing them. They soon reached an opening.

On the other side, the Kaigake Desert stretched for miles, lit by moonlight. Off to their left was a cliff line, highlighted by the backdrop of the moon and star-kissed night sky.

Raynor pointed in the cliffs' direction. A keep with two towers sprouted above the cliffs. Bloomglobes or glimmerstalks showed the location of guards and paths of patrols along the battlements.

"Modra's Keep." He beckoned to them. "Follow me."

They made their way back the way they'd come before Raynor took them to another trail where soaring rock faces peered down from either side. He led the way as if he could see ahead despite the darkness enfolding them, their sole light that of the silver coin of a moon and her court of glinting shards. The scrabble of drake claws on rocks, the beat of kirin hooves, padded zephyr feet, and their breathing was loud in the night, louder in the narrow passage.

An acrid scent hung on the chilly air. Frost couldn't quite place it, but it was there, surrounding them, growing stronger by the moment.

"Stinks here. Even the mounts agree." Meritus stroked his zephyr's downy head. "I got to kick the bolsters to make mine keep going."

"Same here." Dante expertly controlled his kirin with one hand, while holding his long-hafted axe in the other.

"I don't blame them." Saba cupped a hand over her nose and mouth. "It's awful."

"Not this guy." Frost gestured to RnB, the drake's head stretched forward. "He's pushing hard all on his own."

Forms up ahead disturbed Frost's Echolocation. "Someone's up there."

He stopped and aimed The Stunner. "Two people."

"Those are my people," Raynor said. "Everything is fine. We live within these rocks, in these tunnels... what was once the Kaigake Mountains before the first Void Cataclysm broke the world. Those two are guards."

"You didn't tell me you were *from* here," Meritus said. "Only that you worked here."

"You did not ask." The dvergar shrugged. "You have nothing to fear. If I intended harm, my people could have come out at any time." He gestured at the surrounding cliffs. "From anywhere."

The declaration sent a deeper chill through Frost. He kept The Stunner aimed as they forged ahead amid the unrelenting acrid stench. Not even the occasional gust of howling wind through the pass diminished the fetor.

The forms of the two guards remained in position, shifting occasionally as if the guards were tired of standing in one spot. When the group drew close, the guards resolved into two spear-wielding dvergar men outside a cave mouth from which warmth spilled.

"Who goes!" called the dvergar, stepping forward with their spears pointed at the newcomers.

"It is me."

"Zerker Raynor!" Teeth showing in the dark, the taller of the two guards planted the butt of his spear into the ground before him.

"Scout Paedar." Raynor gestured to the man. "Run, summon the men. Send me whichever lookout was on duty at Modra. I will be with my guests at the middle staging area."

"Yes, Zerker Raynor." Paedar bowed and ran off. The other guard took up his former position.

"Leave the mounts and follow me." Raynor leaped off his drake.

Frost dismounted. He spent a few moments stroking RnB's snout.

The drake gurgled at his touch but stared toward the cave. RnB whined and took a step forward, but Frost stopped him.

"I'll call for you if I need you. Go!" Frost pointed to the sky as he'd practiced the night at Dante's barn.

The drake gurgled again, its golden-eyed gaze focused on the cave. After a final whine, RnB took to the air, his shadowy form blotting out stars. He circled once before flying off.

Frost followed Raynor and the others into the cavern. The heat and acrid stench increased, the latter becoming near oppressive. Footsteps echoing with each stride, they rounded a corner. Crackling flames in clay braziers lit an intersection up ahead. Tunnels split off in three directions.

Frost flicked at his nose and sniffed at the stench, which had grown even stronger. As they passed one of the clay braziers, he took a look inside. The flames crackled and licked from wood. Though there was no smoke, the burning wood was the stench's origin.

"What's this?" Frost pointed at the wood.

"Dragonwood," Raynor said. "We grow it in hidden glades. Our ancestors claim its scent is that of a void dragon. Though no dragon has been seen this side of the Dagoda Front since the last Void Cataclysm."

Frost made to argue the point but thought better of it. Mentioning Imanok made no difference to the current situation.

"The smell of burning dragonwood keeps away the corrupted," Raynor continued. "They suddenly began appearing the last two weeks, often slinking into the caves."

Frost tensed at the mention of corrupted, recalling Krator and its minions. He stretched his Echolocation as the group marched through the tunnels, the way lit by torches along the walls. Not once did they encounter any other dvergar.

Bothered by the absence of the natives, Frost had the niggling sense of being followed. Focusing on his Echolocation, particularly on the tunnel behind them, he strained to find a presence. A form. Anything. For a split second he thought he sensed something, but then it was gone. Furrowing his brows, he continued to scan.

A while later, light framed the opening of the tunnel ahead. They had almost gotten to it when Frost became aware of the forms within. At least two dozen of them.

"A bunch of dvergar coming up," Frost mentioned as a way to warn his group.

"My people," Raynor said.

They strode into a cavern the size of a large field, illuminated by braziers and torches. Perhaps thirty dvergar waited inside, each one armed and armored for war. A hush fell across the room.

Raynor motioned for the group to stop. He strode forward. "I promised to find someone who could help us get rid of the ones who have recently brought the Gray Death with them. The ones living inside Modra's Keep."

"What about helping with our corrupted?" someone yelled.

"They have the means to do that as well," Raynor declared.

"What?" Frost's brows climbed his forehead. He leaned in behind Raynor. "That's not true."

Raynor tilted his head. "But it is. I worked for Nakada Masami. I know of your negotiations. But more than that, I'm a cutthroat of considerable skill.

"I have been in the dungeon of Modra's Keep and witnessed Nomarch Setnana Botros torture the young lady for information about you, Drelan Frost of the Blue Sky Network. She raged about you people killing her son, and about an epic zhua. A zhua like the one in your inventory."

A chill ran down Frost's spine. Behind him, his friends gasped.

CHAPTER 20

"Don't do anything, guys." Heart thumping, Frost resisted the urge to bring The Stunner to bear, but he took a step back to give himself a chance if he was left with no other choice. "Unless I'm reading this wrong, it's like he said. If he had bad intentions, he coulda gotten us outside."

"I heard your friend say you were a smart man." Raynor faced them, a smile creasing his wizened features. "I see he was right."

"He could still be leading us to a trap," Saba argued in group chat.

"Like you said," Frost answered under his breath, "we knew it might be a trap even before coming. It is what it is at this point. We do what we gotta do."

Frost focused on the little dvergr and spoke aloud. "What now?"

"Now, you agree to heal our corrupted, if we help you get the girl."

"The girl first." Frost met the dvergr's silver-eyed gaze. A quest revealed itself: **Save The Kaigake Dvergar** part of **The Cure** line.

Raynor's eyes narrowed. "What is there to stop you from flying off when you have her?"

Frost shrugged. "Trust. The same trust we put in you to bring us here before you sprang this on us."

"That is not good enough."

"We're gonna heal your corrupted after we rescue the girl. You have my word."

Behind Frost, the others voiced protests.

"Your word?" Grimacing, Raynor shook his head. "Your word is not enough. I need reassurances and a time. Most people corrupted by the Gray Death do not live for more than four days."

Frost scowled at the insult. "My word's worth a lot to me. If it ain't good enough for you, then we can fight it out right here, right now." He tensed, ready to open fire. "You might win, but your loved ones won't get the help they desperately need, and we'll take as many of you with us as we can."

Raynor studied Frost's face, the corner of his mouth upturned. He was most certainly gauging his people's chances. Unflinching, Frost returned the stare, his eyes dead. Whatever Raynor saw made the dvergr's shoulders droop. The dvergr sighed.

"Fine. But if you cross me, I will hunt you down." Raynor's silver-eyed gaze was cold and hard and swept across them individually. "Every. Single. One of you."

Dante chortled. "That's funny. Seeing that you crossed us first."

Ryne stepped up beside Frost, his haladie in hand. "I relish the threat. But it is one you would regret."

As Raynor opened his mouth to answer, Frost placed a restraining hand on Dante's shoulder and replied, "We can settle this later. Let's get to rescuing Gilda and your people, Raynor."

"Fine." Raynor glared at Ryne and Dante.

"You said you snuck into the dungeon where they're holding Gilda." Frost released Dante's shoulder as the gurash relaxed. "How many guards are there? Can we take them?"

"Six." Raynor held up his fingers to match. "They are not much of a threat. The reinforcements will be of greater concern."

"Alright." Frost nodded once. "I need a few minutes with my friends."

Raynor bowed. He turned on his heels and strode toward the dvergar warriors.

"Are you mad?" Saba hissed when Raynor was out of earshot. "As if the risk wasn't big enough, you go ahead and make a promise you can't keep?"

"Shhh." Frost shook his head. "I'm gonna keep my word."

"How?" Saba pawed at the ground.

"I'm gonna come back with Meritus when we get the spells we need. I said we'd heal them after we got Gilda. After can mean any time."

"Pulling a technicality." Saba gave a slow disapproving shake of her head. "You must like having enemies. I don't."

"I'm with Frost," Meritus said. "Raynor used us first. Put us in a bad situation without asking. Turnabout is fair play."

"We should just lay into them now." Dante hefted his axe.

"Nah." Frost shook his head. "I doubt we'd survive that. We do what we came to do."

"Alright, bro." Dante let out a reluctant breath.

"So, what's the plan?" Saba asked.

"We get in, get Gilda, and get out as fast as possible. We got our maps, so the way back's not a prob." Frost stroked his aether ring. "When we first get in, Saba, your job is to Conceal and scout ahead. Use group chat if you need to warn us. On the way out, we're gonna collapse the tunnels behind us.

"Dante, at that point, you pick up anyone that comes at us from the front. Meritus, you're gonna call out your Servitors. Coupled with Ryne's Mirage, Mimics, and his summonses, that should keep them distracted while we escape.

"And by them, I mean the Battleguards *and* the dvergar. As soon as we're outside, we whistle the mounts. Gilda can ride with me."

"Sounds good." Meritus nodded his approval. The others murmured in agreement.

Frost signaled to Raynor. "Ready whenever you are."

"Good." Raynor's face brightened. "Follow us."

Raynor led them through winding tunnels, the braziers becoming few and far between, the way darkening, the stench of dragonwood sitting heavy on the air. As before, Frost had the feeling of something or someone on their trail. And as before, his Echolocation played tricks on him, the sense of a presence fading the moment he picked it out. His heart rate sped up.

Soon, they were in utter darkness. Their breathing was loud to Frost's ears, as was the shuffle of feet, the rustle of clothing, the clink of armor. They halted.

"We are here," Raynor whispered a few steps away from Frost. "Get ready."

Two forms detached from the group and moved ahead. Something creaked. Light flashed in the blackness, framing a door. Silence and darkness became lovers once more.

Standing in the dark, Frost might have been worried, fearful, if not for his Echolocation. Instead, an electric tingle crept through him. A surge of adrenaline in anticipation of the pending battle.

The creak sounded ahead again. Light framed the door and a dvergr. The dvergr waved them on.

Frost leaned over to Saba and whispered, "I'm gonna tell you to stay here, but you Conceal and go on ahead instead." Out loud, he said, "Saba, wait here and guard this area."

"Okay." Saba moved to the side.

Quickly and quietly, everyone else surged forward. In minutes, they had gathered in a hallway where bloomglobes hung, their light revealing sandstone bricks. When everyone was through, they proceeded deeper into the dungeon, Frost making certain his map catalogued their path. With his Echolocation he picked out Saba's invisible form as she scouted ahead.

They reached another series of halls. Two dead guards were on the floor. It took but a moment for Frost to notice the cells. Cells occupied by dvergar, who crowded the bars, hands held out as they pleaded for help, eyes hopeful.

Some of the dvergar warriors hurried to the cells, imploring the captives to be quiet. They gripped the hands of their loved ones, tried to hug them despite the bars. Tears flowed. The sight tore at Frost.

Raynor tugged at Frost's arm. Sweat trickled down the dvergr's brow. "This way to the ones they infected and the torture chamber." Raynor strode toward another hall.

A coldness settled over Frost. His mind conjured images of Gilda's suffering. Of the dvergar's suffering. Anefet's suffering. He could fulfill so much if he killed Setnana now.

The Comm Orb dinged. It was Saba.

"I found Gilda, but she's in a bad way. Not just torture either. She looks sick, like one of the corrupted.

"And that's not all. It's an ambush. Setnana and her Battleguards are waiting for us near a damned Genesis Engine in middle of the room you're about to reach. I can free Gilda, throw her on my back, and make a run for it with my Aura of the Pack buff, but you guys will have to go all out to distract them."

The mention of Gilda's condition left a sour taste in Frost's mouth. He hoped Saba was wrong. "We got you. Place a couple traps near the hall." Heart a drum, he raised The Stunner, his finger caressing the trigger. He nodded to Ryne, Dante, and Meritus. "Ass-kicking and name-taking time."

The end of the hall drew closer. The dvergar slowed. A scout peeked around the corner ahead and signaled for them to halt.

Frost pushed his way among the dvergar until he was directly behind Raynor. He pressed The Stunner's muzzle to the back of the little man's head. "Why set us up?"

Raynor froze. He raised his hands slowly. "I do not know what you mean."

"Don't play with me." Frost jabbed Raynor's head with the muzzle.

Snarling, the other dvergar backed up with their weapons drawn. A few bows pointed at Frost. Glows appeared around the weapons or hands of casters.

"Move again and he's a dead man." Frost stared them down.

Dante strode up to Frost's right. His crimson skin flared to scarlet. Meritus took up the left. His three Servitors towered around him. Ryne appeared just ahead of Dante. The goblin had summoned a Nightmare and two Defilers. The Nightmare was an ethereal black mass, but slowly it changed shape until it took the form of a giant lupine.

"Answer the question." Frost prodded Raynor once more.

"I-I had no choice." Raynor's shoulder's slumped.

"Explain." Frost growled.

"Th-the zhua." Raynor took a deep breath. "Nomarch Setnana Botros has a mystic with the spells to save my people. She showed me. All she needed was your zhua."

Frost opened and closed his mouth. His thoughts whirled with the idea of someone else already possessing the spells. Someone in Setnana's employ.

"How'd she know I'd come asking for your help?" Meritus inquired.

"She did not. Nakada was to send me to you on the pretense of offering his help to rescue the girl. But then you showed up asking on your own. It

177

was simple, then."

"Nakada. That bastard." Meritus spat to one side.

"Here's what's gonna happen," Frost said. "You and your warriors are gonna walk into the room as if nothing's changed. Your casters and marksmen will attack Setnana's guards. Just like we are. Once my friend makes it back here with the girl, we all get out of here. We'll rescue your people on the way out."

"But what of the corrupted?" Raynor faced Frost, eyes wide. "They're on the other side of the dungeon. My wife and daughter are among them. They don't have much time! They have been corrupted for at least two days already."

"We're gonna help them too, but my girl comes first."

Tears brimmed in the dvergr's eyes. His hands shook. "Thank you."

Frost disliked tricking the dvergr, but it had to be done. He would keep his promise, though. That, he knew.

Raynor turned to his warriors. "We do as he says." The other dvergar bowed to Raynor.

They edged close to the end of the hall. Frost's heart was thumping now. At a signal from Raynor, the dvergar flooded into the room, walking and talking as if nothing was amiss. The casters and marksmen opened fire.

Selecting Homer, Frost held down the trigger, charging the ability, and moved into sight. The hall opened into a large room.

Toward the middle of the room was the Genesis Engine, a large barrel-shaped glass container. Cyan aether swirled within. A company of Battle-guards and one woman clad in royal blue stood a few hundred feet ahead of the Engine. The same woman from Imanok Sanctum.

Nomarch Setnana Botros.

Frost aimed at the Nomarch, lock-on registering a moment later. He released the trigger. Eight Aether Missiles shot forth. Frost followed them up with a Concussion Blast and an Aether Bomb.

Setnana Flickered away from the Missiles. But they still followed. She threw up an Aether Barrier, a luminescent globe surrounding her entire body. A Battleguard leaped in front of her moments before the Missiles' impacts. Explosions rocked the dungeon.

The Concussion Blast and the Aether Bomb landed seconds apart. The

Blast erupted in a circle of white light, staggered a few of the Battleguards, and tossed them into the air. When the Bomb struck, a blue incandescence erupted, setting men ablaze. They careened about, beating at the greedy flames.

The enemy's surprise lasted but a moment. Within seconds, the Battleguards countered. Spells and cannon fire hurtled back across the threshold. Setnana had also recovered. Mimics of herself coalesced and added to the onslaught.

The air between the groups lit up like a battlefield. Fire, Ice, and Shadow Globes zipped back and forth. Electrical Arcs rippled through the air, tearing rents into the ground. Nether Lances and Shadowflame left black afterimages. Flame Walls sprang up. So did Aether Shields and Aether Barriers. Chain Lightning fell on one group or the other, knocking men or dvergar aside.

Meritus and his Shaman flung Mikander's Tears or Blood to heal as needed. The dvergar mystics also had their Servitors out to assist.

An all too familiar screech echoed behind Frost.

He frowned. *RnB?*

Even as the thought crossed Frost's mind, his Echolocation picked out an invisible form, hurtling down the hall. He knew it was RnB, but his mind refused to comprehend the conclusion. The form barged between them, sending a few dvergar sprawling.

"Look!" Meritus pointed as his Duelist cast Fire and Ice Globes.

Off to the left, Saba was galloping toward them. Gilda was on Saba's back, head down, clutching Saba's mane. Even as Saba's legs churned, she pointed her bow toward the Battleguards and loosed arrows. Nock. Loose. Nock. Loose. Wooden, elemental, and Aether Arrows blurred through the air.

"Cover her." Frost aimed at any Battleguard targeting Saba and fired off Aether Shots and Korbitanium Projectiles.

Nomarch Setnana's attention snapped toward Saba. A cloud of blackness suffused her hand, standing out against the backdrop of the Genesis Engine's aether. Frost brought his weapon to bear, but he knew he wouldn't be in time. The world slowed, Setnana's hand rising.

Something unseen slammed into the Nomarch. She went flying to the side.

RnB appeared. The drake's momentum sent him careening into the Genesis Engine, knocking it over.

Mouth agape, Frost could only stare. Saba arrived moments later.

"Go! Run!" She flung her hand out, buffing their group with Aura of the Pack, increasing run speed by twenty-five percent. The buff duration was for an hour.

Chest heavy, Frost turned to run. A last look revealed aether spilling from the tipped over Genesis Engine. The power swirled into the air. RnB's wings flapped above the Engine, the drake unable to extricate himself from the outer struts and supports protecting the glass cylinder and the power inside.

Battleguards loosed spells and cannon fire at the drake. Before the attacks struck, the ground caved in with a sound like thunder, darkness swallowing the Engine and RnB. Cracks raced from the fissure. The Battleguards scrambled away.

Frost and the others fled.

With Saba leading the way, they sprinted down the halls. Frost tried to understand what had drawn RnB into the dungeon. *Had he been following them the entire time?* His eyes widened with the realization and horror that the earlier sensation of something on their trail had been the drake.

The group reached the cells. Frost found himself caught up in the act of freeing the captive dvergar.

A new quest opened and completed beneath **Save The Kaigake Dvergar**, one named **Freeing the Dvergar Captives**. It granted twenty thousand exp and five hundred LDC.

While the dvergar warriors led the old, young, and infirm to the tunnels first, Frost took a look at Gilda. Though her only clothes were underpants soiled with blood and dirt, it wasn't her nakedness holding his attention. That was reserved for the welts, the half-healed wounds, and most of all, the gray splotches marring her normally beautiful cerulean skin.

Something inside him almost broke. A part of him knew she was dying.

"We're gonna heal you." He reached over and stroked her hair. "I promise."

Her eyes were empty. They saw right through him. Somehow, she managed to nod. "I know." Her voice was a hoarse thing, a raspy whisper almost devoid of life's vigor.

"Time to go." Saba trotted toward the doorway leading into the tunnels.

The thought of healing Gilda reminded Frost of the missing empowered spells. But at least he had Benediction. He looked into his inventory. And gasped.

Benediction was gone. Frost spun in a circle, immediately looking for Raynor. The dvergr was no longer with them. Frost cursed himself for not Blessing the zhua, for handing it to the enemy.

******

I have lost everything. Setnana's ears pounded. She wanted to scream.

Fists clenched, she stared down into the chasm, its bottom lit by bloomglobes and glimmerwands. There was no sign of the Genesis Engine or the drake that attacked her. The beast had to be dead. And the Engine was surely buried beneath the rubble.

She became dimly aware of a power surge within her, of aether energy crackling like lightning around her fists. To think that Drelan Frost and his band of sceeves had escaped her trap. She had them all here. And Benediction. Now, she had nothing.

Ihuet approached in that gliding walk of his, sky-blue face as expressionless as ever. "Perihy is almost at Apur. I have ordered Major Neferna and the Sky Swords to prevent him from entering the Crypts."

Those were the last words she wanted to hear at the moment. Setnana shook with the effort to calm herself.

CHAPTER 21

Tightness gripped Frost's chest. "We gotta go back. Raynor stole Benediction." He made to take a step down the long hall when a Battleguard company appeared at its far end.

"Run!" Saba ducked around the corner into the tunnels.

Snarling, Frost brought The Stunner up, but the Battleguards were not yet in range. Growling, he turned on his heels and sprinted after his friends.

When they had gone some ways into the tunnels, Frost turned back and aimed at the distant roof and walls. With a primal scream, both in rage and frustration, he opened fire. The salvo collapsed the tunnel. A cloud of dust gushed out. Coughing, he hurried after the group.

All Frost could think about was Gilda having the Gray Death, losing Benediction, and losing RnB. His plan had gone to shit. He might have rescued Gilda, but she would still die. He wracked his brain for ways to go back and retrieve the zhua, perhaps find RnB alive and well.

But he knew such hope was wishful thinking.

They raced along the tunnels, the dvergar putting out the braziers, leaving the way behind in complete darkness. Finally, they reached the staging area. The dvergar gathered around their loved ones, hugging and crying.

Frost grimaced, a part of him wanting to hate all dvergar the way he hated Raynor. But whenever he gazed upon some child, he lost his resolve. His heart softened. He despised Raynor's deceit, but at the same time he understood.

With a snarl, Frost headed over to where Saba had placed Gilda on the ground among some straw. Meritus was focused on Gilda, brow furrowed, colorful streams of aether whizzing from his fingertips into Gilda's skin. Both Dante and Ryne watched with forlorn expressions. The dvergar kept clear of them.

"How's she doing?" Frost took in the gray splotches. They stood out even more with the improvement in Gilda's light blue skin color.

"I healed the wounds, and cast Purifying Touch, Ameliorate, Suppression, and Rejuvenate on her, figuring since the empowered versions are needed, that the regular ones will help stave off the corruption. They did. But I got no clue how long it'll last." Meritus sighed. "I gave her some dreamweed so she can sleep. She'll be out for another two hours. But eventually, the Gray Death will consume her. I can't do much more. Not without the empowered spells and Benediction." His shoulders slumped.

I'm such a fucking idiot, Frost thought. *If I'd only listened and Blessed the damn thing.* "How much longer does she have?" Frost said aloud.

Meritus shook his head. "I don't know. Raynor said most infected people die after four days. Only Gilda can tell us when they infected her."

Someone cleared their throat behind Frost. He turned to face them. A black-robed dvergr man bowed, his long hair and beard a deep silver.

"I am Elder Agnar, leader of the Kaigake dvergar." The Elder's golden eyes shifted to Gilda and back again. His throat moved as he swallowed in fear. "I am sorry for Raynor's deception. That is not the way of our people. And though he was wrong, and you promised to help us, you now have a corrupted among us. You risk us all."

"You got some fucking balls," Frost snarled.

"Bastard." Saba scowled, her eyes little daggers even as she produced dark robes and a hooded black cloak from her inventory. With Meritus' help, she slipped them onto Gilda.

Elder Agnar bowed. "I mean no offense, and if there was anything I could do to help you, I would."

Frost opened his mouth with the intention to swear some more when flames roared up from the brazier in the middle of the room, causing the acrid stench to flare. He frowned, a spark on an idea forming. A way existed to heal Gilda. The chance was slim, but slim was better than no chance at all. He took a look at Benediction's schema.

"There is something you could do to help." Frost focused on the brazier and its contents. "I'm in need of dragonwood. About fifty pieces of it at least three feet long." It was enough for twenty-five Benedictions.

"Will you leave if we provide the dragonwood?"

"Yes. And I'm gonna still return to heal your corrupted. I got a funny feeling Nomarch Botros won't help as Raynor thinks."

"Deal." Agnar bowed. "I will send my people to gather the wood." He hurried off to the other dvergar.

"Are you thinking what I'm thinking?" Meritus asked.

"Yeah." Frost nodded, a glimmer of hope shining through. "If Nakada wasn't lying about where we can get the rest of the mats and the spells, then we're gonna craft a few Benedictions."

"But they're hierkas." Saba turned her hands, palms up, eyes narrowed in confusion. "Which means we need hierkaneers."

"Who're pretty expensive to hire." Dante added, looking equally bewildered. "Unless you feel one of us can pick up the profession." He gave a dubious frown.

"I doubt Gilda has enough time for someone to level the craft," Saba said. "And we don't have the credits to hire a hierkaneer."

"Which is why I'm contacting Adesh Hamada." Frost was already contemplating the next step. "Blue Sky's got hierkaneers. Meritus, where we gotta go to farm the spells, the forsaken bones, and the void beholder's eyes? We can probably get the void beast blood from the beholders also."

"One sec." Meritus held up his index finger, his brow furrowed. "We can get Empowered Suppression and Empowered Rejuvenate from mobs in the Sands of Salanda, west of here. Of course, there's also Imanok Sanctum. Someone got an Empowered Ameliorate from Grenok the Devourer, the first boss in the Forsaken Crypts, which is where we'll also find the bones and void beholder eyes."

Frost arched his brows. "You trust that source about Grenok?"

"She's always been spot on." Meritus shrugged. "Why?"

"Because there hasn't been a World First announcement for Grenok." Frost stroked his aether ring. "So how'd someone get a drop off him." He paused for a second, brows drawing together as he mulled over the question.

"I can't answer that one." Meritus shook his head. "But if my girl says someone got a drop from him, then they did. And it wasn't just anyone who made the claim. It was Kazuto, the leader of WaR."

Frost nodded, lips forming a tight line. There was a chance the leader of the game's most powerful guild would lie about loot if he intended to keep the real source to himself. But Frost doubted it. He could see a person in that position bragging because no one else could kill Grenok. At least not yet.

"That still leaves the Genesis Engine," Frost mused. "Which means either trying to get to the one buried here *if* Setnana doesn't have her people retrieve it, or going to the Dagoda Front, which we aren't near high enough level to be able to do. Not without help." He ground his jaw in frustration.

"Let's get the easy stuff first and reach level twenty for the Crypts," Meritus said encouragingly. "Worry about the Engine after. One thing at a time, dawg."

Frost let out a slow breath. The moment he'd given himself hope, it had been dashed again. He struggled to keep his frustration in check.

But fear nagged at him. A fear he hadn't voiced. A fear borne of the knowledge that if Gilda died, that if any of them died, they might become invalids, or have some other adverse effects on their brain functions.

Agnar returned with two dvergar carrying chests. He flipped open the lids. "Fifty pieces of dragonwood as requested." The shiny wood was smooth and a dark mahogany brown. "And there is this." Agnar held out a pear-shaped gem laced with blue.

"Where did you get your hands on a skill-effect shard?" Meritus asked.

"One of our enemies dropped it when he died." Agnar looked from the shard to Frost. "He was using a weapon like yours."

Frost reached out and took the item.

Acquired skill-effect shard:

Multi-Lock

Skill:

Homer

Effect: Gives Homer the ability to lock onto separate targets. While charging Homer, aim at a target, and tap the trigger to lock.

Frost was unimpressed. But it was better than nothing. He absorbed the shard.

"Thank you." Without waiting for Agnar's reply, Frost nodded to Meritus. "Take the wood." He also removed Benediction's schema from his inventory. "And this also. Bless it as soon as you can."

Saying the words hurt. He couldn't help but feel like a failure.

******

Setnana prowled at the edge of the fissure, scowling at the Azureguards and the regular soldiers working below. Digging through the rubble proved to be a slow and laborious process. She had to at least salvage the Genesis Engine from this disaster. The thought sparked a smoldering heat deep inside her.

"My nomarch."

Closing her eyes, she willed her rage to subside. *A Botros shows no weakness. Strength always.* She took a deep shuddering breath and turned to face Ihuet.

And gawked.

Raynor was on his knees beside Ihuet, head bowed. He held a zhua in his hands. She did not need to touch it. She knew it was Benediction.

Setnana threw back her head and laughed. When her mirth subsided, she strode over to the dvergr. "Thank you, Zerker Raynor." She removed the zhua from his grasp and smiled at the confirmation.

The Cure
Retrieve the Epic Zhua Benediction
Objective Complete:
Acquired Benediction
15000 experience points
2500 Ignis dominion credits
2500 Khertahka dominion credits

Raynor looked up at her, piteous eyes filled with tears. "Can you cure Inga and Sten, now. Please, Nomarch Setnana."

Anxious to save Perihy, she was on the cusp of denying the man before she changed her mind. "Certainly." She gestured for him to stand. "Follow me."

"What of the Genesis Engine?" Ihuet asked. "We should secure it first."

"Leave men behind to dig it out." She raised the zhua. "I possess what is most important. Have simurghs readied. Tell the Sky Swords and trackers not to let my Perihy out of their sight. We shall be on our way shortly."

"Yes, my nomarch." Ihuet bowed and then glided away. He shouted orders to several guards.

With Raynor waddling beside her, Setnana strode toward where Vindicator Dita healed the wounded. "Dita." Setnana cracked a smile as she raised her prize. "Leave them and come with me."

Vindicator Dita's blue eyes were fixed on the zhua as he approached. His ossicones trembled with anticipation. "Is... is that what I think it is?"

"Take it and find out." Setnana passed the zhua to the grand kora.

Mouth open, Dita turned the zhua in his hand. He caressed the claw at the top. "Praise be to Jerad." He looked up to the heavens.

"Now, we get to see if it works. Follow me." Setnana led them toward the rear of the dungeon where she kept the corrupted imprisoned. Her stomach roiled as they drew closer, the idea of another failure weighing down on her.

When they reached the foul-smelling chamber and its line of cells, she looked down at Raynor. "Find your wife and child."

The little dvergr ran off toward the cells. Corrupted snarled and snapped at him, reached through the bars, while others mewled. It did not take him long to find his loved ones.

They were scrawny, pitiful things, their stone skin chipped and splotchy, brittle in many places. A semblance of sanity existed in their round pleading eyes. They crawled to the bars but could not get past the other corrupted who were craving blood. Raynor stared at them, a hand covering his mouth in horror.

Setnana called for several guards. Using spears, they stabbed at the corrupted near Raynor's wife and daughter. When they managed to bunch them to one side, a guard opened the door.

Inga and Sten stumbled out. The guard slammed the door shut. Raynor ran to his wife and child and threw his arms around them.

"Sergeant," Setnana called to the head guard. "Take your men and help with the excavation." Once the guards left, she turned her attention to the dvergar. "Raynor, move aside so Dita can cure them."

Raynor whispered soothing words to his wife and child and then backed away. Sten clutched her mother's leg. Inga watched Dita approach with wary eyes.

A shiver of anticipation ran through Setnana. She could not help it despite past failures. This was the beginning of a fervent dream to which she had clung.

Benediction glowed. Blue, yellow, and white wisps spiraled up from the zhua's claws. They spun, merged together, and formed a golden ball. The ball shot out and struck Inga.

Golden energy swept across the dvergr's body. A once brittle surface became hard again. Gray rock became beige sandstone. In seconds, Inga was cured. Even as Inga cried out in joy, Dita cast the same spell at Sten.

When Dita was finished, the family hugged and cried. Raynor looked Inga and Sten up and down in amazement.

Warmth suffused Setnana. She wanted to scream in joy. Vindication. Instead, she forced her emotions down and smiled at the family before her.

She heaved a breath and basked in their elation as if it were her own. *This is how it will be with you and I, Perihy.* She soaked it all in. The giddy laughter. The tears of joy. The love.

And then she cut the family down with a barrage of Shadow Globes and Nether Lances.

Vindicator Dita squeaked before slapping a hand over his mouth. "My Jerad, what have you done?" He regarded Setnana with round fearful eyes.

Impassive, Setnana watched the smoldering corpses. "Our possession of the cure must be kept a secret until I am ready. Imagine the leverage it will bring us within the Coalition. The accolades when we save the world. I could not risk them telling anyone. And they would have. Who would not reveal they were saved by a miracle?"

Setnana could see it now. Her goals were within her grasp. For the cure alone, she would at least be named Exarch.

But there was an additional reason for the killing. A message. By the terror writ large upon Dita's turquoise face, the way his ossicones quivered, the grand kora understood.

"Come. It is time to save my Perihy." Setnana stalked away, collected Ihuet and Khafra, and abandoned the diseased, the dying, and the dead.

CHAPTER 22

The dvergar provided Frost with a new drake. A blue one. For all the creature's beauty, Frost could only think of RnB.

After the dvergar and his friends harnessed Gilda to his back by way of a series of leather straps, Frost and the others took to the air, flying west toward the Sands of Salanda. Heart heavy with regret, he took one final look behind him, the gray pearl of dawn creeping across the sky, black smoke snaking up from Modra's Keep.

Refocusing on the task at hand, Frost activated his Comm Orb and sent a message to Adesh Hamada, relaying the dire situation, their need for a hierkaneer, and help locating a Genesis Engine. The Blue Sky leader promised to look into the problem and return an answer as soon as possible.

Though exhaustion threatened to overwhelm Frost, he refused to give in, focusing instead on reaching the Sands. Hopefully, Gilda would be somewhat recovered due to rest and Meritus' efforts. If she could function as well as the corrupted they encountered at the mines, she'd be useful.

During the flight, he found himself whispering to Gilda despite her unconscious state. "You're not gonna die. I won't let you. I'm gonna save you no matter what." She groaned. *Was she awake?* "Gilda? Gilda?" She didn't answer so he snatched a look over his shoulder to where her head rested against his back.

She mumbled something, low at first, but then louder and slurred. Frost strained to make out the words.

"Cow king. Claimed there wasn't." She giggled. "So funny. Mooo."

The incoherent babble continued for another minute. Frost tried to get her attention several times, but not once did she acknowledge him. She drifted into silence.

Frost waited to see if she'd start up again. But she did not.

Eventually, his thoughts shifted to RnB. He missed the drake dearly. Sorrow was a weight on Frost's heart. *Why'd you follow me? Did you feel I needed protection?* Frost shook his head. The idea seemed absurd.

Frost also considered that today was the beginning of his sixth day in-game, which meant he'd been gone from the real world for over two weeks. Questions assailed him. Questions of Mom and Kai's well-being. Questions about Sidrie and the plots she might yet be hatching, her intentions if Equitane became the top Corp, her intentions for the gameborn and Whole Brain Emulation. His mind conjured the worst scenarios, which reminded him of Pops' secret fight against Equitane.

At some point he would ask Gilda if she'd passed off the protocol to her people in the First Ward. And warn her that Sidrie might be tracking their every move IRL.

Shifting his thoughts to Void Legion, he worked out strategies to hasten their leveling. Beneath him, the wheat yellow and ochre of sun-kissed savannas and sands raced by, occasionally broken by patches of greenery and lonesome trees. Toward the north, a river carved a snaking path. Southwest of them was a line of hills.

A cool wind caressed his face as he imagined a quick grind, a smooth run through the Forsaken Crypts, and a cured Gilda, her skin once again the purest cerulean. He smiled at that last. Once she was healed, he would find a nice beach to take her to, one reminiscent of those in Barbados. It would be better than any Virtual Vacation.

A sprawl of stone, thatch roofs, roads, and lanes appeared far ahead, the river beyond them. Meritus' zephyr banked on diaphanous wings and descended. The rest of them followed. With a quick look at his map, Frost saw the town was named Toma. They landed at a copse perhaps a mile from the town and made their way among the trees.

"Why'd we stop?" Frost maneuvered his drake near Meritus.

"For supplies and to rest." Meritus petted his zephyr's owlish head. "I don't know about you, but I'm dog-tired. Gilda's got another hour before she wakes. Getting some sleep is a good use of the time."

Frost made to protest, but he knew Meritus was right. He nodded instead.

"When we wake up, I'll go get the supplies." Meritus dismounted. "Considering how much void beast blood we're in need of, I'll get some empty flasks. Then we hit the Sands." He pointed. "Which're just over those hills to the southwest."

"I'll Conceal my Defilers and have them keep watch." Ryne waved his hand.

Three black-robed Defilers appeared, red eyes glowing within black hoods. They glided away in three directions before disappearing.

Weariness gnawed at Frost, the idea of rest freshly planted in his mind. "Someone give me a hand with Gilda."

Dante was at his side in a flash. Frost unstrapped the harness. Dante eased Gilda from the drake's back. Cradling her in his arms, he carried her to a tree, where Saba flattened grass with her hooves. The gurash lay Gilda on her side and covered her body with her cloak.

Frost climbed down from his mount. "Keep the mounts close in case we need 'em." He guided his to where the first trees hid it, then headed over to Gilda's side. When he took a seat beside her, the need for sleep crashed down on him.

******

Something tickled Frost's nose. He opened his eyes. And stared into Gilda's cerulean and gray face, partially hidden within her black hood.

She had ditched the robes for a pair of baggy beige pants and a mahogany shirt. She also wore leather gloves. Two silver chakrams hung from her belt loop. The circular weapons were at least two feet in diameter, the two-inch-wide blades that made up their circumference etched with glyphs.

Her green eyes met his. "Hey." She smiled, if a bit weakly, and eased away to give him space. She pulled the front of the hood forward a little more, but not before he caught a glimpse of sores.

"Hey." Frost sat up. "You don't need to do that."

"Do what?"

"Hide your face. However you look is fine by me."

"I can't help it." An uncomfortable silence followed before she added, "Meritus said it was time to wake you."

Frost glanced around, the chill of dawn having been replaced by late morning warmth. Dante, Ryne, and Saba were off to one side enjoying meals. The gurash and goblin took bites from chunks of meat while Saba chewed on fruit. The smoked goodness of roasting hung faintly in the air. Frost's stomach grumbled.

"Where's Meritus now?" He didn't see his friend.

"He went off to scout for a bit. He said to give these to you." Gilda held out her hand. Several containers of Korbitanium Projectiles appeared in front of her.

"Thanks." Frost stood, took the ammo, and placed it in his inventory. "How you feeling?"

"Weird. Kinda strong. But still mostly like shit." She shrugged. "But a girl's gotta do what a girl's gotta do."

"We came as soon as we knew where—"

She waved him off. "No doubt. I don't think there's much you could've done to change things anyway." She took a deep, shuddering breath.

Frost fought down the urge to draw her into his arms. Not because he didn't want to, but rather the feeling she didn't want to be touched in that way. Gilda prided herself on being hard, being able to deal with anything thrown at her. "We're working on healing you completely. Mighta been done already if I hadn't lost Benediction. I'm sorry." he hung his head.

"Saba told me what happened in the dungeon. You can't blame yourself for that."

The words did little to soothe Frost. His eyes shifted to an exposed portion of splotchy skin in the space between the top of her glove and the end of her sleeve. "Does... does..." He cleared his throat. "Does it hurt?"

"Not so much hurt as it burns sometimes. Feels as if my insides are all over the place. And there's the sores."

He fought back a grimace so his pain at her suffering wouldn't be mis-interpreted for scorn. "How'd she do this to you?"

"Poured blood she claimed was from a newly-made draconid onto my wounds after she tortured me." Gilda's hand formed a fist. The fist shook. Her dagger appeared. She twirled it, a distant look on her face. "Said she wanted me to feel her son's pain. Wants all of us to feel his pain. She said he died from the Gray Death because of us."

Frost shook his head. "How? We don't even know him."

Gilda put away her dagger. "She blames us because we took Benediction from the Sanctum."

"Damn." Frost let out a breath and shook his head. But there was something more pressing he needed to know. "What day did she infect you?"

"The day before yesterday."

The revelation meant Gilda had two days left if she proved to be like most other corrupted. Frost stepped closer to her and took her hand. She stiffened at first but then relaxed.

He moved to where he could stare down into her face. "We're gonna cure you. Whatever it takes. I made a promise. Remember?"

She smiled solemnly. "I'll hold you to it."

"Please do." He gave her hand a squeeze that she returned.

"I also want you to promise me something else." Gilda stared up into his eyes.

He met her gaze. Something resided in her green eyes. Something alien. Something dark. It slithered behind them like a living thing. Frost fought down a shiver.

"Promise you won't treat me like porcelain. No matter what happens." Gilda's eyes appeared normal once more. "I'm not easily broken. Act as you normally would."

Frost bit his bottom lip. Making such a promise was difficult, but since she asked, he could do little else but give in. He let out a breath. "I promise to be as normal as I can to you."

"I guess that's the best I can hope for." She smiled ruefully and gave his hand a playful tap.

Frost assumed it was her attempt at being normal. He understood how she felt, even if he didn't agree. "Let me grab a bite to eat. When Meritus gets back, we're gonna farm the two spells, level up, and head to the Crypts for the rest."

"No doubt." Gilda nodded once.

"Want me to bring you a plate?" He looked at her, his expression hopeful.

She shook her head. "No, I ate already."

"Alright." He allowed his fingers to linger as he released his grip.

Frost gave her a little smile, turned, took a breath, and strode over to the dead campfire where a pot contained several bits of meat. There was also a bowl of potatoes.

"What up, people." He nodded in the direction of the others.

Busy with their meals, they acknowledged him with nods or grumbles. He picked up a metal plate, heaped some food on it, returned to his spot near Gilda, took a seat, and ate. The food was still warm and had a sweet flavor.

"Frost, you ever seen a cow IRL?" Gilda was staring off at the sky.

He frowned at the odd question. "A cow? Like living, breathing cattle?" She nodded. "Nah, only in pictures. What made you ask that?" He chewed a bit of meat and swallowed.

"A game I was playing named Diablo. There was a boss, the Cow King. It was the funniest looking think ever. Looked just like a cow, hooves and all, but it stood like a human and wielded a great axe."

"Oh." He smiled. "That explains the nonsense you were mumbling on the way here then."

"Huh?" She faced him.

"You were talking about it during the flight. The Cow King… something about levels. Going mooooo." He chuckled. "I figured you musta been dreaming."

She covered her mouth to suppress a giggle. "I'm sorry. I must've sounded crazy."

"It's all good." Frost waved her off and continued to eat.

Meritus returned not long after. He passed Frost a few dozen empty flasks. "I also got you this from the Market." He was holding a skill shard and a Bless.

Frost groaned. "You didn't have to, homie."

"I know." Meritus reached his palm out.

Frost sighed. "You aren't gonna take no for an answer, are you?"

Meritus' reply was a smirk.

"By the time you're done, I'm gonna owe you my life. Thank you." Frost took the shard.

Aether Fusillade
Available at Level 20

Frost opened and closed his mouth. He recalled the list price for the skill. "I'm gonna pay you back, I swear."

"For that one? Oh, I know you are, homie." Meritus chuckled. "That bad boy put a dent in my credits. But it was worth it to stay ahead of the game. Just hurry up and get to twenty already."

"Deal." Frost gave him a pound. He Blessed the shard.

Meritus continued, "I also found a spot with the mobs we need to hunt. Scorpids and molewurms."

"Any idea of their levels?" Frost put the Blessed skill shard and the flasks in his inventory and bit off a chunk of the sweet, tough meat.

"Around twenty if I had to guess. My Bulwark tanked one of each while the Duelist and I killed them. It wasn't too hard. As a group, we'll mop the floor with 'em."

"Sounds good." Frost finished his meal and washed it down with water from his canteen. "Let's do this."

They climbed atop their mounts. Even Gilda, for whom Meritus had bought a black drake. Soon, they were flying over the copse toward the line of hills dotted with hardy vegetation. Beyond the hills was the aptly named Sands of Salanda, a sea of ochre dunes.

Meritus veered left. He took them to a hollow between the end of the hills and the first set of dunes. They landed on a slope amid scraggly brush.

He pointed down below. "The scorpids."

The creatures were similar to the ones Frost had seen near Lothal's east coast except these were the color of stone. They scuttled on eight legs, chitin-covered bodies either shifting sideways or back and forth. Some fought each other, using their one small and one over-sized claw to fend the opponent off while seeking to strike a blow with their barbed tails.

As with other creatures on Marang, the musculature was lacking. They weren't as defined. Frost knew they weren't elite.

"The molewurms are over there." Meritus pointed to the far left at a collection of broken pillars and ruins made from sandstone bricks.

The molewurms had serpentine heads, long bodies closely segmented like earthworms, scaled skin, and two arms on their upper bodies. They had no other appendages and slithered along or sometimes used their arms to propel themselves forward for extra speed.

Frost studied the creatures. "Gilda, what level are you?"

"Nineteen."

Frost's brows shot up. "Damn. That means you were nineteen even before I left Maelpith."

She shrugged. "A girl's gotta do what a girl's gotta do."

"Hmmm, nineteen." Frost stroked his aether ring while working out a strategy. "What other AOEs did you get besides Glacial Eruption?"

"Flame Vortex, Aether Pulse, and Flash Freeze. I especially like the Freeze. Not only does damage but it freezes anything it touches. I also picked up Elemental Snap, which increases my elemental damage by ten percent."

"Sweet." Frost smiled. "I hope you got that Elemental Ignition ready for when you level up. Debuffing enemies so they take twenty percent more elemental damage is amazing."

"No doubt." Gilda nodded. "I can't wait."

"Bet you can't." Frost grinned, glad to see her in better spirits. "Alright, here's the plan. Since we need exp—"

"Not this again." Ryne stomped his boot.

"Wanna let me finish?" Frost arched his brow.

"Fine. Take your time. But I know what's in line."

"As I was saying. Since we need exp, we'll split the group."

"Keeping me out of it," Ryne blurted. "I hate this shit." His green face darkened.

Frost let out a sigh. "Ryne, the molewurms are yours."

"What?" Wide-eyed, the bald-headed goblin stared at Frost.

"Although you won't be part of our group, you still get to kill the molewurms for the shard they hold, while we farm the scorpids."

"I could hug you. You tall purple thing you." Ryne did a little hop step.

"Just don't rub his horns." Dante chuckled.

"Hug me later." Frost smiled at the goblin's enthusiasm and Dante's quip. He eyed the others. "The scorpids are packed closer together and come in groups from what I see. Means we can use the same strat we had for the basilisks. With Gilda's AOEs, this should go pretty quickly.

"And since we gotta do this as fast as possible, I assume everyone has vials?" They nodded. "Good. Pop 'em when we engage."

Without further ado, Frost picked out the vials he would use, taking them from his inventory, and placing them in the pouches on his belt. Each was on a three-minute reuse timer.

Aether Power:

+25 to Aether effects

Protection:

+500 armor

Agility:

+ 10 Agility

Colossus:

+ 10 Strength

Elements:

+25 to Elemental Power

Elemental Resistance:

+25 resistance to all elements

Fortification:

+50 Health

While Ryne flew off toward the ruins with the molewurms, Frost, Gilda, Dante, Saba, and Meritus dismounted and scrambled down the slope to the sands. Any sign of coolness had long since vanished, burned off by the blazing coin of a sun. With sweat beading his brow, Frost drank his vials. The others followed his lead.

Scepter hanging at his belt, Meritus summoned his three Servitors. The gargant and two yurids appeared. He also prepped Mikander's Tears and Blood. The five blue motes of Tears suspended over his left fingertips, the red of Blood over his right.

"Dante, set up by those rocks between us and the mobs." Frost pointed to the area in question. "Meritus, send your Bulwark with him." He turned to Gilda to explain. "Saba and I are gonna pull a bunch of mobs; Dante and the Bulwark are gonna pull aggro off us and tank 'em there. Once they have good threat, we AOE the mobs down. Use Glacial Eruption as a slow also. And Flash Freeze. Rinse, wash, and repeat."

"Got it." Gilda plucked her silver chakrams from her belt loop. She infused them with aether, causing one to glow blue, and the other red.

"Move into range of the tanks whenever you're ready, Gilda. We'll take our spots based off your position." Frost double-checked his ammo while waiting for Gilda.

She strode forward about twenty feet. He, Saba, and Meritus followed.

"Saba, drop traps in front the tanks to help with CC. And keep putting 'em down between pulls."

"Gotcha." Saba buffed the group with Aura of the Pack, the ability making Frost feel as if he could run like the wind. She trotted off to where the tanks had set up.

"I missed this." A smile brightened Gilda's discolored face. She made a motion with her hand as if ushering someone to stand. An Ice Stalagmite grew from the ground ahead of the tanks.

Saba returned to them. "All set."

"I got the left." Frost aimed The Stunner at a group of scorpids. "Ready?" When Saba nodded, Frost caressed the cannon's trigger. "Go."

He fired off a Concussion Blast and then Divergence into the scorpid group. Explosions rocked the scorpids, the sound reverberating in the still air. The creatures let out hissing sounds and charged toward them. Saba's arrows struck mobs to the right with the same effect. Frost picked out a few extras and hit them with Aether Shots.

"Hold off." Frost stopped firing. "Wait for the tanks to pick 'em up."

Perhaps fifteen scorpids charged them, tails swiping back and forth ominously. Their claws clacked open and closed. In his head, Frost counted down the distance.

At least ten of the creatures leaped high into the air. They abruptly changed direction and hurtled toward the ground, claws first. Frost winced, expecting them to slam into the sand, but the scorpids dived *into* the sand, leaving holes in their wakes.

"They didn't do *that* before," Meritus exclaimed.

Brow furrowed, Frost tried to rely on Echolocation, but it only isolated that which he could already see. Then he noticed the anomaly. "The sand," he shouted. "Watch for the slight moving humps in the sand. Soul Scream when they get close."

Subtle rises zipped across the sand toward the group.

Dante twirled his axe. His skin blushed to bright scarlet. He Sentinel Shouted, the sound high-pitched. He followed the skill with the deeper bellow of Soul Scream when the humps were within fifteen feet. The sounds clashed, echoing.

Immediately, the scorpids crashed up through the sand. Their claws snapped and thrust. Dante parried some blows while absorbing others. Axe held out, he spun in circle, aether flowing from the axe's edge in Cyclonic Strike. The moment he stopped, a wider swath of aether appeared, bright white against the ochre sand. The new skill, Scythe.

Hissing, the scorpids became a frenetic mass. Frost delayed the order for a full attack. The first scorpids had lagged behind. Not caught by the taunt of Dante's Soul Scream, they were still aggroed on Frost and Saba.

They hit Saba's Traps. Lightning arced, sizzling across the ground. Chains appeared from the air, snagging the scorpids. Gilda's Stalagmite exploded in Glacial Eruption, coating the scorpids in ice and slowing them additionally.

"I got 'em," Meritus said as if he'd read Frost's mind.

The black-furred gargant Bulwark unleashed a Soul Scream. Within seconds, all the scorpids were attacking the Bulwark.

Charging Homer, Frost aimed, a flash letting him know when he'd locked on. A tap of the trigger and he'd moved on to the next. Within the four-second-charge window he had eight individual targets.

"Let 'em have it." Frost launched Homer. Eight missile-shaped blasts of aether streaked away. A second later, he fired a Concussion Blast. He followed it with Divergence's five-shot spread then bursts of Korbitanium Projectiles.

Saba's arrows blurred into targets. Fire Arrow. Aether Arrow. Ice Arrow.

Gilda flicked up the hand holding the red chakram. A huge vortex of flame billowed around the scorpids and tanks. Partially hiding them from view, the superheated whirlwind swirled one way and spun the other, fire licking out.

In the next instant, she bought her chakrams together. Their glows caressed each other, building brighter and brighter, changing hues to a purplish tint. She drew her hands back, ripping the chakrams away from each other, and then swept the weapons forward. All in one motion.

199

A massive purple ball shot from between the chakrams, crackling and glowing with an electric energy. The ball was the width and height of two men. The Aether Pulse spun end over end, streaked across the distance, and struck among the scorpids, a coruscating purple circle exploding outward with a hum that rose in pitch before it faded.

All of the creatures fell dead. Residual energy crackled around the carcasses.

Large motes of aether shot into the air. They swirled for a moment. In the next second, they split apart and zipped into each group member.

Frost basked in the exp and the Aether Absorption. And marveled at Gilda's power. He'd also gained a point in aether, bringing it to fifty-nine.

"Check for drops and make another pull." A smile appeared on Gilda's face. For a moment she looked like herself.

With a shake of his head and a chuckle, Frost complied. He searched each corpse as fast as he could. He'd almost given up hope of finding anything, when a shard popped up on one of the last few carcasses. "I got one!"

His joy fled in the next instant. His chest sagged. It wasn't a skill-effect shard. "Forget it. It's just a regular Suppression."

"At least we know they drop that particular skill," Meritus said.

"I guess." Frost let out a breath.

Following the same strategy, they ground for hours. Gilda also added Flash Freeze into her rotation whenever the mobs appeared to be too much for the tanks to handle. With a flick of her hand, a blue-white wave swept across the ground. When it struck, it froze everything but their allies within fifty feet.

But the scorpids changed upon every respawn, each time becoming fewer in number, the majority of them diving under the sand and remaining there, not even the hump giving them away. The larger scorpids were the only ones bold or stupid enough to attack.

In the midst of a pull, Gilda let out a whimper and collapsed to the ground. Frost made to rush to her side.

"I got her." Meritus flung the colored balls and streams of several spells in Gilda's direction. "Kill off these mobs."

Without a thought, Frost activated Stand and Deliver. Saba followed his lead with her Arrow Battery. In seconds, the scorpids were dead. Even as the last mobs fell, Frost ran to Gilda's side, fearful of her condition.

Her eyes were closed. She grimaced in obvious pain. Gray splotches covered most of the exposed portions of her body now, some of them with blackness around the edges like mold. Her chest heaved with each ragged breath. The white aura of Purifying Touch, Suppression's yellow, Ameliorate's blue, and Rejuvenate's green commingled around her.

In slow increments her breathing normalized, her chest rising and falling. Her eyes fluttered open. She smiled weakly.

Tightness eased from Frost's chest. He wanted to ask her if she was okay but knew it would be a stupid question. Instead, he helped her to her feet.

"Thanks." She dipped her head to Meritus and Frost. "Now, let's get back to this grind."

"No prob." Frost knew it was her way of battling the sickness. A show of courage. Even if he hadn't promised, he would have still refused to take the moment from her.

"Gotta check for drops." He indicated the carcasses around Dante.

It was then that he noticed he'd reached level seventeen. The increase in strength to forty-two saw him gain an additional one percent in damage reduction, bringing it to six percent. It also added an extra point in vitality, which was now at fifty-eight. Agility was forty-eight, and his aether rose to sixty-four.

He and Dante checked the dead. Not a single empowered spell had dropped. A dozen normal Suppression shards were all they had to show for the grind.

CHAPTER 23

Morning had dragged into afternoon, the sun's swelter beating down on Frost and his group when Frost reached level eighteen. His aether increased to seventy after he'd gained another two points from skill use before leveling up. The constant action, the promise, and Gilda's steady work rate kept Frost from asking after her well-being. But he did keep an eye on her whenever she wasn't looking.

They took a break to eat, drink, and replenish aether. Meritus cast another round of Purifying Touch, Suppression, Ameliorate, and Rejuvenate on Gilda to ward off her debilitation. While she was recovering, Frost absorbed his Aether Barrage skill shard.

Skill Acquired

Aether Barrage:
Cast time: 2 seconds
Recharge: 20 seconds
Consumes: Aether
Available shard slots: 4
Effect: Rapidly fire eight Aether Shots. Can be activated at the start of Stand and Deliver to instantly increase the cyclic rate to maximum. Gain 1.5 percent Aether for each successful hit.

When Frost glanced up from examining his skills, Ryne was riding toward them.

The goblin dismounted next to the group, his expression one of disgust. "I have killed thousands of molewurms, and all I have gotten are two dozen normal Rejuvenate shards. This should not be so hard."

"Been the same here." Frost took a stock of his inventory. He had twenty-six Suppression shards.

Saba stopped chewing on her piece of fruit. "Seems as if Nakada lied to you." Her gaze shifted to Meritus.

"Could be," Meritus acknowledged. "Or maybe he didn't know any better."

"We could keep farming. It might just be an extremely rare drop." Crimson-skinned Dante was sitting cross-legged, his axe beside him.

"Or we can hunt down Setnana and try to steal Benediction." Gilda was standing, staring toward the west. "She's gone to the Crypts to try to find her son."

"What did you just say?" Frost frowned as he watched her.

Gilda's gray splotches were more prominent than at any other time. "Setnana is going to the Crypts to find her son."

"I thought he was dead." Meritus' attention was also on Gilda.

"Same here." Frost stood and strode in front of her.

Gilda's eyes were unfocused, as if she didn't see Frost. The alien thing was there again, a darkness slithering behind the green of her pupils.

A chill ran through Frost despite the day's heat. "Gilda?"

She was still looking through him.

"Gilda."

He raised his voice. "GILDA!"

Her eyes focused on him. "Yes." She gave a little shake of her head. "Sorry. It's just that I feel a need to head west. It's like something's drawing me in that direction. And I think it's the Crypts or something in them."

"Maybe we should go see what it is." Frost licked his lips as the alien thing faded, her eyes returning to bright green. "But that stuff about Setnana and her son. What made you say it?"

"Oh. It was something I just remembered. Her bodyguard, Ihuet, showed up when she was torturing me. He said her son had been found at the Forsaken Crypts. He mentioned that draconids and corrupted were drawn to the place. She said she'd head there once she got Benediction."

"Why would she claim he's dead, then?" Frost glanced from Gilda to the others.

"Could've just been an excuse to hunt you down or get others involved." Meritus shrugged.

"That wouldn't've been necessary," Frost surmised. "She had enough reason with our connection to Blue Sky and the attack on Khafra the Mad."

"Facts." Meritus nodded.

"Regardless," Dante said. "It sounds like we got a chance to take back the zhua and the skills."

"The zhua, maybe." Gilda was focused on the west again. "But not the skill-effect shards. They were consumed by some grand kora mystic Setnana had with her before you guys showed up. A Vindicator named Dita."

"Damn it." Frost pounded his palm with his fist.

"Setnana had a Vindicator down there? We fought a Vindicator?" Saba fixed Gilda with a sullen stare.

"Most likely." Gilda shrugged. "But from what I remember she wasn't all that strong and she was a little squeamish."

"Neither of which matters." Saba's tail swished. "What matters is that we're now likely to have Vindicators after us, who are several times worse than the Battleguards that hunted us previously."

"I'm not convinced the Vindicators have been sent after us as yet." Frost understood Saba's concerns, and typically he would be worried also. But this was not typical. "If the Vindicator was helping spread the Gray Death, I doubt he's gonna be reporting to his superiors."

"We better hope that's the case." Saba stomped a hoof.

"I'm more concerned by the fact the Vindicator used the skill-effect shards." Frost wracked his brain for a solution. "It means our best bet is to continue farming and hope for better luck." Frost opened his mouth to speak again and stopped, brows drawing together. "Unless."

"Unless what?" Saba asked.

"I'm such a fool." Frost shook his head in exasperation.

"What makes you say that, dawg?" Meritus regarded Frost with a furrowed brow.

Frost's thoughts raced. "I been so caught up in trying to save Gilda, what they did to her, and losing Benediction, that I haven't been thinking straight. I completely forgot you told me there's another way to get empowered skills."

204

"Using a hierkaneer to craft them," Frost added in response to Meritus' confused look. "In fact, I don't think they drop at all. I bet the one from Grenok came from a chest. Even the ones we found were in chests in the emperor's room. Not on the emperor himself. I'd be willing to bet the skill-effect shards for empowerment don't drop either. Not naturally."

"Damn, that conversation slipped my mind." Meritus shook his head. "And I stored the info from the books in the Halls of Illumination, but hadn't gotten around to checking it after I got word from Naka Masami. One sec." Meritus' brows drew together. The moment stretched. "I feel bad now." Meritus sighed. His mouth downturned. "I could've saved us some time. Empowered skills work similar to regular item and skill boosts, where artificers imbue an effect into an aether-infused gem, creating a shard. But to craft *empowered* shards, you need high quality gems as well as twenty normal skill-shards of the skill-effect you want to augment."

"We have the shards." Frost's spirit soared.

"And we have the infused gems." Meritus produced a bag from his inventory. "I saved a bunch from the mines. Planned to sell them on the Market."

Meritus reached into the bag and came away with gemstones. They glinted in the sun. There were tourmalines, garnets, topazes, aquamarines, peridots, opals, citrines, and amethysts.

The gemstones all had one thing in common. Aether. Aether glowed within them.

Dante whistled. "Damn, we could be rich if we sold these."

"But not rich enough to afford a hierkaneer," Meritus said. "And we'd have to wait for them to sell."

A glimmer of hope rose within Frost. "All that's left is a Genesis Engine, a hierkaneer, and the rest of the mats to craft a Benediction. We don't need to bother with finding Setnana at all."

"It also means you must reach level twenty like the rest of us," Saba said. "Can't get into the Crypts before then."

"We *could* continue to grind these mobs." Dante gestured to the new spawns. "Exp was pretty good."

Frost took in Gilda's skin. More splotches stained it. Her face was haggard.

"Staying here is definitely safer." Saba pawed the ground. "Especially for two eradae. The Forsaken Crypts *are* in Puria, deep in the Kanpuri Vale. If our experience with Umesh Madara proved one thing, it's that slavery and poaching erada horns is alive and well in the grand kora dominion."

Frost knew of the dangers involved. "Safer but most likely not faster than if we completed quests near the Crypts. I really don't care about the risk. Gilda's got a day and a half if she's like all the others." He didn't want to point out the dire issue, but it needed to be said.

"Why not let me take a group into the Crypts?" Ryne stared up at them, hope shining in his round eyes. "At my level we could clear it easily."

"Not really." Frost shook his head, remembering Zhi Yin's words about the Crypts. "The dungeon scales in difficulty based on the highest person's level when the group enters. So you'd all be facing level thirty-two mobs. And there's no loot from mobs or chests for people above level twenty-five."

Frost's Comm Orb dinged. "One sec. It's Adesh Hamada."

Frost listened to the message. When it finished, he had a quest named **Meet the Hierkaneer** in **The Cure** line.

"Well, that just gave me more reason to take advantage of the quests near the Crypts to level faster. And to beat the dungeon.

"Adesh said there's a Genesis Engine inside. Might be bullshit, but considering there was one in the Sanctum, and the dev made sure to give us a lil info about them before we came in-game, there's a good chance it's true. He's already dispatched a hierkaneer to the Crypts.

"The bigger issue is that the Genesis Engine area will be an Open-PVP zone even if the rest of the dungeon isn't. Which means we gotta get to it first. He also confirmed what Gilda overheard. The Gray Death is rampant in western Puria. Corrupted and void beasts are converging on the Crypts daily."

Saba shook her head and blew out a long, slow breath. "That means an army of Vindicators is probably on its way, if it's not there already. I want no part of them. Not right now."

"A Vindicator army was my first fear also," Frost said. "But Adesh claimed the Coalition has only dispatched a couple of them to help in Apur. The brunt of them went to the Front to face an army of draconids and void beasts led by several draconid generals and two lords."

"Damn." Dante wore a dreamy expression. "That makes me want max level so badly."

"Same here." Frost imagined how powerful he would be then. How strong Gilda would be. The sheer fun he would have completing endgame content with her by his side. The thought of those last two not happening tempered his dream. "But right now, we're gonna take advantage of all this chaos to save Gilda." Frost smiled in her direction.

Everyone agreed. They climbed atop their mounts. From his map, Frost picked out Obuchi, the nearest gurash city with a simurgh, deeper in western Lothal on the other side of the Sands. A few simurgh Velocity Surges would see them in Apur before the end of the day. With joyful cries, the flyers took to the air. Afternoon bled into evening as they flew, the day's heat abating, the sun's orange hues limning heaven's fluff.

Even before Obuchi appeared upon the horizon, Frost noted scarves of smoke twisting in the distance. Meritus pointed. Frost nodded to let his friend know he had seen them.

The scarves grew more numerous, as did orange blooms at ground level. Booms followed. Low thunder like a grumbling belly. Black clouds swarmed this way and that in the sky between the smoke, various colored lights flashing among them. Frost knew what he was witnessing.

A battle. Magic. Aerial combat. All on a massive scale.

Dante's voice in group chat cut through Frost's thoughts. "Hey, I contacted one of my friends when I saw the smoke. Obuchi is under attack. Part of a Lothal civil war.

"General Asamar has staked a claim to become the next gurash Kalarch. Redthorn armies led by him and Umesh Madara have taken several western cities. Goddamned bastards."

"Shit." Frost scowled. "Maybe, we can still sneak into one to get a simurgh."

"Not likely, bro," Dante said.

"Gotta be some other place we could grab one." Frost grimaced. It felt like the world was conspiring against their quest to save Gilda. "We need all the time we can get."

"Sorry, bro, but there isn't." Melancholy eased from Dante's voice. "My starting zone wasn't far from here. I know this area well."

Frost sighed, the need to save Gilda a weight on his chest. "What options we got?"

Dante took a moment before he replied, "Head north toward the Ouroboros Mountains to skirt the fight and fly all night if we have to."

Frost traced the route and was taken aback. "Not only does that take us farther away, but we'd also be flying toward some of the most heavily guarded grand kora outposts."

"I don't see any other way, bro. Not if we're to reach the Crypts by tomorrow morning."

Frost squeezed his eyes tight. That would give them a day at most to cure Gilda. A day versus the chance of being caught up in the civil war. He opened his eyes and let out a slow breath. "Northwest, it is."

CHAPTER 24

"We have arrived, my nomarch." Ihuet's voice woke Setnana. She opened her eyes to the sun's glare and Ihuet's back, his cloak fluttering in the howling wind. Falling asleep while on her simurgh was a testament to her exhaustion despite a determination to remain awake on the flight to the Kanpuri Vale. Tilting her neck from side to side, she worked out the stiffness of being in an awkward position for an extended period of time. She took stock of her surroundings.

A savanna stretched beneath her, sandy roads carving paths through its grassy plains and into the heart of the lush Kanpuri jungle. A few miles before the trees was the Coalition blockade: a long line of tents, banners, and soldiers. Their purpose wasn't to keep anyone or anything out, but to keep corrupted trapped in the vale. Not that it appeared as if any of the corrupted wanted to escape.

She did not care. None of the blockade's rules applied to her. Not when it came to saving Perihy.

Setnana's gaze was drawn to an unnatural gathering of dark clouds above Apur, the stone city that sprawled from one of the Indrati River's massive bends. Thunderless lightning radiated within those clouds. Reminiscent of a voidstorm but for the missing vortex, the sight sent a chill through her.

Her attention shifted to Apur itself. Jutting above the jungle's canopy was the Temple of Jerad's infamous towers. She focused on the pyramid at the city's center. The Forsaken Crypts. It was above the Crypts where the clouds were thickest, boiling with violent radiance.

"Do they still have Perihy cornered?" Setnana imagined her son, teeth bared and bloody.

"Yes. At the cost of over a dozen lives," Ihuet answered. "They say trapping him was sheer luck."

"Good. Fly straight to their location in Apur."

"Major Neferna has advised us not to do so," Ihuet said in his too calm tone.

Setnana scowled at the Blackguard's back. "I did not do as I have done, come this far, to balk, to be denied, or defied."

"My nomarch, I would expect no less of you. But we lost over half the Sky Swords to the void beasts that own the skies above Apur. What's left of Major Neferna's forces are on foot, guarding the boy."

"Even more reason for us to get there as fast as possible." She clenched her fists.

"And if we get shot down and Dita dies, then the cure dies with her. All your sacrifices would have been for nothing."

"Ihuet is right," Khafra added from his seat behind her.

Her shoulders drooped at the truth of their words. Not only were the four of them vulnerable riding a simurgh, but also if the void beasts were numerous enough to wreak havoc on a trained war company like the Sky Swords, then she, Ihuet, Khafra, and Dita stood little chance.

"I have arranged for mounts at the jungle." Ihuet began their descent. "Do not fret, my nomarch. Your son will soon be with you."

Setnana smiled. "Thank you, Ihuet."

******

Over an hour later, she, Ihuet, Khafra, and Dita entered Apur and met two of Major Neferna's scouts. The scouts led them northeast along one of the central avenues, away from the Crypts, and toward the barracks where Major Neferna had trapped Perihy. During the ride they encountered and killed the occasional void beast or corrupted, far from the glut of monsters Setnana had expected.

On one occasion there came a cacophony of roars and screeches, soon followed by the thunder of stampeding feet. But it was from the opposite direction, toward the Crypts and beyond. She was glad for such good fortune. Her sole desire was to cure her son.

Soon, they arrived at the barracks, a building more similar to a fort than she would have anticipated. Sky Swords manned a few of the battlements. Others guarded a large main entrance that featured a portcullis. Her stomach fluttered as she strode into a corridor which opened onto a flagstoned courtyard.

Major Neferna was there to greet them. "Nomarch Setnana." The major bowed to her patron then turned to Dita and offered a slight dip of her head. "Vindicator. I'm glad you arrived safely."

"Thank you for all you have done, Major. I will not forget." Setnana smiled curtly even as she tried to control her emotions. "Is my son secured?"

"I wouldn't say secured." Major Neferna cleared her throat, no doubt nervous over Setnana's possible reaction to any perceived incompetence. "We managed to trap him in a workshop of some kind. He'd fled into this building after fighting and killing over a dozen grand korae outside. A Concealed tracker followed Perihy to the room in question. There, they found him holding several of these."

She held out her hand. A purple pear-shaped jewel sat in her palm. Black and silver energy coiled within it.

"A void shard?" Setnana frowned.

The shard disappeared from Neferna's hand. "They had to be the reason the grand korae were still here despite the evacuation. Either to protect the shards or to retrieve them."

Setnana nodded in agreement. Void shards were an extremely rare and powerful commodity, prized by every armor or weaponsmith. Only hierkaneers could craft them in Genesis Engines.

Neferna continued, "Seeing that the room had no windows and a near impregnable door, we locked Perihy in."

"Smart. Now, if you will, show me to my son." Setnana gestured for the major to lead.

Major Neferna took them through a heavy oak door into a long hall, their footsteps echoing. Various weapons hung from the walls. A statue stood midway down the hall, depicting a robed grand kora warrior bearing dual swords. Amalan Khatri, the Celestial Slayer, a sign read, the greatest blademaster Mikander has ever seen.

Several turns and corridors later, the major stopped before a metal door, its surface dented in several places and bulging outward. She turned to them and put her index finger to her lips.

Something slammed into the door. The frame shook. Setnana started. Dust drifted down from the thick stone walls.

An animal roar reverberated from the room. The thing slammed into the door again.

No. Not a thing. My Perihy.

Heart fluttering at being so close to her son again, Setnana stepped up to the door and placed her palm upon its surface. "Perihy, my sweet boy. Mother is here."

From behind the door came a snuffling noise. A few grunts. Then a burst of gibberish with more similarities to growls and snarls than any language.

"That's right, my sweet. Mother is here for you. To save you. To take you back home. We can visit the orchards, pick some plums or mangoes. I will have the cook bake you a mango cake. We can even play a game of shevla. You would love that, wouldn't you?"

Slam. Boom. A bellow. And then a repeated pounding, the door denting with each blow, dust falling from the bricks, from around the edges of the door itself.

But Setnana was unmoved. She babbled lovingly, reliving precious moments spent with her Perihy. Sweet memories. His birth. His first step. First words. Perihy's love for learning spells. His ear for music and his favorite song, A Symphony of Night. His habit of playing with the drakes.

The pounding stopped. Footsteps drifted away from the door.

Setnana turned to Dita. "It is time." Her gaze shifted to Khafra and Ihuet. "Khafra, you will open the door, charge in, and prevent him from leaving. Use your Diamond Hide for protection.

"Once we enter, I will use Mirage as a distraction. Ihuet, be ready with Shields or Barriers. But I will be the one to hold him still while Dita works. Neferna, close the door behind us." Setnana retreated from the door.

"Be warned," Major Neferna said, "he has a tendency to Conceal."

Khafra got into position, a hand on the metal handle, ready to turn and push the door in. He held up his other hand. Diamond Hide's gemlike surface slid over his skin. He pushed the door and darted inside.

Even as they scrambled after Khafra, Setnana summoned a Mirage of the group. Five copies of them appeared and spread out in the room.

Perihy was across the other side of the workshop, facing the door. Setnana gasped. This was not the Perihy who had fled that night. He was bigger, muscles more developed.

Snarling, Perihy darted toward them, covering the distance in a blur of metallic gray, green, and blue. He'd almost smashed into the real Khafra when Ihuet's Aether Barrier appeared around the dementer.

Before Perihy hit the Barrier, Setnana stopped her son cold with Immobilize, snapping its black chains around his legs and arms. Only to be surprised by his strength as he fought against the ability. Forehead knitted, Setnana poured more power into Immobilize, thickening the chains.

Roaring, Perihy pitched onto his side. His face was a mask of hate and rage, his once bright golden eyes dark beads. His green and blue veins bulged. Slobber flew from his jaws. He rolled and bucked, but there was no escape.

Vindicator Dita strode forward. Benediction glowed. Threads of empowered spells formed, swirling into the golden ball. Sanctification flew from the zhua and into Perihy.

Setnana held her breath. Her heart became as thunder. She was ready to explode with joy, as in her mind's eye, the network of green and blue veins disappeared. The gray metallic skin peeled away, revealing deep chocolate. His disfigured face transformed to the perfect beauty she knew. Dark horns burst through the lumps on his forehead, curling up and back.

He was Perihy again. Unique. Gorgeous. Majestic.

Little of that occurred.

His skin lost its metallic luster, becoming a shade darker than its original color. The veins faded. Horns *did* burst through the two lumps, but they were no longer than an index finger.

Setnana's heart broke. "Nooooo!" Setnana screamed. "Noooooo! Perihyyyyyy! I want my Perihyyyy!" She collapsed to her knees, her spell forgotten. She hung her head, tears blurring her vision.

"Mother?"

Her head snapped up at the voice. The deep baritone. The voice everyone said belonged to a boy who would grow to become a great erada man.

Heart fluttering again, Setnana wiped at her eyes. And gasped.

Perihy was crawling to her. His skin was more ebony than chocolate. The colored veins were gone. His horns were stubs. But his face had a semblance of its old self, even if it were a bit misshapen. His eyes were golden again.

At that moment, she cared not how he looked. This was her son. Perihy. He was still beautiful. He would always be beautiful.

Unbidden tears fell again. But this time, they *were* tears of joy. When she and Perihy fell into each other's embrace, nothing else mattered.

Saving Perihy

Objective Complete.

Her Comm Orb dinged.

The message was from Bakui Assam, voice seething with rage as he demanded that she return to Modra's Keep at once. She did not care. This moment belonged to her. Her and Perihy.

CHAPTER 25

Skirting major cities and signs of battle, Frost's group flew northwest until Puria's snow-capped Ouroboros Mountains rose in the distance to their far right. They traveled parallel to the range. Frost continually scanned the air for any signs of trouble. Every so often he checked on Gilda.

When a swarm of dark specks approached from the direction of the Ouroboros, Frost's breath caught in his throat. The specks grew, and soon enough, their wings became apparent. His chest tightened.

Worry and dread fled when he saw the mounts were kirins, the riders gurashi, flying in a spear formation. The kirin company passed by, cloaks rippling with the large-bladed Crossed Quaker insignia of Lothal's military.

On another occasion the group encountered an erada drake formation, the flyers dressed in Azureguard blue, Khertahka's Dual Katars on display. Puria's drake companies and patrols were conspicuously absent. Thankfully so.

The group veered directly west soon after, headed across the southern edge of Puria. Far to their left, in what would be Northern Lothal, more and more smoke bloomed in different locations, adding to the deepening dusk. Each bloom was accompanied by ruddy glows, fitful light flashes, and angry rumbles.

Frost welcomed the moment when night strangled the day with its black cloak. Under its cover, they would stay hidden from searching eyes and enemies. Military units on the way to battle carried glimmerwands to prevent the occurrence of nighttime collisions and thus could be easily avoided. Frost stretched his Echolocation as far as he could to discern flyers who might be traveling in secret and kept watch for any time something blotted out the stars.

They flew all night, the lights of Purian cities and towns fewer than Frost would have expected. While they had not intended to stop to rest, lapses in Gilda's condition forced their hand. On those occasions, Frost chose remote areas for fear of the hate between eradae and grand korae. Upon landing, Meritus would renew his spells to stave off Gilda's worsening plague. Frost used such times to practice Aether Barrage, the two-second-charge skill firing off eight Aether Shots like a machine gun.

As the first pale sliver of dawn pricked a cloud-filled sky, they finally arrived at the Kanpuri Vale, which marked the border of the Osian nome. Mist like dirty milk spilled across the grassland and hovered above the jungle that spread all the way to Puria's western coast. According to the map, the city of Apur lay a few miles ahead. If Frost had to guess, the city was located where the clouds and mist formed a thick soup. Lightning radiated within the gray quilt in fitful spurts.

Other flyers dotted the sky, but Frost could not discern their identities. The cries and calls of various beasts echoed. Frowning, he glanced behind him. The sky was mostly clear in the east. A golden glow limned the horizon.

Wary of hostile grand korae, they slowed their approach. But their caution proved unnecessary as they encountered many other drake-flying eradae headed in the same direction.

There were also leonine gurashi on kirins, humans on owl-faced zephyrs, furry gargants riding equally massive many-tailed foxes, and yurids who required no mounts, their leathery or feathered wings equal to the task. The flyers spread far and wide. On the ground below, even more people were converging toward Apur atop various mounts.

When Frost took a moment to think, he realized the abundance of player activity made sense. The Crypts were the focus in this phase of the alpha test. He also wondered if there were others in search of mats to craft Benediction and empowered spells. It was a distinct possibility with more players having cleared the Sanctum.

The sun's warmth grew, burning away the mist, and revealing what had been hidden. Frost frowned at activity up ahead, at a gathering of tents. A hiss escaped his lips.

Most flyers were descending toward camps set up in the savanna before the looming jungle greenery. Camps filled with soldiers in green and yellow. Camps with flags fluttering in the wind. Flags bearing a mountain split by a river: The Coalition's Mountain and the Aetherstream.

A drake's screech pierced the cacophony of the other animal calls. A zephyr's scream followed. As did a kirin's hyoo. Armored for war, three flyers speared through the clouds above the area. Atop the back of each sat a warrior wearing intricate silver armor filigreed with gold and green.

Vindicators.

The Vindicators descended until they were above the tree line. There, they took up positions, the zephyr hovering on moth-like diaphanous wings, while the kirin left electrical streaks wherever it went, and the drake flew in lazy circles.

A female voice boomed. "To all approaching the Kanpuri Vale, and even more so to those heading to Apur, Guntur, or Chunar, I am Lieutenant Gillianna Nona of the Vindicators, commander here at the blockade. The Gray Death infection is rampant in this area. There is a very high chance of becoming corrupted beyond this point.

"We have warded off the zone against entry. If you are not corrupted, you must first report to the camps for protection runes. Any uncorrupted who try to pass without runes will be shot down or burnt to a crisp by our wards beyond this point.

"If you are corrupted, you require nothing special to travel beyond this point, nor will passage be denied, but you must still report. Do not fear. We will not destroy you. If you decide not to cross, we will have you escorted to the Dagoda Front. Those are your only two choices of living if you are corrupted.

"If you are not corrupted and choose to brave the area in hopes of treasures, or to help the Coalition find a cure, you do so at your own risk. Those who help find the things we need for a cure will be greatly rewarded."

No sooner had Vindicator Nona said the words than quests popped into IM. Again, they were a part of **The Cure** chain. The quests were **The Forsaken Crypts** and **Help The Coalition Find A Cure.**

"If you are corrupted, do not attempt to return after you pass through. The wards will reject you. Trying to cross them to come back will result in death. Only the clean can return.

"Corrupted will be stranded on the other side until we cleanse the area. Or you will die should the Grendesh Conclave decide incineration is better than risking further spread of the Gray Death.

"This is your last chance to turn away. If you choose to carry on, then may the Divines have mercy on your souls."

"Damn," Dante said over group chat, "she just made that sound so epic."

"Your epic sounds like my awful," Saba retorted.

"Either way, we're going in." Frost directed his mount toward the nearest camp. "Everyone, hoods up until we cross." Considering the many people with their hoods on, he doubted the group would draw attention.

His Comm Orb dinged as he landed. Adesh Hamada left word that Blue Sky's hierkaneer was already Concealed outside the Crypts. The rest was up to Frost.

They joined one of the many lines of players approaching Coalition soldiers who were passing out runes. Player conversation and the snorts and calls of mounts abounded around them. On either side of the lines, merchants haggled everything from weapons to armor to consumables.

Meritus and Saba bought more potions, extracts, and vials off an alchemist than Frost thought they would need. But he didn't blame them. Better to be safe than sorry. The two shared the consumables with the group.

Frost noted the majority of the soldiers were grand korae, the color of the women ranging from yellow to many shades of white, while the men were turquoise, lavender, and even pink. Some shot the eradae scathing looks while others acted as if their cousins did not exist.

"Frost," Dante hissed. "There's a bunch of WaR members two lines over."

Frost matched his timbre. "Keep an eye on them. With the crowds and our changes, I doubt they'll recognize us."

"I hope you're right," Saba said. "We can't afford to fight them and whatever is waiting for us in the vale."

Before Frost could respond, they'd reached the head of the line. A grand kora soldier with a captain's double stripes on his sleeves scowled at Frost and Gilda then nodded to a gurash subordinate.

The lion-faced, brown-skinned gurash, a man who looked as if half his face had melted at some point, stepped forward and passed them silver discs inlaid with inscriptions. "Secure these runes. Lose them and you're dead."

"Understood." Frost slipped his into one of the pouches on his belt.

"Hey, friend." The soldier nodded in Dante's direction. The man's mane was unkempt atop his head but fell in a long braid down his back. He snatched a nervous glance back at his captain and lowered his voice. "My name's Yoshino. Can I beg a favor?"

"Sure thing, Yoshino. And you can call me Chaotix."

"Thank you, Chaotix." Yoshino heaved a slow, relieved breath. "My brother allowed his emotions to get the better of him and led the last company sent to evacuate Apur. All for a woman he loves. He left before I'd returned, before…" He swallowed. "Before I could warn him of what's waiting out there."

"What's his name?" Dante arched his brow. "And what exactly were you going to warn him about?"

Frost's eyes narrowed. Something had frightened this hardened Coalition soldier. He could see it in Yoshino's furtive glances, the dark rings under his eyes, the way he constantly swallowed.

"His name's Sergeant Kazawa." Yoshino paused before continuing. "He's a bit taller than me, green like the forest with a matching mane down to his knees."

"And the warning?" Dante leaned his axe on his shoulder.

"There're… there're monsters taking the surviving townsfolk. Void beasts." The gurash's lips trembled. "Scores of them. They wiped out most of our company. My brother won't fare any better. Please find him and his company. Tell them… tell *him* that she isn't worth it. Tell him to get to hell out of there. To get to this side of the blockade until more Vindicators can come."

"We will," Frost said even before Dante could answer.

219

Yoshino visibly relaxed. "Thank you so much."

IM revealed a new quest. **Find The Missing Rescuers.**

Saba climbed off her mount, her expression one of relief to be on her feet again. Frost smiled. Saba stroked the drake's head. "Yoshino, since we're doing you a favor, I need you to do one for me."

"Certainly."

"Take care of her until I return." Saba held out her reins to the soldier.

"It will be my pleasure." Yoshino took the reins.

Frost glanced sideways at Saba. "You sure it wouldn't be better to have a flying mount just in case?"

"Positive." Saba nodded firmly. "We're close to the Crypts. I'm as fast or faster than anything out here. And since we might be fighting, I trust myself more on the ground than I ever could in the air."

"Fair enough." Anxious to be on his way, Frost turned to Yoshino. "You got any idea where we should begin searching?"

Yoshino nodded. "One of my brother's scouts got hurt and managed to return. He said they were in the forest near the south gate."

"Good enough." Frost turned to the others. "We don't have time to waste, so let's get to it. I still need two levels." Frost kicked the bolsters and set his drake off at a run.

Up ahead, dozens of groups had already entered the jungle. Some flew above the trees. They were now in a race to the Genesis Engine.

CHAPTER 26

They picked their way through the jungle, their breathing and their mounts' footfalls loud to Frost's ears. Despite the lush surroundings, there were no signs of wildlife. No critters. Predators. No animal calls. No birds twittering. Not even the sigh of a breeze. The silence set Frost on edge, more so when a mount hissed or growled.

Heat pressed down upon him. Frost wiped his forehead with the back of his hand. Licking saltiness from his lips, he kept The Stunner aimed and ready.

Frost stretched his Echolocation to its full range as they made their way through the jungle, but he picked up no alarming forms or movement. The majority of the other players had surged toward Apur's eastern entrance while his group had headed south. Saba had Concealed and gone ahead to scout.

Occasionally, they encountered mauled carcasses or corpses. In other spots, they discovered signs of battle. Rent earth. Scorched trees and broken branches. Slices in tree trunks. Blood spatters on undergrowth or staining the ground.

They also found bones. Skeletons. Those were usually accompanied by clothing, armor, or packs. Things that suggested the remains belonged to a player. They found nothing of value, a sign someone had already looted the dead.

Gilda's condition worried Frost. She hadn't spoken in some time.

Her attention was always riveted on the northwest, to the spires of Apur glimpsed through the canopy. The black around the splotches had spread, consuming the gray. He wanted to ask her how she was doing, but at the same time he didn't want to draw attention to her condition. He felt as if the attention would make it worse.

Frost raised his hand for the group to halt. Someone or something was moving their way from Apur. It took but a moment for him to recognize Saba's form.

She appeared about fifteen feet ahead and walked to meet them, tail swishing. "I found Captain Kazawa." She pointed to where Frost caught a flash of Apur's walls through the trees. "He and four others are that way, hiding near a massive tree. There was no sign of the rest of the company."

"Take us to them," Frost ordered.

"You got it."

She led them on a winding route through the jungle. They soon reached an area with dense underbrush and a tree that might take ten men holding hands to encircle. Saba stopped a few dozen feet before the tree, her tail swishing.

A distortion in the air marked when a Concealed person stepped from behind the tree trunk. The size and shape of the form was that of a gurash. Three others followed, also Concealed.

Frost aimed The Stunner down at them. "Another move and you four die. Show yourselves."

Silence hung heavy on the air.

"I won't repeat myself." Frost caressed the trigger. "And tell your fifth not to do anything stupid, Sergeant Kazawa. Your brother, Yoshino, asked us to find you."

Beside Frost, Gilda's chakrams flared to life. Dante's color bled from deep crimson to brilliant scarlet.

But a few seconds passed before the people dropped Concealment. The two women among them wore robes. The men were in armor; one a complete suit of silver, the other a leather brigandine with bronze plates. Emblems of the Coalition's Mountain and the Aetherstream stood out on their chests.

The first woman was a deep blue erada with dainty horns. A scepter hung from a loop on her belt.

The other female was an olive-skinned human, her hair done in a long ponytail threaded with dark wire. The accordion-like surface of a large closed warfan jutted over her right shoulder.

The men were gurashi, both with dark brown skin. The taller of the two had a shaggy blue mane and biceps like thighs. He held a two-handed greatsword out before him.

His counterpart sported a red mane done in a massive braid that fell down his back. He carried an axe that matched his height, its butt planted on the ground. His silver armor was dented here and there and soiled from battle.

"I'm Sergeant Kazawa," a gruff voice said from above them. Sitting on a thick branch, the green-skinned, green-maned sergeant had an aether cannon aimed at Frost. In one smooth move, he leaped to the ground, landing with graceful ease.

Objective Complete
Find the Missing Rescuers
Found Sergeant Kazawa and his company:
5000 experience points
500 Lothal dominion credits

"Who are you?" Sergeant Kazawa cradled his cannon in his tree trunk arms. He had a hard face and harder eyes.

"Just a group of adventurers seeking fortune and a cure." Frost lowered The Stunner. "I'm Lan." He gestured to his friends, each one in turn. "This is Chaotix, Aximand, Meritus, Blaze, and Neru. As I mentioned before, Yoshino asked us to find you. He's worried sick and wants you to return."

Kazawa shook his green-maned head. "I'll return when I complete my assignment."

"Hey, friend," Dante said to the sergeant.

"Greetings, friend." Kazawa nodded in turn.

Dante jutted his chin toward the Coalition soldiers. "Yoshino said you had a whole company, but I only see you five. I'm assuming the rest are either hiding or dead."

"Dead." A pained expression contorted the sergeant's features, softened them.

"So how do you expect to complete an assignment that a full company couldn't?"

The sergeant seemed on the verge of tears, eyes glassy. "I don't know, but I have to try." He took a breath, composing himself, before he glanced nervously in Gilda's direction and looked away. "For my woman, Naora's sake. She was with an earlier expedition."

"You must really love her." Dante's lips formed a tight line. "'Cause it's very likely she's dead and you're going to end up the same way."

"If it is Deluth's wish, then so be it." Kazawa dipped his head. "But I have to keep trying. I've seen the void beasts searching Apur and taking the survivors. And there's something else out there, too. We never got to see exactly what it was, but it ripped through my men. I-I can't leave Naora and those people to that fate. A fate worse than death. I can't leave them to be corrupted."

He paused, the wind's sigh filling that empty moment. "I hate to ask, but will you help me?" Hope shone in his eyes. He nodded to their weapons. "You seem powerful enough to manage."

"We are, friend," Dante said.

"Then you'll do it?" Kazawa's eyes widened with enthusiasm. "Help save the people in Apur?"

"No prob." Frost offered the man an encouraging smile.

IM dinged. Two new quests appeared in **The Cure** line. One was **Rescue The Survivors**. The other was **Reunited**.

"Thank you. Thank you." Kazawa dipped his head several times. "While we do this, we must also kill as many void beasts as possible for Senaty." He indicated the blue-skinned erada. "She's a mystic and an alchemist. She thinks if she studies them that she'll be able to concoct a cure."

"No prob." Frost thought it was unlikely but refrained from voicing his opinion.

Another quest appeared, this one named **Void Beasts**.

Senaty sighed and gave a little shake of her head. "It wasn't my intention to venture this deep into the vale, but I was also trying to talk my best friend out of his mad pursuit of Naora. The others won't say it, but I've told him this was a bad idea."

"Over and over again." Kazawa rolled his eyes.

"And still, you don't listen." Senaty huffed. "You're allowing your feelings for Naora to get the better of you."

"And you're letting your fear consume you," Kazawa shot back.

"We have every reason to be afraid. You saw what the Gray Death did after the last voidstorm. You know how many people we had to kill… to burn in order to slow its spread. It has left western Puria in ruins." Senaty threw her hands up in frustration. "Bah. I won't do this again. But I hope this does not end with me saying I told you so. Or with all of us being corrupted… turning into those things."

"We won't." Kazawa turned back to Frost. "Since we'll be together for a while yet, let me introduce my other friends." He pointed to the olive-skinned human. "This is Varia. A windwalker."

Varia flung her ponytail over her shoulder and bowed with a flourish, her warfan appearing in her hand. Crafted of lacquered paper attached to wooden ribs with a metal outer cover, the warfan was large enough for her to hide behind. She splayed it open, one arm slotted into the back as if she carried shield.

"This is Enatsu, our reaver." Kazawa gestured to the taller of the two brown-skinned gurashi, the one with the unkempt blue mane, bulging biceps, and two-handed greatsword held in one meaty fist. "And Domen, our marauder."

Domen leaned his axe's long haft on his shoulder. He dipped his red-maned head.

"Your friend is not far from the brink." Senaty was staring at Gilda. "By the end of the day she will no longer be able to resist whatever draws the corrupted to the Crypts."

Frost shot a worried glance in Gilda's direction. She was looking at Senaty as if the erada mystic didn't exist.

"I'll be fine." Neither Gilda's voice nor eyes held life. "My friends will see to that."

"I hope so for your sake." Senaty bowed. She mumbled something else under her breath.

Frost swore he heard 'another man with no sense'. And was convinced he was right when Senaty smirked in his direction.

"Let's mount up." Kazawa gestured to his soldiers. He pulled out a whistle and blew. The others copied him.

But a few moments passed before the underbrush rustled. Three kirins appeared, wisps of electric blue and white energy swirling up from all growths of hair. A drake and a zephyr followed. The beasts made their way to their masters. Kazawa and his people climbed atop their respective mounts.

Kazawa surveyed them from his kirin's back, an unruly-looking beast with blue fur, a bushy mane, and long beard. "No matter what happens, we stick to the ground."

"Why?" Frost screwed up his face. "Wouldn't it be that much faster to fly directly to the survivors."

Kazawa shook his head. "We made that mistake already. Anything in the air that isn't corrupted will draw the ire of the flying void beasts once we cross into Apur. That is attention we don't need. Not in the least."

Frost had his doubts, but he acquiesced. "You heard the man. No flying."

"Follow me." Kazawa set off into the jungle.

They followed him, the air thick with heat and the fetor of detritus. Within minutes, they emerged from the trees before the sprawling city of Apur.

Wood, clay, or straw homes spread before them. Smoke billowed into the air in distant areas. A breeze carried a whiff of char and the muted sounds of a battle. A wide flag-stoned avenue carved a path ahead. In the distance rose a great limestone pyramid, its triangular peak seeming to touch the gray clouds within which lightning radiated.

"The Forsaken Crypts," Kazawa said softly and pointed at the pyramid. His hand shifted to the left to indicate another great structure rising above stone buildings. "The Temple of Jerad. That's where most of the survivors are hiding."

He'd barely said the words when several flyers soared from above the trees and into the city. Ten of them in formation by Frost's count. Cloaks with guild emblems fluttered out behind the riders. They headed toward the Crypts.

"Wait." Kazawa held up a closed fist, his gaze following the flyers.

Screeches and cries echoed. A roar followed. Over a dozen drakes and

226

various other flying creatures appeared in the sky. Black and silver void energy crackled around them. They swooped toward the players.

Frost squinted. "Is it me or are there people on those void beasts?"

"On some, for sure," Meritus confirmed.

Blasts of aether shot between the two groups. Whether magic or cannon fire, the attacks boomed.

Something roared once more, closer this time. The sound sent a chill through Frost. A massive form burst through the lightning-etched clouds, its size and wingspan several times that of the other flying creatures. Frost gaped.

It was a dragon. Black-scaled. Beautiful and terrifying all at once. Void energy coruscated from its body, spread along its wings. Its roar reverberated. Even from the ground Frost felt its power pressing down on him.

He found his voice, but it came out in a breathy whisper. "That... that's a fucking void dragon."

"And someone's riding it." Meritus' voice was filled with awe to match that which Frost felt.

"Epic. Just... epic," Dante said.

"No doubt," Gilda chimed in.

The void dragon spewed black lightning. Arcs of silver energy shot from its rider. The attacks blasted through the players. They plummeted from the air.

With a triumphant roar, the void dragon angled upward, its powerful wings beating, and flew into the clouds. The other flying void beasts melted into the sky. Even without being there, Frost knew they had Concealed.

"*That* is why I told you not to fly," Kazawa said.

"Thank you." Frost still eyed the clouds through which the void dragon had gone. Lightning flickered. But there was no accompanying thunder.

"This way." Kazawa pointed down a side street. "We can avoid clashes with bandits trying to prey on people like us by staying off the main roads. If we run non-stop, we can make the temple before the next void beast wave leaves the Crypts."

With that, Kazawa kicked his bolsters, sending his kirin into a lope. His soldiers fell in behind him.

Frost and the others followed. Kazawa picked up the pace, relying on the shadowy confines to keep them hidden. Armor and weapons jangling, mounts snorting, they galloped whenever they crossed the open space between homes or other streets and lanes.

They encountered numerous corpses, most displaying hideous wounds, while others were in various states of decay. Most lay where they had fallen, in an open door, against a wall, sprawled or curled on the ground. Others left bloody trails where the wounded had crawled or had been dragged. The fetid stench of blood, offal, and rot hung in the air. Thick. Cloying. Frost tried to ignore it all, but it made his stomach queasy.

From time to time, the clash of steel, booms of magic, and cries and screams of combatants rose from nearby. As they darted across one street Frost caught a glimpse of a battle several blocks away before edifices blocked his view.

The buildings changed from wood, clay, or straw to bricks the size of Frost's torso. The structures were now also multi-storied, some with as many as six or seven floors.

One thing remained the same. The dead. Carnage. Battle's bloody aftermath. The closer they got to the temple, the more of it they encountered. Whether it was scorched ground or walls, rents in the earth, burned out buildings smelling of char, or structures that were but so much rubble, the tapestry of destruction was on constant display.

"Another few blocks." Kazawa urged his kirin forward, energy crackling from its tufts of hair. "Almost there."

The Temple of Jerad towered above the other structures. It seemed so close yet so far.

Awooooooooooo! A horn blared.

"Oh, Deluth, no!" The fear in Kazawa's voice was palpable. "Run! Run! A void beast wave is coming." He kicked his bolsters violently, propelling his kirin into a full gallop.

CHAPTER 27

Seated in her office, Sidrie studied the holo map of New New York. Covering the entire wall, the map had little green, man-shaped icons to indicate patrols, labeled according to whom they belonged. The DeGens were somewhere hiding in the First Ward's buildings or subway tunnels.

She was certain of it. No other conclusion made sense. Those were the only habitable places they could go. If living in the utmost squalor among the threat of mutated species could be called habitable.

Sidrie allowed her gaze to settle on the giant sea wall that followed the coastline. In ways she wished it wasn't so effective. Or that an overly powerful superstorm would form. It would flush out the DeGens like the rats they were.

"They're always two steps ahead." Keenan Costace's gunmetal eyes were focused on the map. "We gotta find out who their inside man is. He'd be able to lead us to them."

Sidrie agreed with her security chief. Although the Seven and the city had committed more men, droids, and drones to the Bottom Wards after the incriminating video, they still had not located the main DeGen hideout. Not even after Governor Morrison announced a curfew and restrictions on all activities in the Bottom Wards.

None of which mattered when it came to the First Ward itself. Neither the government nor the Corps had any control down there. From early on during the curfews, they learned that teams of at least five men were a necessity. Ten, if they were going underground. The DeGens picked off anything less and were always gone by the time reinforcements arrived.

She wracked her brain, trying to think of a single person in her employ who could be a spy. Anyone who behaved differently, who broke their usual activity patterns. She had everyone monitored. If a person took a piss or sat down for a cup of coffee, she knew about it.

The logical conclusion for the leak was inside the government. Perhaps, the governor's office. Or within the NYPD, SDF, or NAIL. The best solution she could devise was to place them under twenty-four-hour surveillance. Their homes, their work, their means of travel. Whatever it took. The task would be simple enough since everyone and every bit of electronics, except for the First Ward, were linked to the Grid.

And anyone who wasn't on the Grid? They were immediate suspects. She would see to the necessary arrangements before the day was done.

Keenan tapped one of the green icons. "Techs made any progress with those hard drives from the data center? We got a face for this Carlson, yet?"

A holo rose from the icon, a video feed from one of numerous drones. It displayed a ten-man team entering what was once the Kings County Supreme Court, above a collapsed major subway hub.

"They're still working on decryption, and we do have a face. I'll send it to you." Sidrie projected her intentions to Estella through her many implants rather than speaking aloud.

Two images materialized. In the first, dated two years ago, a dozen people posed inside the Barclays Center. The second picture was Carlson, himself, separated from the group. He was a lanky man no older than thirty-five with creepy silver eyes. Sidrie sent the images.

"He's a young one," Keenan said. "I expected some deformed old bastard. Only one person in the entire group resembles the ugly fucks we typically fight."

"The very reason it cannot be made public," Sidrie said.

"Making it public is exactly what you should do." Keenan shrugged. "The common Citizen already considers anyone from the Bottom Wards to be DeGens. Many of those look no different than you or me."

Sidrie shook her head. They had to maintain that fear factor. The idea of DeGens spreading disease and worse. "The status quo must remain. It works in our favor."

"Yes, ma'am."

She knew Keenan did not agree, but he was not one to debate things he considered above his pay grade. Not that his opinion would have changed her mind.

An incoming comm lit up her optics. Austin Carter, the be-spectacled senior analyst for Gameborn Deployment. He would only be contacting her directly if something was wrong.

Sidrie shot a glance over to Keenan. "Are you getting the same call?"

"Yes."

She answered the comm. The analyst was sitting at his desk, a series of holograms arrayed around him. "Good morning, Austin."

"Good morning, Miss Malikah." Mr. Carter licked his lips nervously. "We've got a situation."

"Go ahead."

"It's D600, Miss Malikah."

"What about it?"

"He completed his mission."

"Austin Carter, you did not contact me just to tell me that."

"And then he called the authorities to report the killing and turned himself in," Austin blurted.

Sidrie's gut clenched. "D600 did what?"

"Carried out his mission, then called the authorities while still in the home, and turned himself in."

"I heard you the first time," Sidrie snapped. "Terminate it. This second."

Austin looked away from his screen toward one of the holos. Lit up in green, the holo displayed the DeGen gameborn, D600, a dark-skinned boy in his late teens. The holo turned red. Austin visibly relaxed.

Moments later, he said. "It's done, Miss Malikah."

With a thought, Sidrie had Estella confirm the kill. "Good. Have your techs go over all surveillance in D600's vicinity for anything it might have said. Contact Mister Costace with your findings."

"Yes, Miss Malikah. Right away, Miss Malikah."

Sidrie severed the connection. Worry needled in her gut. D600's assignment had been the assassination of Germaine Peterson, the lead AI engineer at Apex Solutions. *What the hell could have caused the thing to then turn itself in?*

"How do you want to handle this?" Keenan was facing her, those gun-metal eyes studying her face.

"We can try to get ahead of it, float a story about a DeGen killing another engineer." Mind working, Sidrie frowned. "We already use the DeGen's hate for tech and our society as one of the reasons for their terror-ist acts. The silo raids, Constantine's murder, and now this, are all a part of that."

"Except there isn't any news of Peterson's death yet." Keenan shook his bald head. "I checked every channel. They're withholding it. Which means we can't be the first to say anything. We gotta be reactive rather than pro-active. I'll have my sources run down the details law enforcement has and any internal chatter."

Sidrie tapped an index finger on her wrist as she considered his words. "You're right. But I hate waiting."

Keenan chuckled. "You hate being on the defensive, period. But some-times the best offense is defense. And then, you can counter."

Something else bothered Sidrie. "Why do you think D600 did it?"

Keenan shrugged. "Guilt."

"Guilt?" The word didn't make sense to her.

"Yeah. Even the most hardened killer had a conscience at some point. Or questioned what he was doing. Then there's the fact that he's D series."

"The DeGen gameborn." Sidrie scowled. "I warned Dr. Redmond about them. I said they were weak. Too emotional. Every setback we expe-rienced originated from that line. It's past time I end it."

"I don't think being DeGens has anything to do with it."

Sidrie's lip curled. "What makes you say that?"

"I'll start by saying I understand why you choose the D series for that particular sort of work. They're arguably the best since they've been in VR or SR from childhood, a longer time than any of the others.

"But that's also part of their weakness. The games they played offered too many ways they could build attachments, interact with people, experi-ence an imitation of normal life. Feelings.

"Unlike the G series who're adult clones. Blank brains that we fill with whatever we want, and in their case, brains that get to deal with combat situations in SR and out. Just death. No strings. The Gs don't even know what a conscience is. They can be scary as fuck and have issues being around people, but you won't ever have to worry about this sorta thing with them."

"Sometimes, you surprise me, Mister Costace."

Keenan took a bow. "I aim to please, ma'am."

She took a moment to consider all he had said. Changing the program now would be a setback, but it would be worth it in the end.

A part of her regretted not being able to use D Ten Thirty, Setnana Botros, the latest DeGen gameborn she'd singled out for acclimation and training. The other part was glad. She had misgivings when she'd reviewed D Ten Thirty's reactions to its current objectives in Void Legion. Particularly after she had given it Gilda Mordian's location. If those emotions had manifested in the real world, they would have spelled disaster.

Just that quickly, Sidrie projected her intentions to Estella and received a summary of costs. "Going forward, we use only G series for missions. You know them well, so you get to choose. I will have the D series removed from the program."

"Removed?" Keenan's thick brows climbed his forehead. "As in terminated?"

Sidrie nodded. "They serve no other purpose that would justify their cost. We could use the resources on new subjects."

Doubt flashed across Keenan's face. "Could some of them serve in more delicate situations, ones where their loyalties to the company and their feelings are assets? You know… spies."

Sidrie admired his line of thinking. "In any other circumstance it might be a yes, but I already have gameborn serving those needs."

Keenan cracked a pearly white smile. "What if some of them are sent home? According to the DeGens captured and questioned during the assault here, setting the testers free was one of their intentions. I say we make it so the DeGens can try again. Leave a weakness they can exploit."

Sidrie's brows bunched as she followed his line of thought. "And use our plant to discover everything about them, so we can crush them completely." She had to admit the idea was brilliant, and she, herself, had been too close to the situation, too determined to see the DeGens suffer, too intent on giving them nothing, that she had overlooked the possibility.

"Exactly." Keenan nodded. "As for any you don't want to use for that plan… hook them into the combat program. They're skilled. Why let the skills go to waste? The Gs can benefit from better opponents."

"Has anyone ever told you that you are very convincing when you wish to be?" Sidrie regarded Keenan with an arched brow.

"Once in a while." Keenan smiled.

"I'm glad we had this talk. I'll instruct Dr. Redmond to make the necessary changes. Meanwhile, do keep an eye out for any details regarding the Peterson situation, and prep which G series gameborn you think would be best for our next target, Marva Tierney."

"Got it, ma'am." He paused, brow furrowed. "Tierney. She's from Intel, right?" Sidrie nodded. "I'm on it." Keenan gave her the tiniest salute and departed.

The talk about the gameborn and the program made Sidrie think about Void Legion. She still had the issue of the anomalies. She scowled. They reminded her of the DeGens in the First Ward. Ghosts. She hated mysteries.

Her thoughts turned to Dre. "Estella, play the recording from Hotel Manzania."

She did not need to specify. Estella knew the recording. Sidrie had her play it countless times already.

A new holo replaced the map. It featured the inside of a hotel room. Dre was hugging Just Blaze from behind at the window. The rising sun peeked in through the curtains.

Sidrie recited even as the two people spoke. The first was Just Blaze.

"Funny thing is that a part of me finds the risk exciting while another part is scared shitless. Especially since we have to play."

Dre followed a moment later. *"I'd still play regardless. Particularly after experiencing Total Immersion. And seeing Pops. He's worth it all by himself."*

The holo repeated. So did Sidrie.

She had spent sleepless nights studying those words, poring over Alphonso's work, scouring the bits they'd salvaged of Dr. Hank Kim's research on Whole Brain Emulation when he was working for Equitane. She drew to the same conclusion every time.

Alphonso had an NPC in the game to imitate him.

She intended to discover who the NPC was and where it was located. The possibility existed that she might attain all the protocols in one swoop. All she needed was a bit of patience. *Patience.* She ground her teeth at the word.

CHAPTER 28

Screeches, roars, and bestial cries echoed from deep in the city. Urging their mounts on, the group galloped toward the opening at the end of the lane. The sound of their mounts' feet and claws on cobbles was soon drowned out by a loud drum. A rumble. Thunder. Frost recognized the noise immediately. Hundreds of onrushing feet. He shuddered at the idea of so many void beasts.

The group spilled from the lane into the intersection of two wide avenues. Buildings lined the streets. Directly ahead was the Temple of Jerad, a statue of the grand korae's glaive-wielding patron god standing atop stairs that spanned the entirety of the building's facade. Armed people waited on the landing. Every playable race was present among them.

Stacked bricks, logs, furniture, and iron drums and posts covered in spikes formed ramshackle barricades on the approach to the temple. They would be more of a nuisance than a hindrance to void beasts. It was a sign of desperation.

Frost snatched a look behind. The fastest of the void beasts bounded down the avenue. The distance was closing rapidly.

He considered flying over the barricade before he remembered the void dragon. Following Kazawa like the others, he wove his way among the obstacles. Blood and bits of flesh stained the ground and clung to many of the spikes, but Frost saw no corpses.

The people beyond the barricades were waving them on, yelling for them to hurry. Another glance over his shoulder revealed more void beasts than the first time. Scores more. He refocused ahead. People were now positioned where the obstacles began. Within minutes, Frost and his group passed the first group of people and dashed up the stairs onto the landing.

Several of the people around them had the Coalition's Mountain and the Aetherstream on display. Frost figured those were NPCs like Kazawa's company.

Frost eyed the numerous guild emblems. Whether on their sleeves, lapels, cloaks, or a combination of all, many players wore them proudly. The players were aligned in obvious groups, even if mixed by guilds. He counted at least eight groups. The players he had passed soon rejoined them on the landing.

He took special note of the players wearing the Herald of WaR. The insignia was the most dominant atop the landing. WaR members only associated with their own. Their gear was superior to that worn by everyone else.

For the briefest of moments his gaze lingered on a female WaR member who was passing instructions to another. He turned away and hoped she nor anyone else had noticed his eyes widen. Or had noticed him at all.

Although she was dressed in green robes threaded with gold, he could not forget that angular face. The golden-brown skin. The bright hazel eyes. She was Meileen. WaR's co-leader.

Frost whispered into group chat, "Keep an eye out in case those WaR members recognize any of us. Meileen's with them."

"We should get out of here," Saba said.

"Too late for that," Frost replied.

"Newcomers," bellowed a towering silver-armored gargant, his voice like a fog horn, the Herald of WaR standing out on his black cloak. He paused for effect, surveying Frost and his group.

The hair that covered the entirety of his face had been trimmed into an immaculate pointed beard. His features reminded Frost of a picture he'd seen of a buffalo. The gargant's weapons of choice were korbitanium greaves and fists, the latter a pair of hierkas. The Herald was also displayed over his heart, filigreed in gold.

The gargant pointed at Frost's group with his gleaming fist weapon. "Help on the far left with the other Puggers."

"Did he just call us Puggers?" Dante screwed up his face as they moved into position among a motley crew of other players sporting various guild emblems or none at all.

"Sure did." Meritus chuckled.

"Disrespectful." Dante shot a baleful glare toward the gargant. "Never been part of a PUG in any game."

"Pick Up Groups are not *that* bad," Ryne said. "There can be some good talent to be had among random players."

Meritus spoke up. "For every single good player in a PUG, there's five others who have no clue how to play their class, who'll try to zerg a boss, just stand in shit, or cause the group to wipe."

"But that does not make—" Ryne began.

"Don't, lil buddy," Dante admonished. "Just don't."

"Just trying to make you feel better." Ryne's concerned expression said he meant every word.

"I'm glad they think we're trash." Frost eyed the WaR members. "Means they won't be paying much attention to us."

"As good as that sounds, let me hit us with a Pack buff in case we need to run." Saba cast the ability even as she uttered the words. The buff seeped into the group, giving Frost a sense of lightness as if he were the wind itself. "Good to go," Saba added.

A shout from the silver-armored WaR gargant cut off their conversation. "Okay, people, this is it. Remember to wait for them to hit the traps. Ranged, get ready. If you have an AOE slow, stun, stagger or any other type of CC, use it, then go all out.

"Melee, we fight at the bottom of the stairs and our main job is to stop any mobs from getting to the ranged. Mystics, summon your Servitors, and do what you do best: keep everyone alive."

Howling and roaring, the first wave of void beasts reached the barricades. A thrill eased through Frost upon seeing them. An old familiar feeling he once craved. The thrill of a raid.

The void beasts included wolves, arkets, and lamias. Among them were two hulking behemoths with rippling muscles, faces and bodies a mix of bear and bull complete with ridges of horns running down their backs. Black and silver void energy distorted the air around them all.

Frost could easily discern the powerful build of each monster. The enhanced details. They were elite.

He hissed at the behemoths. They were even stronger than the others. They had titles. Resha and Rajan.

"Those two GUMs are gonna tear right through those barricades," he scoffed.

"No, they won't," said a player near Frost. She was a slender buttermilk grand kora whose ossicones twitched as Frost's gaze settled on her. She offered a tight smile. "You'll see."

Frost returned his attention to the incoming threat, expecting the beasts to blast through the makeshift barriers or leap over them. The behemoths slammed into the brick walls. And failed to break a single one of them.

A few wolves and arkets leaped over some logs. Only to be impaled by spikes on the other side. If they leaped too high, they triggered a Trap in the form of an electrical field, causing them to plummet to the ground. The rest of the wave followed the path created by the obstacles.

"What the hell?" Frost stared as the GUMs shook off the impacts and dashed after their counterparts.

"Reinforced and imbued with aether by WaR's engineers." The grand kora smiled proudly. "And the engineers change up the position, height, and pattern of the obstacles every time to compensate for the readjusted AI on respawns."

Frost grinned. He had to admit the strategy was brilliant. Simple but brilliant. He saw the barricades and Traps for what they were now. A maze. A maze that forced the mobs into three chokepoints.

When the first few void beasts spilled from the openings, they triggered the Traps. Chain Lightning flared and crackled. Ice bloomed. Metal chains and shackles appeared, flying out to snare some of the creatures.

All along the landing, the ranged attackers opened fire. Frost joined them. Beside him, Gilda, Saba, and Varia followed suit, their attacks resonating upon release.

The abilities lit the air. Rain of Arrows, Glacial Eruptions, Flame Walls, Aether Bombs, Concussion Blasts, Divergence beams, Arc Lightnings, Static Fields, Lightning Cages, the translucent blades of Gusts and Whirlwinds exploded among the void beasts. Flash Freeze's bluish white waves struck, freezing enemies and barriers alike.

Any time a void beast stumbled or darted from the carnage, it fell to a red Piercer shot. Frost glanced over to see the cannoneer responsible. He was a human and a member of WaR. A demon mask hid his face. His weapon was sleek, long, and completely black like the armor he wore.

In seconds, the majority of the wave was dead. Exp flowed like water, the numbers small but in bunches. He was well on his way to level nineteen. Smoke boiled into the sky. Residual fire and lightning licked at the ground, threaded the air.

Frost almost cheered. But none of the other fighters showed any reaction. He frowned. His answer appeared a moment later.

Resha and Rajan burst through the smoke and flames. As did several other creatures. Roaring, the behemoths lumbered to the stairs, their footsteps shaking the ground.

"Tanks and melee, engage," bellowed the WaR group leader. "Ranged, once aggro is set, single target attacks only to finish them off."

Dante unleashed a howl and Leaped down the stairs. "Time for some action, babyyyyyy. DPS for the win. Pew, pew, pew!"

Frost cackled.

Marauders Raging Rushed to meet the GUMs and their counterparts. A synchronous use of Frenzy, Sentinel Shout, and Soul Scream followed. The slicing spins of Cyclonic Strike and Aether Cleaves left afterimages in the air.

Dementers Spurted in, along with reavers who called upon Onslaught to cover the distance in a flash, while cutthroats relied on Shadowblink. The cutthroats disappeared to reappear behind their targets.

Upon contact, the dementers unleashed Shockwaves to stun and stagger, followed by the blue half-moons of Sonic Blow and the silver of Blade Kicks. Reavers relied on combos of Ravage, Necrotic Slash, Mortal Wound, and Malignant Strike, leaving wounds either infested with disease or bleeding profusely, each one doing Damage Over Time. The cutthroats stabbed and sliced from the rear.

Frost smiled. *The best cutthroats do it from behind,* he thought.

In the middle of it all, Dante's voice rang out. "Get some. Get some. Pew, pew. Balls out, baby. Balls out!"

Blue motes of Mikander's Tears and the red of Mikander's Blood shot from the mystics to the melee. The light green drizzle of Mikander's Rain, a group Heal Over Time, fell over the WaR groups.

On the landing, the ranged chose targets and loosed single attacks. Red Piercers cut through the air, felling monsters. Frost relied on Aether Shots. Beside him, Gilda and Saba unleashed their skills. Soon, the first wave was cleared.

Corpses littered the ground. The area was awash with blood, its metallic stench biting through the acrid smoke.

"Positions!" yelled the gargant.

The melee dashed back up the stairs. Within moments they had returned to their original places, weapons at the ready, sweat pouring down faces that were masks of concentration. Marksmen, this time including Saba, hurried down to the choke points and containment areas to place new Traps.

Huffing, Dante returned, grinning madly. "That was crazy fun. Can't wait to do it again."

The second wave entered the maze. They were made up of many of the same creatures along with basilisks and korbitoises. There were three behemoths this time.

The result was the same. Before the melee departed, the marksmen were setting new traps.

But the next wave was already halfway through the maze. This time, there were four behemoth GUMs.

Frost's breath caught in his throat at the massive creature striding behind them. Gilda hissed. Saba cursed.

Humanoid in form, he was perhaps two stories tall and might have once been a titan. His skin, where not covered by green scale armor, was the color of ash threaded with vibrant red and yellow. Black and silver void energy collected around his hands. His hair was done in a top knot, and his eyes were the brightest blue. The hilt of a massive sword jutted from his back.

IM named him Herzl. A draconid herald.

"Clear the wave as quickly as possible," the gargant ordered. "Saigo and I'll off-tank Herzl. Mystics, your Bulwarks stay here as back up. Shamans with us. Lady Meileen, if you would be so kind as to be our main healer."

"Certainly, my love." Meileen's voice was the same memorable wind chime from the streets of Madurai.

Frost suppressed a gasp. "Meritus, you coulda said that was Kazuto," he hissed into group chat.

"I would've if I had known. This is the first time I'm seeing him."

Kazuto led the way, Spurting down the stairs and over to the far left of the avenue near the maze and a wide side street. Meileen followed by way of Flicker. Bringing up the rear was Saigo, a deep blue gurash in full plate armor, wielding a quaker axe with a blade as wide as his body.

They'd scarcely gotten into position when the void beasts spilled from the openings. The Traps triggered. As before, the players relied on every type of CC as the ranged got to work.

However, the tanks charged in earlier, picking up the behemoths, taking them to the sides. The melee DPS followed soon after.

Now, not only was Frost using his AOEs, but he was feverishly working every other skill. He charged Homer for its complete four seconds, firing off a full Aether Missile salvo.

In the next two seconds he'd charged Aether Barrage, aiming at the nearest behemoth. He fired. Aether Shots spat from the cannon with a drill-like whine. All eight were discharged in an instant. Even as his target let out a plaintive cry and collapsed, he was attacking the next one.

Herzl stepped over, on, or through the barriers, crushing or shattering them. The herald crossed the maze in a few massive ground-shaking strides.

Out of the corner of his eye, Frost saw Saigo point at the herald. In his other hand, his huge quaker axe glowed with aether. With a swift move, Saigo stepped forward and flung the axe sideways and up. Spinning like a massive cyan disc, the weapon sped toward Herzl.

The quaker axe buried itself in the herald's face, destroying his left eye. Mid-stride, Herzl roared in agony. Rage. This, despite the weapon appearing more like a toy than a deadly instrument.

In the next instant, Herzl was *pulled* from his path to face Saigo, who had his hand outstretched. Herzl batted the axe from his eye. Blood fountained. He bellowed again.

Still glowing, and once again spinning, the quaker axe hurtled back down to Saigo, who caught it by the haft. Herzl roared at the gurash, the force of his voice billowing up dust and debris.

"Yoooo, Saigo just used Boomerang Blade. Epiccc," Dante's high-pitched excited voice piped through group chat.

"What's so special about that?" Frowning, Frost watched as Saigo waited, weapon in hand, while Kazuto kept his distance down the street. Meileen positioned herself where she was in range to heal them both.

"It's a reaver skill. And Saigo already used several marauder skills."

The declaration opened Frost's eyes. He wondered if all the WaR members were multi-classing. *How did they handle skills that were weapon-specific?* Boomerang Blade couldn't be one of those, because Saigo didn't have a sword, glaive, or a mist blade hierka. Perhaps they only chose skills that did not require a particular weapon.

The raid was on the final behemoth as an enraged Herzl crashed through the last barricades, sending the obstacles flying. He barreled toward Saigo.

But the gurash didn't wait for the herald to reach him. Instead, he Raging Rushed into the Herzl, stopped before one humongous leg, and delivered a blow to Herzl's upper thigh, which was about head high for the gurash.

Yowling, Herzl swiped at Saigo. The gurash dodged under the blow and Leaped high into the air. The arm passed under him. At the apex of the Leap, he chopped into Herzl's shoulder.

Herzl cried out again. The herald reached back and up for his sword.

Saigo landed. The moment he touched the ground, the gurash Soul Screamed. Abruptly, he took two massive Leaps backward, coming to rest near Kazuto.

Frost re-focused on the last behemoth. Eager to tackle Herzl, he pumped out shot after shot. The idea of fighting such a boss at this early level scattered his thoughts, got him to wondering about Herzl's skills, how hard it hit, the possible strats, the loot. He grinned madly as the behemoth crumpled to the ground.

Frost shifted to face Herzl's massive back. The herald crashed through the buildings on his way down the street after Saigo and Kazuto. In his head, Frost had already worked out his opening combo.

Sword in hand, Herzl threw his head back and let out a mighty roar. The sound echoed. Frost almost slapped his hands over his ears. Herzl took one last look at Saigo and Kazuto and then bounded some two hundred feet away in the direction of the Forsaken Crypts, abandoning the fight.

Frost let out a heavy sigh, his shoulders slumping.

CHAPTER 29

"What the hell happened?" Disappointed, Frost shook his head. "Why'd he bounce?"

"We cleared the waves." The grand kora player stepped up beside him. "Herzl flees every time we do so. No one knows why, but it's the same way each time. He lets out that frustrated roar and makes a run for the Crypts when the last void beast dies."

"What happens if you fail to do a full clear?"

She shivered. "The waves overrun everyone before the herald engages. The void beasts collect the corpses and survivors and head back to the Crypts."

"Damn, I was hoping you at least knew what he did. Or his abilities." Frost sighed.

The grand kora headed down the stairs toward the carcasses piled at the choke points. "I'm just glad for the clear so I can collect some void beast blood."

Her words spurred Frost into action. He hurried after her. His friends joined him among the stinking dead.

Cheers went up, from both the players and the NPCs behind Frost. He turned. Townsfolk poured from the temple doors.

Two quests completed. **Rescue The Survivors** and **Defend the Temple**. Each granted fifty thousand exp and a thousand Lothal, Ignis, Puria, and Khertahka dominion credits.

"Level nineteen. Halfway to twenty already off the quests," Frost said in group chat. "Almost there." He looked to Gilda and smiled. "Let's get this blood and get you sorted."

She barely acknowledged him, which sent a fresh needle of concern worming its way into his gut. Trying his best not to allow gruesome thoughts to run rampant, Frost focused on his immediate surroundings.

While Kazawa, Enatsu, Varia, and Domen had gone up the stairs to greet the survivors, Senaty had remained below, inspecting the dead. If the body was on its back, she would turn it over and look at something on its nape. She also placed blood in glass tubes, added something, and swirled it around. Then she'd destroy the tubes by conjuring flames.

The **Void Beasts** quest completed. Frost gained twenty thousand exp and seven hundred and fifty Lothal, Ignis, Khertahka, and Puria dominion credits.

Frost screwed up his face at the stench wafting from the carcasses. They smelled of rot. Of long dead things.

Wondering what Senaty might be searching for, he steeled himself and checked a corpse's nape. There was some kind of a red mark. A brand, perhaps. It reminded him of two fangs with four teeth in-between. He checked another and found the same.

Although curious as to the brand's meaning, Frost shoved it to the back of his mind. He had a more important task. He set about it, grimacing whenever he scooped a flask into void beast blood. All the other players were doing the same.

Frowning, Frost stopped. Not all the players. The WaR members were missing. He looked to the last location of Kazuto, Meileen, and Saigo. Three full groups of WaR members were riding down the avenue toward the distant Crypts.

A voice in his head said he should be doing the same. They were the best players he'd encountered thus far. Players of that caliber were always at the cutting edge of progression. The chance they might reach the Genesis Engine first was a definite possibility. He had to find a way to beat them to it.

"I've got fifty." Frost held up a flask of the black blood. "Enough for five zhua. Everyone should have about the same, which is more than enough for what I had in mind. Besides, I don't wanna be around when the next waves come. Not without those guys from WaR. I can get to twenty by grinding out the level somewhere else in the city."

Everyone agreed. They hurried up the stairs and got their mounts.

Kazawa strode over to Frost, holding hands with a green-skinned gurash woman in torn robes. The rest of his soldiers waited behind him.

"Lan, this is Naora." The sergeant glanced down to Naora with dreamy eyes. "The love of my life."

"Hello, Naora." Frost dipped his head to her.

"Hey, Lan." She offered him a shy smile.

Frost noticed the gray splotches on her skin. They weren't prominent as yet, but they would grow. Melancholy settled on him.

"We wanted to thank you." Kazawa stuck out a clawed hand to Frost. "Without your help, we wouldn't be together again. And none of these people would be alive."

The **Reunited** quest completed, granting Frost twenty thousand exp and five hundred Lothal and Puria dominion credits.

Frost clasped arms with the sergeant. "It was a pleasure."

Senaty stepped up on Kazawa's other side. "I, too, wish to thank you."

Brow arched, Frost released Kazawa's arm. "For what?"

"For opening my eyes." Senaty smiled and gave a slight shake of her head. "I cursed Kazawa during our time here because he risked our lives over a woman. Over love. I always told him that he was soft. That his weakness for her would be our downfall."

"And it almost was," Kazawa interjected.

"That's one way to look at it." Senaty glanced past Frost, her gaze settling on Gilda. "But I learned that such love is as much a strength as it is a weakness. There are some things a person might never accomplish without strong emotion to drive them. Great things."

"You're welcome." Frost couldn't help a sense of comfort at the sentiment behind the words as well as awe at the statement being delivered by an NPC. *Was it possible that the AI understood emotions? Or had feelings? Was her speech a part of her programming or the AI's independent thought?*

"One more thing." Senaty gestured toward the Crypts. "I found marks on every corpse I inspected. Marks of a void devourer. So named because

247

of their ability to consume void energy, using it to feed on entire cities. It might be the one responsible for the Gray Death.

"Unfortunately, after analyzing the blood, I realize I lack the materials necessary to experiment in order to find a cure or a way to curtail the infection's growth.

"But Vindicator Sadonia had gone to the Crypts for that very reason. Hopefully, she's done better than I, and perhaps you can help each other."

A quest, **Vindicator Sadonia**, revealed itself in **The Cure** line beneath **Help The Coalition Find A Cure**. There were other unidentified parts connected to the Vindicator portion.

"If you find her, show her this and say: Aether is life." Senaty reached out to Frost, turned her hand upward, and uncurled her fingers.

A golden medallion sat in her palm. Adorning its surface was a mountain split by a river. The Mountain and the Aetherstream rose *out* of the metal and appeared to move. The Coalition insignia seemed almost alive. Words curled around the medallion's edge.

"It's an Aetherium Council member's badge. Tell Sadonia she can return it to me here."

"Wowww," Meritus whispered in group chat. "The Aetherium Council controls all the Coalition's research into aether, spells, hierkas, Genesis Engines, and so much more. They're so influential some say they hold as much or more power as the Kalarchs… that they're the true power behind the Coalition along with the Grendesh Conclave."

"Thank you." Frost made to take the medallion. When he and Senaty touched, she grabbed his hand.

She leaned in and spoke so only he could hear. "I hope you succeed. Not only for the sake of many of these people here, but also for Kazawa. He will kill himself for sure when the Gray Death takes Naora. And I'm helpless to stop it." Tears welled up in her eyes.

The words cut deep. Frost took the badge as if it were a precious stone and slipped it into his pocket. He received yet another quest in **The Cure** line: **Saving Kazawa and Naora**. "Thank you. I'm gonna do my best."

"No. Thank you." Senaty bowed. "May Nif guide you and keep you."

Frost returned the gesture. "May Nif do the same for you."

After saying their goodbyes to the others, Frost and his group rode up the avenue toward the Crypts. Sporadic battle sounds and the occasional flash and boom of magic resonated from the direction of the distant pyramid.

"We gotta hurry." Frost kicked his bolsters. "Those WaR members might already be inside. And I'm still not twenty, but the Sadonia quest line should get me there."

Ten minutes of hard riding later, the avenue veered left. A battle unfolded at the base of the pyramid.

A silver-armored human Vindicator was yelling orders. She wielded a warfan that matched her height. "Keep the death knights off us while we deal with the forsaken."

She flung translucent Gusts, fiery Infernal Lances, and Arc Lightning at giant skeletons pouring from the Crypts. Beside her, a mage and a cannoneer launched attacks. All around them, Coalition soldiers battled death knights: skeletal warriors dressed in tattered clothing and armed with two-handed swords or axes.

"Help them." Frost dismounted even as he spoke in group chat. **Locate Vindicator Sadonia** completed. "Gilda, Saba, and Ryne with me. Dante, deal with the death knights. Meritus, keep those soldiers alive."

Frost took up a position to the left of the trio. He fired off AOE attacks into the onrushing horde. Picking out casters behind the undead armed with melee weapons, he chose Homer, selected targets while charging it, and fired eight Aether Missiles. Ryne, Saba, and Gilda unleashed their abilities beside him. Between them, the area before the Crypts became a field of fire and explosions.

"Hold," Sadonia yelled when no more undead tried to pass through the deluge of destruction.

Frost stopped firing. The death knights had also fallen, their bones scattered, skulls crushed.

Another quest completed beneath **Vindicator Sadonia**.

Objective Complete

Crypt Guardians

Defeat the Crypt Guardians attacking Vindicator Sadonia's expedition:

30, 000 experience points

500 Ignis dominion credits
500 Lothal dominion credits
500 Khertahka dominion credits
500 Puria dominion credits

Combined with the exp from the kills and the first Sadonia quest, Frost leveled up.

"Yes!" He fist-pumped. "I made it guys. Level twenty."

"Grats," everyone said.

A weight lifted from him. Finally, he could enter the Crypts to save Gilda.

Vindicator Sadonia approached before Frost could take a stock of his new stats. "Thank you." She regarded them with steely eyes. "But you should not be here. This place is off-limits."

Her gaze lingered on Gilda for but a moment before her eyes narrowed. Sadonia flared open her warfan, hazy energy gathering around its edge as she prepared to attack.

"Senaty sent us," Frost blurted. Frantic, he snatched the medallion from his pocket and held it up. "Aether is life. Aether is life."

The Vindicator's gaze shifted to the medallion for an instant, but her warfan remained open and pointed in Gilda's direction, a translucent haze etched in the empty space around its curved end, the power of the windwalker pushing against Frost as if the air itself lived. With a flourish of her hands, she made the warfan and its power disappear. The weapon reappeared on her back, one end jutting above her shoulder.

Frost let out a shuddering breath. His racing heart slowed. "Senaty said you're to return this to her at the camp."

Sadonia strode over to Frost and took the medallion. She looked it over, grumbled something under her breath, and then let out a resigned sigh. "So, who is it that Councilwoman Senaty has sent to me?" She regarded them with a flat expression.

Frost rattled off their aliases. He kept a straight face beneath the Vindicator's withering gaze.

Sadonia shook her head. "I guess I can find a use for you, since it seems you are here either in search of a cure or because of what's drawing corrupted to this place." She glanced at Gilda.

"The answers you seek are inside. I believe a void devourer named Grenok holds them all. He's the underling of the draconid herald, Herzl, the one who sends his beasts to take subjects for his experiments."

"So, we go in, kill Grenok the Devourer, and get the cure." Frost shrugged. He'd come all this way to craft Benediction and the spells to save Gilda. If a faster method existed to acquire the cure, he was all for it.

A quest for **Grenok the Devourer** revealed itself in **The Cure** chain beneath almost all the others.

"But there is one issue," the Vindicator added.

Frost blew out a breath. He should've known it sounded too good to be true.

"To enter the Crypts, you must pass through a corridor into which infected blood pours. It sprays out like a fine mist. There is no way to avoid it. You will be exposed to a strain of the Gray Death so potent that its effects can appear in minutes. Once corrupted by this strain, you have but an hour to live." The Vindicator held up a square container. Vials of blue liquid were slotted into holes. "Unless you have this serum. It seals your skin, prevents the Gray Death from getting into you."

"So, it's a cure?" Frost squinted in confusion.

"No. It only prevents the infection from getting into you, and only does so for a few minutes while exposed. It cannot remove the plague. If you were to pass through the hall again on your way out, you would contract the Gray Death."

Frost regarded the serum. "You have enough for going and coming, right?"

She shook her head. "I just gave some to several groups like you so I only have enough for you to enter. You will have to find another way out. Also, I'm short one vial for your group, despite one of you not needing it." She was looking at Gilda again.

"We won't be short. The goblin isn't coming," Frost said. "He'll be staying out here."

"Ah." Vindicator Sadonia nodded. She took a step and passed a vial each to Dante, Saba, and then Meritus.

Sadonia was handing one to Frost when a red Piercer shot exploded into her chest. The vial fell from her hands. She went flying.

Frost tried to catch the vial. It struck his hand, spun off, and hit the ground. It shattered. Blue vapor drifted into the air.

CHAPTER 30

"Did anyone see who shot me or where the attack originated?" Vindicator Sadonia struggled to her feet, armor blackened where the Piercer had struck.

Her soldiers were peering in multiple directions, weapons aimed. But there was no one to attack.

"I didn't." Frost suspected the cannoneer from WaR was responsible but wasn't willing to openly accuse the man without proof.

Had the WaR cannoneer intended to hit the Vindicator? Or had he recognized me and the others? Or was the attack just to stop us from going into the Crypts? Stop us from being first to the Genesis Engine?

"What will you do now?" Vindicator Sadonia's voice broke Frost from his thoughts. "It will take me a day to make another batch of serum."

"We don't have a day." Frost shook his head, Gilda's condition weighing on his mind. "There's gotta be another way."

Sadonia shook her head. "There isn't."

"Then I'll just have to risk it." Frost shrugged.

Sadonia's brow wrinkled. "You're going to risk dying or worse?"

"Or worse?" Frost repeated with a grimace.

"There are three results to corruption." Sadonia's voice was flat. "Death is the merciful one. The others are becoming void beasts or draconids."

A hush fell over the group. All eyes were on Frost. Gilda was shaking her head. As was Meritus.

He smiled at his friends. "Nothing worth doing is easy. And there's

253

nothing like a challenge to keep you on your toes. Whether it's making sure Gilda lives or that she doesn't turn into something else, I'm not gonna stop now. If it means I gotta risk what she's suffering, then it is what it is."

Gilda stepped up to him, took his hands, and looked up into his eyes. "You don't have to do this. We can just let the Gray Death run its course, see what happens, and hope for the best IRL."

"Nahhhh. We not doing that. I promised I'd never let you die, remember?" He caressed the back of her hand with his thumb. She nodded and offered a tender smile as he continued. "The fact there's a chance you could die falls under that same umbrella. I also promised to cure you. I keep my promises. A guy's gotta do what a guy's gotta do."

"No doubt." Her smile was wider now. Tears trickled down her cheeks.

"Well, it's decided, people," Meritus said. "We're going in and doing what we came to do. By the way, we need to collect those forsaken bones over there." He pointed to the bones strewn around the area before the Crypt's main gate.

Vindicator Sadonia strode over to Frost and Gilda. "If you succeed, the Coalition will owe you a debt if you return with the cure."

"Not if… when." Frost glanced down at Sadonia. "And I look forward to presenting the cure to the Coalition."

"Very well.' Sadonia nodded. "I shall send word for reinforcements."

A new quest line popped up in IM. **The Coalition's Debt.**

"We have one more thing to do before we head in." Frost envisioned the **Meet the Hierkaneer** quest. It showed the location was just around the other side of the Crypts. He mounted. "Follow me, people. Vindicator, we'll return soon."

Leading the group, Frost rode to the location in question. He saw no one. An Echolocation scan allowed Frost to pick out Adesh's Concealed hierkaneer, so small of stature Frost almost missed the person.

Frost held up a closed fist for the others to stop while he continued on slowly. "Gearmaster Zod, I'm Frost. Adesh Hamada sent me."

Still Concealed, Zod approached. When Zod made himself visible, Frost spun to Ryne.

But Dante was faster still. He'd already snatched up a dark-faced Ryne and was trying his best to calm the goblin.

"A gnome. He sends a bloody gnome?" Ryne's angry voice sputtered into silence, his mouth covered by Dante's hand.

Gearmaster Zod frowned in the direction of the commotion and spoke in a squeaky voice. "Took you long enough." Dressed in leather coveralls to match his dark brown skin, he had a backpack and a belt from which hung various tools. "Any longer and those forsaken were gonna find me." The gnome shuddered.

Another muffled outburst came from Ryne's direction. In the back of his mind, Frost noted he'd gained five thousand exp from the quest.

"What's his problem?" Gearmaster Zod tilted his head to peer around Frost's mount.

"He's happy to see you." Frost offered as genuine a smile as he could manage.

Gearmaster Zod arched a brow. "Doesn't seem like it."

"He is. Trust me." Frost shrugged. "Anyway, I'm just glad you're here. We're about to head in and clear this place. Ryne's gonna be here to protect you. We'll send word when we're ready for you."

"Which one of you is Ryne?" The Gearmaster looked from one to the other. All eyes shifted to the goblin, whose little legs were kicking at Dante. Zod shook his head slowly. "I'm not too sure about that."

Frost turned his hand palm up. "It's either him." He jabbed a thumb back in the direction from which they'd come. "Or you can hang out with the Vindicator and the Coalition soldiers around the corner."

Gearmaster Zod gaped. In the next moment, he'd Concealed. "I'll be here with the goblin."

"Exactly what I thought." Smiling, Frost turned away and headed to Ryne and Dante. Frost lowered his voice so only his group could hear. "Ryne, calm down for a second."

The goblin was glaring past Frost, still struggling to be free of Dante's grip. A long moment passed before Ryne stopped kicking and focused on Frost with eyes like beads.

"I don't know why you hate gnomes like you do," Frost said, "but you gotta chill until we save Gilda. This isn't about a job. This isn't about being the boss. I'm asking as a friend. As family."

A pained expression crossed Ryne's face. He closed his eyes. When he opened them, he let his hands fall to his sides. Dante let out a whoosh of relief and placed Ryne back atop his mount.

Ryne muttered something about robbed and killed before grumbling, "I'll do this for you as a friend and family. For all of you, even though it hurts me." He let out a long, slow, shuddering breath.

"Thank you." Frost dipped his head. "Let's go."

He returned to Gearmaster Zod with Ryne at his side. He introduced them, but all Ryne did was stare poison in the direction of the gnome, who remained Concealed. With a sigh, Frost hoped Ryne would keep his word.

They said goodbye to Ryne, who was as glum as ever. He'd resorted to acting as if the gnome didn't exist. They turned their mounts over to Ryne's care and set about collecting the forsaken bones.

Frost took a look at his new stats since reaching twenty.

Strength: 51
Agility: 56
Vitality: 71
Aether: 80
Physical Attack Power: 164 – 174
Movement Speed: 112
Haste/Attack Speed: 2
Aether Power: 280 – 300
Stagger Resist: 4%
Damage Reduction: 6%

Mouth downturned, he shook his head. His defense was in need of serious work. Eventually, the neglect would catch up to him.

Frost took out the shard for Aether Fusillade. He absorbed it.

Aether Fusillade:
Cast time: instant
Cooldown: 30 seconds
Consumes: Aether
Available shard slots: 3
Effect: Rapid fire four Piercers in a three-hundred-foot range for maximum damage. Piercers can be detonated before impact, causing an explosion in a hundred-foot radius for 50% less damage than a direct Piercer hit. If

secondary activation occurs within 100 feet of a summoned Walker bot, the Walker unleashes Ground Zero, firing five Aether Bombs at the detonations. Ground Zero ability requires bot.

Frost's eyes widened at the skill and the mention of the Walker bot. He looked forward to the day he gained one. He also wished he had a chance to practice the new skill but surrendered to the fact his use of it would have to be a trial by fire.

When they collected enough bones, they headed to the main gate. They passed through the gate, crossed a courtyard, and were faced with a door.

Above the door was a plaque. It read:

Here rests dead kings. There is no sanctuary to be found. Within these tombs, you are no more than a farm animal. Fodder for the undead. Only the appropriate level will see you pass. Only the appropriate level= will see you to the treasures at the top. They are not one and the same. When the question is asked, answer it true. But first, you must face death. Enter at your own risk.

"Sounds an awful lot like a riddle." Saba's tail was swishing.

"It might be." Gilda squinted up at the plaque. Her lips moved, reciting the words.

Frost tried to think of a meaning but came up empty. "If it's a riddle, hopefully we can figure it out in case we need it, but there's no turning back now. Let's get these void beholder eyes, kill Grenok, and finish this. Drink up, people."

He waited for them to consume Sadonia's serum. When they were done, he stepped up, grabbed the handle, and pulled. The door creaked open. He peeked inside. A long corridor stretched ahead to another door.

"Looks like the area Sadonia warned us about. Stay on your toes." Frost ushered the others inside and then brought up the rear after Gilda.

When he entered, the door slammed shut. A foul-smelling black mist sprayed into the air. It filled the room in seconds.

"Get to the other side!" Covering his mouth and nose with one hand, Frost broke into a run.

He could barely make them out as the mist grew thicker. Darker. He followed the slaps and thuds of their feet. The mist soon became choking. It stung his eyes. It felt hot against his skin. The heat grew to flames seeping into his flesh. He cried out.

In seconds, his legs were heavy. So heavy. He felt as if he'd been running for hours. His chest heaved. He tried to stop himself from inhaling, but his burning lungs craved fresh air. His mind wanted him to lie down. His body called for him to rest.

He refused.

"Keep coming, Frost!" It was Gilda's voice. It seemed so far away. "Keep coming."

He pushed on ahead though he couldn't see. Step by excruciating step. He had to make it to her voice. He had to make it to her.

I'm not gonna die here. No way. The people I love are relying on me to make it. If I die. They die. No way I'm gonna let them down. One more step. One more. One more.

He repeated those last words continually. Above his repetition, he heard a noise. Hands grabbed him.

"It's me, baby," Gilda said. "I'm here with you. We can do it."

He held onto her hands, fighting the urge to surrender. And then he was clear of the mist. Clear of the room. Someone splashed him with water again and again.

Chest feeling as if it would burst, Frost opened his eyes. Meritus and Dante held buckets. His friends stood all around him, concern etched upon their features. Tears streamed down Gilda's cheeks.

Frost coughed up black mucus. It tasted vile. Black waste trailed from his feet, running down into a nearby drain.

He froze, staring at his hand. His veins were black. Gray splotches marred his magenta skin, the magenta itself appearing less vibrant. Sickly. Little bubbles had popped up all over him. More formed as he watched.

CHAPTER 31

"Fix your faces, people. Stop looking as if I'm dead already." Frost offered his friends a smile he didn't feel inside. "We're gonna beat this thing."

He knew the poison was eating its way inside him. He felt it. The burning. The way his head ached. And there was this nagging, intermittent ring in his skull, a clink that reminded him of chains. He fought the pain and noise as best he could, driving them to the back of his mind with thoughts of Gilda.

"I hope you're right, dawg." Meritus shook his head, somber voice matching his doleful expression. "From the looks of it, I can't slow down the corruption."

"How can you tell for sure?" Dante squinted at Frost, and then his expression soured. "Is it the way he looks?"

Frost arched a brow. "I look that bad?" He glanced down at the back of his hands. Sores covered his mottled gray and purple skin. *If the rest of my body looks like this.* He killed the thought and resisted the urge to touch his face to see if sores covered it. Brows drawing together, he noticed something else.

He felt stronger. A lot stronger.

"It's pretty bad, bro." The gurash blew out a breath and shook his head.

"Make me feel worse, why don't you?" Frost scowled.

"Sorry." Dante hung his head.

"To answer your question about how I can tell." Meritus was looking at

Dante with lidded eyes, clearly annoyed by the tank's disgusted reaction to Frost. "The best I can come up with is that it's a vision unique to this class. Or maybe the skills. I can see how much a person is hurt, how much of an effect the healing or dispelling skills would have." He regarded Frost with sad eyes. "I'm sorry, homie."

"It's all good." Frost clapped his best friend on the shoulder. "It is what it is. And I'm not worried. Grenok is the first boss. That immediately solves the issue of Empowered Ameliorate. Most likely the void beholders are near him. We quickly clear the rest of the place, send for Zod, get the crafts done, and boom, you'll cure us."

"As if anything has ever worked out exactly as planned." Smirking, Saba shook her head.

"Try your spells anyway, Meritus." Gilda's voice was hoarse when she spoke. "A little is better than nothing."

Frost made to tell her not to worry. But she wasn't looking in his direction. Nor at any of them. Her attention was beyond the little alcove in which they stood.

He suspected he knew exactly what held her spellbound. He felt it. A pull. An attraction like a piece of metal drawn to a magnet. It sucked at him. It led forward and up. He almost took a step in its direction.

"I'll give it a shot. Stay still." Meritus' voice broke Frost from his trance.

Four separate misty threads of aether coiled into the air above Meritus' palm. White, yellow, blue, and green. They spiraled into translucent balls. With a flick of his wrist, he sent the white of Purifying Touch zipping toward Frost. The moment the skill touched Frost, Meritus cast out Ameliorate's blue, Suppression's yellow, and Rejuvenate's green.

When the spells hit Frost, something surged within him. He gritted his teeth, anticipating an increase in agony, a jolt, or maybe an easing of the pain already there, a stop to the annoying metallic clink.

If the pain and burning lessened, he couldn't tell. Colored threads rippled down his arms. Darkness from his veins swallowed them in mere seconds. His magenta skin was still mottled with gray. He still heard the annoying metallic clink. The corruption eating away at his body and mind remained as potent as ever.

As did his sense of extra strength. Power.

Meritus let out a heavy sigh. "Sorry, my dude. I did my best." He hung his head, shaking it slowly from side to side.

"You tried, dawg. Keep ya head up." Frost tapped Meritus under the chin. When Meritus raised his head, Frost smiled. "And shaddup."

"Shaddup," Meritus replied softly, but there was little life to the joke. Nor did he smile.

Frost looked to the others. "No playing around from here on out. No wasting time. Take no chances. Buff and vial up for every encounter. Let's find Grenok and the void beholders."

They answered him with nods and intense expressions. Meritus cast Aura of the Nomarch, increasing their defense and vitality gained from heals. Aura of the Pack seeped into them by way of Saba, the twenty-five percent run speed buff giving Frost that wind-like sensation.

Dante strode to the open doorway. Bloomglobes lit the large room beyond, jutting from the walls at regular intervals. The light illuminated sand and stone for several hundred feet. They had to be on an upper floor, Frost concluded, because silver lights flickered in the distance, revealing the tops of several pillars. Somehow, the clink was even louder now.

When Dante entered the room, the rest of them followed, fanning out behind him. Gravelly sand and shale crunched underfoot. The place was quiet. Too quiet. The clink, clink in the back of Frost's mind made it seem doubly so. The air was dry and smelled of age. And there was something else. A whiff of dead things.

"Saba." Frost whispered in group chat, feeling the urge to avoid disturbing any unnecessary monsters. "Scout ahead until you can see what's down by those pillars."

"On it." Saba faded from sight a moment later.

Echolocation scans revealed her form creeping forward. Frost kept his head on a swivel, The Stunner sweeping one way and then the other. Gilda's chakrams lit up the area with their red and blue glows. Meritus summoned his Servitors. They took up positions around him.

A prickle of anticipation eased through Frost. "Dante, be ready to pick up anything."

"I was born ready, boss." Crescent axe held in both hands, the gurash edged ahead.

Gilda moved up beside Frost. "In the alcove, I felt you watching me. I saw you looking up. You feel it, don't you? The power… the thing pulling at you? "

Frost nodded. He was on the verge of saying more when motion along the walls caught his eye. He turned his head quickly but saw nothing. When he refocused on Saba and Dante, the movement repeated. This time, Frost shifted his eyes alone.

"Stop." Everyone froze at Frost's command in group chat. "We got company. Don't turn your heads. Just look at the walls out of the corner of your eyes. Saba, there's no need to be Concealed."

Six pairs of eyes with glinting silver pupils watched them from each wall. The eyes blinked, ochre lids matching the stone. One of them separated from the wall on a stalk as thick as a forearm. It swayed in the air.

"Beholders." Frost voiced the thoughts he knew had to be in his friends' heads. "Void or otherwise."

"That's not all." Saba was close to the area where the ground looked as if it fell away. "Grenok is down here."

Frost's heart skipped a beat. "Alright, everyone get to Saba." He peered directly at the wall. The stalk withdrew. The eyes vanished. "We won't touch the beholders unless they attack first."

"I don't like the idea of leaving mobs at our backs." Dante was already striding forward even as he voiced his complaint.

"Me neither." Frost checked the wall again while he followed. The beholders hadn't returned. "But I got a feeling we wouldn't've been able to fight those ones here anyway."

"I think you're right." Saba was pointing when Frost and the others reached her side. They were standing at the top of a long set of stairs that ended at an oval landing from which a flagstoned path stretched.

Bobbing up and down, beholders floated out from two alcoves on opposite sides of the landing. Despite maws large enough to swallow a man whole, the round blobs of grotesque flesh were noiseless. A single huge eye occupied the space above their fang-filled mouths, matching the smaller eyes on writhing serpentine stalks jutting from their bodies.

Frost counted twelve beholders in all, six per side. Judging from how highly defined they appeared, they were all elite, which was to be expected in dungeons. Every creature would be like them. He was surprised and glad none of them were GUMs. They formed a line on the landing, blocking the flagstoned path. Void energy radiated around them.

Despite the threat the beholders represented, it was what waited beyond them that drew Frost's attention. In a cavernous opening beneath hanging stalactites, there was a gathering of people, creatures, and a gigantic beast on a stone platform partially surrounded by a black river.

Grenok the Devourer had all the traits of a demon. From the two curled horns on its head, skin of hellish hues, large webbed wings, and clawed hands and feet. The demon's sole clothing was its leather kilt. Black veins bulged at its biceps and boulder shoulders, throbbing with a life of their own.

Frost frowned. Grenok was chained. Shackles the height of a man started below the demon's knees and ended at its ankles. Chains led from the shackles, snaked along the ground, and rose up to meet rungs driven into the far walls. Whenever Grenok took a step, the chains rattled, matching the clink, clink Frost thought had been in his mind.

The demon was facing the Crypts' rear walls. Cyan threads laced the ochre stone, leading up to the massive crystalline stalactites tinted with the same color. The color ended down below, where the tenebrous river flowed, separating the wall from the area upon which Grenok stood.

Among the people and creatures were eight forsaken priests, skeletal features exposed by their ragged robes. They shouted orders, cast spells at those too slow to comply, and even whipped some of their victims.

Four more priests occupied the side of the area closest to Frost's group and farthest from the devourer. But these were motionless. Frozen. Standing at four cardinal points, they were translucent, as if they were Phased like the shadowmancer's namesake spell. Their hands were outstretched above them, curled fingers grasping turquoise bands of color that spiraled up to an orb floating high above them. A column of aether rose from the orb and disappeared behind another set of stalactites.

Back toward Grenok, people and creatures trudged to the black river, herded by the forsaken who whipped any that tried to resist. Crying, screaming, or begging, they reached the platform's edge. When they touched the seething liquid, the victims froze.

A moment later, Grenok's hands glowed bluish-green. Ragged beams shot from them, reminiscent of a shadowmancer's Life Link.

Within minutes, those in the river changed, their bodies losing life's vigor, skin turning a mottled silver and black. They shambled from the river, void energy crackling around them. The priests led the newly created void minions across bridges on either side of the area and into alcoves. Fresh priests appeared, leading more victims.

"IS THIS NOT ENOUGH?" Grenok bellowed, his voice a rumbling peal of thunder. "FREE ME!" He shook his chains.

People and creatures scrambled away from him. The floating orb's glow intensified. Grenok shook his head and unleashed a roar. The sound echoed with frustration, pain, and rage.

"Seems like our boy isn't here of his own free will." Frost squinted at the area and the boss.

"He definitely isn't." Gilda pointed at the four priests. "Looks as if they're helping to keep him imprisoned somehow. Probably diminishing his power."

"We might need to make certain they don't die during the fight," Frost mused. "Protecting them or healing them as necessary."

"What about the other priests?" Dante asked. "The ones doing the work?"

"I'm willing to bet they'll end up being his adds," Meritus chipped in. "Might be best if we kill them."

Frost nodded. "Sounds good. Also, we're gonna have to avoid getting knocked into that river of void energy. Especially you, Dante."

"Shouldn't be a problem." The marauder rested his axe on his shoulder. "I'll just dance using Gravity Crush. It connects me with the Aetherstream, keeps me grounded and immune to knockdowns or knockbacks. When the effect is over, I'll dodge or parry. As long as I don't try a straight-on block, I'll be fine."

Grenok created another batch of void minions. "MY WORK IS DONE. FACE ME, COWARD."

The demon threw his head back and stared up. For the first time, Frost noticed he could see the entire pyramid's walls. Countless stairs, alcoves, and balconies led up and up and up to a ceiling where aether swirled like

264

a turquoise sea.

Frost felt the pull again. Far stronger this time. It originated from somewhere up there.

"IF YOU ARE THE GOD YOU CLAIM, BANISH YOUR WRETCHED PRIESTS AND LET YOU AND I BATTLE!" Grenok roared and shook the chains.

Again, the orb above the Phased priests glowed. Grenok calmed and stalked away, grumbling.

"I wouldn't want to be the person he's talking to." Frost shook his head before continuing with the strat he'd devised. "Tank with him facing us, Dante. Just as a precaution against a knockback. We should be okay unless he does some frontal AOE." Frost eyed the priests. "While you're building aggro, we'll deal with the adds. Other than that, we learn and adjust like any other time. That's about it, unless you got some inside info on this fight, Gilda. Or Meritus."

"None." Gilda shook her head.

"All I know is that WaR's beaten him before," Meritus said.

"Yeah, I was thinking about that earlier." Frost stroked his aether ring. "It's why I believe WaR shot the Vindicator. The Genesis Engine area is Open-PVP. If they get there first and take it, I got no doubt they'll be able to hold it. Their group was OP." He scowled. "Our best chance is to beat them to it."

"A slim chance since they already know the strat for Grenok," Saba pointed out.

"I'll take slim over none." Frost hefted his cannon. "Let's get to it. Everyone back up. Saba, pull the void beholders and run back to us. We won't bother with our current traps because they'll just fly over them. But since the beholders' attacks are ranged, it's gonna force them to come up within line o' sight. As soon as they appear up here... smoke 'em."

They retreated about two hundred feet, leaving Saba alone at the top of the stairs. She glanced back at them, then turned, and in one smooth motion, drew an arrow, nocked, aimed, and loosed. Without looking to see if or when she struck her targets, she Streaked back to the group, body a blur, hooves kicking up dirt and shale.

Enraged screeches echoed from below. Frost inhaled slowly, easing his heartbeat, while he charged Homer. The moment the first few void beholders appeared, eye-stalks waving angrily, Gilda's and Saba's abilities shot across the distance.

Frost locked onto targets with eight quick taps on the trigger. On the eighth, he squeezed. Aether Missiles whooshed from The Stunner, splitting away to their destinations. In the next instant, he fired off Aether Fusillade. Four red Piercers streaked after the missiles.

The combined attacks struck the void beholders in a mass of explosions, ice, and fire. Frost was charging an Aether Bomb for good measure even as Gilda flung her instacast attacks and Saba shot her bow in quick bursts as if it were an automatic rifle.

No enemy passed through the spells or the energy attacks. The fire died. Smoke drifted away.

He eased his finger from the trigger. The charged Aether Bomb winked out. On the ground, the void beholders were writhing masses. Seconds later, they'd stopped moving altogether.

"Loot them and then prep for the real fight." Frost led the way.

They picked among the void beholders' mushy remains, removing the eyes from the stalks. When they had looted them all, the group slunk down the stairs toward Grenok, checking the alcoves against the possibility of more beholders.

Frost stopped when they got to the oval landing, a few hundred feet from the Phased priests. A lump formed in his throat. "Change o' plans."

Now on level ground with the devourer, Frost could properly assess the demon's size. Dante, who was average height for a gurash, a bit over eight feet, would perhaps reach to the devourer's mid-thigh. Frost swallowed.

"Dante, stay with us. Don't engage Grenok unless he comes after us when we're killing the trash mobs. No AOEs. All single target attacks."

"What're you thinking, boss?" the tank asked.

"I'm thinking that although we gotta kill him, he might not really be our enemy." Frost was studying the boss again. "Seems to me that he hates those priests and is likely to be passive at first."

"Cool. I'll be ready to intercept if things go left," Dante said.

"I know this might sound crazy." Frost took a breath. "But I was also thinking maybe we should kill the Phased priests."

"Crazy is an understatement." Saba pawed at the ground. "You see the size of that thing? I thought we agreed they might be blocking his power, which will help us defeat him. Did we come all the way here, staving off death, to wipe now?"

"But what if we don't need to beat him?" Frost argued. "The fact Kazuto got a drop from him without a World First Kill announcement says it's possible. What if killing them frees him and he just leaves."

"Too easy." Saba shook her head. "Someone chained him here for a reason. He doesn't seem too bothered about using innocent people and creatures to make void beasts out of them. What if he's doing this bit in secret, maybe trying to build his power so he can break free and rape the world?"

"I agree with Saba, bro," Dante said.

Frost looked to Meritus and Gilda for their opinions.

"I'm with you, homie." His best friend shrugged. "You know I always got your back."

Gilda smiled tenderly at Frost. "I'm with whatever you decide, but there's something you like to say. 'Nothing worth doing is ever easy.' Remember that?"

Smiling, Frost made to mention it was more Pops' saying than his but changed his mind. "I remember." He also remembered something else that fit in with his idea. Things that were too good to be true.

"Alright, kill the trash then deal with Grenok." Frost took the first step forward, his heart thumping.

CHAPTER 32

Frost neared the Phased priests. They made no move to stop him, but the shift of their eyes said they were conscious, aware of the group's presence. On a whim, Frost drew his Expedition Sword and stabbed at a priest. The weapon passed through the forsaken.

"Looks like we couldn't kill them even if we tried." Frost bypassed the Phased forsaken and continued for another fifty feet along the stone floor with its geometric designs.

He stopped. "While we fight, keep an eye behind in case the priests become active or if mobs come out the alcoves used by the beholders. Saba, wait until a batch of minions have been led away and a new group of priests replaces the old. Single attacks only. Vial up." He followed his own command and drank several vials. "Dante, pick up as needed."

"Got it, boss." Dante strode forward some thirty or forty feet from the group.

The burning and pain within Frost spiked, reminding him it was there. He gritted his teeth against it. Sweat trickled down his face. A glance revealed all the bubbles on his gray-splotched hands had burst and were leaky sores.

He grimaced at the sight. "Get it together," he muttered under his breath. "You're almost there."

The eight forsaken saw the group coming long before Frost or the others were within range to use abilities. Pointing, the forsaken yelled and charged. The victims who had been with them scurried back toward the alcoves.

"Ahhhh. Companyyyy. Playthingggs. Perhaps, he sent you to test me? Or his enemies sent you to kill me?" Grenok stroked his chin, his fiery eyes regarding Frost and his group. "Either way, you will fail, but let us see what promise you hold, if you're worthy of being added to my collection." He stroked his leather kilt.

Four priests Flickered ahead of the others, two with glowing chakrams and the other bearing a haladie. Behind them, two others drew dual katars and disappeared. The final two sprinted forward, long swords bared.

"Drop Traps for the ones that Concealed." Frost tracked the invisible priests by way of Echolocation even as Saba set her Traps. Gilda's Stalagmite rose from the ground. "Those casters will be in range in a sec. Focus fire my target first."

But the four casters remained where they were, allowing the melee to sprint toward the group. The Concealed priests approached fast along either flank.

Frost waited for the hidden forsaken to trip the Traps. *Just a few more steps. Now.*

In that instant, the Concealed forms vanished also. The bodies of the two sword-bearers blurred.

A Chain Snare and a Lightning Trap activated. Gilda's Stalagmite exploded by way of Glacial Eruption, coating the floor in ice. The Traps broke the Concealment, but neither slowed nor stopped the incoming melee.

Understanding dawned. The Concealed forsaken had used Shadowblink while the sword-bearers had relied on a similar movement-enhancing ability, perhaps Raging Rush or Onslaught. Skills whose effects made the user immune to stuns and movement impairment for their duration.

"My Bulwark will get the forsaken on the left." Meritus had barely uttered the words when his black-furred gargant Servitor Raging Rushed to intercept the enemy in question.

Up ahead, Dante had charged in to engage the two sword-bearers. The sky-blue arc of Aether Cleave extended from his axe, cutting into the enemy. In the next instant, he Raging Rushed back toward the group, slamming into the second katar-wielding priest.

"My target." Frost ignored the rest of the fight around him, aiming at the forsaken mystic who was already flinging Mikander's Tears and Blood at his battling counterparts. "I'm gonna stagger him. Y'all do the same to interrupt the other three while we focus fire the mystic the moment my stagger lands. Make sure you get the shadowmancer. The last thing we need are his Mimics or Mirages."

Beside the forsaken mystic, the sorcerers' chakrams lit up brighter. Twin Aether Shields formed around a sorcerer's forearms. A hooded Summoned Defiler appeared next to the shadowmancer.

The enemy's Fire and Ice Globes lit up the air. Shadow Globes, Shadow Flares, and Nether Lances darkened it. The attacks sped toward Frost and company.

Aether Barriers sprang to life around Frost and the others like translucent bubbles tinted a faded blue. Frost unleashed a Korbitanium Projectile, Aether Shot, Korbitanium Projectile, Staggering Shot combo. He immediately began charging Homer, tapping The Stunner's trigger to lock targets. His abilities, Gilda's spells, and Saba's arrows flitted across the distance.

Enemy spells struck the Aether Barriers, exploding in a wave of sparks, melting upon contact, or staining the Barriers with a wash of blackness. The Barriers flickered and waned but held.

Across the field, the sorcerer with the Aether Shields chose to defend the mystic, leaping in front the healer to block Frost's attacks. The Shields guttered and went out when the first Projectiles and Aether Shot struck. Moments later, the ensuing Projectiles pierced the sorcerer's chest. He stumbled to the side.

Frost's Staggering Shot found its target. The mystic stumbled away upon impact. Fire, Ice, and arrows exploded into her torso. A Stalagmite burst up from the ground, impaling her.

Before the mystic fell, Frost used Homer, sending four Aether Missiles a piece toward the shadowmancer and the other sorcerer. Frost shifted his aim to the mystic's would-be protector, blasted him with a repeat of the first combo, and finished him with a red-tinged Piercer. He pivoted to the other two casters, but they were dead.

Shifting his attention to the melee, Frost noted two were already down. The group made short work of the others. Motes of aether drifted into the air before zipping into Frost and the others.

"Impressive, little ones." Grenok chortled and applauded, the smack of his palms echoing. "Now, can you repeat that ten… fifteen more times?" Fangs showing as he smiled gleefully, Grenok raised his clawed hands to either side of his body, shifting his horned head from one side to the other.

Following the demon's gaze, Frost gasped. The floors, stairs, and balconies boiled with motion. Robed bodies. Priests from each level were on their way.

"But first, you and I get to play." Grenok dropped his hands and rolled his head from one side to the other. "I will even give you the advantage of a first strike." He regarded them with lidded, bored-looking eyes.

"I really hate this guy," Dante grumbled. "He's too damned cocky."

"We're so screwed." Saba swished her tail. "Having to beat him is bad enough, but to fight waves of forsaken adds too?"

"Look on the bright side." Frost peered at the alcoves. No priests had appeared yet. "At least the adds aren't GUMS like the behemoths." He smiled at Saba, who rolled her eyes.

Frost turned his palms up and shrugged in response. He nodded to Dante. "You're up. Everyone else, spread out. Grenok looks the type to have some nasty diseases or debuffs, so Meritus be ready with the dispels. Make sure your backs aren't to that river of void energy. Remember the golden rule, people. Don't stand in shit."

Dante strode forward to take up position ahead of the group. "I'm ready whenever you give the word, boss."

Frost nodded. "Meritus, you gotta keep up that Aether Infusion."

"No worries. I got you, homie. I'll cast Korbash's Retribution on Dante at some point also. That should go a long way for maintaining aether."

"Good idea." Frost stroked his aether ring, his mind working, anticipation building. "Also, once we engage, have your Servitors head over to the bridge leading to the left alcove. The Bulwark can pick up adds there with your Shaman healing and the Duelist helping to kill. We're gonna AOE them down on the opposite side first, then finish off yours. Gilda, you're our best DPS. Go all out on Grenok."

"No doubt." She cracked a smile that didn't reach her eyes. Her skin was the grayest it had ever been. The sores were everywhere, leaking fluid.

Frost's chest tightened. The pain and burning came rushing back. He refused to look at his own condition. His body spoke on its own. As did his fear for himself and her. He'd subconsciously allowed himself to be absorbed by the moment, the strategizing, the thrill of the fight to come in order to escape the feeling.

But now, the agony, the despair, returned twofold. He felt lightheaded. His chest and stomach hurt.

In the next moment, he'd toppled over. Someone caught him.

Were people yelling? Wake up? Why? I should just stay here and rest. Sleep. I wanna sleep so badly. When was the last time I had a good sleep?

If you sleep now, chances are you won't wake up.

Just a little nap.

You might not see your mother and Kai again. Gilda'll be gone forever.

Gilda? Mom and Kai?

Frost snapped his eyes open. He was lying on the ground, his head resting on Gilda's lap. She was stroking his cheek, whispering to him. His friends crowded around them.

"Thank God." Meritus pressed his palms together and looked to the heavens.

"What-what happened?" Frost's voice was hoarse, his throat dry.

"You just collapsed." Gilda's eyes were watery, the green flecked with black. "Meritus poured everything into his spells. And you just... opened your eyes."

"How... how long?"

"A minute, maybe." Gilda shrugged. "Less?"

"Damn. Felt way longer. Help me up."

The burning sensation filled him now. And there was something else. Something crawling within him. It felt as if something lived inside and wanted out.

They helped him to his feet. Frost used The Stunner to steady himself. Eyes closed, he drew in deep breaths, fighting a battle within himself, telling himself the pain and burning weren't as bad as they felt. His head cleared. He opened his eyes.

Thunderous guffaws echoed from Grenok. The demon paused, wheezing. He wiped at his eyes. "The mere sight of me made you faint. What shall you do when you feel my power?" He slapped his leg and laughed even louder.

With an effort of sheer will, Frost forced everything but the fight and his purpose to the back of his mind. "Those priests are gonna be here any minute. Let's start before I fall out again."

"You heard the boss." Dante stared at Grenok, skin flaring from crimson to scarlet. "Time for some action. Pew, pew."

The words had scarcely left Dante's mouth when the lion-faced gurash tank Raging Rushed toward the demon, covering sixty feet in an eyeblink. Yelling, he chopped into Grenok's thigh, which was level with Dante's head. Dante spun, and swung again, blade angled upward. A blue arc of aether swept up several feet into Grenok's gut. An instant later, Dante shouted again, the blue becoming a full white half-moon, extending even farther, ripping a furrow across the demon's chest.

Grenok bellowed in pain. His arm swung down, claws extended.

Dante crossed his arms in front of his face, let out a rage-filled cry, flung his arms apart, and stomped the ground. Cyan energy shot out from him in circle some forty feet or more. The ground beneath him cracked, sunk in on itself, and formed a crater. Stone and dirt blasted away.

Frost recognized every skill Dante had used in that brief time. Soul Scream, Aether Cleave, Enfeebling Bellow, Scythe, Sentinel Shout, and that last was Gravity Crush.

Grenok's blow slowed as if passing through invisible sludge. Dante brought his axe up, catching the swipe on the haft. Frost winced, expecting Dante to be knocked away or pummeled into the ground, but Grenok's claws slammed into the haft and stopped. It appeared comical that such a small weapon could stop an equally massive hand.

Frost had already charged Aether Barrage, but before he could shout the command to begin DPS, forsaken dashed from the two alcoves, five per side. "Adds! Gimme a hand, Saba. Gilda, balls out on Grenok."

On the opposite alcove, Meritus' black-furred gargant Bulwark had already engaged. The yurid Duelist remained at a distance, casting spells, while its sister, the Shaman, flung heals.

Aiming at the forsaken on his side, Frost unleashed the Aether Barrage. Eight sky-blue beams rippled toward their targets. He immediately triggered Aether Fusillade's four Piercer spread and then selected Concussion Blast. The red Piercers zoomed away. A second later the glowing white

Blast was on its way.

Saba loosed multiple arrows while Frost charged Aether Bomb and waited for the perfect timing. Her hands blurred. Her bowstring thrummed. Her Fire Arrows and Ice Arrows seemed to meld; such was the speed with which she worked.

A couple of the priests managed to dodge the beams from Aether Barrage. A moment later, the combination of Fusillade and Concussion Blast detonated, flinging the creatures into the air. While the forsaken were suspended, the crackling ball of the Aether Bomb fell in an arc past them. They dropped as the ability exploded.

Frost didn't need to wait for the smoke, fire, and electrical energy to clear to know the priests had died. Motes of aether shot into him and the rest of the group, partially replenishing his stores.

Keeping an eye on the alcoves, Frost joined the fray against Grenok, firing Projectiles, Aether Shots, and Piercers while waiting for other skills to become available after cooldown. He charged Aether Barrage again. Beside him, Saba's bowstring thrummed.

Dante's Gravity Crush had dissipated, and the gurash was now resorting to dodging and parrying Grenok's blows. At times, Dante Leaped into the air above clawed swipes that would split him in two.

Multi-colored wisps drifted from the demon's mottled skin, indicating Gilda had applied the Elemental Ignition debuff. Gilda was a cerulean and gray blur of constant motion as if she danced. She wove her hands in elaborate patterns while casting, chakrams leaving impressions in the air. The Elemental Snap buff rose from her in a muted glow.

Stalagmites burst from the ground, stabbing into Grenok. Their twins coalesced in midair, piercing his chest. Gilda flung her hand forward, unleashing Fire and Ice Globes, quickly followed by an Infernal Spear, which had the appearance of a shaft of igneous rock imbued with lava's hellish hues. But a second or two passed before a gigantic whirlwind of fire engulfed the demon.

"GNATS! Always buzzing. I grow weary." With flames swirling around him, Grenok made a back-handed throwing motion.

Multiple Shadow Globes shot toward Frost and the others. Gilda's Aether Barriers appeared and shattered when the Globes struck them. Grenok repeated the motion with his other arm.

Aiming at Grenok's chest, Frost unleashed Fusillade and prepared to dodge the black Shadow Globe hurtling toward him. He made to Leap away but something snagged his ankle. Panic rose in his chest. A glance down revealed dark shackles with darker chains extending back to Grenok.

The Shadow Globe slammed into Frost. Crying out in pain, he staggered. He felt as if he might collapse.

A moment later, the weakness and pain vanished. As did the shackles around his feet. The glow of Mikander's Tears drifted up from him. Aether Infusion gave him a fresh burst of energy. Frost charged Homer.

Grenok thrust a hand out, his palm facing the group. Blackness suffused it. Nether Lances shot forth, spears of pure shadow.

This time, Frost was able to Leap sideways. A Lance exploded into the area he'd vacated. Energy crackled around the spot like black electricity.

"Good dispel, Meritus." Frost said in group chat.

"Thanks, but I could've been faster."

"Looks like we might have to stun him to get a break," Frost mused.

"Immune." Dante activated Gravity Crush once more.

"Shit."

Before Frost could formulate his thoughts, roars announced two more forsaken groups. He and Saba took up position again. This time, Frost used the already charged Homer.

He and Gilda made short work of the adds. In fact, the fight was so quick that a few Aether Missiles and a single Piercer from Fusillade had no targets. The wayward abilities exploded into the stalactites above. Crystalline spikes crashed into the floor along the bridges, sending up a cloud of dust and leaving fissures in the stone.

When the motes of aether seeped into Frost, he became aware of Overload's availability. He smiled triumphantly. "If you have an offensive Overload ability, use it."

Frost activated Stand and Deliver. His first skill was Aether Barrage, which instantly brought the Stunner to its maximum cyclic rate. Projectiles and Aether Shots roared from the cannon's muzzle, illuminating the air like a battle in a war movie.

Relying on Stand and Deliver's ability to diminish cast and recharge times, he engaged Aether Fusillade, Aether Bombs, and Divergence. The Stunner vibrated in his arms, its discharge a constant drone. Heat emanated from the barrel. He settled into firing Piercer on its new two second recharge time, alternating with Projectiles and Aether Shots.

Saba's attacks joined his. Her Arrow Battery Overload skill had turned her strikes into a veritable storm of empowered and elemental arrows.

Lacking an offensive Overload ability, Gilda had cast Aether Pulse. The humming man-sized purple ball of coruscating arcane elements spun end over end. Her rotation of Globes and Infernal Lances followed.

Explosions rocked Grenok. Pockets of flame bloomed all over him, as well as those tinged with aether energy's crackling electrical residue. His body became a titanic silhouette swallowed by a whirlwind of smoke and flame.

The demon cried out. But this time there was no denying the agony in his voice. Heart leaping with the prospect of imminent victory, Frost continued to squeeze the trigger, going all out.

The cries faded. Smoke and fire dissipated.

Frost stopped firing. He expected the demon topple. He could barely hold in his elation.

"My turn." Grenok's fangs showed in a lopsided grin.

CHAPTER 33

G renok thrust his hand out, palm up. The demon made a fist. Something snatched at Frost. It dragged him, Gilda, Saba, Meritus, and the Servitors to a central point in front the demon but behind Dante.

Still grinning, Grenok raised his foot. Gravity Crush sprang up around Dante. Grenok slammed his foot into the floor with a resounding boom.

Darkness and dust blasted away from Grenok in a circle. The floor itself rose up to form a tsunami of stone, rippling outward.

Frost made to Leap, but he couldn't. He found himself frozen in place, his body refusing to obey his mind's demands.

The wave of stone and earth slammed into Frost and the others, breaking around Aether Barriers Gilda had somehow conjured in the last instant. But the Barriers could withstand only so much. Pain shot through Frost. The debris and darkness rolled over him, and then it was gone, rumbling on its way across the entire area.

Where Grenok stood was awash with Gravity Crush's cyan field. Dante was going toe to toe with the demon.

A clamor rose from the alcoves. Two new groups of forsaken were halfway across the bridges.

"Adds!" Frost warned in group chat.

The stun had lasted for three seconds, but it seemed an eternity. Free at last, Frost took a step toward the alcove and faltered. He felt weak.

Something was sucking at him. At first, he thought it might be the

Gray Death, but a glance revealed a deeper darkness creeping over his arms and body. It ate away at his aether.

The same ailment plagued the others. In fact, it connected them like ebony jewels on a string.

"Get away from each other." Frost did his best to scramble away despite his debilitation. "Dispel us, Meritus. And have your Servitors pick up on the other side."

Certain his friend would comply, Frost turned to the forsaken. He fired off Aether Fusillade and immediately selected Concussion Blast. A second later, he'd unleashed the Blast and began charging Aether Bomb even as the Fusillade exploded.

Saba's attacks joined Frost's abilities. And though he caught at least three of the forsaken, two sword-wielding priests had gotten clear of the AOEs.

They were on him and Gilda in seconds. At the same moment, the debilitation vanished. The death of the three activated Canon Kata.

Using the combined speed of Aura of the Pack and Cannon Kata, Frost dodged his assailant's thrusts. He dashed away, turned quickly, caught the forsaken with a Staggering Shot, and finished it with the rest of the combo. Chest heaving, he looked to Saba, but she had defeated the other forsaken.

On the other side, Gilda had helped Meritus. Forsaken were strewn about the floor near his Servitors.

Aether Absorption saw them regain some of the energy they'd lost. Meritus cast Aether Infusion to help the process.

They made to resume the fight against Grenok when the void devourer flung another round of Shadow Globes and Lances. The shackles followed seconds later, quickly removed by Meritus. Grenok lashed at the air a third time.

Immediately, Frost dropped to one knee, forced down by Grenok's ability. His body throbbed. Inspecting himself, he saw his flesh rise and fall like a heartbeat.

This time, Frost could tell his life force was ebbing. He snatched for extracts and drank heavily. The replenishment from them lasted but a moment before the drain commenced once more.

"Get away from each other," Frost croaked. "Meritus."

He followed his own command. He Leaped perhaps fifteen feet away. But instead of diminishing, the drain increased.

"MERITUS!" Frost screamed in desperation.

"It's some kinda curse that I can't cleanse." Concern rang in Meritus voice. "I used my Overload skill, Ghena's Blessing, which makes all my heals instacast. I'm healing y'all as fast as I can, but I can't keep up. Not even with the Shaman's help. And since you can't use pots or extracts for another minute and change, this is the best I can do."

Frost's mind cleared for an instant. A thought struck him, perhaps borne of desperation. "Everyone, bunch up on Dante."

No one protested. In seconds, they crowded within a few feet of the tank.

The debilitation eased. The life drain was still occurring but at a much slower rate. Meritus' heals refreshed Frost and the others.

"Hit him with everything you got," Frost ordered.

They unleashed hell. Abilities exploded all over Grenok. The demon bellowed time and again. Within thirty seconds, the curse had worn off.

Grenok thrust his hand out again. He cracked a smile.

"Everyone but Dante, use one of the movement enhancers the moment he forms a fist. Flicker… Streak… any of them. That'll eliminate the pull and stun. Then Leap over the wave."

Grenok made a fist.

Frost Strafed and charged Homer at the same time, dashing some sixty feet over to a spot near the left alcove. By the time he stopped, the ground was quaking.

The tsunami of stone, dust, and darkness rolled toward him and the others. Timing the wave, he Leaped high into the air, almost touching the stalactites. He frowned at the crystalline spikes and looked down. Forsaken were emerging from the door to the alcove. The wave of stone and dirt washed away the ground beneath Frost.

But the darkness was higher than his jump. Frost sensed the aether drain even as he fell back to the ground and landed with a thud. The drain lasted but a few seconds, dispelled by Meritus.

"Saba, attack the boss. I got all the adds." Frost aimed above the left alcove, tapping his trigger to acquire targets. He did the same to the right.

Howling, the forsaken charged down the bridge. Frost fired the Missiles. He switched to Concussion Blast and waited.

The Missiles sped to the stalactites and exploded. A rain of crystalline spikes fell on the forsaken. Frost and the others were rewarded with aether.

"Overload!" Turning to Grenok, Frost engaged his Concussion Blast and activated Overload. He fired off Aether Barrage, triggered Stand and Deliver, and unleashed destruction.

The gold and blue ring of Korbash's Retribution emanated from the ground around Dante, stretching out dozens of feet in every direction. Aether swirled into the air, formed motes, and zipped into the players.

In the midst of the Overload skill barrage, Grenok flung Shadow Globes, Lances, and cast Immobilize's shackles. He followed them with the life drain, which Frost had anticipated.

Gritting his teeth, Frost endured the drain for the duration of Stand and Deliver. Meritus healed frantically, the motes of Tears and Blood becoming blue and red streaks.

The moment Overload ended, Frost yelled. "Get to Dante to counter that drain!" Relying on Strafe, he followed his command, resuming normal attacks once the group was bunched together.

"He looks like he's close to death." Saba worked her bow, firing constantly.

"You might be right." Frost studied Grenok.

The devourer's flesh had lost much of its luster. His body was less supple, his muscles atrophied. Black blood poured from too many wounds to count. The wisps of Gilda's debuff still emanated from him.

But it was his eyes that told the story. They were round with fear.

"I hope you're right, 'cause we can't keep this up." Meritus' chest heaved. His words were an echo of Frost's thoughts. "Even with Korbash's Retribution we'll soon be completely dry."

"He changed," Dante's high-pitched voice said in group chat.

But Frost had seen the transformation occur. Grenok appeared insubstantial. As if he wasn't completely there. Their abilities and strikes passed through the demon to explode into the rear wall, blowing away chunks of stone.

"Fuck. He Phased." Frost deflated.

Translucent turquoise beams shot over their heads and into the demon. Four of them.

Frost spun. The four priests were no longer Phased. Their beams had reversed direction from them, into the orb, and over to Grenok.

"Oh shit. That's fucking healing him," Dante shouted.

A quick glance revealed the truth of the gurash's words. Grenok's body was regaining its sheen. The eyes did not appear so fearful. In fact, his fangs showed in a toothy smile.

Snarling, Frost turned back to the priests and unleashed every skill he could.

"No!" Saba cried.

But the priests died to a hail of cannon fire and Gilda's spells. Saba stared at them, mouth agape, eyes wide and filled with horror.

"FREE! I AM FREE!" Grenok's roar shook the pyramid.

Heart racing, Frost spun to face Grenok, cursing himself for his stupidity. He prepared to fight to the death.

But Grenok didn't attack them. The devourer stared down at his shackles. With a look of utter confusion, he kicked. The shackles pulled taut against the rungs embedded in the walls.

Below the rungs, priests rushed out from the alcoves. Not eight. Or ten. Dozens of them. Their focus was on Grenok.

"NO! NOOOOOOOOO!" Grenok's scream was one of fear and desperation. Of terror. Of the denial of a freedom that was so close yet was so far.

Tilting his head, Frost regarded the rungs and spoke in group chat. "Don't let the forsaken get to the area by the orb. I got an idea. Gilda, Flash Freeze Grenok's chains near the rungs."

As abilities erupted all around him, Frost charged Homer. Aiming at the walls and chains around the rungs and the stalactites above them, he tapped to lock on. He waited for Gilda's Flash Freeze. The moment the chains and walls became encased in ice, he fired.

The Missiles shot forth with a whoosh. One after another they blasted into the walls, the frozen chains, and the stalactites. A portion of the wall came crumbling down. The rung fell with it. The chains shattered.

Grenok let out a triumphant bellow. "Thank you, little ones. Thank you, for now. I leave you a gift." A sack appeared, tiny in the demon's humongous hands. He tossed it at their feet. "I look forward to the day we battle at my full strength."

The **Vindicator Sadonia** quest line completed.

Grenok the Devourer

Objective Complete

Get Past Grenok:

50, 000 experience points

2000 Ignis dominion credits

2000 Puria dominion credits

2000 Khertahka dominion credits

2000 Lothal dominion credits

2000 Nimri dominion credits

Grinning, Frost picked up the sack. "And that, my friends, explains why there hasn't been a World First Kill for him."

When he looked inside the sack, he immediately picked out the Empowered Ameliorate shard along with other treasures. His heart leapt.

"Thank you." He nodded to Grenok, feeling a sudden kinship.

Grenok strode across to the other rung and snatched it from the wall. "HERZL! I COME!" Chains clinking, he dashed toward the wall, scaled it, and crashed through an alcove.

The cacophony of battle ensued. Magic lit up the balconies. Bodies went flying out and down, splashing into the river of void energy.

"Look." Gilda pointed, her voice a husky whisper like death brushing across paper.

A great circular ethereal beam extended from the floating orb down into the middle of the area. Within the light, two translucent pillars formed a sky-blue doorway taller than any of them.

From the door stepped a gargant in elaborate silver armor. His body was incorporeal. As if he were Phased. His golden eyes focused on them.

"You have done well, travelers." His voice was deep, his accent thick. "However, this is but one step if you are to ward off the coming of the next Void Cataclysm." He pointed up.

"Above us, a treasure awaits. A Genesis Engine, one of the most powerful artifacts in Mikander. An artifact used to reshape the world itself.

"You can gain use of it. Or perhaps can take it with you. But only if you can get to the roof before the crazed devourer destroys all before him. Grenok has never reached the top before, but today might be his day."

Frost glanced up. He saw no way they could catch up to Grenok. "How do we get to the roof before him?" Frost stepped forward.

The Genesis Engine and the pull gnawing at him filled his thoughts. But more than that was hope. Life. Love. A chance to save himself, and even more so, to save Gilda.

"Through this portal. But in order to use it, you must have the key." The gargant gestured. A wide-bladed sword appeared in his hand. Smoky wisps drifted from it. He turned the blade and placed its point into the ground. His hands rested on the hilt, chest high. "I am Keymaster Gudbrand. To use me, you must solve a riddle. Answer incorrectly; you fail. Take too long; you fail. If you fail, you cannot use this portal and must find another way up. Try to force your way past me; you die."

Frost looked to Gilda. In her eyes, he saw his thoughts reflected. This had to be Pops' handiwork. "You up for this?"

"No doubt."

"Go ahead." Stomach fluttering, Frost nodded to the Keymaster. The result here could be the difference between life and death.

Keymaster Gudbrand cleared his throat. "You people are easily herded, chasing after treasure like it is sweet grass. But here it ends, for only a diablo awaits. There is no grazing to be had, no cud to be chewed, no king to be crowned, no hidden level to reach. Or is there? You have twenty seconds."

Frost stared at the gargant and then at Gilda. His mind drew a blank. He made a gesture of helplessness.

Gilda stepped up beside him and took his hand. Their fingers entwined. She smiled at him, a twinkle in her eyes. "What would you do without me?" She faced the Keymaster. "There is no cow level."

"Welcome." The Keymaster dipped his head. His blade disappeared. A silver light bloomed in his palm. The light drifted into the air, hovered, then zipped into Frost and the others, striking them on their right hands. "You have taken the first step toward joining the ranks of the Sapphire Phalanx."

A new main quest became available. **The Sapphire Phalanx.**

Frost frowned. Not only was he ignorant of the Sapphire Phalanx, but he also felt no different. When he turned his hand, the back of it was covered by a tattoo of a silver ball with a sapphire edge. The tattoo itself appeared three dimensional, popping out from his skin. His friends all had the same tattoo.

Keymaster Gudbrand held up his hand. He also had a tattoo, but flames encircled his, appearing to caper as if blown by a wind. "The mark is visible only to other Phalanx members."

"Sounds cool," Frost said. "But what is the Sapphire Phalanx?"

"Guardians of Mikander. The ones who will fight when the true war begins." He stepped aside and beckoned them toward the portal. "The Genesis Engine awaits."

Squeezing Gilda's hand, Frost suppressed the need to let out a cheer. They weren't done yet. "I need to bring someone else to help us use the Engine. Will you let them in?"

"If it is your command." The Keymaster bowed slightly.

Practically dancing with anticipation and excitement, Frost looked to Saba. "You're the fastest of us. You gotta get Gearmaster Zod and Ryne."

"You forgot about the poison at the entrance?" Saba's tail swished.

Frost bent and reached into the sack at his feet. He pulled out a stack of vials like the ones Vindicator Sadonia had given to them. He passed them to her. "These should help. Off you go."

Left speechless, Saba tucked away the vials into the pouches on her belt. She turned and galloped away.

"I'm surprised she didn't ask what if WaR had already done this bit and went on up." Meritus was watching the dresdor, who was little more than a blur. She disappeared up the hill.

"We'll find out soon enough." Curious, Frost turned to the Keymaster. "Gudbrand, has anyone else used you before today."

"No."

A weight lifted from Frost's chest. But a part of him itched to go through. Not only because the cure was at hand, but also the pull. It was stronger than ever. It demanded that he step into the door. Frost stroked his aether ring, fighting the need, impatiently waiting for Saba's return.

To pass the time, Frost decided to question Gudbrand about something that had piqued Frost's interest in Mikander's lore. "Keymaster, this true war you mentioned… exactly who's the enemy?"

"To answer that in a way you would understand, I would have to tell you a story. The story of Mikander's birth as it was passed down to me.

"Eons ago, the Divines battled each other for dominion over this universe. During this First War, two Divines, Marang and Sienne, fell in love. But Korbash, Sienne's old lover, became jealous. Korbash tracked Marang, waiting for his target's weakest moment, the moment Marang and Sienne were together.

"Korbash attacked. To save Marang, Sienne leaped in front of the spell and was wounded. Marang lashed out, injuring Korbash, but he, too, took a blow in the process.

"Space around them destabilized from the release of such magics. They fell through a voidhole and ended up in a part of the universe so remote that it lacked the primordial energies from which they drew. Too grievously wounded to travel or to summon aid, they soon realized if they did not help each other, they would perish.

"To heal, they needed more void and aether energy than their wounded bodies could produce. They pooled their power, creating a world around their bodies, creating Mikander. From their flesh came the land; their blood formed the seas; their breath made the air; their void and aether energy birthed Celestials upon the planet.

"They named their first born the Ashuras, who were primarily aether-based, and the Daevas, who were of the void. These were the gods and goddesses we know today.

"The Divines tasked them with creating new life whose cycles innately produced tiny amounts of aether and void energy. The Ashuras and Daevas were to collect this power, returning it to the Divines' slumbering bodies, healing the Divines until the day they were strong enough to return to their old home.

"Millennia passed. The two factions grew stronger, eventually feeding on their own creations rather than passing on the energy to their progenitors. The thirst for power took root.

"And thus began the Celestial Wars.

"The Daevas wanted to harvest aether and void energies to ascend to immortality. To become Divines. The Ashuras wanted to destroy the Daevas so they alone could rule. The two sides fought until only seven of each were left when there were once hundreds.

"Seeing their imminent extinction, they called a truce. They copied their masters, created lesser beings, the races you know today, and left them to find their way. Then, they cast a spell upon themselves to induce a slumber like their progenitors. But with one difference.

"A trigger for an Awakening.

"When enough void and aether energy had gathered in Mikander by way of their new creations, seeping down to the slumbering Celestials by way of Mikander's aether and void currents, the accumulation would cause an Ashura and a Daeva to wake. Their sole purpose would be to gather the energy, deliver it to their progenitors, and return to their sleep until the day the Divines stirred.

"But an alien race, the draconids, were in search of a way to save their dying people. In a last desperate effort, they chose to follow an old myth. They flew their armada into the voidhole and crashed on Mikander.

"Here, they found a world with abundant void energy. The very thing they needed to live.

"Using parts from their ship, they built the Genesis Engines to harvest aether and void energy and to terraform Mikander, transforming it from a world dominant in aether to one that could support their revival, one primarily of the void. With promises of power, they allied with the once great titans from the north and set about carving a home out of Mikander, enslaving its people. That began the Titan War.

"Wishing to defeat any opposition, the draconids unleashed voidstorms, the concentration of void energy corrupting the land, creating the namesake beasts. This influx of power upset Mikander's balance. It triggered an Awakening.

"When the two Celestials rose, the Daeva, Deluth, and the Ashura, Kitu, had but one purpose. To harvest the world for the Divines. They took no sides. Every living thing was considered fodder. The first Void Cataclysm was born. After they ravaged the world, the Celestials returned to their resting places.

"The surviving draconids made an adjustment. They would unleash only one voidstorm every fifty years, and rely on the spread of the Gray Death to fulfill their needs.

"They placed triggers in the Genesis Engines which would release power attuned to the corrupted, compelling them to go to the activated Genesis Engine above all others. There, the corrupted could be harvested or collected for transport to the Akufa dominion.

"The Phalanx's job is two-fold. One is to prevent another Cataclysm by dispersing aether and void energy, maintaining a precarious balance. The second is to stop the draconids. Our enemies are the most powerful void beasts, the draconid heralds and overlords, and the very Celestials who would strip Mikander bare."

"Epic," Dante declared.

Frost agreed.

"I have a question," Gilda said. "If the land is made from the bodies of the three Divines, why're there only two continents named after them?"

Gudbrand smiled. "Before the first Void Cataclysm reshaped the world, Marang was actually two continents. What you know as the Dagoda Front was once an ocean. The Akufa dominion began its life as Sienne."

CHAPTER 34

Saba returned minutes later with Gearmaster Zod and Ryne on her back. The gnome and the goblin looked thoroughly disgusted at having to be so close to each other. When they saw Frost, they both stared, mouths agape, before catching themselves.

Frost sighed. Judging from Gilda's appearance—the oozing sores and blotchy skin—he knew he didn't make for a pretty sight.

Trying to guess how much time they had left, he checked on Grenok's progress. The devourer was about halfway up and did not appear to be slowing. He had to be sprinting up the floors while decimating everyone and anything in his path.

"Keymaster Gudbrand, you mentioned that we're the first to solve this riddle and get access to this portal, what do the others do?"

The gargant pointed up to where the battle raged. "They follow him. Eventually, he will face a draconid general just before the top. He has yet to win that battle."

Frost deduced WaR's strategy. They had followed Grenok, allowing him to engage first, and only helped when it was safe. He was certain they had devised a way to see Grenok defeat the general, granting them access to the roof.

He glanced up again. Grenok had covered two more floors. Depending on when WaR freed him in their instance, they could reach the Genesis Engine first. They could be there already.

Fighting down dread, Frost regarded his friends and explained his thoughts. "We don't have much time. If any at all." Grim expressions met him. "Dante's gonna be the first one through the portal. Everyone else be ready to fight if WaR's up there."

Hefting his axe, Dante strode up to the door. He limbered his shoulders and stepped into the light. His body faded. Frost and the others followed.

They reappeared in a square area atop the pyramid. The portal remained, but Gudbrand was gone. Gray clouds boiled overhead. A light mist fell. They spread out quickly, weapons aimed or held ready, prepared to defend or attack.

The place was empty of people or monsters but not the Genesis Engine.

The large barrel-shaped glass cylinder occupied the center of the area. Inside was a platform like a plate of some sort. Azure aether swirled within the glass, touching here, drifting there, darting, slowing, coiling. It was as if the power were alive.

And it was to the Engine Frost was drawn. He took an inadvertent step in its direction before he stopped himself.

"Yes!" Frost pumped his fist. He turned and hugged Gilda, giddy with joy and excitement. Jubilation went up from the others.

But not Gilda. She held onto him, her body shaking. It took but a moment for Frost to realize she was sobbing.

Whispering soothing words, he stroked her hair and horns and let her cry. He recognized the release of pent-up emotions. Perhaps even more than happiness, there would be relief.

"Gimme a sec, let me hand the Gearmaster the schemas so he can get to work." Frost held her a little ways from him and stared down into her eyes. The corruption was still there, living within them, but he imagined how it would soon be gone.

Sniffling, Gilda nodded. "No doubt." She scrubbed her cheeks with her palms. "I'll stay here for now 'cause the way that thing wants me to come can't be good."

Frost understood, but he would let nothing stop him now. As he strode toward the Gearmaster, he took note of his surroundings. A massive double-sided door was set into the far left wall.

On the right wall, a faint greenish-blue glow caught his eye. The luminance emanated from a set of symbols. Straining, he made them out.

Void Gate.

His heart skipped a beat. Pops would be inside that room.

He raised his voice for all to hear. "Although we're here first, we can't let our guard down. Saba, drop some traps by that door. The rest of you get ready in case WaR shows up." He could hear the battle within the pyramid but had no idea how close Grenok was to the top.

The group hustled to comply.

"Gearmaster Zod." Frost stopped beside the gnome who was busy inspecting the Genesis Engine. This close to the Engine, Frost had a sense of comfort. He felt as if he needed to climb inside and rest. "I need you to make these." Frost passed the schemas to the gnome.

Zod's eyes bulged. His mouth formed an O. He looked from Frost to the schemas and back again. "I-I heard rumors of this, but I thought they were just that… rumors." His head shifted from side to side as he read. "By Anzu, is there any chance you have the materials?" He looked to Frost, eyes shining with expectation.

Frost puffed up his chest. "We do." He turned to his friends. "Bring the mats, people."

They hurried over and deposited the materials near Zod. Each had its own pile. The infused precious stones, bejeweled skill shards, and korbitanium stood out in comparison to the dragonwood, forsaken bones, void beholder's eyes, and vials of void beast blood.

Gilda got close to Frost again, casting nervous glances at the Engine. Her voice was little more than a hoarse whisper when she spoke. "I've never felt anything like this. It's like the aether itself is talking to me, telling me to get into the Engine."

Frost swallowed. "I know exactly what you mean." The aether now hovered on the side of the glass closest to them, coiling lazily.

"So much. So much," Gearmaster Zod chittered as he rushed to-and-fro, inspecting the items. He picked up a gemstone and held it up to the light. "Flawless." He let the gem fall into his palm.

"Perhaps enough for twenty zhua. And only Anzu knows how many empowered skill shards." Zod regarded Frost, expression intense. "Do you understand what you have here?"

"Ummm… an epic zhua that could cure the Gray Death?"

"Yes, but do you understand how?" The gleam of excitement shone in Zod's eyes.

"The spells?" Frost shrugged, thoroughly confused now, but no less intrigued.

"Bah, you state the obvious, but not the seeeecret. Void energy! Hierkas are the only items that can take void shards. They are the only way normal beings like us can handle void energy. *That* is how spells are empowered rather than simply boosted."

Frost recalled the black and silver river. And the mutations. "But isn't void energy bad?"

"Is aether bad?" Zod arched a quizzical brow. "Think of them as opposite sides of the same coin."

"Point taken. How do we get our hands on void shards?"

Gearmaster Zod screwed up his face as if Frost were a complete dunce. He gestured. "We have a Genesis Engine. They tap directly into the Aetherstream, which, despite its name, is really a combination of aether *and* void energy." He tilted his head. "That last is a secret very few know. From the Aetherstream, we draw both energies to imbue gems, making them flawless, and then infusing them further to create void shards."

"How long's the entire process gonna take?" Frost checked the door to the area. Grenok sounded a lot closer now.

"I'm not sure." The Gearmaster shrugged. "There's no telling with hierkas and other genesiswork items until the process begins. Usually, the more powerful or higher level the genesiswork item, the longer it takes to craft. Some can be instant. Some in minutes. Others can take hours."

"We don't have hours." Though muffled, Grenok's roars were closer. And if Frost strained, he thought he could make out the ring of steel on steel.

"Luckily, the zhua and the shards are relatively low level despite their power." The Gearmaster was arranging the materials in groups. "Even the hierka, Benediction, starts off very low, but can grow with its user to perhaps become one of the strongest weapons in all of Mikander."

Frost liked the sound of that. It meant the other weapons were the same.

Zod appeared thoughtful. "There are rumored to be other more powerful hierkas, ones that contain weapon souls. But I have yet to encounter any of those. Nor do I know what weapon souls can do. Or if they really exist." He shook his head and snorted. "There is also another issue when it comes to crafting." Zod strode up to the Genesis Engine. He put his hand out.

A display appeared, floating in the air in front Zod's fingers. It had more in common with a holo than anything Frost would have expected. The display was filled with buttons beneath which were words in a language Frost did not recognize.

"As with anything else, it requires aether." Zod worked his fingers across the display, selecting various buttons. "And I only have but so much aether. I will have to rely on Replenishment and your mystic to speed up the process. And I will still need breaks. Genesiswork crafting is already exhausting. Doubly so when one has to make this many."

"No prob." Anxious for the job to be done, Frost stroked his aether ring.

He wanted himself and Gilda cured more than ever. And as soon as possible. The connection between the corruption inside him and the urge to climb into the Genesis Engine was disconcerting. No. It was downright scary. He shuddered.

"First, we must scan the schemas to load them." Gearmaster Zod jabbed a button. A light beamed from the console, appearing on his chest as a thin horizontal line. One after the other, he held up each schema to the light.

"Then we have copies processed for insurance." He pressed another button on the virtual console. A slit at the bottom of the Genesis Engine spit out several schemas.

Gearmaster Zod waddled over to Frost and passed all but one set to him. "May I keep these for myself for future use?"

Frost took the others. "Sure. It's the least I could do."

"Thank you. Thank you." The gnome bowed profusely before returning to the console. "And now, we begin." His fingers worked the buttons.

An image popped into existence beside the console and rotated slowly. It was a replica of Benediction, complete down to the polished korbitanium claw, which topped a wooden staff etched with glyphs. Several more joined the first. They showed skill-effect and void shards.

"I need one of you to load in the materials from the piles I arranged. The ones for a single zhua first, then once I have crafted that, we will do the shards to match one by one." Gearmaster Zod tapped the display.

A section parted seamlessly near the Engine's middle. The circular platform slid out, but the aether itself still hovered inside the cylinder, enclosed by glass.

"I got it." Dante strode over, picked up the materials, and placed them on the platform. When Dante was done, the platform slid inside. The section closed.

"Stand back." The Gearmaster shooed them away before taking a seat. The console and the images vanished. "Once I tap into the Aetherstream through the Engine, a field will appear around the Engine and myself. No one else can be inside. I'll also be meditating to keep my aether up. See that I'm not disturbed. Any interruption ruins the process, and the materials are lost. It could even cause the Engine to go boom."

"You heard the man." Frost backed away and gestured for the others to do the same. "Ryne, Dante, and Saba, keep watch on the entrance in case we gotta fight before he's done."

"I hope we are long gone before it comes to that," the Gearmaster said. "If an offensive spell strikes the Engine, the explosion might kill us all."

"We'll keep that in mind," Frost assured him.

The others went off to do as Frost had instructed. He, Gilda, and Meritus waited. The pain and burning within Frost were becoming near unbearable.

Gearmaster Zod's eyes were closed. Aether rose from him like a celeste mist. It drifted over to the Genesis Engine.

When the Gearmaster's aether touched the Engine, the structure lit up and began a hypnotic hum. The aether inside the cylinder reacted, forming a solid band several shades darker than that belonging to the Gearmaster.

A cerulean glow appeared beneath the Engine, forming a circle. The hum sped up. The radiance spread until it touched the Gearmaster. There, it stopped. The humming grew louder. Faster.

"Look." Gilda pointed at the cylinder.

But Frost had already seen it. The materials had lifted off the platform and were now spinning. The individual parts coalesced, one after the other. A shape formed. One as tall as a man and thick as an arm.

Frost squeezed Gilda's hand. He hadn't even realized he was holding it until that moment. Nor could he remember when he'd taken it.

In minutes, the craft was finished, the glow and hum diminishing. Inside the cylinder, standing on end, was a Benediction. Frost fought back tears, his hand covering his mouth.

"Infusion." Chest heaving, Gearmaster Zod opened his eyes. "Take the zhua, then place six gemstones from the pile to the right onto the platform. The brightest ones. Those are the best quality candidates."

"Get it, Meritus," Frost urged his friend to take the zhua. "It's yours."

After Meritus cast Infusion on the gnome, the human mystic strode over to the Engine. The slot within the platform opened, as did another down the cylinder's side. The zhua floated out to him.

Meritus took the weapon reverently. He turned to Gilda and Frost, grinning like a big kid, and held it up.

"The gemstones," the Gearmaster called.

Meritus picked up six of the most vivid gems. Their colors and types varied. He piled them on the platform and then rejoined Frost.

"Thanks, dawg." Meritus clutched the hierka close to his chest. "You don't know how much this means to me."

"Shaddup." Frost chuckled and extended his fist. They gave each other a dap.

The next few minutes felt like an eternity. Crafting the void shards played out in the same fashion, except black and silver void energy rose up to commingle with aether. The power poured into the gems, making them brighter and the trapped energy denser. Two infused gems joined to form one shard, its outward color changing to a shade of purple. Black and silver coiled within the shard like a cloud.

"Another Infusion," Zod instructed. This time he did not appear as spent as when he crafted the zhua. "And place the shards into the weapon slots."

Meritus removed the void shards from the Engine. He turned the hierka until three slots were visible about chest high. When he'd placed the third shard, Benediction gave off an ethereal glow.

"And now the skill shard materials for one empowered spell," Zod said.

Meritus did as he was told. The crafting process was the same. He absorbed the skill-effect shards when they were done.

After the third shard, Gearmaster Zod detached himself from the Genesis Engine. "I need a few minutes to replenish. Then we can begin again. But first, let's see the zhua in action."

Everyone gathered around, almost breathless with expectation. An electric energy hung in the air.

With the moment at hand, Frost couldn't help questioning himself. *What if it don't work? Maybe, I should have him cast the original spells first just to be sure.*

Or maybe you should just get it over with before that damned demon and WaR spoils it all.

Frost took a calming breath. Palms sweaty, he nodded to Gilda. "Heal her first."

"You sure?" Meritus screwed up his face. "Because you—"

"Do it."

Gilda stepped away from everyone. She lifted her hood. Gasps echoed all around. Sores covered her face. They bubbled and boiled and oozed. Her skin hung in strips in several areas.

Frost refused to look away. She locked eyes with him and smiled. He could only imagine how much worse he looked. He met her smile with the warmest one he could manage.

Meritus brought the zhua up. The weapon glowed. Threads of white, blue, and yellow snaked up from the clawed fingers. They swirled together, spinning faster and faster, growing denser until they formed a golden ball the size of a man's head.

The ball shot out and into Gilda. Golden energy raced across her body.

Frost gaped at the ensuing change. The sores disappeared. The gray fled. Her skin regained its cerulean luster. Her flesh became supple. In seconds, the Gilda he remembered was standing before him. Beautiful. Whole.

The group let out a whoop. They ran to hug Gilda, but her words stopped them in their tracks.

"After Frost." Her smile and the twinkle in her eyes warmed his heart.

When the spell struck Frost, the burning diminished first, quickly followed by the loss of pain. Warmth suffused him. A soothing warmth like taking a shower in water that was the perfect temperature.

He glanced down at his hands. His skin had regained its magenta shade. And he definitely felt more powerful than he did prior to his ordeal. On a whim, he checked his stats.

Strength: 51

Agility: 57

Vitality: 71

Aether: 120

He tilted his head to one side. The aether was wrong. Very wrong. He double-checked and confirmed he was still level twenty. He had eighty aether when he leveled.

Stroking his ring, he tried to make sense of the change. Even with as much skills as he'd used during the Grenok fight, his aether should not have been that high. He was certain of it.

A barely discernible throb made him glance toward the Genesis Engine. He no longer felt the magnetic pull, but he sensed the great power within the machine.

"You two are the first to experience Sanctification," Meritus declared, breaking Frost from his thoughts.

Grinning, Frost bowed to his best friend, his concerns forgotten. The group hugged, laughed, cried, and slapped high fives.

Until Grenok's fearsome roar shattered their jubilation.

CHAPTER 35

"Grenok's almost here!" Filled with renewed panic, Frost dashed over to the Genesis Engine even as Gearmaster Zod took a seat. Frost loaded the materials for another zhua. "Meritus, take over here. We need as many zhua and shards as we can get."

"No worries. I got you, dawg."

Leaving Meritus to it, Frost hustled over to where Gilda and the others faced the massive double doors. At best, Grenok was only a few floors down. All that was left was for the demon to defeat the draconid general. Frost hoped the demon would lose, but he wasn't willing to bet his life on it.

"Saba, Dan, and Ryne, I'm gonna need y'all to hold the fort while Gilda and I take care o' something." Frost eyed the Void Gate. If there was any chance to talk to Pops, he needed to get on with it.

"Now?" Saba swished her tail. "You have to do something now?"

"Go ahead, bro." Dante held his axe ready, gaze focused on the door. "We got this."

"Like Dan said. Go ahead." Ryne summoned several Defilers and a Nightmare. A Mimic of the group also appeared. "We got this."

"Thanks." Frost turned to Gilda. "Follow me." He ran toward the Void Gate.

"I wondered about this." Gilda stared up at the glowing symbols.

"I noticed it as soon as we got up here." Frost's aether ring vibrated. "Let's go in." He took a shuddering breath, grabbed her hand, and stepped into the portal. Light suffused him, and in moments, he had passed through to the other side.

"Pops!" Frost grinned at the sight of his father's ethereal form hovering above the map of Mikander.

Tension fled Frost's body. Tears welled up in his eyes. Both of sorrow and joy. He could stare at that face, the large nose, the bald head, the full beard sprinkled with silver, the smiling eyes, and never grow tired. Pop's clothes of choice this time was a white ninja outfit.

"Son." Pops returned the grin. "Hey, Blaze." Pops waved at her.

"Hello, Mister Taylor."

Frost wished he could run over and hug Pops. But he remembered too well the first time he'd tried to touch his father. The thought and the ghostly form sobered his emotions, but it also brought on a question.

"Pops, is there a way to transfer you back?"

"Transfer me back? As in WBE?" Pops was frowning.

"Yeah."

"I don't think Uncle Kim ever got that far. But you'd have to find him and ask to know for certain. If he's still alive. You can start with finding that out. When last we spoke, he was on his way to meet Carlson, the leader of the Lifers. Blaze can contact them."

Frost made up his mind to follow Pops' suggestion. If there was the slightest chance of getting Pops back, he had to pursue it.

"There's also the matter of my body and brain." Pops was stroking his chin. "Not having them might present an entirely different set of complications. But let's not get caught up in that just yet. One thing at a time. Baby steps. For right now, I'm ecstatic being able to see you here."

"Me too." The potential obstacles to return Pops from the game dulled Frost's enthusiasm, but he had no intention of giving up. "It was tough getting here, but we managed it thanks to Gilda's research and knack for riddles and puzzles. At some point you're gonna have to give us the exact rundown on the others."

"Wish I could." Pops raised his hands in a helpless gesture. "But I only designed Imanok Sanctum. The other dungeons were created by different devs. Best I can do is to tell you that the puzzles and secrets they added were based on a list of games I gave them. Most of which you already know.

"I would make it easier for you if I could, but that's a bit of the game I can't meddle with. Not without Estela becoming aware. Which means I'd get caught and would most likely be deleted. The good news is that not every dungeon has something to solve."

"Thank God for that," Frost said.

"You'll be fine if you continue playing the way you've been. Especially if you collect the other epic hierkas like Benediction to get you through early game. They'll be good until you acquire normal legendaries or other genesiswork items from epic all the way to genesis." Pops drifted over to a position beside the map. "Now, first things first, is Theresa okay? What about the twins and Kai?"

"Everyone's fine for now. Mom is up and about. The twins are healthy and are gonna be here soon. Kai is back to her old self, enjoying Munsters and Minions."

"Good. Good." Pops stroked his chin. "What's Sidrie been up to?"

The mention of the woman's name set Frost's blood to a boil. "She made me return to the game when I wasn't ready. She went back on her word.

"She tried to make herself look good, saying she's paying me two hundred grand a year to alpha test, even made certain we got our Green Cards renewed, but all that matters is that she didn't let me spend more time with Mom."

"Two hundred grand in credits a year?" Pops whistled. "She'll stop at nothing, that woman. I'll think of some ways you can put the credits to use to get from under her clutches. An escape plan. For now, just act normal."

"Alright."

"That alright doesn't sound convincing. I can tell when you'll be stubborn. But that'll just cause more problems. Play along. Let her think she's winning. There's a bright side to these things. You just need to grow up and see it.

"If there's one thing you should've learned from this, it's that you can't give everyone the benefit of the doubt. You can't think everyone will live by the morals you do. Especially not Sidrie."

"You're right." Frost hung his head.

"I raised you to be honest. Some people feel that lying and cheating are the way to go. That the end justifies the means."

"I'll keep that in mind." Frost tried to push the bad thoughts from his head.

"What about the first protocol?" Pops asked. "Was it delivered?"

"It wasn't." Gilda pursed her lips and shook her head. "When I went to make the delivery, something felt off, so I waited. Good thing I did. Equitane security showed up. I'm pretty sure they have people following me now, rather than just relying on the drones and cams."

Frost slapped a hand to this forehead. "Damn it. Sorry, Gilda. In the rush to save you in-game, I forgot to warn you. Mom said she thinks they got everything bugged."

"Of course, they do." Gilda shrugged. "It's why I told you the walls have ears before we left the room."

"I wondered if that was what you meant." Frost shook his head.

"Don't beat yourself up." Gilda touched his hand. "You're new to this. We have to be as careful IRL as we are in-game."

"Agreed." Pops nodded. "Having said that… Gilda, our Gridrunner contacts in-game are still secure. As long as we control the protocols, Equitane won't be able to crack the anomalies. Use the contacts to make arrangements for delivery IRL. And to pass a message to Carlson about Dr. Kim's fate."

"Gridrunners?" Frost frowned.

"Name of the Lifer group fighting against Sidrie." Pops smiled. "Catchy, ain't it?"

"Yeah."

A frown settled on Pops' face. He stared off at nothing. "You weren't kidding when you said there wasn't much time. Grenok is about to defeat General Iblis. Some players from a guild… WaR… are helping the devourer. I was wondering when someone would figure out that fight." Pops floated over to them. "Quick, touch me to receive the second protocol."

They reached out to Pops with the hands that held aether rings. As their hands passed through him, the particles that made-up his form swirled, formed threads, and trickled into the rings.

Frost felt new code added to the old in his head. The lines melded. In seconds, it was over.

"Hurry! Go! We'll meet again at the next location." Pops gestured toward the Void Gate. "You don't want to be up here when Herzl and Grenok clash. See you soon. I love you, son."

"I love you, too, Pops." With a last look at his father, Frost smiled sadly. "See you soon."

His Comm Orb dinged, the stentorian voice rising from it.

WORLD FIRST KILL

A group, led by Kazuto Morow of the WaR guild, defeated Ibliss the Stormraiser, a draconid general who had captured the Purian city of Apur and was using its people for experiments in the Forsaken Crypts. As a reward, the Coalition has bestowed the title of Crypt Conqueror unto Kazuto Morow and his group members, Meileen Elune, Saigo Thrall, Vash Quickdraw, and Aizen Shadowblade.

Frost and Gilda stepped back through the Void Gate. He made to yell to Meritus and Zod, informing them it was time to flee. But they were no longer near the Genesis Engine.

"They're back," shouted Meritus.

The group stood perhaps a hundred feet from the double doors. A blow landed on the door with a resounding boom. Another followed. And another. The doors shook. Stone and debris fell from the walls.

"Here I am, Herzl! Face me now!" Grenok's bellow reverberated from the pyramid's interior.

"Get to the portal." Frost Strafed toward the sky-blue doorway. The others were ahead of him.

A roar echoed from above them. A panoply of lightning illuminated the gray murk. The black-scaled void dragon swept through the clouds, the beat of its wings buffeting Frost, billowing his cloak. This close, the dragon was the size of a building.

IM named it Ebonwing.

Upon Ebonwing's back sat a man in green armor, his hair done in a top knot. A sword hilt jutted above one shoulder. Void energy crackled around both dragon and man. As the dragon spread its black wings, slowing its descent, the 'man' proved to be none other than the draconid herald, Herzl.

The dragon settled to the ground, the Genesis Engine between it and the door. It threw back its head and unleashed a roar. Herzl remained upon its back.

"Let's go," Gilda implored, tugging at Frost's arm. "The others are gone already."

Frost placed his hand atop hers without taking his eyes from the scene before him. "I have to see this. Just give me an Aether Barrier and join them."

"As if I'd leave you alone. I promised not to let *you* die either, remember? We'll watch together." She cast an Aether Barrier around them and summoned her Aether Shields upon her forearms.

The double doors blasted outward. Grenok charged through, a mass of muscled demonic flesh, wings spread wide. Behind him, Frost made out Kazuto, Meileen, Saigo, the mask-wearing cannoneer, and one other WaR member at the shattered doorway.

Grenok slammed a foot into the ground, sending out a wave of darkness and stone. A moment later, he flung Shadow Globes and Nether Lances.

The void dragon spewed a bar of black energy. Herzl drew his sword.

The world seemed to slow, the spells creeping toward their targets and the Genesis Engine between them. They struck the Engine.

The world turned white. Searing heat washed over Frost. His ears rang. Something snatched him up and tossed him back through the portal.

Frost and Gilda materialized on rock-strewn ground. His armor, skin, and clothes were singed. Gilda's were the same. Chunks of stone fell around them.

He thought a person was speaking to him. Many persons. If those slurred noises were voices. His ears were still ringing.

Hands fussed over him. They hustled him and Gilda away from the falling rocks.

Frost allowed his gaze to follow the arms up to faces. Meritus and the others were speaking to him. Yelling, he thought. Their mouths moved, but the words stretched. The disorientation lasted a few seconds more before the world adjusted.

Blue motes of Mikander's Tears settled upon Frost's skin. In moments, he felt refreshed. The ringing diminished to nothing.

"You should be good now, homie," Meritus said.

"Thanks." Frost looked to the group who were staring at him and Gilda.

They were standing at the bottom of the stairs just outside of Grenok's area. The portal was gone. So was the orb. Stone and debris continued to fall, covering the ground where the priests had been. A gaping hole had replaced much of the roof.

"That, is what happens when attack spells strike a Genesis Engine," Gearmaster Zod said. "The power is multiplied several times."

"Does that mean Grenok and Herzl are dead?" Gilda took up a position next to Frost, staring up at the hole.

"I doubt it." Zod shook his little brown head.

"And the WaR members?" Dante rested his axe's haft on his shoulder.

"I saw them at the doorway to the roof." Frost followed the path of a curtain or cloth as it swirled down. "If they're as smart as I think, they avoided the explosion."

"Then its past time we leave before either Herzl and Grenok return, or before WaR has time to regroup outside." Saba was already halfway up the stairs. She raised her voice. "And I know one thing, you always accuse me of being too cautious, or scared, but think about our battle in Modra's Keep. We're lucky we didn't blow ourselves up."

"This is one time I agree with you." With a chuckle, Frost followed the dresdor.

As they made their way out, Frost looked to Meritus. "How'd we do on the crafts?"

Meritus sighed. "We only got two more Benedictions with a complete set of spells for each."

"Damn." Frost winced. "I was hoping for more, but they'll have to do. Pass them to me, please."

"What's the plan for them?" Meritus handed the shards and zhua to Frost along with a few Bless vials.

"I promised one to Adesh Hamada. The other… well, we all have **The Cure** quest that needs completion." Frost sprinkled the golden Bless fluid on the items.

"Too bad the Genesis Engine got destroyed," Dante said.

"Yeah. But I just might have a solution to that." Frost told them his plan.

CHAPTER 36

They departed the Crypts to a sky awash with evening's rosy blush. Frost sent word to Adesh Hamada of their success and asked the man for one more favor. He thanked the Blue Sky leader for Gearmaster Zod's services and gifted Adesh the other Benediction and a set of schemas. Gearmaster left to deliver. After retrieving their mounts, they rode to meet Vindicator Sadonia.

For Frost, the small amount of time spent with Pops was a tease. It made him hunger for more. There was a way for them to spend a day together. He just had to find it.

When they got to the front of the Crypts, there was no sign of Vindicator Sadonia. A Coalition captain was calling out orders and directing a full company of new troops. More were flying in atop various mounts in a sky empty of void beasts.

Frost rode over to the company's leader. "Hi, captain, you happen to know where I might find Vindicator Sadonia?"

The captain jabbed his thumb behind him. "She's back at the Temple of Jerad with the other corrupted."

"Thanks." Frost urged his drake forward.

"Is it me," Gilda asked, "or did that just sound like he said Sadonia is corrupted?"

"That's what I got from it. Let's hurry." Frost kicked his bolsters and sent his drake galloping toward the looming temple.

When they arrived, they navigated their way through the barricades.

Mostly new players had taken up position on the stairs. But there were still several with the Herald of WaR.

Frost tried and failed to see Senaty or Kazawa. Instead, he picked out Enatsu's dark brown skin and bright blue hair atop the landing.

He rode to the gurash. "Hey, Enatsu, you got any idea where Sadonia is? A captain said she was here. And where's Senaty and Kazawa? I gotta speak to them also."

"This way." Enatsu beckoned them on with an over-sized clawed hand.

They followed Enatsu to the temple's front door where they dismounted. Enatsu drew a scarf up over his leonine face, paused, and then pulled the door open.

A stench wafted out. Rot. Death.

Frost slapped a hand over his nose and mouth. Somebody retched.

Enatsu held up his hand. "Wait a moment to get accustomed to the smell."

"There's no getting used to that." Grimacing, Frost shook his head. "Just take us to them."

Without another word, Enatsu led them inside. Bloomglobes illuminated a long corridor with rooms on either side. People occupied the rooms and most spaces, sprawled on the floor or huddled in corners. A dirge of despair echoed from the mouths of the suffering.

The corridor opened into a large room with marble floors, pillars, and elaborate carvings and architecture along the walls. Numerous corrupted were here also. At the head of the room was a brightly illuminated area. A set of stairs led up to a statue of Jerad, the grand kora god dressed in full sorcerer regalia, including two oversized chakrams.

"By the statue." Enatsu pointed.

"Thanks." Frost dipped his head to the gurash. "Do me a favor?"

"Anything." Enatsu was staring toward the stairs, sadness etched upon his face.

"Get a few people from outside and have them gather up all the corrupted into this room."

Enatsu frowned. "Are you certain?"

"Yes."

"Right away." Enatsu ambled off.

Frost headed toward the stairs, his heart burdened by the suffering around him, and yet, he was calm. Everything would be fine.

Senaty was the only one standing. Kazawa was seated on the stairs, Naora's head cradled in his arms, as he whispered and rocked her. Vindicator Sadonia sat with her back against the statue's calf. Gray splotches marred her skin.

"Hey, Senaty, Kazawa, Vindicator Sadonia, Naora." Frost stopped at the bottom of the steps.

"Nif be praised! You returned!" Senaty looked up to the heavens, her face tear-streaked.

"We did."

"I had a feeling when I saw the explosion." Senaty smiled.

Vindicator Sadonia pushed up to her feet. "How did you manage? Did you get—"

"I'll tell you all about it later." Frost nodded to the Vindicator and Naora. "Right now, let's focus on curing you two and everyone else."

Kazawa's head snapped up. "What did you say?"

Frost smiled at sergeant. "We're gonna cure her. Well, Meritus is." He gestured to his friend.

"You hear that Naora?" Kazawa looked down at her and lovingly stroked her face. "The gods heard our prayers."

"Just set Naora down and give her a little space." Meritus took up a position beside Frost, Benediction in hand.

After Kazawa did as asked, Benediction glowed. Sanctification's white, blue, and yellow threads snaked up the head of the zhua's clawed fingers, swirled together, and spun until they formed a golden ball, hovering in the air. The completed spell zipped across into Naora. Meritus flung blue motes of Mikander's Tears moments later.

Naora gasped. Her back arched. Golden energy flushed across her body. Sores and infected skin washed away, leaving radiant green. Mikander's Tears struck her and seeped into her body.

Moments later, Naora turned her head, smiled, and sat up. Kazawa dashed to her side, snatched her up, and bawled like a babe.

"All praise be to Nif." Senaty joined her friends.

In the back of his mind, Frost became aware of a quest completion for

Saving Kazawa and Naora. It granted twenty thousand exp and a thousand LDC.

But Meritus wasn't done. While the three basked in each other's company and good health, he cast Sanctification on Vindicator Sadonia, who was staring at Naora in wonderment.

A veritable shower of praise followed. Sadonia and Senaty thanked the entire group, but paid special homage to Frost and Meritus.

"Hey!" Ryne shouted from behind them, his basso voice shattering the celebration. "You have company."

Frost turned his head. Corrupted filled the room behind the goblin, Zod, Enatsu, Domen, and Varia. Murmurs drifted from the crowd amid moans and groans.

Smiling, Frost eyed Senaty and Sadonia. "You said the Coalition would owe us if we got the cure." He gestured to Meritus. "You mind starting, homie? Get Enatsu and the others to help."

"You got it, dawg." Meritus and the rest of the group headed down the stairs to the crowds.

Frost spoke to Sadonia and Senaty as the soldiers and his group directed the people to form lines. "How bad is the situation with the Gray Death?"

Vindicator Sadonia looked to Senaty, who nodded slightly. "We curtailed the worst of it across most of Marang by slaughtering tens of thousands, but some believe it is the first part of a new draconid offensive. Some religious zealots think if we don't stop the Gray Death altogether, that we might be seeing the start of a Void Cataclysm. The last Cataclysm was over a thousand years ago and brought about the formation of the Coalition, which would eventually help to save Mikander."

Frost remembered the Keymaster's words. He wondered if Sadonia or the others knew how right they might be. "What if it was possible to provide Coalition mystics with other Benedictions and the necessary spells? What if we knew how to acquire schemas to craft more? What would it be worth to the Coalition?"

"Are you serious?" Vindicator Sadonia glanced at Senaty.

"Serious as death."

"Very well," Sadonia said. "I hope I'm not speaking out of turn, but I would think our leaders who sit on the Grendesh Conclave would give anything within reason. Personally, I would need to contact my superiors, who in turn might need to speak to one of the Viziers or a Kalarch to say for certain. Council member Senaty is more equipped to give a better answer."

"Vindicator Sadonia is correct." Senaty was studying Frost. "Credits. Land. Titles. Gifts. Any and all are quite possible as a reward. But the final decision would rest with the Conclave, no matter what the rest of the Coalition might want."

"Considering the nature of the situation, you think there're things the Conclave might refuse?"

"Yes." Senaty shrugged. "None of you are of noble birth, so they would not raise you and yours to Exarchs or Nomarchs, if that was your hope." She paused, expression thoughtful. "I could have you named as Aetherium Council Emissaries. It is an influential position."

Frost winced, thoroughly unimpressed. "Sounds like they'd try to deny what we've accomplished."

"Not deny," Senaty corrected. "Diminish. There are those who would say we would eventually obtain the cure on our own. Or those who'd advocate for Meritus' capture and the forcible use of the spell... by any means necessary."

Frost scowled. "That's bullshit."

"I am simply telling you the reality of the situation." Senaty shrugged. "My word and that of Sadonia *will* carry weight. And your selfless act would be recognized. Anything the Grendesh Conclave considers to be within reason would be granted."

Within reason. The words rubbed Frost the wrong way. He decided to test the statement. "Do you know who I am?"

"Lan?" Senaty's brows drew together in confusion.

"Drelan Frost, to be exact." He waited to gauge their reactions.

Silence reigned for a moment, broken only by joyful outbursts as Meritus healed another person. The faces of the Coalition members became deathly serious. They shared a knowing look.

"Son of the late, Anefet Frost, the Hand of Freedom." Sadonia nodded, lips pursed. "I see it now that I look closely."

"And those?" Senaty jutted her chin toward Gilda and the others. "Are the other members of the Blue Sky Network group wanted by Nomarch Setnana Botros and Demipho Pansa for robbery, attempted murder, and murder."

Frost scowled. "We didn't rob anyone. We weren't responsible for the deaths of any patrons, and we sure as hell didn't try to kill Khafra. I'm certain Adesh Hamada has contacted the Coalition to claim sole responsibility for the events in Kituan." That last had been a part of the deal Frost made with Adesh in exchange for a Benediction.

Senaty had her arms crossed near her waist. Her index finger tapped her wrist. "Witnesses placed you there."

"I was investigating my mother's murder."

Vindicator Sadonia spoke. "Murder? She died during a raid on Niba led by the grand korae and the slaver, Umesh Madara."

"Yeah, murder. Umesh Madara might have been involved, but I discovered the plot ran deeper." Frost stroked his aether ring. "The Coalition had pardoned Blue Sky before, but then came after them again because of supply raids, an attempt on Kalarch Voculo's life, and supposedly for spreading the Gray Death." He met their gazes. "You know the last part is a lie. The rest of it is also. And even if you believe I'm Blue Sky due to my association with Adesh Hamada, you see the trouble I went through to get the cure."

"Some might claim it was all a ploy by the Network itself," Senaty argued.

Frost snorted. "You don't believe that. The ploy was the Black Hand using propaganda to set up my mother and Blue Sky. The Black Hand had to stop Blue Sky from disrupting the Hand's slaving operations. And what better way to do it than to manipulate the Coalition into doing their dirty work."

Their faces became masks. Frost knew he'd struck a chord.

"So, the Black Hand has been playing you." Frost arched a brow.

"There is still the murder of Nomarch Setnana Botros' son, Perihy," Senaty said.

Frost smirked. "We had nothing to do with her son. She blamed us because we took Benediction from the Sanctum before she could acquire it to heal him of the Gray Death. Regardless, he's alive."

The women shared looks of incredulity.

309

Frost smiled. "I'm certain she's gonna announce his miraculous survival soon. Here's what I want.

"Lift the bounties off me and mine. Pardon us. Provide us with ten thousand credits of every dominion. Give us plots of land at a location I pick where we can build anything we choose. I'm not going to ask you to pardon Blue Sky again, because obviously there're too many Coalition members set against them. And there's Adesh's crimes.

"Give me a chance to clear the names of my mother and the other Blue Sky members. I'm gonna expose the Black Hand and its operatives, reveal who leads it. I intend to kill Umesh Madara. In exchange, you get the cure and the schemas."

"I might be able to broker such a deal." Senaty was nodding appreciatively. "But when I present it, some might require an act of good faith."

Frost gave her an incredulous stare and gestured to the room. "Meritus healing all these people isn't enough? Saving y'all wasn't enough?"

"It's more than enough for us," Sadonia conceded. "But we don't have the last word."

"Fine. This should convince everyone else." Frost smiled inwardly. So far things had gone as he'd envisioned. He took a completed Benediction and three empowered spell shards from his inventory. He handed them to Senaty.

The Aetherium Council member gasped. Her eyes grew wide. She looked from Frost to the items and back again. She absorbed the shards.

"I will make arrangements immediately. You shall have what you asked for. If you will excuse me?" Senaty moved off to the side.

Certain she was speaking to the Grendesh Conclave via Comm Orb, Frost turned his attention to Meritus. Within minutes, all but one quest in **The Cure** line completed. Frost leveled to twenty-one and gained a wealth of new credits. Down in the room, Meritus had almost Sanctified everyone.

He took a stock of his stats with the new tier of four attribute points per level from twenty-one to thirty.

Strength: 55
Agility: 61
Vitality: 77
Aether: 124

He now had five percent stagger resist. He made a mental note to improve his armor and jewelry for better defense.

When they exited the temple, **The Coalition's Debt** completed. Senaty informed Frost that the Grendesh Conclave and the majority of the Coalition leadership had voted to pardon him and his group. They had also granted them ten thousand credits of every dominion that was part of the Coalition. Land would be made available where they requested, as long as no previous claims existed. Confirmation arrived via Comm Orb.

WORLD FIRST

DECLARATION

A group led by Drelan Frost has cleared the Forsaken Crypts, and helped the Coalition obtain a cure for the Gray Death. As a reward for providing the cure, the Grendesh Conclave has bestowed the title of Aetherium Emissary unto him and his group members, Meritus Killgain, Saba Nerubi, Gilda Mordian, Dante Blackblade, and Ryne Waldron.

Cheers went up outside. Frost grinned from ear to ear. Gilda threw her arms around him. The other group members slapped each other high fives. Ryne had a look of awe on his face.

Frost's jubilation was tempered by the sight of Kazuto, Meileen, Saigo, the masked black-armored cannoneer, and a human in expensive robes toting a storm lance. The five WaR members strode up the stairs.

In response, Frost's group arrayed themselves around him. Frost casually raised The Stunner to a more viable position for attack.

Kazuto bowed from the waist to Senaty and Vindicator Sadonia, but his eyes remained on Frost. He all but ignored the others. "Congrats. I had to come see who it was that beat me to a world first. For a second time. I also heard you killed a few of my guys. First was Cardiac, after you left Maelpith, and then three initiates near the Jurojin."

The human with the storm lance scowled at Frost. He had hair so blond it was almost white. His face was angular, hard, and vaguely familiar.

Frost made to speak. To defend his actions.

"It's okay." The gargant dementer held up a massive hand encased in a korbitanium fist. "The initiates don't matter if they died that easily. Cardiac, on the other hand, was one of my officers." Kazuto shot a scathing

311

look toward the stormcaller, who hung his head. "No way he should have lost to the likes of you."

Realization dawned, but Frost gave away nothing. He found himself to be unusually calm.

Kazuto continued, "But maybe that's what he gets for not killing you in your little cave on Maelpith. I must say, though, his death, and now this second World First, makes me curious about your skill. How about a duel?"

So someone did go in the chest after all, Frost thought. Aloud, he said, "Not interested."

The masked cannoneer chuckled. "I told you he was a Care Bear."

"So, you did Vash." Kazuto wore a mocking smile. "Is Vash right, Drelan? Are you a Care Bear? Are you the kinda guy who runs from PVP, who'd love it if there were no Open PVP zones, and who's scared of a little blood and guts? The kinda guy who gets mad at PKers?"

"Ask Cardiac." Frost smirked at the stormcaller.

Kazuto growled. His arms dropped to his side. Meileen rested her hand on his arm, her eyes pure ice as they regarded Frost. The others shifted into battle stances.

Frost and the others responded in kind. On the far end of Frost's group, Ryne had summoned a Defiler and a Nightmare. Frost regarded Kazuto with dead eyes.

Councilwoman Senaty stepped between the groups, but she was staring at Kazuto, the corner of her lip upturned. "Be the first to raise a weapon against anyone and I will set the Vindicators after you."

The moment stretched. Kazuto guffawed. "Consider yourself lucky this is a Safe Zone. I'll see you around, Drelan." He bowed to Sadonia and Senaty. "Good day, Vindicator. Good day, Councilwoman." He turned on his heels and stalked away, his people following behind.

"Watch your back with that one." Senaty stared after the WaR members. "I don't know how much it will help, but I'll make certain your Emissary medallions are crafted before you leave the camps."

Frost barely heard the words as he studied the WaR members. They were the kind of players he despised. "Hey guys, how would y'all feel about being in a guild again?"

"I knew you were going to do it." Dante was beaming. "Soldiers of Chaos, for the win."

"Actually, I'm gonna give us a new name." Frost watched the WaR members fly off. "Care Bear Company."

"Oh, damn." Meritus grinned. "Shit just got real."

CHAPTER 37

Setnana grimaced at the Grendesh Conclave's announcement. The pardon. The cure. Drelan Frost had ruined her plans yet again.

But at least she had Perihy once more. Nothing could change that now. He was different. Stronger. A lot stronger. Quiet. Brooding. But he was her Perihy.

He was seated behind her, dressed in the best clothes she found in Apur. A hooded cloak hid his face. He'd asked for weapons. A set of katars and a storm lance. She wondered after the request but allowed it.

Her simurghs landed in the courtyard at Modra's Keep, their wings kicking up dust. The Sky Swords arrived moments later.

A dozen of Bakui Assam's personal Blackguards and three of his Azureguard companies were there to meet her. Not the man himself. A slight, as usual.

The Blackguards passed orders from him, stating only her closest advisors were to accompany her. Her Sky Swords and others were to remain in the courtyard.

With Perihy and Vindicator Dita at her side, she followed six Blackguards down into the Keep's bowels. Ihuet, Khafra, Neferna, and Perihy were behind her. Six more Blackguards brought up the rear.

Bakui Assam's voice had trembled with rage when he demanded her presence in the Comm Orb message. Yet, she had no fear. She was calm. Serene.

When the guards marched toward the dungeon's torture chambers,

cold fingers slid down Setnana's spine. For a moment she considered order-
ing those with her to attack and for her men upstairs to fight. She and her
people could flee. *But where would we go?* She shook off the idea. She would
see this through. *No weakness. Strength always.*

The lead guard gestured for them to enter the chamber. When the
group complied, only half the guards followed.

Upon entry, Setnana schooled her face to calm at the spectacle before
her. Neferna hissed. Dita gasped. Neither Khafra nor Ihuet reacted.

Strapped to racks near the far wall were two of her men. Naked. Ser-
geants left in charge of the Genesis Engine excavation. They had been
stretched unto death, legs soiled by their shit.

Not far from them was Bakui Assam, dressed in black robes that offset
his violet skin, his eyes little beads of assessment. But he wasn't alone.

Exarch Aishani was with him. Her face wore a frown, thin lips downturned. Her buttermilk grand kora skin was paler than usual.

When Bakui Assam spoke, he did so with the leaden weight of his
authority. "I am glad you returned, Setnana. Imagine my surprise when I
arrive to find you gone, off on some quest to save your son, according to
these two. A corrupted son. Or worse, if I am to believe one of them. And
why shouldn't I? When I find holding cells filled with corrupted dvergar."

Setnana remained quiet. As did everyone else.

"No words, then?" Bakui Assam clasped his hands behind his back. "To
add to the madness, I discover the accident with the Engine. But wait." He
held up a finger. "Not an accident. The dvergar attacked you in an attempt
to recover their loved ones." The man's face darkened. "What were you
thinking, you dumb bitch? Your idiocy came at the price of my Engine."

"I am no one's bitch." Setnana's hands formed fists at her side. She
strained to keep her voice even. "And you mean the Black Hand's Engine,
don't you? Unless… you really mean *your* Engine, which would explain the
absence of Shadows."

Bakui Assam became livid. "You heaping pile of lupine shit. To whom
do you think you speak? You are who I say—"

The man's face parted at the mouth, a horizontal slit appearing. The
upper half of his head fell to one side. Blood splashed Aishani.

Perihy appeared next to Bakui Assam's corpse even as it thudded to the ground. His Mirage was still beside Setnana.

The guards made to move, but Perihy was faster still. In a blur of motion, he was among them, katars flashing, lightning energy crackling from his storm lance. He, himself, was a storm.

Setnana turned to the door. The first guard who poked his head inside caught a Nether Lance to the face. Fighting erupted from outside as Khafra, Ihuet, and the rest of her men joined the fray.

It was over in seconds. All of Bakui Assam's men were dead.

"That went smoother than I anticipated." Setnana hawked and spat on Bakui Assam's corpse.

"What have you done?" Aishani was standing with her hand covering her mouth, eyes like saucers.

"What have *I* done, my dear?" Setnana smiled grimly. "I have begun the thing we dreamed of. Made the first step. Which was to take his place as Exarch."

Aishani was shaking her head. "But Benediction. The cure. We needed it to proceed. And with the Genesis Engine—"

"We have a Benediction." Setnana gestured to Dita, who produced the zhua. "We have the cure. I will inform the Fingers. They will be pleased to know we can match the Coalition on that front. I will also tell them of the Genesis Engine, so they can send Shadows to collect it. Gifting the Engine to them, and my deed here, should let them see our value."

Aishani was frowning. "You keep mentioning the Engine. You really don't know, do you?"

"Know what?"

"Follow me." With those words, Aishani led them through the dungeon to the chasm.

When they reached the chasm's edge, Setnana saw that glimmerwands illuminated the bottom. There were numerous bones. The Genesis Engine was nothing more than a shattered cylinder and dented or broken struts.

"How?" Setnana began.

"That was the same thing we asked." Aishani shrugged. "We concluded the Engine must have exploded when the men were trying to dig it out. Your men said that wasn't the case.

"When we arrived, we found them upstairs. Or what remained of them. They were deathly afraid of the dungeon, claiming some monster was down here. They blamed it for the bones. We placed men here and waited but saw no sign of any creature."

Setnana found herself thinking about the drake. *Had it survived? It couldn't have. Not buried under all that rubble.* She dismissed the thought. Of more importance was the destroyed Engine.

For all of a second she considered not telling the Fingers. But a part of her knew they would find out eventually. And they would send Shadows for an entirely different reason.

"When the Fingers ask, we blame this on Bakui Assam," she said. "I will tell them that I assumed he had informed them of the Engine, and I was simply following orders by bringing it here. I do not know how it was destroyed, but once I realized Bakui had not revealed its presence to them, I recognized his betrayal. I slew him for it."

She smiled. *Yes, that story will work. It most certainly will.* She saw it all clearly now. She would move up in the **Ranks of the Hand,** and was well on her way in the **Road to Kalarch.**

CHAPTER 38

In ethereal form, Sidrie stood outside the strange doorway atop the Crypts. Void Gate, read the symbols carved above the door. The symbols nor the door no longer glowed as they did when Frost and Gilda had gone inside.

Sidrie had tried to step inside, but she'd merely passed through and ended up on the other side of the wall within the Crypts itself. That room was a Guardian area, featuring a low level draconid general.

"Why isn't it working?" Grinding her jaw, she tried again.

"It's the protocols," Zhi Yin said through voice chat. "They're rejecting you."

Sidrie glared at the Void Gate. Another protocol transfer into Frost and Gilda was the very reason she'd ended up here. The glare became a frown.

"Zhi, check every dungeon to see if there are more of these Void Gates."

Minutes passed.

"Yes, Miss Malikah, there are more. Dozens of them."

"Let me guess. We cannot penetrate any of them with surveillance."

"We can't," Zhi confirmed.

"Your job, and the job of every tech we have, is to find a way in."

"Yes, Miss Malikah."

She craved to find out what the gate hid. She had an idea, more of a hope, a fervent wish, but she tempered it as she had learned to do over the years. An idea came to her. Perhaps she could find another use for Alphonso's clone. Maybe it could help solve this mystery.

"Miss Malikah."

"Yes, Zhi?"

"Dr. Redmond just called in. He said you're to come immediately."

Sidrie arched a brow at the demand. At the same time, she knew whatever had the man speaking out of character had to be serious. With a thought, she logged out of the game.

CHAPTER 39

Early the next morning, Frost, Gilda, Dante, and Meritus landed outside the underground home of the Kaigake dvergar. Elder Agnar and several other dvergar waited at the main tunnel entrance, the Elder's long silver hair and beard standing out among his peers. All of the dvergar wore black.

A notification popped up in IM.

Servers will be brought offline in 30 minutes for an update. Get to a safe location.

"I hope everyone saw that," Frost said in group chat as he dismounted. "Let's at least get this done before shutdown."

"In position on the ridge overlooking the keep," Saba said. "Place looks abandoned. I haven't seen a soul. Ryne and I'll keep watch in case anyone shows up."

"Alright." Frost strode toward the dvergar.

"We are honored by your presence, Emissary Frost." Elder Agnar bowed. "I did not expect you to return."

"First, just call me Frost. Second, I gave my word that I'd come back to cure your corrupted."

The Elder's head bobbed up and down. "Pyrini be praised."

"Lead the way." Frost gestured to the cave entrance.

He also had another more pressing reason for his return: the chance of getting his hands on the Genesis Engine. He knew it was a long shot. Most likely Setnana had recovered the machine from the cave-in. But it was worth a look to be certain. Not for the first time he found himself wondering if RnB had somehow lived.

They made their way down into the belly of the dvergr home by way of the braziers, the scent of burning dragonwood filling the air. The Elders brought them to a large room occupied by several dozen corrupted.

On one side were those who were docile or enfeebled by the Gray Death. On the other were those chained to a wall. They seemed more beast than dvergr, often growling and snarling.

"There were some who transformed completely." Elder Agnar gestured to the corrupted. "They became draconids or void beasts. We were forced to kill them, but a few escaped. We were able to track them north until they entered Puria."

"Meritus, you and Dante handle things here." Frost nodded to the corrupted in need of healing. "I'm gonna check for the Engine with Gilda."

"Alright." Meritus headed toward the docile dvergar with Dante following.

"Elder Agnar, is there a way through the mines and into the dungeons other than the tunnels we destroyed?" He'd sneak in through the keep itself if he had to, but it wouldn't hurt to inquire about an easier way.

"Yes, there is." The Elder beckoned to a dvergr, who ambled over. "Scout Paedar will show you the way. But be careful, there might be corrupted or worse down there."

"No prob. After you, Paedar." Frost gestured for the scout to take the lead.

After an uneventful trip, they stood in the keep's musty central dungeon within the glare of Frost and Gilda's glimmerwands. The place was empty. Still hopeful, Frost treaded over to the chasm where the Genesis Engine had fallen.

He held up the glimmerwand, but the fissure was too deep for him to see the bottom. Frost retrieved another glimmerwand from his inventory, activated it, and threw the radiant stick down into the hole. He took another and tossed it a dozen or more feet from the first.

The glimmerwands spun end over end for what seemed an eternity, illuminating rocky walls and dirt. They clattered to the bottom, the sound echoing. The light revealed a host of white things strewn about the bottom.

"Are those bones?" Gilda asked from beside Frost.

"Looks that way." Frost squinted. "Yeah. Definitely bones. I see a few skulls."

Gilda pointed. "Found the Engine."

His gaze followed her finger. Jutting up from the rubble was the shattered remains of the Genesis Engine. The struts were bent or broken. Half the cylinder was missing.

10 minutes until server shutdown.

Frost sighed heavily. "Ah well, now we know." He offered a silent prayer for RnB.

"Hey, Frost," Saba said. "You have got to come up here and see this."

"On my way." Frost trudged back toward the mines.

As he and Gilda made their way outside, Frost couldn't help the feeling that they'd missed a golden opportunity. The Genesis Engine would have given them the upper hand. Particularly with the group being on WaR's KOS list.

Meritus was done curing the dvergar by the time Frost got back to his friend. **Save The Kaigake Dvergar** completed, granting twenty-five thousand exp and a thousand LDC. They said their goodbyes and prepared to leave.

5 minutes until server shutdown.

"You really need to hurry up," Saba implored. "Like, get up here ASAP."

Curiosity piqued, Frost led the way out at a jog. They mounted and flew above the ridge.

Saba was waving frantically to them from a spot to their far left. "Up there." She pointed to where a cliff rose from the ridge to form a steppe.

60 seconds until server shutdown.

"What is it?" Frost asked.

"Just go. Hurry. But be careful."

Frost directed his drake up the cliff. His mount cleared the top, giving him a good vantage of a large opening set against another cliff face. Frost gasped. His heart became a drum.

A massive red and black creature basked in the sun. Void energy radiated around it.

"Fuck me," Meritus exclaimed. "That's a damn baby void dragon."

322

"That's RnB." Frost landed on the steppe.

The server shutdown.

******

Dre woke to bright lights and hands helping him from the pod. He took a minute or two to get his bearings and steady himself. A tech passed coveralls to him. Dre stepped into the clothes and zipped them up.

It was at that moment he realized Dr. Redmond was there with the tech. The doctor's face was deathly serious.

Dre's chest tightened. One thing came to mind. "What's going on? Is Mom okay?"

"Your mother went into premature labor."

Thanks for reading! A little message from the author.

If you enjoyed this book, then I humbly ask you to leave a review on Amazon. Visibility is everything. And it helps us authors know we're doing something right.

To chat, for ARCS, free swag, news, and to just hang out and talk to me, join the **Void Gate, my Facebook group**.